The Red Cross of Gold IV

"The Hesperian Dragon"

Assassin Chronicles

by

Brendan Carroll

The Hesperian Dragon is dedicated to everyone who has ever had the desire to meet or be a dragon.

The characters are fictional and any resemblance to real persons alive or dead is unintentional and coincidental.

Brendan Carroll can be reached at http://redcrossofgold.blogspot.com/ for comments or questions.

Preface

"Let any man having knowledge of why these two should not be joined in Holy Matrimony speak now or forever hold his peace," Simon pronounced the words that Lucio had been waiting for. The Healer looked up from his book of Sacraments and gave the required pause before continuing.

"I object!" Lucio announced just before the priest continued with the ceremony.

A general murmur of surprise ran through the congregation gathered in the Chapel of Glessyn followed by the singular sound of the song of the Golden Sword of the Cherubim when the Chevalier du Morte, drew the blade from its scabbard. The Italian cringed and felt perspiration running down his face and neck into the stiff collar of his tuxedo.

"Brother…" Ramsay uttered one word of warning and pressed the tip of the blade against his back. "Mind your tongue."

"What is the basis of your objection, Sir?" Simon ignored the Knight of Death and directed this almost casual question at the best man.

"He does not love her as I do, Father," Lucio said in spite of the danger.

"On your knees, Brother!" Mark Andrew ordered and took his arm just above the elbow, twisting it painfully.

Lucio went down without a whimper. He was helpless against the man. He was ill. He was dying.

"And you have proof of this, Sir?" The Healer asked and closed the book of Sacraments, allowing his hands to drop into the folds of his priestly white frock.

"I do!" Lucio answered through gritted teeth as the groom took a hand full of his hair and pulled his head back. "Look at her, Father! Look at her! Look what he has done to her!"

"I see nothing amiss with the bride, Sir," Simon smiled as he spoke, again acting as if nothing were wrong. "You are overwrought, Brother."

"The veil!" Lucio shouted. "Raise the veil!"

"How dare you accuse me?!" Ramsay asked and stepped between the priest and his best man. "You are nothing! A street urchin. A filthy dog."

"Look at her!" The Knight of the Golden Eagle gasped as the groom yanked his hair and then pressed the point of the blade against his side, directly where the pain was worst of all.

Simon stepped down from the platform in front of the bride and took hold of the floor length veil made of heavy, white lace. He pulled the veil from the bride's head and her tiara fell to the floor. Lucio cut his eyes to the left and felt the blade enter his flesh.

5

He screamed at the sight of the lifeless bride. Her bedraggled blonde hair tangled with weeds and briars, her face nothing more than bare bones and bleached teeth, her hollow eye sockets staring straight ahead.

"I see nothing amiss here," Simon announced as he surveyed the grisly face and replaced the veil, letting it fall over the horrible sight.

"I warned you, Little Brother," Mark spoke softly to him, leaned close and pushed the sword deeper into his side.

The pain was unbearable, hot and searing and he heard the sound of ripping cloth as it emerged through the back of his coat. He screamed again and grabbed the blade in both hands.

The groom let go of his hair and placed one boot against his midsection, wrenching the blade free, gashing Lucio's hands deeply in the process.

The Italian fell crumpled to the cold stone floor in front of the altar.

Simon resumed his place in front of the altar and opened the book.

Ramsay wiped the blood from the sword on his white sleeve and put the sword away before kneeling beside his bloody best man, searching through his pockets for the ring.

Simon resumed the ceremony as if nothing had occurred when Mark resumed his place beside the silent bride.

Lucio got onto his hands and knees and began to crawl toward the open front doors where he could see green trees and bright sunshine. As he crawled past the pews, the guests cursed him and spit on him and threw rotted fruit and vegetables at him. Some of the men kicked at him, sending new pains coursing through his side where the blade had pierced him. When he reached the doors, he fell again, down the steps and into the dirt at the base of the stairs.

"Sir! Are you all right?" A woman's voice speaking Italian pierced the darkness and pain.

"He killed her!" He gasped. The face of an elderly woman wearing a white scarf over her head drifted in the darkness above him. "Help me."

Instead of answering, she disappeared and then he felt himself being lifted from the ground.

"No! No!" He protested. "Let me go! Meredith!"

But they did not let go and he felt his strength run out into oblivion as he was carried from the street onto the sidewalk in front of his apartment building in Naples. The last thing he heard was the distant wail of an emergency vehicle's siren.

Chapter One of Seventeen
Gabriel, make this man to understand the vision.

Sir Philip Cambrique, Seneschal, Chevalier du Orient, reluctantly sought out the company of Grand Master Edgard d'Brouchart in his study. Normally, he would not have bothered him in his privacy. The balmy night breeze engulfed the restored Roman Villa and the French Knight like a comfortable glove, insulating him somewhat from the chill growing in his heart. The smell of the sea hung in the air and he could hear the calls of seagulls flying somewhere in the darkness above. The Master was completely engrossed in a sheaf of dog-eared papers, yellowed and smudged with thousands of fingerprints from long years of use. Philip sighed as he perused the numerous papers scattered about the Master's desk. He had tried, time and time again, to bring the Master into the twenty-first century, but had failed miserably. The obstinate Frenchman still insisted upon shuffling through ancient manuscripts and printouts in spite of the fact that he had a state-of-the-art computer system on the desk in front of him, collecting dust. The best that the Master could manage was to obscure the monitor screen with sticky notes covered with scribbled handwriting. He complained that his fingers were too clumsy for use on a keyboard and he detested the point and click system. He wanted something he could hold on to, he said, something that didn't look like an Egyptian dung beetle. Philip assumed he meant the mouse, which vaguely resembled a scarab.

Sir Edgard squinted at the ancient writing on the paper under the light of the brass and stained glass reading lamp on his old mahogany desk through an over-sized, silver-encased magnifying glass. The big, red-haired man laid the papers down and sat back in his chair, causing it to squeak ominously.

"Brother Philip," he said simply as his second in command took a chair in front of the desk, clasping his hands in his lap.

The tall, thin Knight looked up at the ceiling, blinking his dark eyes rapidly as was his peculiar custom when he had something distasteful to discuss with the Master. D'Brouchart had always assumed that this was the way the man organized his thoughts before speaking, especially when he had some heavy matter on his mind. He finished up a note, tore it carefully from the pad and placed it atop another note on an antique spindle while Philip made ready to speak.

"My Prince," Philip spoke softly and focused his eyes on him presently. "I would speak to you concerning your decision to send Sir Dambretti on this mission with Sir Ramsay. I do not believe that the circumstances warrant his presence in light of his... his new status."

D'Brouchart nodded, he had expected this. The Knight of the Golden Eagle was no longer immortal and subject to the uncertainties of life to a much greater degree than the other eleven members of the Council of Twelve. It was Sir Philip's duty as his second to point out possible flaws in his logic whenever necessary.

"Our Knights are not bound by the desire to live, Brother, but rather by the willingness to die in the service of Christ. Brother Dambretti has always been at risk as are we all," d'Brouchart countered. "Please do not remind me of the mistake I made. I have suffered much on that account."

Philip drew a deep breath. He had not come here to chide the Master concerning Dambretti's condition. The Master had thought the Italian dead when he had bestowed the gift of mortality on the traitorous ex-Templar, Philipe Devereaux. No one could hold him responsible for what had happened. There had been little choice at the time.

"He has not passed on his mysteries and has sent his apprentice back to the Academy without proper authority. The boy, Stephano Clementi, is barely eighteen and has completed only three years service next month with his Master. He is far from ready to assume a seat on the Council and he cannot be expected to take Sir Dambretti's Mystery under the circumstances. It would be prudent that one of us receive the mysteries from the Knight of the Golden Eagle until…the situation is rectified. Should some unfortunate incident occur, that is to say, something that would put Sir Dambretti's life in jeopardy, one of the other members should hold the Mystery in safe-keeping until they might be restored to him, God willing." The Seneschal lowered his head and paused to see how his introductory words were being received before continuing.

D'Brouchart nodded thoughtfully. Philip was reluctant to speak on this subject. Dambretti could be killed or die at any moment and, if so, he would take the Mystery of Isis and Osiris with him to the grave. He would not linger in the suspended state between life and death until Sir Ramsay could attend to him. There would be no opportunity to take the Mysteries before releasing his soul. The Divine Knowledge would simply die with him. An unacceptable risk. The only remedy for the Italian Knight's dilemma would be the death of the former Templar who had once been apprenticed to Hugh de Champagne. Then Dambretti could, once again, receive the gift of immortality. There could be only twelve. Dambretti's situation was unprecedented in the history of the Council. Never had a Knight of the Council lost his immortality and remained alive.

"Sir Ramsay and Sir Champlain would be able to accomplish the task of finding Devereaux with the assistance of Sir de Lyons or Sir de Bleu with much less… worry, if Sir Dambretti were to remain here where he would be… safer. In no way do I mean to discredit his desire to do his duty in this matter, Sir. He fully understands what is at stake here," Philip said and then paused again. He would have only one opportunity to present his concerns and he wanted to make his points very clear. "Brother Lucio's presence is not essential to the mission. And, further, I believe that his judgment is clouded due to his personal interest in the outcome. He may possibly jeopardize the mission's success. I would ask, with all due respect, that you reconsider your choices of the members of this mission. My recommendations are Sir Ramsay, Sir Champlain and Sir de Lyons. Sir de Lyons has not yet seen much work in the field, your Grace. He would benefit from the experience, especially in the company of two such seasoned soldiers and he shows great promise regarding his political and practical views. He would retain his objectivity in regard to the outcome. Meanwhile, de Bleu could hold Brother Dambretti's Mystery for him until the mission is complete."

D'Brouchart could see the logic of the Seneschal's reasoning, but he, too, had personal reasons for sending the Golden Eagle with Sir Ramsay. The Master could not remain objective either. For one thing, he wanted to know, once and for all that the matter of the Chevaliere Sinclair was settled between them before he restored the gift of the Tree of Life to Lucio Dambretti. He could no longer risk the integrity of the entire Council of Twelve because two of his Knights were constantly at each other's immortal throats over the favors of a woman. The time was drawing near when he would need all of them to do their duties without outside interference and internal contentions distracting them from their purpose. If the matter between them was not settled, then one of them would have to go. He had thought that Sister Meredith's acceptance of Mark Ramsay's proposal of marriage had settled it, but that had not been the case. And then he had resigned himself to losing one of them by way of the deadly challenge Lucio had made upon learning that he had lost Dame Meredith to Sir Ramsay. But that, too, had failed to settle the matter as neither of the Knights had killed the other during the fight. Now the problem remained in a somewhat modified version. He had lost Lucio Dambretti in a very unexpected turn of events. Even though the Golden Eagle still lived, he would not be able to continue as a member of the Council of Twelve in his mortal state. If the mission failed, one of the remaining eleven members would be forced to take on his Mysteries indefinitely, but it would be preferable to losing the mysteries altogether. Unfortunate, but necessary.

If the contention between Ramsay and Dambretti remained, though the mission was successful, it would be highly distasteful and regrettable to have to inform the Knight of the Golden Eagle that he was to be relegated to one of the remote outposts even if Philipe Devereaux had been successfully eliminated. It would be a hard thing, but he had done harder things in his life. Much harder.

"I had a call from Brother Lucio earlier today," Philip continued when the Master did not respond immediately and looked down at his hands. Philip had always liked the Italian personally. Lucio was impulsive and a bit profane at times, but he was very personable and always dependable in a pinch. "He wants me to speak to Brother Ramsay concerning Stephano. He wants Sir Ramsay to take on Stephano as his apprentice since Sir MacLaughlin will be leaving him soon for reassignment in the Middle East."

"That may be possible,"   d'Brouchart pursed his lips.   Major MacLaughlin would be transferred to one of the outposts in the Middle East to take command of a small company of Templar soldiers. His current status as Knight disqualified him from serving as an apprentice. "Sir Barry has been very concerned about the young man since John Paul left for Scotland. They are very close. Much like Brother Lucio and Brother Ramsay were... at one time. If Sir Ramsay will have him, then he will be more closely tied with John Paul in the future. It may be a good thing. It may not. We will see. I will think on it."

"And Brother Lucio also mentioned that he may need the services of our physician,"   Philip added as a footnote.   "He said he was feeling... poorly."

"*Oui*?" D'Brouchart frowned. Feeling... poorly? Already! "Do you mean to say he has taken ill?"

"Yes, your Grace. I have dispatched Dr. Blum to his residence in Naples,"   Philip nodded.   "I sent Sir Champlain with him. He knows the way."

"Good."

D'Brouchart was disturbed by this news. In spite of their differences and their disagreements, he was very fond of the Italian. They had been bickering and arguing together for almost eight hundred years. It was easy to get used to someone after that long. In fact, he missed the man terribly and they had only been back in Italy a few days, but Lucio had gone home to Naples immediately upon their return from Scotland and had not been back to the Villa since. Lucio's presence at HQ had been an almost daily occurrence before the incident, but the Grand Master had allowed him his time alone. It must have been very hard for him to accept two devastating events so closely spaced. To lose his status as one of the Council of Twelve and then the woman he loved all in less than two days! "Ramsay is due in Sunday?"

"Yes, your Grace," Philip told him.   "His wedding is set for tomorrow."

"Good."

The Master set his jaw. The marriage would be done and that part would be finished.

"Your concern for Brother Dambretti's safety is understandable, but he will be in good hands with Ramsay and Champlain to look out for him. I will give some thought to the other. We may transfer the Mysteries temporarily. I will pray on it."

Philip sighed. Lucio's gift was of incalculable value. He wondered what it must be like to be able to see, to actually see, the human soul. And then there were his other, less well understood secrets. Philip was not quite sure what it was that Lucio did. He knew that he read and translated documents for the Master, but why? The Seneschal had no idea how this task had come down to Lucio or if it had anything to do with his mystical knowledge of Egypt. If they lost the Golden Eagle, who would be able to translate all those old scrolls and documents in the treasury? Who would be able to look on the face of a stranger and say whether his intentions were true and honorable? Who would be able to infiltrate the enemy's ranks and find the chinks in their armor if not Dambretti? Who would be able to make him laugh in spite of himself with his blasphemous utterances if not Lucio? Philip got up slowly and turned to leave the room. He had made his bid and lost. Dambretti would go with Ramsay in pursuit of the Golden Key.

The Grand Master watched the Seneschal go. He could almost feel the man's disappointment. He knew how much his second enjoyed the company of the Golden Eagle. It would be a devastating loss, but they had lost many good men in the past. They would lose more in the future. Lucio's best chance for survival and re-instatement lay in his association with Sir Ramsay now. He would have to buck up as they said and come in line or else... d'Brouchart knew that he could not tell Lucio his thoughts. The Italian was too volatile. If he thought that his entire future lay in Mark Andrew's hands, then he would surely jeopardize the mission, if for no other reason, than to prove a point. That point being that he would owe nothing to Mark Ramsay. The scene in front of Mark Andrew's house on the day he had told Lucio of Sir Ramsay and Dame Meredith's impending marriage had been extremely taxing. The Golden Eagle had actually threatened suicide and then murder and had then almost, but not quite, cursed God, along with himself. His words and actions should have been more severely punished, but the Master had allowed him his rage for a few moments before bringing him into line the only way he knew how. Lucio was hardheaded. A few well-placed punches were sometimes necessary to get his attention. D'Brouchart did not regret what he had done to the man. It served a double purpose. It added humility to Lucio's punishment and it served as an example to the others. Blasphemy and impetuosity could not and would not be tolerated among the members of the Council of Twelve.

Sir Philip let himself out of the room and started up the long walk leading back to the main building. He needed to gather his papers from the office there and take them back to his room. He looked up when one of the younger boys who served as a valet for the Grand Master, came running toward him down the walk. Running on the walkway was strictly forbidden.

Philip held up his hand and the boy skidded to a stop in front of him. The boy was about fourteen and almost hysterical. His dark eyes were wide and his face was flushed with excitement. He was also in training at Sir Barry's academy and would be a Knight in the field one day... if all went well.

"Hold, son," he addressed the boy sternly. "What is the meaning of all this noise?"

The boy looked up at him with wild eyes, full of fear.

"Sir Cambrique! You must come quickly!" He whispered loudly before he turned and dashed back toward the main building without waiting for a reply.

Philip considered going back for the Grand Master, but changed his mind. He would see what all this was about before disturbing the Master again. What he had, at first, taken to be boyish exuberance was something else. What new curse had descended upon them now?

Just before he reached the sun porch along the rear of the main building, he saw what was wrong.

Louis Champlain, Knight of the Golden Key, pushed his way through the double doors leading from the main hall onto the porch beside the pool, in his arms hung the limp body of Lucio Dambretti. Dr. Blum followed close behind him. Brother Lucio was feeling much worse than 'poorly'. He looked to be seriously ill or dead. Philip thought ironically that perhaps his concerns had become prophecy. He rushed down the walk toward them.

Champlain glanced at him and then hurried away toward the Infirmary without saying anything. The Knight of the Golden Eagle's head rolled limply from side to side as Champlain walked. The expression on the big Knight's face was one of total despair.

Philip caught the doctor's arm.

"What is this?" He asked in alarm.

"He was delirious when we arrived, Sir. A troupe of medics and a fire brigade were already there trying to convince him to come down from his apartment and he was... well, he wasn't cooperating very well. Brother Louis had to intervene... physically. I thought they were going to press charges, your Grace. I had to sedate him. He thought us some enemy or another and was well ready to fight us both as well as half of Naples," the English doctor did not sound happy. "He could tell us nothing of what was wrong. He seemed to be in a great deal of pain in the abdominal region. I had him brought here for further examination and I'll need to run some tests. I didn't think this was possible, Sir Philip. He is a member of the Council. Is there something I should know about Sir Dambretti's condition?"

Philip just stared at him. He would have to disturb the Grand Master after all and he was unsure of how much to tell the physician. The Seneschal turned to the excited young man still weaving and bobbing next to him.

"Go tell Master d'Brouchart to come to the Infirmary at once on my authority," Philip told the boy in a low voice. "Tell him that I sent you. Tell him it is his Golden Eagle. And... hurry!"

The boy started off at a fast walk.

"Run!" Philip shouted after him as he, himself broke the rules and ran after the doctor.

(((((((((((((<O>)))))))))))))

Sir Philip sat stiffly in the gray metal chair facing the Grand Master as he scowled into space above the Seneschal's head. They were in the small, sparsely furnished office of Sir Charles Blum, MD, poor Knight of Solomon's Temple. One of the few Knights stationed in Italy who was not a member of the immortal Council of Twelve, Dr. Blum did not associate with them freely. He was a good doctor and had served the soldiers well for many years at the outposts before being brought to work, at Sir Barry's request, in a state of semi-retirement for the convenience of the students and staff assigned to the compound. Not an easy task. The boys were always getting themselves into trouble. Philip and the Grand Master had been debating whether to call Ramsay to Italy at once or wait until Sunday.

"There will be trouble in Scotland, if we call him away before the wedding," Philip told him. "Sir Ramsay will not be happy to put off the marriage."

"That will be regrettable for the both of us," d'Brouchart agreed heartily with his Seneschal, but could they afford to take chances with the mysteries of the Golden Eagle? The Grand Master had been undecided whether to have Ramsay remove the secrets from the Italian immediately or to wait... a while, but this turn of events was causing him to lean toward the former. "Brother Ramsay will get over it. He will do his duty."

Philip nodded. Sir Ramsay had never shirked his unappreciated work for any reason. Nor had he ever heard the Knight complain of any assignment and he had listened to seemingly endless complaints from many of the members of the Council in the past. They complained, but they did what they had to do. Ramsay never complained. He simply followed instructions. It was very difficult to tell what the Knight of Death was thinking. But then, Sir Philip did not actually want to know what the Prince of the Grave might be thinking. The Seneschal shuddered at the thought of Ramsay's list of titles. King of Terrors. Prince of the Grave. Knight of

13

Death. Alchemist. He silently thanked God he had no such titles attached to his own name, no such duties and no such mundane work. The duties of the Knight of the Orient were quite enough for him. The most important thing now was the recovery of the Stone, Champlain's Golden Key and, in the process, the death of the traitor who had stolen them.

Dr. Blum opened the door and came into the office carrying a large brown envelope. He slid a stiff sheet of plastic X-ray film from the paper cover and clipped it on the light board above his desk. Again, Philip had to sigh; the doctor was as bad as the Master, preferring to use outdated medical equipment when he could have had anything he asked for. The X-ray equipment at the Infirmary dated from the 1980s and the doctor had refused to allow the Order to purchase a CT scanner for him. He did not want to go back to school and learn how to use it. He could have used any number of modern medical computer programs, but he stuck to the old ways.

"I have never seen anything quite like this." The doctor frowned at them; his French was heavily accented by his clipped British style. "Do you care to tell me what has happened to Sir Dambretti now?" The doctor reached for a very expensive cigarette in a box on his desk. Philip frowned again. Smoking physicians, the height of irony!

D'Brouchart looked at the black and white picture of Dambretti's internal organs. It meant nothing to him. There were light patches and dark shapes, what looked like ribs and perhaps the Golden Eagles' heart in the upper center of the frame.

A very bright, white object about the size of an English pea was located near the lower right side of the frame.

"What is that?" the Master asked and raised his chin somewhat. He did not like modern medicine, but it had certainly come a long way from the Dark Ages. He did not care for doctors, in general, but Dr. Blum was a very necessary commodity for most of the residents of the Villa, even though he was a bit arrogant at times.

"Perhaps you should tell me," Dr. Blum suggested and looked at him expectantly. "It looks like a large gall stone."

"That is common, is it not?" Sir Philip leaned forward to look at the object in question. "Stones. Sir Ramsay only recently suffered from a kidney stone...." his voice trailed off abruptly when he remembered that Sir Ramsay's stone was very different than a normal kidney stone and had, indeed, been the result of strange and magickal workings. Was this another one? Was it possible?

"Common enough in... the regular army," the doctor avoided the word mortal as averse to immortal. "Not common at all in Knights of the Council of Twelve."

"Sir Dambretti has lost his... status as a Knight of the Council," d'Brouchart said almost casually, as if this sort of thing happened every day.

"I see." Blum let out a disgusted sigh and sat down in his chair, looking at them suspiciously. "I didn't know that was possible without being fatal. With all due respect, good Sirs, you must be forthcoming with me or I can be of little service." The man raised one eyebrow skeptically as he exhaled a plume of smoke over their heads.

He knew how it worked for them. They were not subject to every day diseases and illnesses. When one of them lost his 'status', as d'Brouchart called it, that meant that they had gotten themselves destroyed beyond the point of recuperation and had most likely lost their heads as well, to the one called the Prince of the Grave by many of the soldiers. The Knight of Death, *Chevalier* Ramsay. Dr. Blum shuddered at the thought of the Kavorkian Templar, as he called him in private, but made no comment. He did not approve of their methods. He had been a Templar for over thirty years, and he had seen a few of the Council members come and go, but he'd had no part in the passings of any of them. If their so-called Mystic Healer, Sir Simon d'Ornan, could not help them, then they were declared beyond help and the Chevalier du Morte was called to do his 'duty'. He never saw the bodies of the Knights they had lost. In fact, he had never even been officially informed of their demise. How he would have loved to do an autopsy or two. He'd heard of the fairly recent deaths of three members of the Council and he'd seen their replacements, but he'd heard it through the proverbial grapevine. Thomas Beaujold, James Argonne and Hugh de Champlain all gone within the last fifteen years or so. There were many rumors about their deaths, but no real facts to be had. The Council of Twelve had their own way of taking care of things. Usually such changes were absorbed in the status quo with few ripples, but recently, the introduction of a female Knight only proved that things were not always as immutable as one might assume within the Grand Council Chamber. The Knights were not beyond reproach, nor were they exempt from the follies of mortal men. Some of the displays he had witnessed here in the Villa gave proof to the idea that they still had one foot in the Dark Ages. In fact, one of the most brutal exhibitions he had ever witnessed had been perpetrated in broad daylight in the common area in front of the Blessed Mother's alcove. The victim had been none other than the Italian Knight himself, who now lay in the ward room, waiting for treatment. The doctor still had occasional nightmares wherein he relived the day that Sir Barry of Sussex had 'killed' Sir Dambretti in some bizarre form of extreme corporal punishment by stringing him up and beating him with a wooden rod in front of the entire assembly, including the boys at Barry's school. He'd made a concerted effort to learn the reason for it, but nothing had come of his inquiries.

Now he was puzzled, to say the least, by this development concerning the Knight of the Golden Eagle. What did this mean 'lost his status'? Had he lost his title as well as his immortality? Had the Golden Eagle flown the coop? He almost smiled at the irreverent thought and then caught himself before he made a serious mistake. He might be a member in good standing and a long time Templar, but he was still subject to most of the same rules and laws as the rest of them. Certainly, he did not want to get on the Grand Master's bad side. Sir Barry was bad enough to contend with when one of his students was ill. He just wanted these two out of his infirmary.

"Only in rare circumstances," Philip answered his question without elaboration. "What can be done for him? You must treat him as you would treat one of the students."

"I would normally suggest surgery," Blum told them. "But that is not a gall stone, Brothers." He indicated the bright spot with the tip of his cigarette and tilted his head back as he blew another long streamer of smoke into the air.

"If it is not a gall stone, then what?" d'Brouchart asked in consternation, clearly aggravated by the doctor's seeming reticence to just come right out and tell them what was wrong with the Eagle.

"It is not in his gall bladder, for one thing," Blum told them and leaned his chin on his hands. "It is in his appendix." The Grand Master certainly had never learned much about anatomy in all his long years.

"Oh, then this is better, no?" D'Brouchart looked relieved, though he knew very little about the gall bladder or appendix. Internal organs should remain internal at all costs. That was all he knew. All he wanted to know. "So what is the problem? Can you not remove the... thing?"

"The appendix can be removed simply enough, appendectomy, but there are no such things as..." the doctor paused to make air quotation signs before continuing "... appendix stones, so to speak. The condition known as appendicitis, which is an inflammation of the organ itself, usually occurs earlier in life, say... eight hundred years plus or minus younger, in his case. It is usually caused by some sort of blockage in the appendix," the doctor actually smiled. "But it is not usually accompanied by such a large obstruction as to show up so clearly on X-ray. What has he been eating? Rocks?" The doctor swiveled his chair about, stubbed out his cigarette in a stainless ashtray and pulled a small colored brochure displaying very basic outlines of internal organs. He placed it on the desk and slid it toward them. "The main symptom of appendicitis is pain in the lower right abdomen. Here." He tapped the paper with his left index finger. "There is also fever, loss of appetite and nausea. Occasionally, vomiting, of which I believe we found evidence in his apartment, but it was difficult to say whether this condition brought on the vomiting or his rather large intake of alcohol sans food. His apartment was quite cluttered with empty wine bottles. He is a heavy drinker, is he not?" They shook their heads in a mutual lie. "At any rate, surgery is the standard treatment to avoid infection and a possible rupture. I need to remove the appendix as soon as possible since a ruptured appendix can sometimes be fatal."

"And you can do this, no? Here, in the infirmary?" the Master asked, but looked perplexed as he chose to focus on the man's silly question about eating rocks as a way of not dealing with the real problem. He had no idea what the Golden Eagle had been eating. Knowing Lucio's taste for rich foods, there was no telling.

"I can remove his appendix, yes," the doctor nodded. "But there are other... things."

"*Oui?*" Philip leaned forward slightly. What other things? He didn't want to hear about any other things. He did not like doctors. And he particularly did not care for Dr. Blum. The man was too... arrogant.

"He also appears to have scarlet fever." The doctor raised both eyebrows at them and shook his head, eyeing them accusingly. What on earth had happened to Sir Dambretti? Dambretti was the only one he ever talked to and that, most recently, had been about the health and welfare of his young apprentice, Stephano Clementi. The Italian Knight was congenial most of the time and had a wicked sense of humor and they had even gotten drunk together once or twice on the eve of some fast or another when they had been confined to HQ for some reason or another. The Italian seemed a bit less aloof, more down to earth than the rest of them.

"*Oui?*" d'Brouchart asked. He was unfamiliar with these things as well. Disease and pestilence! Still common enough, even in the face of all the modern miracles of medicine, but he rarely gave them much thought. He had heard of this sort of fever long ago, but what it meant was lost on him. He wondered why the doctor had not already administered something for this. Surely, the man had some pill or elixir to take care of a fever! Was he a complete idiot? He would speak to Sir Barry about the man at first opportunity.

"Scarlet fever is another illness common to childhood. It is caused by group A beta-hemolytick streptococci bacteria. He has the rash, the high fever, chills, in addition to the abdominal pains which are common to both diseases," the doctor continued. "Where has he been? Some third world country?"

"Yes, he has only just returned from America," Philip nodded his head vigorously. He did not like this at all. Scarlet fever was rare in this modern age. Only in a barbaric country such as the New World would such a thing still be common. He had heard of many such diseases and pestilence coming out of America. He shook his head sadly, remembering what Christopher Columbus, himself, had brought back to Europe from the West Indies. An insidious disease that still plagued most of the civilized world. Something that proved, once again, that the company of women is a dangerous thing. But then, so was the company of men. The explorers had traded one disease for another, leaving small pox with the Indians, bringing syphilis home to their wives. Philip had to force himself to return his thoughts to the present situation.

"This brand of fever is rarer these days than in ages past. It usually starts with a streptococcal infection in the throat and goes from there. Again, it is more common in children. It's treatable with antibiotics, but I cannot perform the surgery while he has this infection. It would be very dangerous. The fever could cause complications during surgery."

"And?" D'Brouchart prompted him when he stopped. Where had Dambretti picked up a bacterial infection? Scotland? In the evil red water, no doubt. He would need to call Scotland and warn them about this. John Paul and Ramsay's cook could be infected was well.

"I will have to treat him for the fever first and then do the surgery, but if his appendix should rupture before I can safely perform the appendectomy, he could develop peritonitis which can be quite fatal to... mortals." The doctor grimaced at the use of the word mortal "In the event that his appendix ruptures, we would have to transfer him to a larger facility. One better equipped to deal with such complications." The two Knights grimaced at the suggestion of an outside agency. "If I operate on him in his present condition, I could lose him on the operating table as they like to say on the telly," he gestured toward a rather large antique TV console set against one wall of the office. "There could be very serious complications and our facilities here are rather... primitive in comparison to a modern hospital." The doctor coughed and reached for another cigarette and his gold lighter. "It is inadvisable to anesthetize patients with high fever unless it is absolutely necessary, you understand," he paused and they both nodded affirmatively while thinking negatively. "I am more accustomed to treating sprains and bruises and an occasional broken bone. Surgery is... well, I would do it if I had to." He looked at them expectantly. It would be interesting to look inside an eight hundred year old body, but whom would he tell? It would make a good paper, but, oh well, he had given up all of the glamour and prestige of his profession when he had joined the Order. He had to stop thinking like that. It was a good thing Sir von Hetz was not there. The doctor had heard that the Knight of the Apocalypse could read minds! What a pleasant thought that was...

"I see," d'Brouchart nodded. "So there is distinct possibility that he could die?"

"Actually, there is a very good chance that he will if he continues to deteriorate and pick up diseases as he goes," the doctor said flatly as he twirled the lighter deftly in his fingers, fascinating Cambrique. Had the man not been listening to him? He turned to trace the outline of Dambretti's shadowy appendix on the film with the unlit cigarette. "His appendix is much enlarged and greatly inflamed already. It could rupture any moment and I would be forced to remove it before he is ready. The risk would come with the possibility of complications as I said before."

D'Brouchart narrowed his eyes and peered at the bright spot on the X-ray suspiciously.

"When you remove the..." he gestured toward the X-ray with one finger. "... obstruction, I will want to see it."

"Sir?" The doctor looked at him in amazement.

"You heard me, Doctor!" d'Brouchart said shortly and stood up. "I will see the Golden Eagle now." He turned to Philip. "Get the Ritter on the phone for me, Philip."

The doctor's face fell. The Ritter! Not the Apocalyptic Knight. He would have to mind his thoughts. God was punishing him now. D'Brouchart reached across the desk, took the cigarette from the startled man's fingers and snapped it in half. On his way out, he slammed it on the floor and crushed it under his foot, uttering one word sarcastically "Impudence."

(((((((((((((<O>)))))))))))))

The Knight of the Golden Eagle was flying, truly flying without benefit of wings or any other extemporaneous trappings. He was simply gliding over a landscape full of blue flowers that stretched away on all sides toward the horizon. Birds sang in the meadow and millions of bees and butterflies worked the flower petals. In the grass below him and among the flowers he saw many things. Old things and new things. Things that had happened long ago and not so long ago. He wanted to stop and set down at some of the sights, to study them more closely, to talk to the people he recognized there, but he had no control over his journey. He even saw himself along with some of the other Knights in scenes from long ago. Many of the events he saw involved Mark Andrew Ramsay, always present or nearby. Had they really been so close? But he had no time to ponder this question properly before being whisked away to another scene.

It seemed that something or someone was pulling him along. Someone he could not see held his hand and kept him from falling to the ground below. They came to a hollow in the meadows where a fountain with seven heads rose up from the ground with golden water steaming from each head. Sparkling liquid flowed from the fountainheads into seven urns and thence from the urns into seven streams. In the middle of the fountain stood a woman dressed in pure white. Her hair was also golden and the mists of the waters spraying from the fountain hid her face. The woman stepped from the midst of the water and stood before him. In her hand she held a bouquet

19

of violets, purple amaranths and delicate white lilies with pink centers. He took the flowers from her and she held out her hand to him. She drew him back toward the center of the fountain with her. The cool spray fell onto his face, golden droplets clung to his eyelashes, sparkling in the sunlight. He turned to see another woman, dark of complexion with dark hair and small, black horns protruding from her temples. She led a great red dragon on a slender filigreed leash. The dragon pulled back on his chain, twisting his hideously horned head to and fro, but for all his great size and obvious strength, he could not break free of the thin chain that held him.

Lucio looked into the face of the flaxen-haired woman.

"Behold the Hesperian Dragon comes to the fountain! Thrice times seven he must drink of the golden waters," she told him and handed him a silver sword, then nodded toward the dragon. "Make him drink!" she commanded.

Lucio approached the dragon with his sword in one hand and his Egyptian dagger in the other. The dragon reared its head above him and pulled back on the chain, rolling its huge eyes in fear. Dambretti looked up into the red eyes of the beast and felt the blood leave his face. This was no ordinary beast! The dragon drew in a deep breath and snarled at him, preparing to scorch him with its flaming breath. The Knight of the Golden Eagle raised his sword, swung desperately at the white throat of the red dragon and d'Brouchart fell onto the floor.

"Master!" Philip cried out in alarm and bent to help the Grand Master to his feet. Two men dressed in white uniforms ran forward to restrain the patient on the small bed.

A moment before he had been lying on his back, out of his mind with fever and chills, shaking and shivering, with his head thrown back on the little pillow as if he would die at any moment and then suddenly, he had come off the bed, swinging at the Grand Master as he had leaned over the bed railing to look at his face.

"Saints preserve us!" d'Brouchart said under his breath as he climbed to his feet in a most undignified manner.

The two attendants were still struggling with the Knight and finally had to have the assistance of both the Grand Master and Philip to help them, before they could strap his arms to the bed rails. He was delirious again, speaking aloud in Italian now and making every effort to free himself of the restraints.

"*Mio fratello*!" Lucio called to one of his Brothers. Which Brother was unclear.

"Yes, Brother!" Philip leaned close to him. "I am here."

"The destruction of the dragon is upon us! He must not drink of the fountain! You must not join with the virgin, my Brother, my Brother! She is my wife. My wife! *Santa Maria, Santa Maria*! Help us, Holy Mother!" he cried out in Italian and his voice cracked as if he would break down in weeping.

Philip turned to look at d'Brouchart in dismay. Lucio was speaking of the dragon, saying that the dragon had come to kill them. Then the identity of the Brother was made evident when he began to speak directly to Sir Ramsay as he told the Knight of Death that he could not marry the virgin. The last part was most disturbing. "She is his wife?" Philip frowned. "What does it mean?"

D'Brouchart motioned for the orderlies to clear the room. When they had retreated, he leaned close to the head of the bed once more, avoiding the range of the Knight's unsecured legs and feet.

"Lucio, my son," he said in a low voice. Philip had never heard him call the Knight by his Christian name. "What dragon? Why can Ramsay not marry the virgin?"

"The dragon must drink twenty-one times from the golden fountain, Brother," Lucio looked at him as he spoke, but did not truly see him. "The virgin must be married to the second. The twins must be of the Eagle and the Dove. She cannot marry you, Brother. The dragon will win! Shrive me, Brother, for I am dying."

D'Brouchart shook his head. This did not make sense. The Golden Eagle was out of his head with the fever. Delirium, he had witnessed this before.

Philip stepped forward and hit the Knight on his shoulder, answering his request for confession.

"Padre, I am lost. What am I to do? What am I to do with this knowledge?" Lucio did not confess. Was he talking about his mysteries of Isis and Osiris?

"What knowledge?" Philip looked at d'Brouchart. This was not a confession. It was a question. D'Brouchart shrugged. Perhaps Lucio was truly dying and wanted to pass his mysteries on to one of them.

"You must do as you always do, my son. The Will of God," d'Brouchart answered Lucio in Italian.

A terrible pain gripped the Knight and he fell back on the bed, rolling his head and breathing hard. The Grand Master turned away. He could not bear to see him suffer and felt that it was, at least partially, his fault.

"Get Ramsay on the phone!" D'Brouchart told Philip as they hurried from the infirmary. "He must come at once. The wedding will have to wait." The severity of the Golden Eagle's condition finally convinced him that they would have to take the mystery before it was too late.

Dr. Blum, who had been standing in the hall, waiting for them, looked up when he heard this last order. First, the Apocalyptic Knight and now Ramsay. Perhaps he wouldn't have to do anything for the Knight of the Golden Eagle after all, but he would insist that they take him somewhere other than his infirmary to do the dirty deed! He would not allow it to happen on his watch.

(((((((((((((<O>)))))))))))))

Simon covered John Paul with the comforter on Meredith's bed and stepped back, allowing her to bend over him, feeling his forehead. The boy's parents had not asked him to leave and he was thankful for that. This did not bode well. Something had happened to upset the boy tremendously and it seemed to have something to do with the Knight of the Apocalypse. Von Hetz had gone off to the chapel earlier, alone. Something that Mark Andrew had strictly forbidden. Simon had warned him not to go, but had not offered to go with him. Furthermore, he had failed to inform Ramsay that the German was defying his orders. Now he regretted his laziness and his reluctance to be near the Ark of the Covenant. He had no desire to return to the Chapel. He'd not been back since he'd had the distinct honor of carrying the relic from Ramsay's home to the little chapel down the road. It was becoming more and more imperative that they get the chapel back in order and seal the crypts where the holiest relic in the entire world now resided.

"He has not been eating well," she said off-handedly, bringing the priest's attention back to the fifteen year old boy lying semi-conscious on the bed. "He refused his lamb chop at dinner. I wonder if he has not been eating at all these past few days. He would only eat the vegetables and would not drink his milk either."

"I'm sure that he is in good health," Simon leaned closer to look at the boy's face. He lay with his eyes closed, dark lashes resting on his cheeks. The image of his father. It was only when his bright blue eyes were open, that the difference between them became evident. "He has had too much excitement perhaps. The Ritter is also concerned about all that he has been through recently. John's age must be considered. We have all been... under stress."

That was the understatement of the year. The boy had recently witnessed the murder of his own half-brother and then gruesome beheading of the murderer at the hands of his own father. He had come home from Ian McShan's house smeared with blood. The Healer had seen the brutal method the Knight of Death employed when one of them was in need of final correction and it had left him shaken and ill for days every time. Simon shuddered at the thought of this seemingly innocent young man being involved in such a thing. Although he kept his opinion to himself, he felt that John Paul was more suited for the clergy than the Council of Twelve and could not imagine the boy ever replacing one of the Knights. They were,

22

after all, a fine lot of killers. Simon considered himself a Healer, a counselor and a priest first and foremost, but he'd taken quite a few lives himself in battle. If John Paul Sinclair-Ramsay was ever going to become a warrior monk in the service of God, then he had a lot of changing to do.

Mark Andrew returned to Merry's room dressed in his usual black attire, interrupting Simon's thoughts. He went directly to the bed and looked down at the boy who had so unexpectedly interrupted his bath with Meredith. The bath he should not have been taking with her. The embarrassing scene that had been witnessed by Simon of Grenoble, of all people. The wedding was tomorrow, but... his cheeks burned anew when Simon looked up at him.

"How is he?" Mark Andrew asked quietly.

"He's sleeping," Simon said softly. "He said something about the Ritter and the Dragon and..." Simon stopped short. Merry looked at him sharply.

"Elizabeth," she added what he did not say.

"I heard him," Mark Andrew said darkly and shook his head. What did the boy know of Elizabeth? "What does it mean?"

"I don't know," Simon also shook his head. "Let him rest. We'll ask the Ritter."

"Where is the Ritter?" Mark finally locked eyes with the Healer.

"He went to the chapel," Simon admitted. "To check on the crypts. He said there was more water to be drained and..."

Mark Andrew was out of the room before he could finish speaking. Simon looked at Merry in surprise and then jumped when the phone rang, startling both of them.

Simon yanked the receiver from the set beside the bed. "Ah, *oui*?"

"Brother Simon?" Philip Cambrique's voice sounded strained and far away.

"*Oui*," Simon answered shortly. He did not have time for this. Mark Andrew was most likely on his way to the chapel. Ramsay had not been back there since his duel with Lucio when the crypt had been completely flooded with eerie red water rising up from somewhere in the substructure. They had managed to keep him away only because he had been unwilling to go in his heart. Simon needed to go with him now. The Grand Master had ordered him to stay here and help Sir Ramsay see after the great treasure in the vaults below the church. Von Hetz had volunteered to stay and help, thereby allowing John Paul to spend some time with his mother. If something were amiss at the chapel, he needed to be there.

"Where is Sir Ramsay?" Cambrique asked.

"He is not here at the moment," Simon told him without elaboration.

"Listen very carefully, Brother," Cambrique's voice changed a bit and Simon's heart lurched. More trouble.

"Tell Sir Ramsay to come to Italy at once. The wedding will have to be postponed. Our Brother is very ill. He may not last long. Brother Ramsay must come immediately without delay. Do you understand?"

"Yes, I understand." Simon answered and looked up at Merry who stood with her hands on her hips, watching him. She could read his face clearly. She narrowed her eyes at him.

"You and the Ritter von Hetz are to remain there with the Chevaliere," Philip continued. "Tell him to bring Sir MacLaughlin with him."

"*Oui*," Simon's calm voice belied his feelings. He wanted to ask questions. What had happened to Lucio?!

"Brother?" Philip paused. He had expected a more concerned response from the Healer.

"*Oui*?"

"Is something wrong there?" Philip sounded very weary and equally suspicious.

"No, everything is fine," Simon lied and then crossed himself and looked at Merry apologetically.

"Go quickly then and find him, Brother," Philip told him and the phone line buzzed.

"Let me guess," Merry frowned at him as he hung up the phone. "More bad news?"

"*Oui*."

Simon felt his most recently lost depression return at ramming speed. "But you must trust me for the moment, Sister; there is no time to explain now. I will be back shortly and then we will talk. Stay here with John Paul and see to his needs."

Merry opened her mouth to protest, but Simon laid his index finger against her lips and looked into her eyes. If she could not trust Simon, she could trust no one.

"All right," she said resignedly and turned back to the bed where her son lay curled on his side under the fluffy white comforter. He looked well enough for the moment, but something had disturbed him greatly. John Paul had always been the picture of health, physically, at least. She reached to brush away the grass sprigs and remnants of drying soap bubbles from his hair. One of the purple flowers from the meadow was entangled in his dark locks. He had lost his battle with the wolfhounds over the bath. She wondered how many more battles he would lose before it was all over.

Chapter Two of Seventeen
And I prayed unto the Lord my God, and made my confession

Mark Andrew approached the steps of the chapel slowly. The skin on his arms and the back of his neck prickled and he felt cold at the sight of the place where something evil had issued from the depths and tried to claim both Lucio Dambretti and Meredith Sinclair. The question of what had attacked them and where it had come from was still unanswered. He would never forget the stormy night when they had brought the Ark of the Covenant here to the crypt at Glessyn chapel and placed it in the tombs. He had not been back to the place since. Before the Ark had come to rest here, he had never given much thought to the task of keeping up the old place other than routine maintenance. It was just something he did. Something he was supposed to do. Brother Simon and Sister Meredith had been able to talk him out of coming back after the flood... much too easily. He knew in his heart that he had to face his new found fear of the place and get on with his caretaking chores. Putting it on Brother Konrad's shoulders was unacceptable. He would deal with this problem as he had always dealt with problems in the past. He would face it head on, no matter what the outcome. Just going inside the stone structure now, took every ounce of fortitude he possessed.

Konrad von Hetz' BMW was parked in front of the chapel. The old place was as tranquil as it had always been on any bright summer's day. Birds sang in the ancient oaks surrounding the building and squirrels scampered under the trees, searching for acorns. He caught sight of a hedgehog disappearing around the corner of the building and there were deer tracks in the soft earth beside the drive. The atmosphere was bright, fresh and cleansed. Every trace of the storm had disappeared except for a few long, wavy piles of leaves left behind when the water receded. A light breeze brushed the hair from his face and exposed the white braid with its immovable silver trinkets, causing them to jingle slightly as he walked. He touched the white braid instinctively, silencing the jingling earrings embellishing it. He kept forgetting it was there and it never failed to surprise him when he saw it in the mirror. He silently drew the Golden Sword of the Cherubim from its black scabbard with his right hand and a jeweled dagger from one of his pockets with his left hand as he stepped through the open doors. Exactly why he did this, he could not say. There was nothing particularly threatening in sight.

The chapel was cool and dim and utterly silent. Empty. His footsteps echoed hollowly in the high ceilings. He looked up at the carved bas-relief on the columns supporting the arches above his head and passed by the smooth marble altar where he had retreated from the reach of the red, boiling water that had pulled Lucio from his grasp during the flood, remembering his own fear and how he had been unable to save the Italian. There were stripes of dried mud and piles of leaves on the stone. Left there by the same red water that had almost killed Merry when she had been swept away in the torrents outside the chapel. But if Lucio had not been incapacitated by the flood waters, the Grand Master might not have thought him dead and had he not thought the Golden Eagle dead, John Paul might have been lost. If the Master had not agreed to trade the Tree of Life for John Paul, they might not have found him in time to save him. It was a hard thing, weighing the value of one life against another and he chastised himself soundly for even thinking about it in terms of worth. It was within God's purview to decide who should live and who should die, not his.

Thinking again! He had vowed to give it up entirely. The whole thing had been the will of God. The will of God. That was what Lucio always said. He shook his head and the earrings jingled again.

"Dammit!" He cursed himself for thinking and then crossed himself for cursing in the church before continuing down the aisle.

The heavy wooden door at the base of the bell tower stood open. He paused at the door and shuddered. The faint sound of water dripping somewhere below drifted to his ears. A thin layer of silt still covered the stone floor and stairway leading down into the tombs below the chapel. The red glow of a torch flickered on the rough walls at the bottom of the stairs. Mark took a deep breath and stepped softly down the stairs. He felt as if he were descending into Hell, itself. Here, the silt on the risers muffled his footsteps and he could hear the sound of his own heart reverberating in his ears.

At the bottom of the stairwell, he stopped and looked left and right. The torches were lit in the black iron sconces along the walls. The flames swayed in the slow current of air that flowed through the corridor. He drew another deep breath then walked even more slowly toward the crypt where the fallen Templars lay in their stone coffins. It was in this chamber that the Ark sat on the altar below the wooden cross stained with his own blood. He kept his weapons raised and his back to the stone wall, moving sideways. He did not want to see the chamber again, but it was his duty. It was his job. He should have been here instead of the Ritter in the first place. Von Hetz and Major MacLaughlin had been working on the chapel and crypts for days without his help. If something had happened to the Ritter, it would be his fault. The utter silence did nothing to relieve his anxiety. If the Ritter were down here somewhere cleaning, then there should have been noises.

The stone archway into the tomb loomed dark against a rosy backdrop. Water continued to seep from above into the floor where a thin layer still remained in the lower depths. It sloshed around his boots, making soft slurring sounds as he moved forward under the curved stones carved with Celtic symbols of an age long past. He ducked under the low arch though he did not have to do so, it was above his head, but he was, by now, half crouching with the sword and dagger raised defensively in front of him as chills began to race up and down his backbone. His breath came in short, ragged gasps and his knees felt weak. The sound of a slight rustling noise caused him to jerk around to the right. Nothing! Another noise and he spun left. Nothing! The candles on the altar guttered in an unfelt breeze and a rush of cold air almost took his breath away. He swung the blade in front of him at nothing. A short involuntary shriek erupted from his lips followed by an equally involuntary invocation to the Holy Virgin when a rat scuttled across the floor near the wall on his left. Rats! They must have moved in after the storm. A shadow loomed suddenly behind him, but when he spun around, nothing was there that could have made it. He was finding it difficult to deal with the fear that crushed his heart. It was not something he was accustomed to. Normally, he would know exactly where the enemy was and who the enemy was and he would do what he had to do. Normally, the only emotion he had to deal with under trying circumstances such as this, was anger. But he was not angry now. He was afraid.

He steadied himself on the first of the ancient coffins, also covered by silt and squinted into the gloom. His heart caught in his throat at the sight of the Apocalyptic Knight lying supine on the coffin lid directly in front of the altar. The dark Knight lay with his sword clutched to his chest and his booted feet crossed as if he were dead. Mark Andrew started forward and thought he heard another rustling. This time, directly in front of him. Another rat was sitting up on the chest of the downed Knight. A relief and a terror at the same time.

Mark drew back his left hand and threw the dagger at the rat, spearing it neatly from the Knight's chest. It squealed loudly and splashed into the water on the floor at the foot of the altar. Von Hetz did not stir.

When he reached the Knight, he was greatly relieved to find that he was only sleeping. His chest rose and fell in a regular pattern. Mark Andrew went around the coffin to find the rat and pulled his dagger from the disgusting creature before throwing its lifeless carcass across the room toward the door. The rat slapped against the wall and splashed into the water on the floor.

Mark Andrew frowned when von Hetz snored and then nudged him gently on the shoulder with the hilt of the dagger.

"Brother?" His voice echoed in the chamber.

Von Hetz came awake suddenly, reaching up to take hold of Mark Andrew's wrist in an unexpectedly fast move while, at the same time, bringing the dragon sword up and then down on his shoulder with the edge

27

resting at the base of Mark's neck. Ramsay stumbled back away from him in alarm, narrowly missing a collision with the object on the altar behind him. Von Hetz yanked him back in time to save him from the terrible presence beneath the stained cloth covering.

"Don't touch it!!" von Hetz shouted at him and then slid down off the coffin to face him.

They stood staring at each other, wide-eyed in the gloom. Both of them breathing hard after the two closely spaced near misses. To touch the Ark, even by accident, could be certain death, or so the Holy Scriptures said, and neither of them wanted to test the scriptures' validity.

Mark Andrew let go a long sigh of relief and blinked rapidly, trying to calm himself.

"Brother, this is not a good place for napping," he said after a moment when he could speak again. He sheathed his sword and replaced the dagger in his pocket. "It's old and full of... memories." The Knight looked around the crypt and shuddered.

"That is very true," Von Hetz agreed and then spun around with his sword held up as if listening for something.

"What is it?" Mark asked him quietly.

"Nothing," Von Hetz whispered and clasped his wrist again, much to his surprise, yanking him forward roughly. "I thought I heard voices earlier."

A skittering noise echoed through the crypt and Mark found himself suddenly stumbling along after the taller man as he was dragged forcefully from the tomb, down the corridor and then shoved ahead of the dark Knight up the stairs. The fear he'd felt upon entering the old place returned tenfold as a contagion of unexplained terror gripped his heart and they ran like two frightened children. By the time they reached the apse of the chapel, Mark's heart was racing out of control and he felt as if the devil, himself, were right on his heels, chasing him.

He stopped only when he reached the altar where he supported himself with one hand, trying to calm his heart to a more tolerable rate. If these frights kept up, all of his hair would be as white as the alien strands above his right ear. He pushed himself off the altar and turned back to face whatever they had been running from.

Von Hetz stood at the open doorway to the bell tower gazing back into the stairwell, as if listening for something again. The Apocalyptic Knight's face was frozen in unmasked terror.

(((((((((((((<O>)))))))))))))

"Mama!" John Paul opened his eyes and sat up suddenly, causing Merry's heart to jump into her throat. She had been dozing in the chair near the bed. John Paul had been sleeping peacefully. Now he was wide-awake and staring straight out the window in the far wall. The look on his face frightened her.

"What is it, John Paul?" She asked him when he turned his crystal blue eyes on her. What if something had happened at the chapel? What should she do? She couldn't leave John Paul here alone and she had no idea where Major had gotten off to or where Bruce Roberts was.

"My Master is home?" He asked and blinked at her as a chill draught of air brushed her face from the open window. She went to close the window and came back to sit on the bed beside him.

"The Ritter is at the chapel, John," she told him and managed a smile in spite of her own fear. "Have you been eating right, sweetheart? Are you hungry? Can I get something for you?"

"Yes, no, no," he nodded and then shook his head. "Papa is home?"

"He's at the chapel, too. And so is Brother Simon. They're all fine."

John Paul did not look convinced. He frowned and Merry was amazed at how much more he looked like his father when he frowned. Was there none of her in him at all?

John Paul looked up at the ceiling, crossed himself and began to speak in a low monotone voice.

"All this evil is come upon us: yet made we not our prayer before the Lord our God, that we might turn from our iniquities, and understand thy truth. Therefore hath the Lord watched upon the evil, and brought it upon us: for the Lord our God is righteous in all his works which he doeth: for we obeyed not his voice."

This was more than she'd ever heard him say in one sitting. But these were not his words. They were from the Holy Scriptures. Merry did not know chapter and verse, but she knew enough to recognize the scriptures when she heard them.

"John Paul?" She found her voice and leaned toward him, reaching for his hand.

"O Lord, according to all thy righteousness, I beseech thee, let thine anger and thy fury be turned away. Now therefore, O our God, hear the prayer of thy servant, and his supplications, and cause thy face to shine upon thy sanctuary that is desolate, for the Lord's sake. Amen. Amen. And Amen."

Merry stood up. John fell back on the bed and turned his face toward the wall. After a moment, he looked at her again and asked for a glass of water as if nothing out of the ordinary had happened.

$$((((((((((((<O>))))))))))))$$

The Ritter von Hetz waited impatiently for the Grand Master to come to the telephone.

"Brother?" d'Brouchart's deep voice sounded in his ear.

"Yes, Master." Von Hetz' eyes darted around the library at the faces of the people who stood watching him.

"I would ask you a question," the Master's tone was one of deep aggravation.

"Yes, your Grace?"

"The Stone?" D'Brouchart said shortly.

"The Stone?" Von Hetz frowned and Mark perked up at the mention of the Stone. Were they talking about the damnable Stone again?

"What did you do with the Stone, Konrad?"

"Well, Sir, Brother," von Hetz started then stopped before adding quickly "We fed it to Brother Dambretti."

Silence. Mark Andrew looked at Simon in surprise. Simon shrugged and shook his head.

Merry was speechless. They had fed the Stone to Lucio? Why?!

"Why?" The Grand Master echoed the question in Mark's head.

"I saw it in a vision, your Grace," von Hetz admitted reluctantly, feeling foolish somehow.

"Let me speak to Simon of Grenoble."

The Apocalyptic Knight grimaced and handed the phone to Simon who took it hesitantly.

"Is Mark Ramsay on his way to Italy?"

"Ah, no, sir, not yet, your Grace."

Simon looked pained. He had forgotten to tell him. He had found the two Knights in such a state when he had reached the chapel; they had only just gotten back to the house. He had not had time to even find out what had happened to them, but he knew that something was definitely amiss.

"Do as I have said, Simon!" d'Brouchart almost shouted at him and he held the phone away from his ear, gritting his teeth and frowning. He could not remember the last time he had made the Master angry.

"Yes, your Grace," Simon answered miserably.

"Do not delay. There may not be much time." The connection was cut.

Simon replaced the phone in the cradle and looked at them apologetically. His heart was very heavy with the news he would have to impart to them now. The Grand Master's agitation could only mean one thing.

"I have bad news," he said in a low voice and then threw himself down on the hearth. He sat with his elbows on his knees, holding his head in his hands.

"Lucio?" Merry asked in a small quiet voice.

Simon nodded and Merry sank to the floor in despair. Her mind had done nothing but roam back and forth over every possibility imaginable since Simon had gone off to look for the Ritter and Mark Andrew. Lucio's condition had been first and foremost in her mind. She was terribly worried about him and felt responsible for his current dilemma.

"Is he dead?" Mark Andrew cast a dark look at her and voiced the question she did not. Mark had known Lucio longer than anyone else and he knew that the Italian was given to heavy bouts of drinking and deep depression. He had seen him suicidal on more than one occasion. The defeats that his Brother had suffered lately were most likely the worst things of a personal nature that had ever befallen the Knight of the Golden Eagle. Suicide was not out of the question.

"No... not yet," Simon looked up at them, shaking his head.

Von Hetz crossed himself. Had he done the wrong thing? Had they killed him by feeding him the Lapis Philosophorum? Was that why the Master was so angry?

Their misery was made complete by an unearthly scream emanating from the upstairs hallway.

"John Paul!" Merry shouted. She was the first on her feet, but the last one out the door into hall as all three Knights responded to the cry.

John Paul was no longer in Merry's bed. He was in the corner of her room between a heavy wooden chest and the wall, with his knees drawn up in front him. His bright blue eyes were wide with terror and he stared past them at a point near the door. He had taken off all his clothes and violent chills wracked his body as the three Knights pulled him forcefully from the floor and carried him back to the bed. Mark Andrew pulled the covers around him and felt of his forehead.

"What is it, my son?" The Ritter asked as he leaned over him, holding one of his hands.

"Elizabeth," he answered though chattering teeth. Merry pushed the German and the Healer out of her way and felt of his face and his arms. His skin was cold. His fingers were blue. He closed his eyes and continued to shiver and shake while Mark tucked the comforter tighter around him. His clothes were strewn around the room as if he had thrown them about wildly.

Mark Andrew looked at Simon for help. Elizabeth again!

"Elizabeth," Simon repeated the word softly and chewed his bottom lip thoughtfully.

Von Hetz moved to the foot of the bed and stood looking down at the boy. His face was unreadable.

"Sister," Simon caught Merry's arm. "Find Bruce and bring some water and a bottle of red wine." Merry looked at him as if he were crazy.

"Meredith, please do as Simon asks," Mark Andrew urged her toward the door. "He knows what he's doing."

"He needs a doctor, Mark Andrew!" She told him angrily. "John Paul is not one of us."

"Simon will say," Mark told her and shoved her forcefully from the room. "No doctors!"

Merry stood in the hall staring at him briefly before he closed the door in her face. She raised one hand to pound on the door, but the Ritter opened it suddenly and caught her wrist. She was still not used to taking orders from anyone.

"Three Knights beat one Queen, Sister," he told her and gave her a shove toward the stairs. "I will stay with them."

Merry cursed them all soundly as she started for the stairs and the requested items, but the Ritter had a point. If she brought the wine and the water, they would have to let her back in.

"I can do nothing for him!" Simon said quickly when she was gone. "He is not ill. It is something else." The Healer turned from John Paul to Mark Andrew. "The Grand Master has commanded you to come to Italy at once, Brother."

"I canna go t' Italy," Mark told him and shook his head. He picked up John Paul's limp hand and checked his pulse. "I canna leave th' boy like this. His mother wud nevar furgive me." Mark Andrew was clearly upset now. "Wot th' hell is goin' on, Simon? Why does he keep sayin' 'lizabeth?"

"I can't answer that, Brother, but you have no choice in the matter," Simon told him. "Lucio may be dying and you will have to do your duty before he does. John Paul will be in good hands."

"Lucio!" Mark spat the name as if it were distasteful. "Th' mon has caused me nothin' but trouble. Let 'im die and I say good riddance."

"You have to take his mysteries," von Hetz spoke up. "And the Stone. The Stone is with him. You cannot be serious."

"The Stone!" Mark shook his head and looked down at the floor. "Why'd ye do it?" His anger was dying in the face of hopelessness. He would have to go. There was no other alternative.

"We... Brother Simon and I... had the same vision," von Hetz answered and looked at Simon. "The Knight on the white horse. Your brother, Luke Matthew. He showed us what was to be done for Brother Lucio."

Simon did not correct the Knight. He had not seen Luke Matthew. He had seen John Paul with the Stone. Or had it really been Luke Matthew? He remembered it clearly now. But no, he'd had two visions. Now he was confused more than ever.

32

Mark drew a deep breath and closed his eyes. His brother. Luke Matthew. How could it be so and why now? After eight hundred years?

"The wedding?" He asked and opened his eyes.

"Will have to be postponed until you come back," Simon told him as John Paul moaned softly on the bed, causing them all to look down. The color had returned to his formerly pale face, but he clutched his stomach and rolled onto his side whispering the dreadful name again, but did not open his eyes.

"Why does he keep saying Elizabeth?" Mark asked more calmly and cast an accusing glance at von Hetz.

"I don't know, Brother," von Hetz answered, but refused to meet his eyes. He did feel somehow responsible for John Paul's malady.

"You must hurry now," Simon almost pleaded with him and placed one hand on his arm. "The Grand Master is waiting for you and he is not happy. You must break the news to Sister Meredith. I don't envy you your task, but the Ritter and I have been commanded to stay here. You are to take Major MacLaughlin with you. We will see after the boy. You need not worry on that account."

"No doctors here!" Mark told them. "If he does not improve, bring him to the Villa and let Barry decide. The doctors at the clinic understand."

Simon nodded, but wondered how they would be able to move the boy if he became even worse than he already was. He touched the boy's forehead. Fever. The Master might have to contact the Vatican and arrange an air ambulance for him. It would cost them...

Merry returned to the room with a pitcher of hot water and a bottle of wine. She immediately felt of John's face and then scowled at Simon.

"Sister," Mark turned to her. His voice was low and ominous. He looked at her from under his brows. It was not a good thing to see. "I would speak to you... alone."

Merry's scowl turned to one of dawning dread as she scanned their faces. She didn't have a chance against all three of them. Whatever it was, she didn't want to hear it. Mark Andrew had not called her 'sister' in a long, long time. This was an official address. It meant he was about to tell her something concerning business and the look on his face meant it was dark business. They had sent her on a wild goose chase for the wine. Tears welled up in her eyes and she brushed them away angrily. Why were they still leaving her out of everything?

"What now, Mark Andrew? What have ya'll done to John Paul?!" She asked angrily and backed away from him. Her response was personal in spite of her willing it to be otherwise.

He took her arm roughly and dragged her from the room as if she were a disobedient child. The Knights of the Council of Twelve had never been much on tact, nor had they ever been gentle men. Simon was the closest thing to a gentle person among them and he was given to violent rages and dizzying sick spells when pushed to the limits of his endurance. And especially, they had never been easy on one another. Now she was nothing more than one of them. Furthermore, Mark Andrew had never been easy on her before she had become one of them.

She didn't want to leave John Paul. She fought with Mark Andrew all the way down the hall to his room where he shoved her inside and then slammed the door. The sound echoed through the house and Simon shuddered before reaching for the wine. He pushed out the cork with his thumbs and turned it up, taking a huge swallow before handing it to von Hetz. He was very glad the task of telling Meredith that Mark Andrew was about to leave before their wedding had not fallen to him.

Von Hetz turned up the bottle and took over half of it at once. He set the bottle on the table and sank to his knees in front of Simon and crossed himself.

"Forgive me Father, for I have sinned," he said and bowed his head.

Simon was astounded. The Apocalyptic Knight had only just confessed earlier the same morning.

"Go on, my son," Simon told him automatically as he reached for the bottle again. He took a drink above the German Knight's head. Sacrilege! Drinking during confession...

"I have had impure thoughts and I have lain with a woman. I have consorted with demons and I am lost," von Hetz' words tumbled from his lips in a rush. Simon almost sprayed him with the wine.

"No!" Simon cried and backed away from him. He collapsed in the chair beside the bed and turned up the bottle again before continuing. "That's ludicrous! I will not listen to this. You will not make a mockery of the confessional, Brother!"

Von Hetz looked as if he would break down completely.

"You will hear my confession, priest," he said darkly. "Do not accuse me."

"What you say is ridiculous," Simon told him again and then asked "What woman?"

"She was not a woman. She was a... dream... more so a nightmare," Von Hetz told him.

"Then it was a dream, Brother. Not a sin," Simon told him desperately and perked up a bit. "We do not have to confess our dreams. This is not the time..."

"But it was... so real," Von Hetz shook his head. "I have never had such a dream. The scriptures say that as a man does in his heart..."

"No! It was not in your heart, Konrad. It was in your sleep. We all have dreams, Brother. Even I have such dreams," Simon admitted and looked away from him. The subjects of his dreams were not open for discussion. "I will not hear it." The Healer pushed himself from the chair and walked from the room. The wine had done him no good. He felt the familiar nausea roiling in his stomach. He was about to see the wine again.

Von Hetz reached for the bed and pulled himself up to sit beside the boy. He placed one hand on his forehead. John Paul opened his eyes and looked at him briefly before grimacing and clutching his stomach again as if in pain. The pink in his face had darkened to red patches resembling a rash of some sort. Von Hetz was truly puzzled. John Paul was simply feeling everyone's pain. An empath and not surprisingly so. Everyone knew the boy was practically telepathic. Empathy would not be a far stretch.

Had it been a dream? Was Simon right? That Simon would have such dreams was surprising, indeed. He had not thought it possible, but he had never given much thought as to what the Healer might dream.

"Uncle," John Paul said softly and opened his eyes.

Von Hetz was wracked with pain for the boy. He had been lying in unholy slumber beneath the chapel when the boy had taken sick and the idea filled him with guilt and remorse. That Simon had refused to shrive him of his sins had shocked him to his foundations. This whole business shook his faith.

He slid to the floor and crossed himself, looking up at the ceiling.

"I am lost O Lord. Tell me, tell me what I should do with this knowledge?" He asked for divine guidance in his native tongue. In growing alarm, he realized that he needed help in order to understand what to do with the knowledge he had gained from his association with John Paul and the visions he had concerning the situation at hand.

"You are not lost, Konrad," a disembodied female voice drifted into his mind, familiar, yet not, telling him that he was not as lost as he thought he was. At first, he thought Merry had returned and overheard his prayer, but when he turned he saw that he was alone. Then he realized that the voice had spoken to him in German and that the voice was that of the girl who had come to him in the dream in the chapel. His blood ran cold.

John Paul moaned again as another pain wracked him and he began to cough and choke. Von Hetz dragged him from the bed to the bathroom and held his head while he threw up. A splotchy red rash had developed on his back as well as his face and arms and he was shivering with chills and fever. The German had seen this before. He pushed scenes of horror from his mind.

((((((((((((<O>))))))))))))

Lucio was having a very bad day. He was not in the Villa, nor was he anywhere he recognized. The place was dark and hot and he could hear something breathing somewhere behind him, but he could not see it. It sounded very large and very inhuman. He could not move his arms. They were tied at the wrists. Again! Not Again. And he heard someone talking to him. Someone was always talking to him. Matins! It was time for his prayers at Matins, but he could not say his prayers in this place. It smelled of sulfur and burning oil and it was hard to breathe.

A voice came nearer to him. Almost in his face, but he could not see the face. He recognized the voice. Hugh de Champagne, late Knight of King Solomon's Wisdom. As hard as he tried, he could not will his eyes to open. They felt matted shut as if from a sickened sleep.

"You have sinned against your Brothers, sir," Hugh told him in a raspy voice. "It is time for you to repent and beg forgiveness."

"I have done nothing," Lucio answered him.

"You will say your prayers. Thirteen paternosters, Brother," another voice spoke up from his left side. Sir Argonne. Also deceased.

Lucio pulled on the bindings holding him in place. He had died and gone to Hell. This was his punishment. But he could not pray in Hell. It would be blasphemous. Sacrilege!

"You will repent." A different voice and his eyes flew open. Mark Ramsay stood in front of him with the golden sword. Of course! This was the plan, was it not? "And then you will be the best man."

"I will not," Lucio told him stubbornly.

"But I saved you from the dragon, Brother," Mark Andrew told him and smiled at him. "The water in the church. The dragon. You remember?"

"I will not repent," Lucio told him.

This was not hell. It was the dungeon in Rome. The Inquisitors were there, only this time they were Templars.

"Say your prayers!" Mark held the sword's point against his stomach. "Say your prayers and I will cut out the Stone."

"No," Lucio shook his head.

Mark Andrew pushed the sword into his stomach and he screamed. "No! No! No!"

"What do you suppose he sees in his sleep, Sir?" Dr. Blum looked up at Sir Philip in consternation. He had done nothing to cause Dambretti's anguished outburst in Italian.

"Who can say?" Philip grimaced as one of the attendants hooked up yet another small bag of potent antibiotics to the IV tubes beside the Knight's bed. "When will you be able to release his arms?" Philip had been watching him struggle against the straps on the bed for hours. He was tired of it. He only wanted it to be over one way or another.

"We can't let him go," Dr. Blum shook his head. "He will not stay in the bed. We have to keep this medicine flowing, Brother. He needs this antibiotic and the fever is dehydrating him. He won't be able to fight off the infection on the floor."

"Can't you give him something for pain?" Philip got up yet again to press his hand to the Knight's forehead. His skin was hot and rough with a bright, red rash. The fever was very high. The rash covered his arms and his back and he had been coughing and choking and throwing up nothing but foam.

"I have given him everything I dare to give him, Brother," the doctor shook his head. "It is up to God now. If we give him anything more, he's likely to go comatose, no doubt. That would not be good. Also, he needs to wake up. If we can get this fever down, the delirium will pass and then we can see if he is ready for surgery."

Philip nodded. How long would it take? How long could he withstand such a fever? It had been a very long time since the Seneschal had sat beside a sickbed. In fact, he couldn't even remember the last time he had been around someone seriously ill. Grievously wounded, perhaps, but not like this.

"Brother!" Lucio said suddenly and opened his eyes and looked around wildly.

"Yes?" Philip leaned over him.

"Did you get the Stone?" he asked desperately in English.

"Not yet, Brother," Philip told him.

"Then do it now," Lucio said. "I will say the prayers. Just do it now."

Philip raised both eyebrows. The Knight was not talking to him. He was talking to someone who was not there. Someone in his dreams. Philip wondered what he wanted him to do.

"Our father, who art in heaven, hallowed be Thy name," Lucio began the first paternoster as Mark Andrew pushed the sword deep into his stomach. The sword was almost a relief in comparison to the pain the Stone was causing and he only wanted the thing out of him.

Dr. Blum shook his head and checked the small bag of antibiotics hanging from the stand.

"Perhaps he is getting better," he said. "He doesn't seem to be in as much pain as before." He turned to the attendant who was cleaning up the trash from the medicine's wrappers. "Take his temp again and let me know if there is any change." The doctor gave Philip a nod and then left the ward.

"Perhaps," Philip muttered his belated agreement with the doctor, but did not believe it. He sat down again in the chair and crossed his legs. He listened to the Knight repeat the prayers. The Paternoster, over and over. It was an uncanny sound in the harsh lights of the infirmary. Occasionally, Lucio would stop praying and inquire about the stone.

Chapter Three of Seventeen
We have sinned, and have committed iniquity

Merry turned on Mark immediately after he closed his door.

"How dare you treat me like a child!" She said angrily, backing away from him. "I have the right to know what is going on."

"I am not treating you like a child, Sister," he said miserably and tried to approach her as she backed away from him around the bed. "Time is short and I have no choice. I am trying to be… professional with you."

"Professional? What? Which profession? Are you going to assassinate me or cook me up in your lab? No choice in what?" She asked several unreasonable questions before getting to the root of the matter.

"I have been summoned to Italy," he said abruptly and reached for her hand. His only attempt to console her was rejected when she stared at his hand as if it were a snake.

She drew back from him in disbelief. "Italy! How can you leave at a time like this?"

"I've been commanded. I have no choice," he tried to maintain his objective demeanor. God. Order. Family. He did not want to leave. She didn't understand even though she had taken the very same vows herself. Americans! The provisions of the change he had won for the Rule had not changed the loyalties of a Knight of the Temple of Solomon. He had no choice. Mark Andrew distinctly remembered going over this with her several times when he had been teaching her about the Order. "Meredith, you know the drill. I taught you myself."

"John Paul is ill!" She retorted angrily, ignoring him. "You would leave your son to go to Italy? He could die!"

"I would. I will. I am," he said simply and turned away from her. She would settle down after she thought it over. He went to his dresser where he pulled out one of the drawers and began to pile things on the dresser making ready to pack a bag. The motion was rote, well-practiced. His mind was near blank.

"Mark Andrew!" She shouted at him from across the room.

He had no idea what to say to her. And he was not in the mood to argue. So… he ignored her. Not a good thing to do.

"Mark Andrew!" She said again and walked deliberately to where he stood with his back to her, yanking at one of the drawers that had become stuck on the slide bar.

When he ignored her again, she punched him on his upper arm as hard as she could. Not a good thing to do.

He spun on her and took her by the shoulders, backing her toward the bed where he set her down forcefully on the mattress. He stood blinking at her for several seconds, before he turned back to his work on the stubborn piece of furniture. It came free and he took out a single black tee shirt.

She bounced off the bed and was up again. She grabbed the shirt away from him and flung it across the room in frustration. He went after it, shaking his head. He went to the door and shouted into the hall for Major MacLaughlin, knowing full well that his apprentice would not be able to hear him, but he did not want to shout at her. Anger was not what either of them needed. He understood why she was angry, but he could do nothing about it. No doubt his anger toward the Italian matched or exceeded her own and he wanted to add nothing more to it.

"Mark Andrew!" She shouted at him again and tried to drag his bag from the bed to the floor. "You can't leave now! What about the wedding? What is this all about? Why are you abandoning me when I need you the most?"

"I have to go, Meredith," he said quietly and caught hold of the bag, pulling it back. He did not want to go. He wanted to stay and have their wedding. He was already angry that the wedding he had waited so long for was going to be postponed... and for Lucio Dambretti whom he had asked to stand as his best man at her insistence.

"Why?!" She almost screamed at him. Totally out of control now.

She did not want to be shouting at him. After all they had been through... The words he had pounded in her head over and over again during her training came back to haunt her. God. The Order. Family. Little had she thought it would be so hard to live up to those words now. Fighting with him was not what she wanted. Lucio was alive, he was strong, he would last one more day. Eight hundred years? One more day would not matter! It was a pathetic ploy that Lucio had concocted to pull Mark away from her. To postpone the wedding at all costs. A trick. A sick joke. Lucio had lived forever and he picked her wedding day to die? It was preposterous. She didn't buy it for a minute and she couldn't believe that Mark would fall for it.

Every time she watched him walk away something happened. If it weren't for John's illness, she could have gone with him. They could have stayed at the Villa until the crisis passed and then went on to Greece or Monaco for their wedding and honeymoon. They wouldn't have a license anyway, so what did it matter? But he had to go. He had no choice. At least he could have held her a moment... consoled her just a bit... He was working on the jammed drawer again, trying to get it back in the dresser. It wouldn't go so he yanked on it.

The drawer came free and all the way out of the dresser, dumping its contents on the floor at his feet. Socks and tee shirts went everywhere.

"Damn it!" He cursed and bent to pick up the socks. Another mistake. She took advantage of his awkward position by throwing herself at him, shoving him to the floor. He went down on his hands and knees amidst his wayward footwear. She pushed him over on his back and sat down on his stomach, knocking the wind from him.

"Don't ignore me, Mark Andrew!" She shouted as she leaned over him and pinned his hands to the floor above his head. "I won't have it! Answer me. Why do you have to go now? What about our wedding? Lucio would not come for you. He wouldn't even answer your letter and he refuses to come to the wedding. We asked him to be your best man. Remember? And he refused you! Do you know how badly that hurt my feelings? How can you leave your son, your own flesh and blood, who could be dying for all you know, to go off to see about Lucio Dambretti? He tried to kill you, for God's sake!"

Mark's anger with Lucio was brought to the surface by her angry words. Everything she said was true. Why should he go? He owed Lucio nothing! Lucio, his Brother. After all they had been through and Lucio had tried to take her from him... would still take her if he got the chance. But it was not Lucio he was going for. The Grand Master had commanded him. He had a duty to the Order. He had to go.

"I have no choice, Merry," he said and pulled his hands from her grasp easily. He caught her hands as she struggled with him and pulled them to his chest. "You are missing the point. I may have to kill him yet."

"No! Goddamn it! You're missing the point," she countered and glared at him. "If you leave now... if you go... I swear, by God, that I will..."

She did not get to finish her oath. It was something he would not abide. He took her wrists and flipped her over with minimal effort and held her there as she had held him only moments before.

"Thou shalt not take the name of the Lord thy God in vain, neither shalt thou profane the name of thy God."

"How dare you quote scriptures to me, Mark Andrew," she spoke through gritted teeth at him and struggled fruitlessly to get clear of him. "And what does God say of your wife? Therefore shall a man leave his father and his mother, and shall cleave unto his wife."

Mark's eyes snapped with anger. That did it! He'd cleave his wife, by God! He'd cleave her in twain.

"Ye 're no wife o' mine. My wife wudna profane th' name o' God and speak to 'er husband like a common whoor," he told her darkly and let go of her hands, intending to release her completely. But before he could move, and before she could think better of it, she slapped him as hard as she could manage while lying on her back.

Mark froze momentarily and she yanked free of his grasp. This was the way it had always been between them. Had they reverted back to this? Violence? When he made no move to speak, she tried to hit him again and he grabbed both her wrists in one hand, bruising her no doubt in the effort to control her.

"Get off of me, goddamn you!" She shouted and he put one hand over her mouth. Everyone would hear her if she kept it up.

She continued cursing him, though her voice was muffled by his hand.

He let of her grabbed her hands and then leaned forward, replacing his hand with his mouth, kissing her while she still tried to scream at him, but it worked. She suddenly relaxed under him and kissed him back. Would it always be so?

"I would not leave you of my own accord," he whispered in her ear after a moment. "You are my light and my life. Why do you do this to me, Meredith?"

Merry wrapped her arms around him and began to cry into his hair as he kissed her again. Her anger was gone and she wanted only to be held and kissed and loved. Nothing else mattered... at least not for the present.

"You will be the death of me or I of you before this thing is over," he said. "Meredith, if you don't..." His words were cut short when she kissed him again.

(((((((((((<O>)))))))))))

An hour and a half later, Merry stood on the front steps with Simon, watching silently as Major MacLaughlin threw two bags in the trunk of the Mercedes. Von Hetz had stayed upstairs with John Paul. Mark Andrew glanced up at them once, but did not wave or say anything. He opened the door and sat down under the wheel while Major got in on the passenger side. Within seconds they were gone.

Merry drew a ragged breath and turned away. She had a terrible feeling that she would never see him again. The weight of the world seemed to settle on her mind and she was developing a headache on top of everything else. Something she had not experienced in a very long time. Simon followed her inside. He had said nothing during the entire time Mark Andrew had been taking his leave of them.

Simon wanted Brother Ramsay to stay almost as badly as Merry did. He had a very bad feeling about his mission. He did not know if it was the news about Brother Lucio or if it was a feeling of ineptitude concerning John Paul's condition. Simon had not wanted to tell Merry that the symptoms seemed to indicate scarlet fever, something he had seen before in children in days gone by, though usually much younger than John Paul. The Healer still felt that John's illness was psychosomatic in nature. He was almost positive that the boy was experiencing a sympathetic illness, possibly related to Lucio Dambretti. John Paul had even mentioned Lucio by name during one of his bouts of delirium. Mark Andrew had carried the boy from Meredith's room

41

to his own room and put him in the bed, tucking him in carefully and then standing over him for a short while before leaving. The boy seemed to be improving, sleeping better now, but he still had a rash and fever. Simon had wanted to say something meaningful to Mark, but nothing came to mind. Whatever Mark had been thinking, it was probably better left unspoken.

Bruce Roberts caught up with them in the entry hall when they closed the doors.

"Dame Sinclair?" Bruce asked hesitantly. "I need to ask you something."

"Yes?" She answered distractedly. He had hardly spoken more than two or three words to her since she had come to stay at the house. She had the feeling that he did not care for her presence. Perhaps he was afraid his job was in jeopardy.

"Master John Paul," he began and then glanced at Simon.

Simon nodded to him and continued on up the stairs leaving them to their privacy.

"What about him?" Merry asked somewhat anxiously.

"He asked me t' fix somethin' fer him," the man told her. "Before he took sick."

"He asked you?" She hardly thought it possible.

"Yes, mum," the cook nodded. "He wanted somethin' called 'pulse'."

"Pulse?" Her frown deepened. "For what?"

"To eat." The cook raised both gray eyebrows. "I have never heard of it."

"Pulse," Merry repeated and looked at the floor, then back up at him. "Did he say anything else?"

"As a matter o' fact he said 'Prove thy servants, I beseech thee, ten days; and let them give us pulse to eat, and water to drink," Bruce quoted John Paul's words. "Scriptures, I believe, mum."

"Yes, it would seem." She nodded. Scripture again! Did he not know anything but scriptures? "When did he tell you this?"

"This mornin' before he went out t'wash th' 'ounds," Bruce told her. He stuffed his hands in the pockets of his jeans and shrugged. "I've been lookin' through th' cook books oll day. I thought I wud make some fer th' lad's supper... wot 'aver tis. Moight cheer 'im up. I canna find it mentioned any wair except in th' scriptures."

"I will ask Brother Simon about it," Merry told him. "If it is scripture, he will know it."

"Aye," Bruce nodded. "Just let me know wot tis. I'll fix it up fer 'is supper. Moight broighten 'is day."

Merry nodded and forced a slight smile for the man who hurried away back to his kitchen.

Simon went directly to his room and closed the door. He had missed his prayers twice already and he needed time to think. There would be much to do here. First of all, they had to make sure that John Paul was not seriously ill. He did not understand John Paul's mystical connections to his father, the Ritter and Brother Lucio, but he knew there was something mysterious and wonderful between them. And had the boy not appeared to him in his own dreams, as well? But how could a dream or vision leave something solid behind? How did John Paul or Luke Matthew or whoever or whatever leave him the Philosopher's Stone? A vision and yet the Stone had been real! He thought back over the vision he had experienced in the meadow when the Knight on the white horse had given him the stone and told him to feed it to the Golden Eagle.

The Healer forced himself back to reality. There was the matter of helping the Ritter get the chapel ready for sealing, and Sir Philip had instructed him to contact Barry of Sussex for the boy's lessons. They did not want him to get behind in his studies and lose his place in the Academy. The Grand Master had also tasked him to supervise an extensive search of the burned out McShan place for the Golden Key. He would receive help for this. They had already searched the two rooms at the Inn where the ex-priests had stayed while they negotiated with the Grand Master. Von Hetz had been in charge of that one. It had been very hectic, but it had been done quickly and quietly with the help of the Grand Master's influence. He got on his knees beside his bed and crossed himself before bowing his head over his clasped hands.

He had never found the opportunity to talk to Mark Andrew about his feelings concerning the wedding and he had been spared... for the moment. Justice would prevail whether they wished it or no. If Lucio was correct... He would be expected to perform the ceremony sooner or later, the ceremony that he was now dead set against. The words the boy had said to him were crystal clear. 'Join her to the second, by whose seed she shall conceive again and shall in time bring forth a reverend off-spring of double-sex, from whence an immortal Race of most potent Kings shall gloriously arise!' These words were from the Tractate of Hermes. He recognized it because it was one of the things he had been studying with Jacques de Plessier when he had been trying to learn more about the red tincture.

As he knelt beside his bed trying to focus on his prayer, another bit of the Arcanum came unbidden to his mind. 'Now he makes haste to bind and betroth himself to the virgin bride, and to get her with child in the bath over a moderate fire. But the Virgin will not become pregnant at once unless she be kissed in repeated embraces.' Twenty-one days! The Donum Dei. Twenty-one days. Thrice times seven. The Hesperian dragon would have to drink from the golden fountain. The Tractate of Hermes and the Donum Dei was mixed, mingled and mangled in his mind. What he had thought pertained only to the concocting of the alchemist's secret formulas held a double meaning. Why did this come to mind? Of course! Simon opened his mouth in wonder. Had not Mark Andrew and Sister Meredith been in the bath together when John Paul had run to find his father? But the virgin will not become pregnant at once... Simon did not have the divine inspiration and knowledge necessary to sort these things out. He needed help with the technicalities. He needed Dambretti or Mark Andrew to tell him what it all meant in common terms. Neither was available, nor would he have been able to ask them had they been there in the room with him. Such delicate matters. Lucio's letter had said many things. And was not Mark Andrew hurrying, making haste, to marry her? Why?

The writings of Hermes. If Lucio did not understand it, then none of them did. All Simon could know was that it would be a terrible mistake for Mark Andrew and Sister Meredith to be married before it was sorted out. And had not God now intervened, just as Lucio had always said. God's will. God's will could not be changed. God's will would be done regardless of their actions or inactions. The greater plan, the divine plan of the One Great Identity.

"Father, what can I do? I am only a poor Knight of Solomon's Temple. What good is this knowledge if I am not allowed to act on it? I am lost, Father," Simon prayed as he looked up at the ceiling.

"You are not as lost as you think you are, Father Simon. I will help you," a woman's voice spoke to him. He stood up abruptly and turned to see his door standing open. Merry stood in the open doorway.

"What did you say?" He asked her.

"I didn't say anything," she shook her head and her cheeks turned red with embarrassment. "You were praying. I was about to leave... the door was open. I'm sorry I interrupted you."

"Yes, I was, I mean it is no problem," he told her and licked his lips. Nausea threatened his concentration. "I thought you said I may not be as lost as I think I am. I didn't know you speak French."

"I didn't say anything. Much less in French. I don't speak French, Brother," Merry told him and then a shiver coursed through her. "It's cold in here." She looked about and wrapped her arms around her shoulders, shivering involuntarily. "I didn't know Scotland was so chilly in the summer."

Simon looked around the room in confusion. It did seem too cool in the room. The windows were closed. "It's not... usually, Sister."

"I'm sorry I interrupted your prayers," she apologized again. "I came to ask you something regarding the scriptures."

"Go on, then, please," he offered and sat down on the edge of the bed. "I'm sorry that Mark Andrew had to leave."

"Me too," she said and shivered again. "What is 'pulse'?"

"Pulse?" Simon made a wry face. "You mean like blood?"

"No, I mean like something to eat," she almost laughed and then shuddered. Blood! She had seen enough blood lately. "John Paul told Bruce that he wanted some pulse to eat. Pulse and water."

"Really?" Simon's eyebrow shot up. "For how long?"

"Ten days, I believe. What is it? Why?"

"It is what the prophet Daniel asked of the prince of the eunuchs in Babylonia. The head eunuch was called Melzar, in the first chapter of the Book of Daniel. When he was brought to live at the palace of Nebuchadnezzar in Babylon. It meant he did not want any meat or profaned food. He wanted only herbs and vegetables. And he refused the King's wine and asked for water. A grave insult."

"Why?" Merry shook her head again. She had never heard this before.

"He did not want to defile himself," Simon went on. "In ten days, he made himself and his friends wiser than all the philosophers and magicians and astronomers in the entire kingdom. He found favor in the sight of God and God gave him the ability to interpret dreams..." Simon's voice trailed off. "Wait a minute..."

Simon got up and hurried past her into the hall. She followed him down the hall and then down the stairs to the kitchen to where Bruce was fussing over the stove as always.

"Bruce!" Simon startled the old man with his urgency. He turned to face him, obviously afraid.

"Did John Paul say how long he wanted to eat this pulse?" Simon asked him the same question.

"Aye, Father," Bruce nodded. "Ten days. Th' lad said 'e wud eat it fer ten days."

"Ten days..." Simon repeated the words.

"Wot ist, Father?" Bruce backed away from him.

"Your name. What is your name?" Simon took him by the shoulders.

"Bruce Roberts, Sir, you know me. I warked at th' Villa for whoile," the man said quietly, staring at him as if he had lost his mind.

"Yes, yes. I remember, but your name... your middle name..." Simon asked him. The scriptures from Daniel had sparked a trivial, but unsettling memory in his mind.

"I do, Sir, but..."

"What is your middle name, my son? You do have a middle name, don't you?"

"Melzar," Bruce told him and bit his lip in chagrin. He hated his middle name. It had caused him much suffering in his youth. "Me moother. She was ollways readin' th' scriptures. She told me she'd been lookin' fer somethin' different when I was barn, sir. I was the youngest of twelve brothers."

"Melzar," Simon whispered the name, nodded and let go of him. At once, his demeanor changed completely and he smiled at the frightened cook. "Vegetables and herbs. A vegetarian diet, Bruce. That's what the boy wants. It shouldn't be a problem. No meat, no milk, no eggs or cheese."

"Aye, sir," Bruce sighed in relief. "Thot will be nae problem though it sounds a moight unhealthy fur a growin' lad."

"Don't worry. It will be all right," Simon said brightly, turned on his heel and took Merry by the arm to lead her from the kitchen. This was incredible. Melzar. Bruce Roberts' middle name was Melzar! He remembered it from some of the files he had helped Armand with only recently when Bruce had transferred to Ramsay's service from the Villa. The same name as the Prince of the Eunuchs in Nebuchadnezzar's palace. It was all very fascinating. Was John Paul to become a prophet then? An interpreter of dreams? He had to tell Sister Meredith what he had seen in the vision. He was her son. She had the right to know.

"I need to see that letter from Brother Lucio again," he told her as they hurried back down the hall and up the stairs. This time he went to her bedroom.

Merry followed along behind, completely aghast. What was he doing? She wanted to ask him, but he was muttering to himself in French and there was no time. Within moments she had located the letter and handed it over.

"The Treatise speaks of the union between Sol, the Sun, and Luna, the Moon. It also speaks of the Dragon and the Lion who are one and the same as Sol and all these refer to Mark Andrew..." Simon's voice trailed off. "Mark Andrew is the Dragon after all," Simon nodded to himself and then looked at Merry as she plopped onto the floor in front of him. He held up one hand when she started to speak. He didn't want her to interrupt his chain of thought. The Dragon would have to drink from the fountain twenty-one times. But why? And what would be the purpose? Did it mean that he would have to lay with Merry twenty-one times or did it mean something else? Simon looked at Merry. She raised both eyebrows and leaned toward him, looking extremely innocent at the moment. It was impossible to ask her how many times she had been with Mark Andrew since they had been in Scotland together, or if they had been together while she was in training for the Knighthood? Certainly they had had enough opportunities to be together in nine years to accomplish twenty-one consummations even though no one might have guessed. They may have kept up a secret liaison in order to keep the peace with Brother Dambretti, but he could not ask her such a question. Surely not. He began to read again. "It speaks of the union of the Crow and the Lion and their offspring, John Paul..." Again he stopped to think. Was the twenty-one times perhaps the number associated with the conception of John Paul? He needed Lucio to translate this for him. The last line was extremely disturbing. "The powers of darkness will be set against us, my love. They will try to keep us apart and if they are allowed to succeed, we will all be in serious trouble." Simon looked up at Merry again and she frowned. "It could mean anything," he said at length, perceiving the look of anxiety on her face. "Surely if the powers of darkness are keeping you and Brother Lucio apart, could they not, possibly, also be keeping you and Mark Andrew apart as well?"

Where he had been convinced that Merry should not wed Mark before, now he was uncertain again. He pressed his fists against his eyes. He was not qualified to say. He needed more data.

((((((((((((<O>))))))))))))

Chevalier Ramsay sat in a very uncomfortable chair next to Sir Dambretti's bed in the infirmary ward at the Villa in Italy. He had been sitting there with his arms crossed over his chest watching the comings and goings of the orderly attendant with a very sour expression on his face. He had not expected to be placed on watch at the infirmary like a common soldier. It was outrageous. He was a Knight of the Council. This was not proper at all, but the Grand Master had insisted. The men at the infirmary had been avoiding the Knight of the Golden Eagle's bed ever since the Knight of Death had arrived. The medical staff gathered in the corners of the big room, whispering and glancing at him from time to time and he was not happy. He had to assume that it was because he was wearing the Golden Sword at his side, but what was he to do with it? Put it in his pocket? Put it under the bed? His purpose there was as obvious to them as it might have been to his Brothers. A literal Death watch.

Their stares were getting on his last nerve. The third time he caught them staring at him, he got up and pulled the sword from the scabbard and sat down with the naked blade across his lap as if they weren't there. He examined the edge of the blade closely, running his thumb down it and then sucking the blood off of his thumb before glaring at them. That had gotten rid of them for several hours which he'd spent in total boredom, staring at the plain white curtain that was half drawn around the bed of the sleeping

Knight, nursing his sore thumb. But the pain served to give him something to do at least. Suffer.

Lucio, on the other hand, slept fitfully. His face, neck and arms were covered by a red rash. He alternately burned with fever and then broke out in profuse perspiration, shivering and shaking and mumbling in his sleep. He was hooked up to an intravenous bag and his wrists were strapped to the bed rails to keep him from hurting himself. From time to time he would yank on the straps and roll his head, but that was about all he had done. The night was wearing on and the hands on the clock on the far wall were not moving. Twice he had gotten up and checked the damned thing to make sure it was not broken. Mark Andrew's head dropped and his chin rested on his chest. He closed his eyes and drifted off to a restless sleep.

A dream placed him before a tremendous fountain with seven heads, each one rising up above the last, in a stair step fashion. Each circular tier sprayed golden streams of water into the air. The water rose up and curled back on itself. Lucio stood in the center of the fountain with a beautiful, golden-haired maiden. Mark could see them through the curtain of water. The woman was speaking to him in a language he did not understand. Lucio walked through the water and stepped outside the fountain's perimeter, soaked to the bone. The Knight was dressed in a Templar uniform, black this time, with a red cross on the shoulder of his surcoat. He drew his sword and Mark Andrew tried to retreat from him, but a golden chain around his neck held him in place. He drew in a deep breath as Lucio raised his sword preparing to strike at him. He closed his eyes and waited for the death blow, but nothing happened. He opened his eyes again and found that the sword had become a golden cup full of clear water.

Lucio held the cup to his lips, but before he could drink, he pulled it away. "You would drink from the fountain?! I think not!"

"No... yes! Yes," Mark Andrew pleaded with him. He was suddenly desperate for the water.

The cup was gone and Lucio had the sword again. He pressed it to his neck. "You will not drink from the fountain. And you will never have the virgin bride. She is my wife, Brother! It is the will of God."

Mark tried to get away again, tried to break free of the chain that held him. It was slender and seemingly frail, but he could not break it.

Lucio stepped forward, dipped slightly and swung the blade around imitating his own method for taking heads. Just before the blade connected with his neck, he shouted, startling himself awake. He looked up quickly to see if anyone had been watching. No one was in sight. He turned his eyes on Lucio and was startled to see his dark eyes open, staring at him through the railings of the bed.

"Brother?" Ramsay asked quietly and leaned toward him. "Can you hear me?"

"Is it over?" Lucio asked him in a raspy voice.

"You tell me," Ramsay sighed in disgust and leaned back again, misinterpreting the question.

"I am dying. There is no need to pretend," Lucio told him flatly. "Is the wedding over? Is it done?"

"There has been no wedding. You have seen to that, Sir," Mark answered angrily and the Italian smiled. His eyes were bright with fever in his splotchy face.

"She is my wife, Brother. It is the will of God," Lucio told him and rolled his head back on the pillow to stare at the ceiling. He let go a long breath and then began to pull the bonds on his wrists again as pain wracked his body. Mark could not believe he was hearing the exact words from his nightmare. His anger flared and he diverted it to the infirmary staff to keep from leaping on the bed with Lucio. It would not do to attack a dying man no matter how angry he made him. Dambretti was delirious. It was foolhardy to give credence to the words of delirium and fever.

"Medic!" Mark shouted and stood up quickly, flinging the flimsy curtain aside.

Two of them appeared almost magically from beyond the doorway and stopped to stare at him.

"He is in pain," he told them brusquely. "Bring him something! Laudanum. Liquid if you have it. Or if you have no morphine, then opium will do…" he paused when the man cleared his throat loudly and looked at his partner, rolling his eyes. "If ye dunna think ye can prepare it, I'll do it meself. Whair's the med'cine chest?"

"The doctor has left no orders, Sir," one of the men told him hesitantly. "We can't…"

Mark stepped forward and took one of them by the collar of his white uniform.

"Dunna make me angry, Brother!" He told him through clenched teeth. "Ye wud call yerself a man of med'cine? I suggest ye get to it."

He released the man and the other one caught him. They scurried off together. Mark was instantly sorry for having ill treated them. It was not their fault. The infirmary was meant for the laymen and students. His own presence profaned their purpose.

Presently, they returned, but stayed by the door. The sleepy-eyed doctor came to speak to Mark Andrew.

"I can't give him anything more for pain, Sir," the doctor told him irritably and looked closely at Lucio who was moaning and pulling on the straps. He had already cut himself on the nylon cords. Blood stained the pads on the binders. "It would be dangerous to over medicate him in his present condition." Dr. Blum straightened up and cast a contemptuous look at the Knight of Death. He did not like what the man did for a living. And he did not like seeing him there with his golden sword in his infirmary. It was a place for healing, not hacking.

In spite of all his own self-recriminations, Mark's temper asserted itself. The doctor's attitude was intolerable. He stood slowly and drew the unwelcome sword. The doctor's mouth fell open and he stumbled backwards into the curtain. Mark smiled at him wickedly and then used the blade to cut the straps on Lucio's arms. The Knight of the Golden Eagle turned onto his side immediately, curling into a ball, clutching at his stomach with both arms, pulling the IV from his vein in the process. An alarm attached to the device began to beep and Mark stepped toward the shocked doctor.

Dr. Blum turned to leave, but Mark caught his arm and pulled him back, pressing the tip of the blade under his chin, holding him in place with one hand.

"Ye call yerself a mon of med'cine? I will nae aboide yur dungeon techniques," he said. Lucio's predicament reminded him of his own similar experience a few weeks prior. "I'll tell ye wot, sair, if ye dunna wish t' be doctorin' yerself, then ye best be goin' aboot yer business before ye make me truly mad, Brother. Bring 'im something fur pain. Now, move it!" Mark shoved him away with the last three words.

The doctor drew a sharp breath, turned on his heel and left the ward muttering something about ill-bred Scots and mystic bullshit.

(((((((((((((<O>)))))))))))))

The telephone next to Sir Philip's bed rang and he sat up, rubbing his eyes. The clock on the table read four AM. What had happened now? He snatched the phone from the cradle.

"*Oui?*"

The voice on the other end was speaking rapidly in French accented heavily with English.

"He did what?!" Philip swung his feet to the floor.

More almost unintelligible ranting flowed from the receiver.

"I'll be right over," Philip said tiredly and hung up the phone.

Why had they provoked Sir Ramsay... again? Didn't they have any sense at all?

(((((((((((((<O>)))))))))))))

At midnight John Paul woke up. He sat up in the bed and looked around.

"Mama?" he asked the dim figure curled in a chair beside his bed.

She sat up, rubbed her eyes and turned on the bedside lamp.

"John Paul?" She blinked at him in the dim light. "Are you all right?"

He nodded his head. "I'm thirsty," was his answer.

"Are you hungry?" She asked him, hoping that her imagination was not playing tricks on her. He looked absolutely fine. Like nothing had ever happened. There were no signs of the red discoloration that had spread from his head to his toes and no signs of the fever he had developed along with the rash.

He nodded again.

"Do you feel like getting up?" She asked another question, as she stood up and stretched her arms over her head.

John Paul threw back the cover and climbed out the bed. He looked around at the room, frowning. This was his father's room. He did not understand how he had come to be here.

Merry took his hand and led him into the darkened hallway. The wind moaned around the eaves of the old house, but not with the strength they had recently witnessed. The light of the moon shown through the high windows above the stairs. At such times, Merry thought she could grow to love it as much as she had loved her home in Texas. Mark's house actually possessed much more character than hers had and its history only added to its charm. She had heard several of the Brothers complaining that the house was haunted, but she had never seen anything here to make her believe it. Mark Andrew had worked hard to keep it in good repair. Of course there were some areas that were off limits. The parlor wasn't the only room closed off and locked, but if those areas were as well kept as the rest of the house, she would have loved to explore them. There was a door in the hallway between the library and the kitchen that she suspected might be a formal dining room. There were two rooms, also locked on the third floor and the attic was locked as well. If she had the good fortune to actually wed the indomitable Scot, she intended to explore the entire house top to bottom and make use of every nook and cranny. What the place needed was more light and he had said that she could spruce it up any way she liked with the exception of the library and his lab in the cellar. She actually liked the library the way it was and had no intention of spending time in his spidery den in the cellar.

She had already forgiven him for leaving. Her anger had been misdirected. She would ask him to forgive her when he returned. What she did not understand was Simon's peculiar behavior. He was waffling on his support of her marriage to Mark Andrew. Hadn't he just told her himself that the two Knights were interpreting the old documents each in their own favor?

And what had he said about the will of God? It could not be changed, hurried or argued. The will of God would be done.

At the foot of the stairs, they were greeted by a sudden draught of cold air that caused chill bumps to rise on her skin. She rubbed her arms with her hands and looked about, expecting to see an open window or door, but everything was closed up tight. One of the wolfhounds trotted out of the library to sniff at them as they traveled on toward the kitchen. The big dog followed them, snuffling in the dim hallway. A single light above the sink cast deep shadows in the corners and behind the appliances and furniture.

"Have a seat while I see what I can scare up," she told John Paul as he sat down at the table, quietly watching her. "Bruce said he fixed up some pulse for you." She glanced over her shoulder at the boy, but the mention of the word did not seem to affect his expression at all. She went to the refrigerator and removed a plastic-covered bowl filled with lettuce greens, spinach greens, shaved carrots, black olives and sliced cucumbers. "Would you like some dressing on your salad?" She looked back at him.

"Lemon juice," he answered.

She brought the bowl and a bottle of glacier water to the table.

He looked in the bowl and then up at one of the cabinets. Merry watched as he got up silently and then went to open the cabinet. He took down several small metal boxes and brought them to the table. Inside the tins, were a variety of dried herbs. Tarragon, parsley flakes, oregano, chives, sage and basil. She sat down at the table with another bottle of the water and watched him as he sprinkled a little of this and a little of that in his bowl. After applying a bit of lemon juice, he made quick work of the salad. When he was done, he made the sign of the cross in the air and bent his head to pray silently.

Merry leaned her chin in her hand and watched him with great interest. He had grown at least three inches since Christmas it seemed. It was such a relief to see his beautiful smile again, to see that he was growing into a very fine young man without her help apparently. She had the feeling that it wouldn't have mattered if he'd been raised by wolves, the results would have been the same, yet she wondered why he seemed to have made a psychic connection with the Ritter and Mark and even Simon, but not with her.

When he finished his prayers, she broke the silence by speaking first..

"Your father had to go to Italy," she told him.

He nodded briefly as if he knew this already.

"Brother Lucio is ill," she said.

Another nod. Of course, he already knew this. He seemed to know everything already.

"We had to postpone the wedding."

52

This time he did not nod, but raised his eyes to the ceiling and smiled slightly, shocking her somewhat.

"Does that make you happy?" She asked.

He nodded.

"You don't think that your father and I should be married?" she asked hesitantly. She had never thought to ask his opinion of her impending marriage to his father. She had taken it for granted that he would want his birth finally legitimized. That he even had an opinion about it had never occurred to her. Perhaps he did not realize the importance of it, but he now seemed to have an opinion and she wanted to know what it was.

He shook his head slightly. "Too late."

"It's not too late, John. Don't you want us to live here together here... as a family? You and me and your father?"

Another negative response. He looked at her from under his brows, blinking rapidly as if it pained him to think of it.

Merry jumped when the wolfhound suddenly sat back on his haunches and howled.

"Shut up, Matthew! Or Luke! Or whoever you are!" She snapped at the dog and placed her hand over her heart.

John Paul looked at the dog sternly and it trotted out of the kitchen back toward the library.

"Matthew," he told her the dog's name. How he could tell them apart was beyond her.

"John Paul," Merry began again and tilted her head slightly to study his face as he sipped the water. "Do you know Elizabeth?"

He nodded and continued to drink, a cool breeze swept through the kitchen and chills ran up her arms. The house was drafty. It needed some weather stripping, obviously.

"The queen," he continued his brief narrative and looked up at her. "Mother." He shook his head. "A long time dead."

Queen? Mother? Queen Mother? Dead?

"Elizabeth is a queen?" Merry was confused. "You mean Queen Elizabeth of England?"

"Yes, maybe," he said, paused and then added. "Mother, but not of England."

"Who's mother?" She asked.

"My brother's," he said and gave her a broad smile. "Mother. Brother. Sister. And wife."

"Good grief," Meredith muttered under her breath as she tried fruitlessly to get her water bottle's cap back on it. He was extremely frustrating. "Which is it? She can't be all those things."

"Some can," he insisted and then pressed his index finger to his lips. "No talking now, Mother."

His answer was not clear. Perhaps he was just trying to classify her. But how did he know Elizabeth? She had been dead for... eighty years? Another cool breeze brushed her face and she jerked her head toward the back hallway. "Matthew?" She called the dog. She thought he had gone back to the library. He had gone back to the library. "Luke?" she called and two dogs trotted down the hall from the library. They stopped and looked at her in confusion. She shivered. Her imagination was playing tricks on her. The two hounds sat down and waited, expecting a snack from John Paul or a remnant from John Paul's bowl.

Merry decided not to pursue the subject of Elizabeth with John Paul until another time.

Things were going to get complicated when Mark returned. Simon didn't want to perform the ceremony any longer, but she hoped Simon would change his mind before Mark found out. She sat watching John Paul while he found a bowl of peaches in the refrigerator for dessert. When the meal finished for the second time, John repeated the prayers and stood up. She followed him back to the front hall, prepared to escort him back to bed in his father's room, but he kissed her lightly on the cheek, told her not to worry and then disappeared down the hallway toward the ground floor bedrooms in the back of the house where his own room was located was next to Simon's. He apparently had no intention of going back to Mark Andrew's bedroom. Her disappointment made her realize that it was she who needed an escort.

Another draft of cold air brushed her face as she hurried up the stairs. When she reached the top step, she heard one of the dogs howling in the library. A scratching noise made her feet and her heart freeze. The noise seemed to be coming from the hallway to her left. Only Mark's room was that way. Merry cursed softly under her breath, berating her imagination and started down the central hall toward her own room. The noise erupted again and she stopped.

It sounded like one of the wolfhounds was locked in Mark's room and was scratching on the door to get out.

Merry frowned as she tried to remember whether they had closed the door before going downstairs.

"All right, Luke!" She said, steeling herself against her own fears. "Or Matthew!" she added loudly as she walked toward the door. "Master Ramsay's going to be mad at you if you jumped on his bed..." she continued talking more to steady her nerves than chastise the dog. The noise became even louder when she stopped in front of the door and put her hand on the doorknob. She felt the brass vibrating and saw the door moving slightly as the scratching intensified. Her heart seemed to be skipping every other beat. There was no whining or howling or snuffling noises that usually accompanied the big hounds wherever they went.

She drew a deep breath, held it and yanked the door open. A chill blast of air struck her face for one brief instance and then nothing.

No dog. Nothing.

At first she heard nothing as the blood rushed past her ears and then she heard a sort of high-pitched whine that seemed to be emanating from within her own head. With a short shriek, she turned and fled down the hall to her own room. Inside, she twisted the bolt lock with trembling fingers and then collapsed against the wall. Her heart was racing. If only Mark was there, he could explain it all. It seemed that his home missed its master and resented her intrusion. Her nerves were getting the best of her. Perhaps this was why she had overheard some of the boys at the Academy asking John Paul if his father's house was really haunted. Ghosts? Mark certainly had enough of those in his past to fill the entire structure. She wished desperately that John Paul would talk to her. Not quote scriptures. Just talk to her.

She undressed quickly and put on one of her warm, flannel gowns before kneeling on the floor by the bed. As she mulled over John Paul's attitude toward the impending marriage, her thoughts returned again to Simon's words and the things Lucio had said in his letter. She felt like the whore he had called her in his moment of anger, but she had caused that. She had broken one of the rules, provoking him to anger, furthermore she had caused him to break a few more before he left. But now she simply needed someone to tell her what to do. Just what to do. Where to turn. For once, she wanted help and there was none to be had. Simon did not have the answers after all. Perhaps she should consider speaking to the Grand Master about it.

"Father?" She looked up at the ceiling and called upon the Creator, whom she felt would not be listening to her at that moment. "I am lost. I need your guidance. What shall I do with all this information? None of it makes sense."

The question Simon had accused her of asking in French echoed in her mind almost as if he were there speaking to her. 'You may not be as lost as you think you are.'

Chapter Four of Seventeen
Neither have we hearkened unto thy servants the prophets

The days wore on in relative serenity and the days of September passed, unseasonably warm and sunny. Merry was surprised by how quickly they fell into a routine in Mark Andrew's absence. The Ritter rose earlier than the rest of them each morning and had his breakfast in the kitchen with Bruce Roberts before going off to Glessyn Chapel to work on the repairs. Merry, Simon and John Paul ate together and then Simon took charge of John Paul in the library. They used the computer to correspond with Sir Barry at the academy and John Paul was given lessons to study and assignments to complete under Simon's supervision. Merry spent the first part of her morning in her room studying her own documents and records, making notes, meditating and praying. She finished off the mornings by taking a long walk in the meadow with the wolf hounds. There had been no repeat of the strange noise in Mark's room. Nor had there been any other unexplained occurrences and she'd elected not to tell anyone about the incident.

At noon, they all met together for lunch and then after more prayers, Simon accompanied the Ritter back to the chapel to help him with the heavier work there. The matter of re-hanging the doors was no small feat and neither of them were carpenters. A pair of local craftsmen were employed to repair the hinges and door frame, but refused to go inside the church when von Hetz asked them to inspect the bell tower windows. He and Simon had been forced to repair the heavy windows on their own, at least temporarily. John Paul would go out with the dogs into the meadows in the afternoons, playing and running with them. He never seemed to grow tired of the big dogs, nor they of him. Merry took to sitting by her open window upstairs, where she could watch him. She was afraid to let him out of her sight and she never got tired of seeing him at play, imagining him to be a little boy again. She had missed a great deal of his life between the ages of seven and fifteen and those were lost years eternally regretful. After almost losing him twice, she felt that, should anything happen to him again, she would simply die. But since he had climbed from his bed at midnight four nights ago as if nothing had been wrong, nothing more had happened that gave her any cause to worry. He continued to eat only vegetables garnished with herbs that he applied himself and without butter or dressings other than lemon juice. Everything was quiet. Almost too quiet.

Mark Andrew called her every day, sometimes two or three times within the space of a few hours. His conversations were always brief and to the point. He would ask about John Paul, the chapel and her health. She would inquire about things in Italy and he would tell her that things were improving without elaboration and she knew it was a lie. He would comment that he was bored and that he wished to be home with them, say that he loved her "I love you, Meredith. Don't be forgetting that." And then he would hang up. Sometimes barely half an hour would pass before he called back with some question about this or that or some instruction concerning the house or grounds that he wanted her to pass on to Bruce Roberts or Simon. It seemed he only wanted to hear her voice and she found it very difficult to find anything to say to him other than a murmured yes and no. They had very little in common even after sixteen years and everything they had been through together. Striking up a conversation with him was almost impossible. What would they talk about? Old times? The Order? The weather? She wanted to ask about Lucio, but did not dare. She wanted to pour out her concerns and worries, but couldn't bring herself to dump more on his head. She wanted him to tell her what was on his mind, but then was afraid he would. When Mark Andrew spoke of Dambretti, he called him 'your Brother' and never by his name and his comments were laced with profound revelations such as 'your brother is sleeping' or 'your brother is awake' or 'your brother is having his bath'. Merry wondered if another sixteen years would pass and leave them with the same strange silence between them wherein they had nothing meaningful to say to each other.

(((((((((((((<O>)))))))))))))

Mark Andrew was going crazy with boredom. He found himself calling home for absolutely no reason with nothing to say. But just hearing Meredith's voice on the other end was a comfort. And it was something that Lucio could not do. It was the one thing that separated him from the Italian in their mutual miseries. He could call her and Dambretti could not. A petty thing in reality, but it kept him going. He wished desperately that Merry would tell him what she was thinking. He knew very well that she wanted to ask after Lucio's health, but dared not. And spitefully, he refused to volunteer any real information about Dambretti's health to her. Simon, on the other hand, had called him several times and he'd given him the full report. All she had to do was ask Simon. The bloody Healer would fill her in, but he wouldn't.

The infirmary personnel had petitioned off a part of the ward room with hanging, draw-curtains and had given him a regular bed and a small desk. A television he never watched, hung from a rack in the ceiling and a phone, which he used quite often, sat on the bare desktop. A pad with innumerable alchemical scribblings lay on the desk. He tried to recalculate several of his old formulas and came up with a few new ideas to try when he got home, but this was a fleeting pastime. He read a few medical journals supplied from the doctor's office and brushed up on the latest discoveries in science from a supply of magazines provided by Sir Barry. Some of those were quite surprising, but he had trouble keeping his mind from wandering back to his current sorry predicament and who was the cause of it. As his familiarity with the phone increased, he considered asking Simon to help him purchase a personal cell phone with a private number just to keep in touch with Merry. They had offered him a lap-top computer, but he had declined. They had offered to bring him a Gameboy, computer games, puzzles. He had declined. They were desperate to find something for him to do besides sit and watch their every move when he was not on the phone. One of the orderlies had ventured to offer him a number puzzle.

"Wot the divil wud I be doin' puzzlin' over numbers, mon?! If ye bother me again, I'll number somethin' fer ye!" he had shouted at the terrified man. "Whattar ye tryin' t' do? Rehabilitate me? Leave me be!"

He felt as if he were in prison. The only respite he was allowed from Lucio's immediate vicinity was when he went into the bathroom and closed the door. He spent a great deal of time in the bathroom staring at himself in the mirror and he took numerous showers for lack of anything better to do. Only Sir Barry came regularly to visit and drop off magazines. Champlain had come to sit briefly three times, once each day, but they had very little to talk about. Sir Louis would dutifully utter a paternoster for Lucio or with him, if he was awake and then sit a little longer, twiddling his thumbs and then he would leave again. The big, Frankish Knight was obviously eager to get on the road in search of his missing Key. He also felt he owed something to the Knight of the Golden Eagle since it had been Lucio who had taken most of the blame for the loss of the Key. It was customary that the appointed leader of the missions take the blame for everything that went wrong as well as the glory for anything that went right.

The Grand Master came very early in the mornings and sat by Lucio's bed looking at him. Lucio did not like this when he was awake, but he was rarely awake early. He had always been a late riser. He spent most of his time sleeping, talking in his sleep, moaning and groaning and the only time he got up was to make the orderlies happy and then he would spend more time sleeping. He was too weak to take care of himself properly, but protested loudly every time someone came to change his clothes or his bed linens. Baths were torturous affairs, laced with much vulgar Italian. But the medical attendants were extremely patient with him. The fever came and went. The rash progressed. The redness left him and then his skin began to peel, making him itch and complain whenever he was awake. The doctor and the other technicians and medical staff avoided the ward as if the Knights had the plague. They wanted nothing to do with Lucio or his constant companion who kept a sword at his side day and night, often pacing the long room for hours on end, swinging the wicked sword at imaginary adversaries, practicing his swordsmanship without a sparring partner.

Mark Andrew was hardly in the mood to converse with the Grand Master, but sat with him dutifully each morning while he stared at Lucio. It was nerve wracking. Lucio developed a nasty cough on the third day and made it virtually impossible for either of them to sleep for more than an hour or two at a time. The pain continued in his side and every time the potent medicine the doctor had prescribed began to wear off, he would moan and groan and Mark Andrew would pace the floor, waiting for them to come with more of the drug they were giving the impatient patient to ease his distress.

Meal times at best were awful. They brought Mark a variety of food and plenty of wine, but he had no appetite and the wine served only to deepen his depression and darken his countenance. Lucio could eat much of nothing without throwing it all back up. Clear broth. Gelatin. Water. Mark drank to take the edge off of his temper. Then they would have to deal with not only a grumpy Knight of Death, but a partially intoxicated Knight of Death. They stopped bringing the wine and plied him with fruit juice until he lost his temper again and threw a bottle of Strawberry-Kiwi punch across the room.

"Strawberry! I hate strawberry! And wot th' divvil is a kee wee?! A liquefoied faery?!" He had shouted at them, sending them scurrying after a bottle of Scotch, whereupon he had gotten entirely drunk and completely trashed the bathroom in a fit of uncontrolled rage when he found all the towels damp from his repeated showering.

Lucio, on the other hand, had to be made to eat at different times whenever they could force him to stay awake. He did not want the food and he was already beginning to lose weight. His face was showing signs of the ravages of the fever and the lack of solid food. His cheeks looked sunken and there were dark circles under his even darker eyes. The heavy drugs that they were giving him at Mark's insistence caused him to be groggy and unable to control his movements well. His hands shook when he tried to drink and he was constantly spilling things on himself and begging for wine or beer or anything with alcohol. Mark was actually shocked to learn that his Brother was, indeed, a severe alcoholic and had he been a mere mortal for any length of time, he would have been in serious trouble even without the scarlet fever and appendicitis. Mark was too nervous and too aggravated to help him and Lucio never asked him for anything anyway. The floor around Lucio's bed was being scarred down to the unfinished wood by Mark's constant re-arrangement of the chair he sat in as he perpetually moved it to various positions around the bed. He could not seem to settle on one place to sit whenever he did sit with the Knight of the Golden Eagle. He did most of his actual sleeping in the chair with his chin on his chest and they had found him more than once curled on his side on the floor holding his sword as if it were a small child. Oftentimes he would awaken from some nightmare or another and find Lucio staring at him from large, feverish eyes. Another unnerving development. By the end of three days, Mark was completely undecided as to whether Lucio was really dying or even close to death as the Grand Master insisted. He was beginning to suspect that the Master had withdrawn his approval of his impending wedding and was using the current situation to keep him and Merry apart.

The worst possible thing that could have happened to him had happened. He could not have imagined anything more terrible. He had lost the opportunity to wed Merry and then had had the misfortune to be confined with the very reason why he had lost his opportunity in the first place, leaving him with nothing to do and plenty of time to think about it. Mark Andrew was not accustomed to thinking; he was accustomed to doing. He had always found it hard enough to cope with the few minutes a day when he found himself with nothing on his schedule to do. Of course, he had no real schedule, but he had certain things that he did at certain times and these things occupied his mind when he was at home. He had meals and prayers and his work in the laboratory and his work at the chapel and his reports to the Council. He had time with his dogs and time with his apprentice for study and he read a number of small, daily newspapers from the local towns around Lothian and a few reports sent to him from Italy. He rarely watched television unless someone talked him into it or his rugby team, the Border Reivers, was playing. He occasionally listened to music whenever he drove a car or had occasion to enjoy live performances. If anything occurred that he needed to know about, someone would tell him. Other than that, he was lost to international current events.

He supervised the care of his estate and listened to the problems of his servants or servant, as the case may have been. The rest of his time was spent in the mundane cares of life such as brushing his teeth and sleeping. At present, he had no use for the Italian newspapers from Rome and Naples and even less interest in the French newspapers from Paris that the infirmary staff read and offered to share.

Sitting and thinking was not a fit occupation. He had no use for thinking. Thinking only led to depression or rash actions. His only hope was getting through this ordeal, taking care of the upcoming mission and getting home to his soon-to-be wife and son and incorporating them into his daily schedule.

It seemed his only outside interest was that of keeping up with the people he considered friends, such as Simon d'Ornan and, since losing Lucio in that small category, only Merry and John Paul fell into something vaguely akin to family. It was the first time he had ever realized that he had no friends. Over eight hundred years and he had no friends! In the beginning, he'd had his brother, Luke Matthew, but even as a child, he remembered no friends. After Luke had died, he had been with Lucio and then Simon and then Simon and Lucio and then Lucio and Simon. Interspersed along the way, he'd had several apprentices, but he had learned the hard way that apprentices were sources of much heartache if he became attached to them. Since the loss of Christopher Stewart, he'd decided to put as much distance as possible between himself and his apprentices in order to avoid the inevitable pain of losing them. He had only Simon now and his relationship with the Healer was strained. Simon was his confessor. It was very hard to be friends with one's priest. The time he had spent from Friday night until Tuesday morning seemed like an eternity and made him realize just how much he missed Lucio's antagonistic friendship. Had things been different, they could have passed the time talking or perhaps playing chess whenever Lucio was awake, but now they did nothing to pass the time, but try to ignore each other's presence.

He had spent several hours reflecting on the events that had led him to this sorry pass. And those events were even now becoming muddled in his brain. Only the more outstandingly horrible portions remained clear to him. After an extended bout of requisite melancholia, he pushed those thoughts aside only to be assuaged by a sense of depression wherein he wallowed in self-pity for several more hours, examining how he may have succeeded in his attempted suicide. He had to assume that his failure had been due to three factors. First of all, he had failed to pass on his mysteries to anyone else and there had been no one to pass them on to anyway at the time. Second, he had modified the words of the ritual meant to release his soul from his broken body, something he had never done before. Third, he had not cut his own head off, but had tried to run his blade through his heart instead, while such a wound might have caused temporary death and a great deal of anguish, it would not have been severe enough to render him incapable of recovery. In the future, should the need for suicide return, he would have to pass on his mysteries first and then say the exact words of the ritual before inflicting a more potent method such as leaping into a volcano or perhaps devising a guillotine workable by remote control or a timer. The review of his failed attempt at suicide inevitably recalled the reason he had done it and that caused him a great deal of pain at the memory of the terrible death of his former apprentice, Christopher Stewart. This line of thinking led him to wonder again if he had caused Christopher's death by not allowing his servants to call in a physician to tend to him. By extension, these thoughts made him even more angry and depressed about being there with Lucio because he felt that, had Lucio gone on to his home in Lothian as he had ordered him to do instead of taking Merry on a fantasy trip at a local inn, perhaps Christopher Stewart would not have been killed. Inevitably, this thought led to even darker thoughts about the fact that Meredith and his

Brother, Lucio Dambretti, had betrayed him and now here he sat, nursemaiding the Italian, knowing perfectly well that, should Dambretti survive, he would still be after Merry and he should have simply killed him in the chapel and been done with it. It was no wonder he spent very little time thinking! All this mental exercise precipitated a series of calls to Merry wherein he wanted to ask her forgiveness for rethinking these old grievances, but he had been unable to voice his true reasons for phoning her. Instead, he gave her silly instructions for Bruce's housekeeping or needless messages for Simon or the Ritter concerning the chapel's care.

He had pushed these thoughts aside after hearing her voice for the third time in as many hours and tried to formulate a plan for tracking down Philipe Devereaux as soon as Lucio was able to leave the infirmary. Certainly he wanted to get the Devereaux mission out of the way while he was away so that he did not have to go home and then come back again. In addition, he was absolutely convinced that Lucio would recover from his affliction... whatever it was.

Once he was home and the wedding accomplished, he would not be leaving again for a long time. Or at least, not without another command from the Master. Devereaux was a loose end. Louis' Key was a crucial matter that had to be dealt with and quickly, but he could see nothing pending in the near future beyond these issues. He was impatient to get home and show Merry what it was to be a Scot and teach her to love the land as he did. To teach her that he was not without some basically good qualities deserving of her love. There was no doubt in his mind that she would become as attached to the land as much as he was... in nae toime atoll and that an attachment to Scotland would, by extension, strengthen his hold on her and make him just a little more important than the Italian.

There were hundreds of things he wanted to tell her when he called. Places for her to go and things for her to see. Food to try, books to read, but the words never came out. Each time he called, he changed his mind because he could not bear to think of how foolish it all might sound. He wanted to talk to her about taking over the management of the household for him and he wanted her to take over John Paul's tutoring so that the boy could remain in Scotland with them as a family for at least a few years before going off full time to Barry's Academy. He would take on another apprentice to train in the lab and then, of course, Merry would also need an apprentice. He wanted to talk to her about some of the young men at Barry's school. He'd sent for their jackets and looked over the available prospects. There were three in particular that he wanted to recommend to her. She would need his help to choose a suitable candidate and she had no experience in such matters. Then there was the matter of a new groundskeeper and a handyman. Bruce could stay on as cook. He owed the man. And perhaps he could convince Simon to stay on with them in Scotland and make it his home as well... fur a whoile.

Merry loved flowers... roses in particular and he had plenty of room for flowers. They could build an arbor perhaps or a greenhouse. Simon was known for planting gardens from time to time and seemed to have a green thumb. John Paul would benefit greatly from the Healer's friendship. They would be one big, happy family. Simple. The time he had spent thinking along these lines had been the best part of his stay with Lucio, but had taken less than thirty minutes.

His thoughts eventually returned to the mission he would soon be sent to carry out with Lucio and Sir Champlain. Devereaux would no doubt be a formidable foe since he now possessed the gift of immortality. The thing tended to lend a bit of bravado and carelessness that mortal men were unlikely to possess. Certainly, he would be less afraid of them. He remembered seeing Devereaux sparring with Sir Barry of Sussex at the Villa on several occasions. He was an exceptional swordsman and could outshoot almost anyone at the range with the exception of Sir Montague. His fighting skills at hand-to-hand had put his former Master on the ground more times than not. Barry had even employed the former apprentice to help him teach the boys how to fight with lances, maces and swords. He had even designed the lesson plans for Sir de Lyons classes in the care and use of several ancient weapons including the longbow, the crossbow and throwing stars. The man had even gone so far as to have a tattoo on his chest that said 'Approach with Caution!' in three languages. Mark had never cared for the impudent apprentice, but he would definitely keep the warning in mind when he next approached him. Perhaps, if God was with them, the man might never even realize that Death had come for him before he was doing time in Hell.

That was Mark's plan. Simple. Surprise him and kill him before he knew what was happening. Some would call it murder. But he considered it justice. As far as he was concerned, once a Templar, always a Templar. He had been totally against allowing the ex-apprentice to leave the Order in the first place. He had wanted to send him into exile or possibly to one of the outposts as a traitor and be done with it. Of course men left the Order all the time under honorable conditions. They retired, they went elsewhere, did other things, but they remained in touch and loyal... to the Order until the day they died.

Devereaux had sworn an oath to the Order as apprentice that was a bit different than the regular recruits. He knew it was a life-long commitment. He knew the only way out of his responsibilities to his Master and the Council was death. If he did not become a Knight before he retired, he lived out his life in service to the Council in some direct form or fashion. It was just like a wedding vow: until death do us part. The only exceptions had been a few men like Major MacLaughlin who became Knighted officers in the regular Templar Army. His pension would be a bit larger than the regular officers, but such exceptions were few. Why had the Grand Master gone soft? And worse yet, d'Brouchart would hold him responsible if anything happened to Lucio while he was in charge of the mission. This line of thinking brought on more depression. Was he truly now his Brother's keeper? Why? He had not given away Lucio's gift. Why had d'Brouchart cursed Devereaux with the Golden Sword of the Cherubim? Why hadn't he cursed him with the Silver Axe of the Vikings? Or the Egyptian Dagger of Horus, Sir Dambretti's knife? Or the Blue Barrel of the Forty-Five, Sir Montague's pistol? Why did it have to be his sword? He knew the answer. He was the Assassin. It was his job.

So far, their search had turned up nothing, not a clue, as to the location of Champlain's Golden Key. When they found only an empty titanium box at the Inn with a smashed lock, the Grand Master had naturally drawn the conclusion that the Golden Key had been taken by Philipe Devereaux. John Paul had affirmed his conclusion with a brief nod. They could not even be sure that the Stone Simon had received from the Knight in his vision was, indeed, the Stone. It was possible that Philipe Devereaux still had possession of the Stone as well as the Golden Key. No matter. They knew for sure that Devereaux had possession of at least one thing they had to have back and that was Lucio's gift of immortality. That, alone, would have been enough to warrant a search and recovery mission. They would track him down. The man would die. Hopefully, they would be able to recover the Key and possibly the Stone, if the man still had them. These thoughts helped his feelings somewhat. At least they were less depressing and more self-gratifying. Thinking of killing someone had taken his mind off his present misery for a few hours. But it had been impossible to plan anything in that regard. He had no idea where Devereaux might have gone after leaving Scotland. Sir Philip had told him that they hoped to have a fix on him within a week or two. Mark Andrew felt guilty for allowing thoughts of murder to cheer him up. And he spent a goodly amount of time on his knees, in front of the damnable chair, praying for forgiveness when Lucio was asleep.

In addition, thinking of killing Devereaux had caused him to think of killing in general, which had brought back a number of memories he did not want to recall and he had sunk into another round of depression, again blaming Lucio for everything. Eventually, he had just cleared his mind of thought and sat staring at the wall for hours without thinking at all. Just waiting.

Lucio, on the other hand, was having his own problems. He could not get a grip on reality. The world faded in and out for him and sometimes when he woke up, he forgot who and where he was for several long, panic-filled minutes. The few minutes he spent out of the bed were excruciating exercises, which ended in humiliated defeat at the mercy of the Orderlies. They were so bent on rushing him around, he suffered much unnecessary pain under their hasty care. And the hospital gown. A nightmare in and of itself. It was always twisted and always ended up somewhere other than where he needed it most. When he had a clear moment, he would wonder why Mark Andrew was there almost every time he opened his eyes. And then he would remember what had happened and know why the Knight of Death was there. This was even worse than the confusion. They wanted to make sure he did not die without passing on his mysteries. What a comfort that was in his hour of need. The pain in his side was dreadful and the medicine they gave him, made him drift in a miasma of muddy oblivion for hours, but it never lasted long enough. The food was terrible and he had a sore throat. His tongue was swollen and his body ached from the fever. He had pains almost everywhere else in addition to the one terrible spot in his lower right side. Nothing had ever been worse than this. Even the terrible pains he had suffered from the various wounds he had received in the past did not compare with this uneven ride through the endless halls of Hell, drifting in and out of consciousness and in and out of pain. And always, every time he looked at Mark Andrew he was either drinking something or pacing the floor swinging his sword, no doubt practicing for the blow that would take his head! Worst of all, he had heard Mark remarking to Sir Barry that he didn't think the illness was serious and suspected that it was mostly for show. Somehow that remark hurt his feelings over and above everything else. Why had Mark Andrew never trusted him? But then, why should he?

The doctor got on his nerves, the medical personnel got on his nerves, the Grand Master's visits especially got on his nerves and then Mark Andrew's incessant presence drove him up the wall. He did not want the man in the same room with him, reminding him that he was mortal and that he could die and that everything he was, everything he had ever done would go for naught. Unlike Mark Ramsay, he'd not even had one child in all his long life. Not even one sorry bastard to carry on his bloodline. Nothing!

And where was Simon? Simon was his only friend, now that he had lost Mark Andrew in that regard. But Simon had heard his confessions too many times. There were times when he could barely look the man in the face. How could Simon be his priest and his friend? Surely Simon had little respect for him by now. And with all the events that had taken place so recently, Simon was probably totally disgusted with him. He only wished that Simon could understand how he felt about Merry and what the prophecies meant. If only Simon could look into his mind like the Apocalyptic Knight... but that wouldn't be fair to Simon. Simon could never understand. Simon would never understand. It was impossible for Simon to understand the love between a man and a woman. At times, he felt sorry for Simon in that regard, but at other times, he envied him the peace of mind he must have enjoyed at not having to worry that the company of women is a dangerous thing.

The only consolation he had, when he was clear-headed enough to remember his own identity, was the fact that Mark Andrew and Merry had not had the opportunity to carry through with the wedding. Perhaps all his suffering was for that purpose alone. If that were the case, then it would be worth it in the long run. The will of God. Always the will of God. And Karma... and destiny... and....

(((((((((((((<O>)))))))))))))

Sir Philip was called away from his prayers in the chapel by an urgent request from the Grand Master. Edgard d'Brouchart paced the floor of the Council Room waiting for him.

"Sit down!" the man said gruffly when he entered the room and waved one meaty hand at the empty chair in front of him.

Philip took his usual seat at the immediate left of the head of the U-shaped Council table and looked at the man expectantly. The Master was obviously greatly perturbed.

"I have had news," d'Brouchart told him, but continued to pace with his hands clasped behind his back. "It seems that the boy has been appearing to Simon and the Ritter in visions either as himself or as Ramsay's dead brother, Luke Matthew. This apparition was who told them to feed the Stone to the Golden Eagle and he has made many declarations concerning the Arcanum and the prophecies in the Revelation of St. John of Patmos. It makes me wonder at the sanity of my Knights when they choose to keep such things from me until I pry them out. These things can have tremendous... repercussions!"

"Yes, your Grace," Philip nodded when he paused. The news surprised him greatly. Imagine that. The boy... a prophet!

"It is possible that the boy is delving into things in which he has no business," d'Brouchart mused more quietly and stopped briefly to stare at him from bloodshot eyes. "He has convinced Simon d'Ornan that Dame Meredith is to be kept away from du Morte at all costs. That according to the prophecies, she is to wed the Golden Eagle instead. But the Ritter is convinced that she is already pregnant and with twins, no less! And, further, that these twins belong to Mark Ramsay. Now, tell me, my dear Brother, when and how did that happen? No!" he said, throwing his hands up in exasperation, before Philip could say a word. "Don't tell me how... I want to know when our venerable Knight of Death had time between going mad, dueling with the Golden Eagle, taking care of the Chapel and everything else he had to do, tell me just when he managed to woo our Dame Meredith into his bed... again. He certainly is a busy fellow. But then, you did not know

66

that he had gone mad, did you? That he was apparently strangled to death by his own hair and that at the time, it was not attached to his head? And now? Simon has changed his mind and believes that she is not pregnant after all. He believes that the Ritter jumped the gun as they say."

"It is possible that Brother Konrad was mistaken, your Grace," Philip answered softly and shook his head. He was truly amazed. Strangled by his own hair? Not once, but twice had Ramsay been strangled by his own hair. Why was this not in the records? He would check with Armand immediately. "A very tricky business, interpreting dreams and visions. Deciphering prophecies and whatnot. I would not presume to try. And you say that John Paul is influencing their actions? How so?"

"Yes, yes!" d'Brouchart threw up his hands again and spun to face Philip. "It seems that they neglected to tell me about the worms and that damnable braid of hair he used to wear with the silver earbobs. About it taking on a life of its own and choking him to death or some such. Simon was quite vague, mind you... but there are strange things afoot in Scotland! I am quite aware of the words of the Donum Dei and the descriptions of the worms etceteras, etceteras, but I am appalled at this turn of events. I had no idea that these things were so very... very..." He paused again, searching for the correct word. He slammed his fist on the table, causing Philip to jump. "I didn't think they would be so literal! Now Ramsay has a patch of white hair in his head that can move about on its own, the which cannot be cut from his head by any blade, by the by. Magick! Sorcery! Fie! Fie! And fiddle-dee-dee! Further, the silver trinkets are hopelessly entwined in this mysterious lock of hair, the which he claims is not his hair. Demons! Specters! Great God Almighty, preserve us from Satan and his minions. Would that I could understand it all. Mine eyes have led me astray and mine heart doth weep so at the treachery of the lustful heart! Deliver us, I pray from the wiles of lovers and Scotsmen!"

"Saints preserve us!" Philip whispered the words and his eyes widened. He now wondered about the Master's sanity. He'd not heard the man in such an uproar in ages.

"I have seen it myself," d'Brouchart spoke more quietly after a few moments of silence and seemed to calm down somewhat before finally sitting heavily in one of the burgundy leather chairs at the side of the table. "When I went over to see the Golden Eagle this morning, du Morte was sleeping and I took the liberty of examining his hair. I ventured to touch it and I was... it felt... like... it was like no hair I have ever encountered. He almost pulled that cursed sword on me when he woke up and caught me leaning over him. Damn his Scottish ass to hell, Philip! I wanted to cut his scalp from his head in the manner of those poor bastards on the American frontier. Let him put that in his pipe and smoke it. He vexes me, Philip, he vexes me. For an age on an age, he has vexed me to the bone and I? What have I done to deserve this treatment from a Brother? Why nothing, I assure you, good Sir. Did not our roots entwine so deeply within the earth's good heart, I would put him out of his misery myself. And fie the Italian as well! Have I not kept him close all these years? Kept him and loved him and for what? So that he could entangle himself with his Brother's wife? Oh, the world has grown colder than ever for an old man. We have not advanced here one iota. Did I not know better, I would look to see Tiamat in the Heavens come evening. "

D'Brouchart fell silent and Philip waited for him to go on with a look of pure astonishment on his face. He had never heard the Master speak this way about one of the Brothers of the Order and he hardly understood half of what he was saying. The reference to Tiamat made his blood run cold. He did know something of her.

The Master poured himself a glass of brandy from a decanter on the table. Philip sighed as he realized that the Master must have been here for quite some time, pacing the floor, drinking heavily. Not in years had he done such a thing.

"I had thought we had come to the sixth chapter of the Donum Dei with the production of the Stone in Ramsay's body," d'Brouchart continued after the burn of the liquor left his throat. "The black Stone, which he originally... passed was taken by the two thieves, but I now see that we have progressed much further. We are into the fifth chapter. The worms have already been brought forth. And the Stone has passed from black to white in the stomach of the boy. He must have taken it from those hapless idiots whilst they were sleeping and swallowed it because Simon told me that he appeared to him in a vision and gave him the Stone, which was by then perfectly white. Now they have put it into the body of the Golden Eagle. The water in the chapel, the red water that flooded the crypt, fulfilled the rest of the sixth chapter and Dambretti was made red by the waters. Now he is nurturing the Stone from white to red. Of the bitterness in his throat the color is taken, from his body the redness, and from his back pure water! Just as the fifth chapter has foretold. Understand the Gift of God, receive it and hide it from all unwise Philosophers. I have given the Gift of God, which was hidden, to the thief and taken it from the Golden Eagle. Damn my soul to Hell!"

Philip was totally confused. He knew nothing of the Donum Dei and the Alchemical Art. Worms. Stones. Pure water? Animated hair? He was lost.

"Know ye that this red of the art is the Crow," d'Brouchart almost moaned aloud. "I had thought Mark Andrew was the Crow and that his son was the Head of the Crow, but Lucio is the Crow. And I have done wrong."

"Master," Philip could say nothing more. He did not understand, but he did know that the Master was being too hard on himself. "You cannot have done wrong. What you did, you did in good faith. God's will be done. You are the instrument of God. Therefore, whatever you have done has been at His bidding."

"You are a good and loyal friend and Brother, Philip," d'Brouchart almost smiled at his second and seemed to relax somewhat. "There are three circles of digestion according to the Tractate of Hermes. The first was the extraction of the Stone from the dregs in Mark Andrew's body by sweat and labor. And the second was his son John Paul and called the Restoration and speaks of the flood and the deluge, which occurred at the Chapel. But this was a gentle digestion without pain. After the flood, the body of Lucio lay without his spirit and without motion and without pulse. He was then ready to receive the Stone. He is the third circle of Digestion. The Stone passed through his stomach and is now in his appendix. It says that it be moved by the Feverish and most gentle heat of dung, lest that the things volatile fly out, and the Spirit be troubled at the strictest Conjunction with the Body. The Stone is exactly where it should be. The boy is a prophet and if not a prophet, then a sorcerer of exceeding great power." The Master's eyes lit up with sudden realization and he pointed one finger at the ceiling. "God has sent a Messenger amongst us, Philip and we did not know. I have been blind. The boy is a Prophet!"

Philip sighed. The Grand Master had talked himself through the dilemma. The great, red-haired man slapped the table again, this time with no small satisfaction. He looked up a Philip smiling broadly.

"All we need to do is get the Key back from Devereaux and we will be back on track," he summed everything up. "I must go and see the Golden Eagle. Ramsay must not marry the Dove."

"But, your Grace…" Philip, who had been relieved momentarily, was astonished at this final announcement. He stood with the Master. "This will not set well with Ramsay. His wedding to the Chevaliere was set for Saturday past. He is already very disturbed that it had to be postponed. And you are proposing to send him with Brother Dambretti to retrieve the Key. If you now make known that he is forbidden to marry Sister Meredith, he will most likely be in a state. It may even be dangerous to send them off together. Surely he will kill the Italian."

D'Brouchart's smile faded.

"Mark Ramsay could have killed Brother Lucio in that chapel," Philip continued quickly in the void. "Have no doubt, Sir. The only reason that Brother Dambretti's head is still attached his neck is because Sir Ramsay did not want to kill him. My God, Sir! They have been like father and son, like true brothers, closer than friends for eight centuries. If Mark Ramsay decides that Lucio Dambretti must die, then the Golden Eagle will die! If you are right about this, and I have all confidence that you are, then you will certainly condemn the Italian to death if you make your knowledge known to them before they go. I beg you, Sir. There must be some other way. These things you speak of have come about of their own accord by the will of God. Isn't it possible that you really have nothing to do but sit back and watch the will of God play out before you? Is it possible that you need not... interfere?" Philip said the word and then cringed inwardly; expecting an explosion to follow, but the Master simply narrowed his eyes thoughtfully.

"You may be right, Brother," d'Brouchart nodded. "Simon said something that I believe may be of use to remember and apply to this situation." He leaned toward the Seneschal and lowered his voice conspiratorially. "We are not here to ensure that the prophecies are fulfilled, we are simply here to fulfill them. I will not say anything that would upset our dear Brother Ramsay. It will not be necessary and God forbid he should send that braid to choke us in our sleep," d'Brouchart laughed and Philip's mouth fell open slightly at the jest. "The prophecies cannot be unmade. They are the will of God. And besides..." the Master paused and Sir Philip looked at him expectantly. "I don't believe that du Morte could handle being more upset than he already is. He would simply explode into a mound of haggis."

(((((((((((((<O>)))))))))))))

Tuesday morning dawned a rare day in the Scottish countryside. The sun was up and shining brightly on the meadows, the winds resembled spring breezes and the smell of hay and wild flowers filled the air. Simon found himself dreading his return to the Villa. He had grown used to the wide-open spaces and the comfort of Mark Andrew's big house. He corresponded with Jacques de Plessier daily. Jacques was continuing the deciphering of the documents he had gleaned at the monastery in France and Simon listened to him talk about the contents of them with feigned interest. He did not have the heart to tell his apprentice that it was all for naught. At least it kept the man busy as there were no other, more pressing, matters to deal with at present. He finished up his morning session with John Paul and wandered out to the patio to sit in the sun. He could see Sister Meredith as she walked with the dogs far out on the meadow. It was hard to believe that they had been through so much evil only so recently. Merry looked like a small girl out in the field with the hounds running to and fro around her.

In spite of the beauty surrounding him, Simon was troubled. He was not sleeping well. His dreams were full of fleeting shadows and things just beyond his reach and understanding. The Ritter rarely spoke to him any more. The man seemed to be totally preoccupied with cleaning the chapel and the crypt below it. Almost obsessed. In fact, Simon had been hard pressed to convince the Knight of the Apocalypse that he should go over with him in the afternoons to help out. Never-the-less, cleaning was progressing nicely. Almost all the silt had been cleaned from the stone coffins and the lids replaced over the bones and remains in the tombs and the Grand Master would be coming in a few days to bring a new cover for the Ark. He thought it just as well that Mark was gone and had not stayed to help with the cleaning. Seeing Christopher Stewart's corpse had been quite horrid. Not to mention Beaujold, Champagne and Argonne all in varying states of decomposition. He shuddered at the memory of it, but what could they do?

The Master would oversee the sealing of the crypt. Something that Mark Andrew had protested loudly. He did not want the crypt sealed. He had been caring for it for hundreds of years. Ramsay did not like change. As far as he was concerned, the crypts belonged to him. They were his responsibility. And even though Mark Andrew had not wanted to go back to the chapel after the incident with the red water and Brother Lucio, he still did not want the crypt to be sealed. Instead, he wanted the Ark to be moved. He didn't care where it went. He just wanted it gone from his chapel and he even expressed this thought on several occasions by telephone to the Ritter, who had listened to his complaints without comment. Simon knew that the Ritter had subsequently suggested that it might be wise to move it to Switzerland, but the Master had rejected the idea for reasons known only to him. Simon silently agreed with Mark and the Ritter. There were better places.

The worst part was that everything had happened so suddenly. Mark was hardly over his bout with the kidney stone and the madness, before he was called away to Italy. That he had been sorely disappointed had been quite evident. What would eventually happen, only God knew. But Mark Andrew was his friend. Not just his Brother, but a true friend. Sometimes it was hard to separate the friend from the Brother and vice versa, especially when he was acting in the capacity of a priest and confessor.

Simon was also troubled by the Ritter's aborted attempt to confess his dream. What had he been thinking? If they had to start confessing the crimes and sins they committed in their dreams, he would be a very busy priest indeed! The Ritter had never mentioned it again, but he seemed distant now and somehow changed. It was nothing Simon could put his finger on, but there was something hidden or something irreconcilable in his mind.

Simon also worried about the visions he had received in which John Paul had appeared to him as himself and then as Mark Andrew's dead brother. The Grand Master was convinced that it was the boy who was manifesting himself as Luke Matthew Ramsay. There were things there that were puzzling. The man had mentioned his dreams. 'Beware the phantoms of the night, Healer! Thy father will mourn thee sorely shouldst thou fall prey to this abomination. Woe unto your dreams!' His father would mourn

him?   It puzzled him greatly.   What abomination?   What dreams?
Furthermore... who's father?

(((((((((((((<O>))))))))))))))

Konrad von Hetz had been very busy. Working diligently to get the
crypt ready for sealing. He wanted to get it done and be gone. His work
there was taxing with the presence of the Ark so near. The object weighed
him down and oppressed him, but he blocked it from his mind as best he
could and tried to ignore the ever-present spirits that hovered near it. He had
gradually become aware of their presence more and more over the last few
days. They were unseen and unheard, just beyond his conscious perception,
but now he was growing more and more sensitive to their whisperings and
flutterings. He did not want to know more of them. He wanted nothing to do
with them and he felt they wanted nothing to do with him... except for one.
There was another presence in the chapel that had nothing to do with the Ark.
Or, at least, he felt it had nothing to do with the Ark. He wondered if Mark
Ramsay knew of this spirit, or presence, in his beloved old chapel. He made
a note to ask him about it sometime. He was hard at work sweeping off the
top of the last of the stone coffins in the immediate vicinity of the Ark when
he heard again the girlish giggle he had heard on the first day he had come
here alone.   He glanced about the dim interior of the tomb and finished
brushing the grit into the dustpan before setting it on top of a coffin. He
would deal with the presence this time. He would not be taken in as before.
It was an abomination! He would exorcise the spirit as he had exorcised
many such things in the past.
    "Show yourself," he said sternly into the seemingly empty chamber.
    The girl stood up in the center aisle. The same place he had first seen
her. She wore the same flowered dress and her wavy, red hair fell on her
shoulders in lustrous cascades.
    "What do you want, girl?" He asked.
    "I have come to help thee, Konrad," she told him just as she had said
the first time he had seen her. She spoke in High German.
    "Get thee behind me, Satan," he whispered and walked toward her.
"Be thou gone, thou unclean spirit!" he spoke more loudly and drew his
dagger from his belt. Holding it upside-down in front of him, the guard and
hilt making the sign of the cross.
    "Unclean?"   She laughed at him.   His stern countenance and
unflattering words did nothing to turn her aside. "Thou wouldst insult me,
Ritter, but to no avail. I know thy mind. I know thy heart."

"You know nothing of me." He stopped a few meters from her and waited. He had made up his mind to send her away if she returned. "Turn from me evil spirit."

The girl laughed and the smell of freshly baked bread and wild flowers filled the air. She walked slowly and deliberately toward him.

"Wot is it that ye be wanting, Konrad?" She asked him softly as she came within striking distance, now she sounded like Mark with a distinctively Scottish lilt. "Would ye be wantin' t' kill me?" she looked up at him and he tried to look away from her eyes. They were so deep... so green... so lovely. "I think not, sair."

"Elizabeth," he said her name aloud and the sound of it echoed slowly through the crypt. The dagger dropped to the floor. He snapped back to reality. "Get thee back into the darkness from whence thou came. In the name of Christ Jesus, be gone!"

"I am yours, Konrad," she smiled at him, speaking German again and he drew his sword. The invocation of the name of Christ should have worked. He wondered if she might be of the same ilk as the spirits hovering about the ark after all. They were not ghosts, but something else. They were something entirely different. Something with which he had no experience.

"Elizabeth," he said her name again and she stepped closer. He held the sword between them. She did not flinch at the sight of the black and silver blade. She took hold of the naked blade with her bare hand, pushing it aside as if it were a feather.

"Elizabeth," he said once more before she closed in on him, wrapping her arms around his waist, laying her head on his chest just as she had the first time he had seen her. "I am lost," he muttered and closed his eyes.

"You are not as lost as you think you are, Konrad," she told him.

Chapter Five of Seventeen
O Lord, to us belongeth confusion of face

"Good news, Sir!" The doctor greeted d'Brouchart at the front doors of the infirmary. "You won't believe this!"

D'Brouchart frowned at the man. He seemed overcome with joy. What had happened? Had Ramsay died? Had he and the Golden Eagle finally killed each other? He thought nothing short of this would have made the doctor happy.

The Master had never heard so much complaining from anyone, about anything in several hundred years, as the complaints made against Ramsay by the good doctor. Ramsay was too loud, too rude, too restless, too silent, too demanding, too arrogant, too moody, too neat, too frightening, too grumpy, too nosy, too... everything. And the doctor's complaints were rooted in the truth. The Grand Master knew that Ramsay was unhappy; he did not need the doctor's report to confirm it. Ramsay did not want to be in Italy. D'Brouchart had never had the occasion to work closely with Mark Ramsay for any length of time in their long history of association, but he had learned a great deal about his Knight of Death in the past few days.

First and foremost, he had learned that he was very lucky that Mark Andrew lived in Scotland. He had also learned that Mark Andrew did not like Italian food and that he drank too much Scotch and that he freely associated dirt and rats closely with doctors. He had nightmares almost every time he closed his eyes and he was hardheaded, impulsive and narrow-minded. He despised television, did not care for radios, could not abide ignorance and had no developed sense of humor. His reading preferences were limited to ancient manuscripts, alchemical textbooks and scientific journals, which he muttered about as he read, disagreeing with the authors apparently. He was intolerable of even the slightest hint of impudence from subordinates. He had a bad habit of scowling from under his brows, tapping his teeth with his thumbnail and he spent too much time in the shower. He hated strawberries, didn't care for raw onions and he did not know his basic tropical fruits. He had no apparent hobbies or interests outside of alternately dozing in chairs and pacing the floors. He didn't know and didn't care about world events and he did not want to know anything that did not relate directly to the Order or Scotland. And last and most exasperating, the man believed that the infirmary was infested with Brownies as if such a thing were a common occurrence.

The Master was not unfamiliar with the beings that inhabited the ethereal planes, but his knowledge of Italian faeries was a bit lacking. Such things were not near as prevalent as they had been in the past. D'Brouchart had employed Sir Philip to look that one up for him and had learned that Brownies were supposedly a part of a race of mythical creatures known as the 'Wee Folk', allegedly inhabiting the country sides of Ireland and Scotland. A pesky group of little people with nasty habits. Ramsay had requested a set of glass wind chimes to keep them away from the ward. Sir Philip had provided him with the chimes, but he still insisted that Brownies were stealing the toilet tissue and towels from the bathroom. How on earth had he missed all these quirks in the man he had known for over eight hundred years? If there were Brownies in the infirmary, then the Scot had brought them in his luggage!

Sir Ramsay's temper deserved a study all its own. It was barely suppressed and he often reverted to speaking with such a heavy Scottish brogue, it was difficult to understand him at all. The infirmary staff was terrified of him. He had even accused the doctor of practicing satanic rituals in his spare time and had, subsequently, made a formal request that the doctor be investigated for use of Black Magick, Sorcery and Voodoo. And all of this in less than four days. The man spent too much time thinking! But then, the Knight of Death was under stress. He did not want to be there with Lucio Dambretti. He wanted to be home in Scotland with Sister Meredith no doubt. Another problem yet to be resolved and Mark Ramsay seemed to have more problems than was any man's fair share. If d'Brouchart could have found a nice, bloody insurrection to send him off to, things would have been better for all involved.

D'Brouchart crossed himself sub-consciously as he followed the doctor to his office and waited while the man closed the door.

"Look at this, Sir," Dr. Blum said excitedly and pointed to another X-ray sheet clipped to the light board above his desk. "We just took this one a few hours ago."

The Grand Master squinted at the film. There was no sign of the bright obstruction in the picture of the Golden Eagle's internal workings. He sat back in the chair in alarm.

"Where is it?" He asked suspiciously.

"I don't know," the doctor let go a long sigh and beamed at him. "I have never seen anything like it. It's gone! Vanished! Poof!"

"Poof?" d'Brouchart shook his head. "That's not possible."

"No, it isn't. But you see it is not there." The doctor pointed to the place where it had been. "And the pain has gone as well. Not only that. His fever is down and the rash has disappeared. He is still peeling a bit and weak from lack of food and the effects of the fever. But there will be no need for surgery. And, thank the Lord in Heaven, he can go home and recuperate there with the help of his apprentice."

"Did it...pass?" D'Brouchart asked, wrinkling his nose as he recollected the words he had quoted from the Tractate of Hermes to Sir Philip. The stone was to be processed in the slow heat of digestion: dung.

"Excuse me? You mean did he pass the object through his intestines?" The doctor frowned at the question. He was appalled at the Grand Master's lack of enthusiasm for his good news. "I wouldn't know, Sir, but I would have to assume so, though I couldn't be sure. I haven't looked at his elimination chart this morning."

"But you are his doctor! Don't you people keep up with these things?" D'Brouchart asked in growing alarm.

"We had no reason to suspect anything. High fever tends to restrict the natural functions of the body. I will check his chart and get back with you on that," the doctor said defensively. "You might ask your Sir Ramsay about it. He's the one who has been with him night and day. If he got up to the bathroom, then your Knight would know. Of course, pain is also a symptom of blocked intestines as is nausea and vomiting. It is possible that the obstruction was partially blocking his bowel and he was throwing up from time to time. If he did pass the blockage, then he would most likely remember the occasion. It should have been... explosive. But then you can ask him yourself. Sir Dambretti is awake and lucid. Perhaps he can tell you more than I."

D'Brouchart sat pondering how he might ask such a thing of the Golden Eagle.

"Is there some chance it might have gone somewhere else?" He asked almost hopefully.

"The obstruction?" the doctor asked, growing somewhat aggravated. What was with the obsession with the obstruction? "Not likely, Sir. Of course, there is no way to know what it may have been composed of. It could have simply dissolved. That would be one for the record books," he muttered under his breath. "Not likely," the doctor ventured a small, dry laugh. "But I can release him this afternoon and you can be assured that he will be more than glad to go. And I will not be sorry to see him leave since that will mean his companion will be leaving as well."

This was good news and bad. He had come to the infirmary try to speak with Lucio concerning the prophecies and was glad to hear that he was over the fever and out of pain, but the Stone... They had to have the Stone. He also wanted to discuss the Arcanum with the Golden Eagle. It was, after all, his mystery that was concerned with the Treatise of Hermes. But the Stone!

"See to it that he is released as soon as possible. I would speak with Ramsay first," d'Brouchart told him and stood up. The doctor led him out of the office and down the hall to the ward occupied by the two Knights.

Mark Andrew stood up when he came in. He had been sitting in a chair near Dambretti's bed.

Lucio looked at him from beneath a scowling brow. What had they been doing, the Master wondered. Sitting and staring at each other?

"Brother!" D'Brouchart actually smiled as he approached the bed and extended his hand to Lucio. The Knight took his hand and kissed his ring.

"Your Grace," he said flatly. His face was covered with a whitish, powdery looking film as if his entire skin had died and was now coming off. They had put some sort of lotion on it. He looked awful, but his eyes were full of their usual devilish gleam.

"The doctor tells me you are well," the Master nodded to him.

"Yes, so I'm told," he said shortly.

"He will release you this afternoon," d'Brouchart assured him and then turned abruptly to Ramsay. "Brother Ramsay."

"Yes, your Grace?" Ramsay perked up at this news. It was over!

"I would speak to you alone."

Mark's countenance fell.

A few moments later found Mark Andrew pacing the steps in front of the infirmary.

"Wot in God's name air ye askin' me, yer Grace?" He grumbled the question and stopped to look up at the Grand Master, who stood on the top step looking down at him. "I dinna go in th' water closet with 'im and we didna discuss th' outcome! In point o' fact, we've discussed nothing together since I've been 'ere."

"We have to have the Stone, Brother," d'Brouchart tried to reason with the Scot.

"Then I suggest ye fetch the plumbers, Sair," Mark retorted and looked at him in wonder. "And 'ave them commence t' diggin' in th' ground warks."

D'Brouchart nodded and made a face.

"We will meet later on tonight to discuss the mission," he changed the subject abruptly. "I expect news this afternoon of Devereaux's location."

Mark stopped pacing and drew a deep breath. This was a much better subject.

"Then you are still planning to send me on this mission?" he asked, though he already knew the answer. The brogue vanished.

"The man must be found. The Golden Key must be returned to Sir Champlain and the Golden Eagle's gift must be restored. You cannot fail me in this, Mark," d'Brouchart lowered his voice. "You must work out your differences with Brother Lucio. He is still one of us as long as there is breath in his body. And you must make sure that he does not lose his life in the process. It would be a hard thing to replace him. I am not ashamed to say that I have missed him and I didn't think it was possible, but it is true. In

77

spite of his irreverence and his straying from the path, he is a good Knight and true to the Order. He does not shun his work and he is... refreshing. He gives me diversions, if you will."

"You place a great burden on me, Sir," Mark said darkly. "How do you know I won't kill him myself? I have never been able to control the man."

"You are too attached to him to kill him. Is he not like one of your damnable hounds? Would you kill it if it chewed your slipper? Tell me, Brother.... what would you do without him? What would your life have been without his... influence? He was your Brother long before you knew Sister Meredith. In the end, you will both do as God wills."

D'Brouchart turned abruptly and left him on the steps, retreating inside the infirmary from the combined glare of the midday sun and the Knight of Death.

The Grand Master found Lucio out of the bed, searching the room for his clothes. He held the hospital gown close around him with one hand and looked at him questioningly. D'Brouchart sighed and began the uncomfortable task of questioning him about the Stone, stammering and stuttering around the question he needed to ask.

"It is difficult, Brother," he said after a few minutes of getting nowhere. "I need to know if you passed the Stone. Did you check your... bowel movement for... inclusions?"

"*Che cosa e` esso?*" He frowned. "No, your Grace. I did not look at it at all. Was I supposed to?"

D'Brouchart grimaced and shook his head.

"I thought you might have noticed or felt something... unusual," he muttered and shook his head in defeat.

"I did notice one thing, your Grace," Lucio told him and then lowered his voice. "The quality of the paper here leaves much to be desired. I should think we might afford something a little... gentler on the bottom, eh? I have used softer cornshucks."

D'Brouchart raised one eyebrow in consternation.

One of the attendants came in carrying the Knight's clothes, neatly pressed on a hangar.

"Aha!" Lucio smiled as he took the clothes from the man and checked them over. "It's about time."

He took his clothes and disappeared quickly into the bathroom, leaving the Grand Master standing in the room with the attendant.

D'Brouchart turned slowly and headed back toward his office. He would have to do no less than what Mark Andrew had suggested. He hurried away in search of Sir Philip and Sir Ramsay. They would have to call the plumbers.

Simon leaned back in the chaise lounge. He had a few minutes before lunch and the warm sun on his face caused him to linger on the patio. He yawned and closed his eyes. A cool, almost cold wind brushed his face and ruffled the blonde hair on his forehead. Simon opened his eyes and looked into the eyes of Mark Andrew, Chevalier du Morte.

"Father!" Mark Andrew took his hand. "You must come with us at once!"

Simon of Grenoble's eyes widened. Sir Ramsay looked panic-stricken. What was wrong now?

He looked around the deserted sanctuary. No one else in sight except for the three of them. Where were the others? Why had no one come for prayers?

"They are coming to arrest us all. You included," Sir Boniface blurted.

"Who is?" Simon shook his head. Why? He had done nothing wrong!

"It has been decreed by the Holy See!" Ramsay told him brusquely and tugged on his arm. "Brother Edgard sent us to get you."

"I haven't... I don't..." Simon turned away from them, looking back at the altar where he had been preparing to say the early mass.

"You must hurry, Father," Sir Ramsay insisted. He would hear nothing of his protests.

They turned back toward the aisle, dragging him along with them. Simon only then realized that the two Knights had come into the sanctuary wearing their swords and daggers. Sir Boniface held a mace in his left hand.

"Weapons are not allowed at mass, my sons," Simon said inanely, eager to put aside the panic he felt welling up in his heart.

They almost made it to the front doors before a troop of Provincial soldiers burst through the open doorway, heading directly for them in a rush, weapons drawn. Simon stumbled back when Sir Ramsay grabbed him and shoved him out of the way, drawing his broadsword. The first soldier to meet them fell at the hands of Ramsay, speared through and through on the golden blade. The second soldier fell as the side of his head met with Sir Boniface's mace. Blood sprayed into the priest's face, shocking and horrifying him.

They were killing each other in the sanctuary! He was unable to comprehend fully what was happening. Two more soldiers rapidly replaced the first two, but Sir Ramsay hacked his way through them to meet the fifth, who fell back in terror at the sight of the enraged Templar in a blood-spattered, white mantle. Sir Boniface dropped the heavy mace, unsheathed his own broadsword and reached back for Simon, dragging him forward roughly. He opened his mouth to cry out, but his shouts were cut off as two more soldiers made their way around Sir Ramsay and fell on the frightened priest. One of them ran his blade through Sir Boniface's back and out through his stomach, while the other hacked at the side of his neck from the rear. Another spray of bright red mist hit the priest full in the face and he shrieked in disgust and anger, trying to grab the blade from the soldier who had killed the Knight of the Serpent. The soldier pushed him aside and brought the blade down on the exposed neck of the fallen Templar. Simon caught himself on a candelabra. Sir Ramsay was still fighting with more of the soldiers in the center of the transept. The two soldiers advanced on him and he heard Sir Ramsay shouting something in his strange Scottish dialect just before a gloved hand slammed into his temple causing the world to fade away in a blinding white flash of pain.

Simon jerked awake with a shriek and looked around Merry's patio. Two crows sat on the glass-topped table, eyeing him warily. One of them had a dead lizard hanging from its beak. He waved one hand at them and they flew away in noisy protest. He sat up and rubbed the side of his head where the soldier in his dream had hit him. He imagined that there was a sizable lump there and when he looked at his hand, blood was smeared across his palm. He patted the spot again gingerly and found a small cut over his left eye.

"*Sacre bleu!*" he muttered and pushed himself up in the chair, looking around suspiciously. What had happened? Had he hit himself? Or had one of the crows been trying to make a snack of him?

And the dream? So realistic. He remembered every word, every moment as if it had actually happened only yesterday. Nothing like it had ever happened in reality! Why would he be dreaming of Sir Boniface? The man had died in France in 1307. Killed by the soldiers sent to arrest the Templars in France on the order of the Pope, but Simon had not been present at his murder. Simon had not even been a Knight at the time. He had only just been recruited to the Order by Sir Edgard as a priest. He had missed the entire affair, the arrests, the imprisonment and even the flight to Scotland due to an unfortunate twist of fate that had left him very near death, comatose in fact, for almost two weeks. He'd not thought of Sir Boniface in decades. Sir Boniface had been his predecessor as Knight of the Serpent, but that had been seven centuries ago! The entire series of events surrounding the fall of the Templars were but a blur to him. One minute he had been a simple priest for the Order in the Languedoc and the next, he had found himself waking up in Scotland with the remnants of the Knights Templar who had fled the persecution and thrown in with Robert the Bruce against England. He didn't even remember the trip to Scotland. Now he was here again and he had forgotten how beautiful it was on a good day.

The Healer stood up and looked around. Sister Merry had already returned to the house and it was time for lunch. He wondered how John Paul's diet was coming. The boy had been eating only fruits and vegetables since Mark Andrew had left them. This would be the fourth day. Six more to go. He went into the house and found Bruce Roberts hurrying down the back hall.

"Father Simon," the cook greeted him at the door. "There is a call for you in the library, Sir."

Simon nodded and went to take the call.

Sir Philip was excited. "The Grand Master asked me to call. Sir Dambretti has recovered and is out of danger for now. He thought you would want to know."

"Yes, I am grateful for his consideration."

"The Master will be coming to Scotland in a few days to seal the tomb," Philip told him. "It is ready, *oui*?"

"*Oui*. Almost," Simon told him. "And Sir Ramsay? Will he be coming also?"

"No. He will continue his assignment," Philip would say nothing more of this. "Is the Ritter available for the phone?"

"No, he hasn't returned from the chapel yet. Perhaps he will call you?" The Ritter usually came back just before noon and waited for the call to lunch while reading and answering his own e-mail. It was eleven thirty.

"Tell him to return to Italy at once. Bring the boy with him," Philip instructed him. "The Master is concerned about the boy's studies. We have had news concerning the thief. The Master feels that the boy will be safer here at the academy."

"I see," Simon grimaced. Sister Merry would not like this.

"You and Sister Sinclair will stay there and wait for the Master," Philip told him.

"*Oui*," Simon nodded to the phone. He did not want to face Merry with this news.

"Is everything well there?" Philip asked.

"*Oui*," Simon answered shortly. His 'vacation' was over. Strangely enough, they had been truly enjoying themselves except for the nightmares.

"Go with God," Philip responded and then hung up abruptly.

Simon reluctantly replaced the phone on the charger.

As he expected, Merry did not take it well, but the Ritter, for the first time in days, seemed to cheer up a bit and Simon thought the man was actually going to smile.

"It will be good to get home for a while. My old Cookie will have given up on his Master returning, I'm sure, and gone off to work in town. I'd to have to replace him," the dark Knight had told them before sitting down to eat. He had come back to the house shortly after the phone call in an extremely agitated state. He fully intended to make the argument once more for transporting the relic to Switzerland before returning there himself.

Merry had been unable to tell John Paul that he would be leaving. He had been having such a good time, it seemed. She felt they were all abandoning her. First, Mark Andrew and now John Paul and the Ritter and she had never heard von Hetz refer to anyone in such an affectionate manner. He was obviously very pleased and relieved to get away from Scotland. She had protested that he should stay in Scotland long enough for John Paul to finish his cleansing diet, but the Ritter would hear nothing of it. They would make sure that John continued his diet uninterrupted. The Master had given the order and the Ritter would obey.

But when Simon broke the news to John Paul, he had taken the news with his usual bland expression and then smiled at his mother and patted her arm as she had hugged him as if to say 'It'll be OK, mom'. The Ritter reported to them that the Chapel was ready for sealing and that there was no need for Simon to go there after he was gone. In fact, he had stressed the point several times within a short period. Enough to send up red flags, but Simon had been relieved to hear the news and would not allow his curiosity to overrule his common sense. He did not relish the thought of going there alone. The place seemed to be full of spirits and not all of them were benevolent. He did not envy Mark Andrew's job at all. But a sense of melancholia overcame him as they ate their meal in silence and though von Hetz had not been much of a conversationalist, he would miss the Knight's presence and the comfort of having him nearby. The Grand Master would no doubt expect him to return to Italy once the crypt was sealed and he hated to leave Merry alone in Scotland, but someone would need to stay until Mark Ramsay returned. Perhaps he would be allowed to stay a bit longer if he voiced his concerns just so. And then there was the unsettled business of the wedding and whether it was to be or not to be. Again, the will of God would prevail.

(((((((((((((<O>)))))))))))))

"That is preposterous!"

Lucio Dambretti stood up suddenly, slamming his fist on the table in front of him to accentuate his outburst.

"Sit down!" d'Brouchart told him sternly and the Knight of the Golden Eagle complied reluctantly, glaring at the man with barely suppressed rage.

"The situation is critical," d'Brouchart continued. He looked from Ramsay to Champlain to Sir Philip and back at Dambretti.

82

Mark Andrew's face was unreadable and Champlain looked pained. Lucio looked awful. He was pale and thin. Not something they were used to seeing in the normally robust Italian. He seemed to have trouble breathing. His eyes were dull and he appeared to be suffering from a headache as he kept squinting and pressing one hand to his forehead. In fact, it seemed that his entire frame seemed about to buckle with exhaustion as if he had become a palsied old man.

"Devereaux has been in Monaco," d'Brouchart briefed them. "He apparently came into some money and since he took none from us, I have to assume that he has sold the Key to a third party. Furthermore, it didn't take long for him to go through it. He has gone back to France, apparently penniless. Fortunately, we have also learned that a certain fellow by the name of al Sajek bought the key from him during a hasty transaction in Greece. The man in question poses a whole new problem. Al Sajek is an anomaly. It seems he is a Shiite Muslim of considerable wealth. An odd sort, with light skin and deep green eyes said to be a native of Yemen. A collector of rare antiquities and a shrewd businessman to boot. Further, it is rumored that he is a member of the ancient order of Assassins. I trust you will all remember who they are...? The order was never fully recognized by the followers of Mohammed in general and was dismissed as a group of heretics. It seems we had more in common with them than we realized." The Master paused, waiting for this bit of information to sink in.

No one said anything. The Assassins were always considered heretical and persecuted by official Islam. Their doctrines were maintained in secrecy and known only to themselves. The only thing that the Templars knew about them for sure was that they were very dangerous, held some strange beliefs about Jesus Christ and his crucifixion and also believed in reincarnation. Their paths had never crossed in any official capacity, though the truth of the matter was that the Templars and the Assassins had shared the same fate. Not only did they have commonalties in regard to belief systems, they had common interests in Jerusalem and the treasures buried there. They also had common enemies and that alone was enough to make them strange bedfellows. The Assassins did not look forward to the second coming. They dreaded the end of the world when they believed that their faith would disappear from the Godless earth. Even though many of the Assassins' beliefs closely mirrored their own, the Templars, in general, refused to admit this. The Assassins also delved into esoteric studies and it was rumored that they practiced rituals and rites associated with *the Necronomicon* or the Book of the Dead, a book recently attributed to a modern author, one H.P. Lovecraft. Whether Lovecraft had invented it or inherited it was still a matter of debate amongst the various modern schools of occult thought. Some dismissed the thing as fiction. Others had elevated the book to such an extent that it now had a cult following. It mattered very little to the men sitting around the table what the world thought. *The Neconomicon*, the Book of the Dead. Whatever one chose to call it was very real and its true followers were very dangerous. They had their own goals and their own agenda, which did not include any plans that might have been construed as benevolent or in any way beneficial to mankind in general.

Ramsay's heart sank. He did not have time for this! He only wanted to get home. He did not feel very confident about chasing some mystery man with unlimited means, trying to repossess the Key. It would be a difficult task indeed and could take years. An Infidel. Of course! How could it have been otherwise? Sooner or later they had to get involved. Just when he thought things could get no worse, he would find himself pitted against long-dead specters from the past. The Assassins! He knew them, but his dealings with them had never been pleasant. He kept his comments to himself.

"At present, he is in the United States. In Florida, attempting to invest in a bit of real estate no less. Apparently, he is planning to build a resort," d'Brouchart continued.

Mark Andrew's face fell even further. What was he thinking? Of course, things could get worse. America! Not America. Not again! And Florida? Was that not some tropical jungle with crocodiles and swamps full of snakes? Why not send him looking for the Fountain of Youth while he was there? A resort? He would like to resort to something... something very violent.

"He has such holdings throughout the world. The Pakistanis are known for their incomparable skills in the world of business. I have consulted with Sir Montague in this regard. However, I am convinced that Sir Philip's knowledge will be of use if the man is, indeed, a member of this secret cult. Sir Philip has studied the secrets of the Sumerians and the Babylonians and these are the sources of the Assassins' occultism."

Mark Andrew sat with his mouth partially open. Babylonians? Sumerians? Assassins? Occultism? He had thought the Brownies infesting the infirmary were bad, but this... He pressed one hand to the side of his head and closed his eyes. He was the Assassin. He wanted to assassinate someone, anyone. Lucio! And maybe Champlain as well for losing his Key in the first place.

Sir Philip coughed and picked up his glass of water. The Knight of the Orient was shocked to his foundations. That he was being called on to go on a mission was unthinkable. *The Necronomicon*. Just the mention of the thing sent chills up his spine. He was unprepared. Philip knew the truth about the Necronomicon. It was included in his mystery. He also knew that Lovecraft's version of it, while containing some truths, was not nearly as detailed as the original, nor did the author call it by its correct name, but it mattered little. A technicality. The Babylonian Book of the Dead was nothing like the Egyptian Book of the Dead. The latter concerned itself with the methods and techniques involved in successfully navigating the Underworld after death in pursuit of blissful immortality, but the former concerned darker methods and techniques for manipulating the occupants and powers ensconced in the Underworld for darker purposes. He licked his lips nervously and glanced at Mark Ramsay. The man sat with his hand pressed to his face with his eyes closed as if he were bored. It must have been nice to be that self-confident. He had never been on a mission with the Knight of Death. No one had ever called on his mystery for anything... for any purpose.

"Many prophecies and riddles have been unfolded for us and, yet, we remain in the dark," the Grand Master continued. "I have summoned your son home from Scotland, Sir Ramsay, in order that he may more safely resume his studies here with Sir Barry. We have made some adjustments in order to ensure that no interlopers may invade our sanctuary with such ease as this... thief has done. It will not happen again. The Ritter will also be returning with him. Simon d'Ornan will stay on in Scotland until the work there is completed, at least, mayhap he may stay longer..." He looked at Ramsay who raised one eyebrow. Simon would be a good choice to leave in Scotland. At least his baser self-interests would be more easily put to rest if he knew Simon would be there with Merry rather than one of his more energetic Brothers whom he had learned to trust so well by way of Lucio's example. He would not have to worry about Simon betraying his trust. It would be impossible.

Mark Andrew nodded his head slightly in approval of his suggestion.

"Brother Ramsay and Brother Louis will depart at once for France to seek out Philipe Devereaux and we shall be done with him. Brother Lucio will stay here and make inquiries concerning this al Sajek fellow. Once we have sufficiently corrected the... problem with Devereaux, we will proceed with a plan to recover the Golden Key. I will go to Scotland and take care of the business there. I have not decided on the full complement of the mission to recover the Key. That will depend on what the Golden Eagle learns. We will discuss it more after point one is accomplished. There will be no further discussion of these plans." He cast a meaningful glance at Dambretti and then turned up his glass to finish off his wine. "We will meet back here as soon as your mission is accomplished, du Morte. I would have the thief's head, Brother! I must be absolutely sure that he is dead this time."

"Yes, your Grace," Mark nodded and then glanced at Lucio, but the Italian was staring at the wall with his arms crossed on his chest. The pronouncement that he was not going had crushed him and he was not well in spite of what he and the doctor said. They all turned their attention suddenly to a noisy procession beyond the windows in the courtyard. The plumbing company had arrived with more equipment and was proceeding across the grounds beyond the swimming pool with a heavy-duty backhoe. They were digging up the plumbing. Looking for the Stone.

Chapter Six of Seventeen
and I am come to shew thee

John Paul's departure along with the Ritter von Hetz had been a quiet affair with few tears and even less speech. Merry had seen her son down to the Ritter's car, kissed him goodbye and hugged him tightly. Only now, while she stood forlornly on the steps next to Simon did she actually cry. Simon took her arm gently and guided her back inside when the car was out of sight. The news that Mark Andrew would be going straight to France had not helped her feelings. Simon had no words of comfort that could ease her grief, and he knew she was still in a quandary about whether she had done the right thing by accepting Mark's proposal.

She had gone straight up to her room, apparently intending to cry it out in solitude. It was just as well. The Healer found himself again on the back steps admiring the new stone and brick patio. It needed something. Flowers, perhaps. He walked around the perimeter of the paving stones, casting an appraising eye on the lay of the yard at the rear of the big house. There was no shrubbery to speak of, no flowers or flowerbeds anywhere. There were no trees and no vines. No landscaping, only a few old gnarly trees next the house on the east side. Too stark and sterile for his taste. He was more accustomed to the overgrown dwellings of southern Italy and the small French villages where everything was crowded together in interlocking gardens, courtyards, vineyards and walkways shaded by old growth trees. Where endless vines and ivies of every possible variety profusely entwined every nook and cranny in both urban and suburban areas, softening angles, hiding incongruities in the architecture and making things seem more comfortable. The rambling old house needed more greenery and more color than the sparse few shrubs clinging fitfully around the foundations. Blue, white and purple would complement the gray and brown exterior of the house quite well. And maybe some pink. And perhaps a fountain or at least a stone birdbath. Yes, he was glad the Master had suggested that he stay longer. He needed a rest and a diversion after all the excitement. It had been many years since he had tried his hand at gardening and it would give him something to do with Sister Meredith. He was worried that she would not appreciate his company and would see him as a watchdog or a chaperone. He liked her immensely and wished that she might like him enough to count him a friend as well as a Brother.

He went back inside to consult with the cook concerning the availability of local gardening supplies. If he could get the thing started, he knew Merry would come around eventually and the activity would be good for her, too. They needed something 'normal' to do. Simon talked to Bruce at length and then went to the library to sign on to the Internet. He would need a plan and information about flowers that might thrive in Scotland.

((((((((((((((<O>))))))))))))))

Merry sat silently in Mark's bedroom, surrounded by his unseen presence, trying to gain some insight about the situation in which she found herself. She wanted to embrace the room and hold it to her breast and tell it that everything would be all right, something that she knew she would never be able to do to its resident. He would not be happy when he came home. He would never be happy.

His room presented a different view of the countryside. From his window the front drive and parking area were clearly visible at the front of the house and beyond that stretched the meadow, marred only by a small, darker green hummock as far as the eye could see to the west, bordered by shady forests on the north and the south. The woodlands north of the house was filled with gullies and washouts leading down to the river and beyond the trees on the south side was the highway leading north to Edinburgh and points beyond. She stared out over the green, yellow and blue landscape, not seeing it, thinking of John Paul and all that had occurred in the past few weeks. That she and John Paul could have ever come here to live with Mark Andrew as a family now seemed like a fleeting pipe dream. Questions plagued every waking moment. She had been a fool to ever think it could be so. All the news from Italy had been disappointing, except for the bit about Lucio's recovery. Merry had not realized how much she had been hoping that Mark Andrew would come home soon. But come home to what? Another rejection? Another bout of rage and depression because she would now have to tell him that she could not marry him until things were sorted out? But Simon had told her not to worry. He had told her that all would go as God willed and that the situation was out of their hands. She had spent a long time in prayer, handing the problem over to God and asking for His guidance. Simon had said that if she would do this, then it would be all she had to do.

The phone calls from Mark had ceased coming at such regular intervals since the day before and she had to assume that at least he had been released from the terrible boredom he had been suffering in the infirmary with Lucio. That was some bit of comfort. Her attention was arrested suddenly as she realized that someone was walking up the long drive toward the house. Someone carrying a bag and she was quite close. How had she overlooked her?! She sat up straighter and squinted at the figure silhouetted against the lighter colored rocks of the drive. Mark Andrew's home was the only destination at the end of the drive. Whoever was coming would end up at the front door in a matter of minutes.

Merry got up quickly and went to check herself in the mirror. She had been crying and her eyes were a bit red and puffy, but she looked otherwise presentable, though she was in no way prepared to greet guests at the door. She hurried down the stairs to find Simon. He was in the library at the computer looking at flowers of all things. She told him they were about to have company and dragged him toward the door over his protests, maintaining that she did not feel up to fending off a stranger, lost or otherwise.

Merry stood back while Simon answered the knock on the door.

He opened the door hesitantly and stood blinking against the bright sunlight that streamed in from behind the visitor standing on the front stoop. Merry strained her eyes trying to get a glimpse of her face.

"Yes?" He said after a moment of silence. "May I help you?

"I am looking for Mister Mark Ramsay," the girl's voice was sweet and melodious and sounded almost as if she thought they had been expecting her. The slight Scottish brogue betrayed her local origin.

"He isn't here, child," Simon smiled at her. "I am… we are friends of his. Perhaps we can help you with something?"

The girl turned slightly and her face came into view. Young, very young. Red hair. Green eyes. A pleasant expression. Merry's curiosity was piqued immediately. Who was this beautiful girl and why was she looking for 'Mister' Ramsay?

"I was told that he would be able to help me," the lovely girl smiled at them. "That he owned the McShan place just down the road. It recently burned to the ground?"

"Oh, yes," Simon nodded, frowning slightly. "I believe he does… or did… own it." The Healer looked around at Merry for help.

"Won't you come in?" Merry stepped forward to extend her hand. The girl dropped her bag on the step and accepted the hand. She could not have been more than eighteen or nineteen years old. Her skin was fair with a smattering of freckles splashed across her small nose. Her long hair gleamed golden in the sunlight. "I'm Merry Sinclair."

"Elizabeth," the girl told her as she shook her hand vigorously. "Elizabeth McShan."

Merry's throat closed up momentarily. Elizabeth! Coincidence or something else?

Simon picked up the bag as the girl stepped inside the entry hall. Merry exchanged a bewildered look with him and they both shrugged in unison behind the girl's back.

"What a lovely home," the girl exclaimed and stood looking up the stairs as if she expected someone... Mark, perhaps, to come down to greet her. "I had no idea."

"Ah..." Simon was at a loss for words. "You are related to Ian McShan?" he finally asked.

"Yes. I was," she turned her eyes on him and an expression of profound sadness replaced the smile. "He was my..." her voice trailed off. "What a beautiful lamp!" she turned her attention on a brass floor lamp with glass marbles embedded in the shade. "Is it from the sub-continent? I have been away, you see. I haven't seen him in many years. Now I have learned that he was killed in the fire."

"I'm so sorry," Merry apologized. She quickly passed by her and went on to the library. The girl followed her and Simon brought her bag. "Please come into the library and make yourself comfortable."

"I had been intending to come for a visit," the girl continued. "But now... it is very unfortunate."

"*Oui*," Simon set the bag on the floor. "Very unfortunate. We were all saddened by the loss of a good neighbor. Most dreadful."

"Yes, very unexpected," the girl nodded.

"Won't you sit down?" Merry gestured toward Mark's favorite chair. She was at a total loss at what to say. Elizabeth! Elizabeth McShan. A granddaughter... perhaps? Surely. Mark had never mentioned that Ian had grandchildren or even children for that matter. A million questions ran through her head at once. How had she gotten here? They were a long way from the nearest town. And what did she want? Did she know who Mark Andrew was? She had called him Mister.

The girl sat in Mark's chair and looked up at her.

"I feel lost," the girl told her. "I'm afraid I counted on Ian too much. What am I to do? I thought Mr. Ramsay might help me."

"Oh, I'm sure you are not lost," Merry tried to comfort her. "Surely we can help you in some way. Would you care for some... tea?" Merry asked inanely and looked at Simon.

"I'll go," he said shortly. He was at an even greater loss. His face had no color and his eyes were filled with an expression Merry could not name. He looked as if he had seen the devil, himself. He recognized her voice. It was the same voice he'd heard in his room speaking French to him.

As soon as Simon disappeared, the girl began to cry. Merry sat down on the footstool in front of her and took one of her hands. "Will Mr. Ramsay be home soon?" She asked hopefully.

"No," Merry shook her head. "He will be away for quite some time, I'm afraid. What can we do for you? Did you walk far?"

"Just from the highway," the girl sniffed and pulled an embroidered linen handkerchief from her dress pocket to dab at her eyes. "I'm sorry for crying, Miss. I was so shocked to hear... to see..." She began to cry in earnest, burying her face in her hands, sobbing loudly.

Merry got up and sat on the arm of the chair.

"I'm sorry," she said. What would Mark say about this? This was his great-granddaughter. Did she know it? Did he?

"Ian was all I had left," the girl continued, answering one of Merry's unspoken questions. "I don't know what to do now."

"Where is your grandmother?" Merry asked, testing the water. She had to get rid of the girl. It would never do to have her here.

"I don't know," the girl shook her head. "I don't know where she went. The man who gave me the ride out said that she was not home when the fire occurred and that perhaps she went to stay with her sister."

"You are welcome to use the phone," Merry offered and stood up. "We could give you a ride, perhaps back to town? You have other relatives?"

"No," the girl shook her head. "Just Ian. My grandmother is very old and ill. Her sister lives in Wales. I have no money... I don't know what to do."

Things were rapidly getting worse. Wales? How far was that? South of London? She couldn't think.

"I'll go and check with Simon," Merry told her desperately. "He'll know what to do."

She rushed from the room down the hall to the kitchen in search of the answer man. The girl's story didn't quite ring true, but what should they do? Was she really Mark's great-granddaughter and, if so, why did she refer to her grandfather as 'Ian'? Did Mark even know she existed? Surely, he did. He was so secretive about everything personal. He would not have mentioned it to her at any rate. But when had they ever had a moment to just talk to each other? She had no idea how much Mark knew about her, but she was rapidly learning that she knew very little about him. It was entirely possible that she would never know much about his life. Technically, she was 45 years old though her physical aging had stopped nine years earlier, but Mark had been twenty-five or so at the Fall of Jerusalem in 1187. He had a few years on her. Twenty-plus lifetimes he had lived and Meredith Sinclair was involved in only one of those. He could have had hundreds of children, thousands of grandchildren by now. To think that he might have had only one son with one surviving relative to date was the truly incredible part of his story. His story. History.

Mark had lived much of recorded History and yet he seemed, on the surface as simple as any man she had ever met. Perhaps even less complicated than her pharmacist back in Waco. How had he come so far with so few strings attached? Mark was the ultimate Buddha in her mind. Even in his madness and his suffering and his anger, he had let go of more than any other living soul with the exception of his fellow Council Members. Certainly, they had found some way to let go of the material world and yet, one slip and he had fallen back into the mix. She had been the cause of that slip. She had set these things in motion. She and her idiotic ideas. Now she was living in his house, eating his food, drinking his wine and yet, he was not there. Just as he had not been there in Waco. He was there only in her heart. Would it always be so with them? Would a day ever come when they might have peace... together?

She had learned very little about him even during the years she had spent under his instruction before she became an initiated Knight of the Temple. Mark had made sure that they were never alone. He had been his own best chaperone. In fact, he had taken great pains to stay away from her during that time except for business, lessons, training and meals. She had thought it another of the Master's games when he had assigned her to Ramsay for her training. She had thought perhaps that the Master expected her to change her mind or expected her to be unable to keep her vows with Mark so close at hand. But she had been wrong about the whole thing. The Master had, indeed, known what he was doing when he put Ramsay in charge of her training. None of the others could have been entrusted with such a tedious task. Only Ramsay had the strength and internal discipline needed to avoid another entanglement with her, romantic or otherwise. If Mark Ramsay had not suffered a complete loss of memory in Texas sixteen years earlier, he would never have fallen in love with her in the first place and none of this would have happened. In this case, however, hindsight was more than twenty/twenty. Hindsight ensured her of the fact that the Hand of God was involved in everything. These things had happened as part of a Greater Plan and she was totally convinced that she was part of that plan, just as Dambretti always said the Will of God is in everything and everything is in the Will of God.

Likewise, this girl's appearance was no coincident. It would be up to her and Simon to determine what path to take now.

(((((((((((((<O>)))))))))))))

Mark Andrew was glad to get away from the Villa. Going anywhere was better than staying in the hospital with Lucio and he was ecstatic that Lucio had not been sent with them. In fact, he felt almost giddy, as if he were walking on air to be rid of the Italian's glum presence to remind him of all his most recent troubles. He was also glad to have something to do other than call Meredith every hour or so, having nothing to say and hearing the same from her. He was not completely disconnected with the modern world.

He went out from time to time... to Edinburgh, London, Paris. He saw people walking around, talking constantly on their phones. Yes, he saw them, but he always wondered what they were talking about. He wondered that anyone could carry on phone conversations for hours and he had to think that Merry felt the same as he did about it or else she would have talked more when he called her. Face to face was better when things needed to be said. Phones were more for emergencies, brief messages, that sort of thing in his opinion.

He had been expecting the worst as far as the current mission, but the Grand Master had decided that he and Champlain would go alone. Mark liked it simple. Two men. A simple execution. No complexities in store. No surprises. That was how he would try to keep it.

They flew into Barcelona, rented a car there and crossed the border into France from the south. The roads had little traffic and the hilly terrain was dotted with very old homesteads and vineyards. The Languedoc area was still somewhat economically depressed in spite of a recent resurgence in popularity for tourists from America, retaining its pastoral qualities, primarily the realm of wine makers' grapes and quaint cottages. The region had once been the home of the Cathars who had been almost totally obliterated by the Inquisition in the eleventh century. Ramsay shuddered at the thought of those dark times. He had been passing through this very same area just prior to the dissolution of the Templar Order. He remembered it quite well. They were not far from the ruined church where Simon d'Ornan, then Father Simon of Grenoble, had been taken prisoner by the Inquisitors in spite of his efforts to save him.

He winced aloud, causing his companion to glance at him in surprise, when he remembered the browbeating he had received from d'Brouchart for losing Simon, but he had certainly deserved that and more after all was said and done. The thought of that failure threatened to bring on a new round of depression and he pushed it from his mind. He had enough to worry about. He hadn't thought about those failures in years.

Now that he was back in this place for the first time in ages, he realized that very little had changed since then. Only the modern highways and power lines, a few of the more modern buildings and the presence of mechanized farming equipment along the road reminded him of their present mission. Philipe Devereaux had returned to his family home near *Montagne Noire*. He picked up the slip of paper with the map and description of the property he was looking for. They would park the car down the road and walk in. They were in the middle of hiking country. No one would pay any attention to them if they carried backpacks.

The sooner he could get this over with, the sooner he could get home. There was a good possibility that he could manage at least a few days with Meredith before they would be off again to find the man who had purchased

Champlain's Golden Key from the soon-to-be late Philipe Devereaux. Perhaps there would be enough time for the wedding and Simon would be there already...

(((((((((((((<O>)))))))))))))

Philipe Devereaux slouched in a chair in front of his small television, watching the evening news, drinking directly from a bottle of cheap red wine. He had done a lot of drinking lately, but it didn't matter. Nothing mattered. He couldn't even get good and drunk anymore. His happiness at having achieved his goal had been short-lived. He was alone now and had no money, nor any plans for the future. What had he been thinking? The Order had been his life for the better part of his thirty-three years on Earth. After the Order had given him the boot, he had been consumed by an unquenchable desire for revenge. Now that he was immortal, he was lost. What should he do? Where should he go? He was no better off than before. He even wished he had that maniac, Michel Barres, to talk to and strangely enough, he missed Ramsay's son, whom he had kept hostage for a few days. He had no direction. Nothing to keep him occupied and he could not get his mind off the bright-eyed boy who had acted more like a companion or co-conspirator than a prisoner in the short time they had traveled together. What the attraction was, he couldn't figure out. John Paul's very presence had been like a breath of fresh air, a spring breeze. Just being in the same room with him had been comforting. Looking into his eyes had been nothing short of euphoria. He shuddered every time he thought of what must have happened in Scotland after he had left. There was no way he could find out if d'Brouchart had rescued the boy or not.

All he was able to learn was that the body of a certain Michel Barres had been found at the scene of a mysterious fire in a rural area of Southeastern Scotland. The body of the elderly resident had also been found, but it was uncertain as to the cause of the fire. The intruder had evidently shot the old man in a botched burglary and the old man had killed him with a bayonet before the house burned to the ground. A bizarre crime, the news report had said. They had no idea how bizarre it must have truly been. Devereaux was quite sure that no bayonet had caused Barres' demise. Ramsay had killed him. Simple. There was no mention of the boy or anyone else. Not even the old lady who had lived at the house. Oddly, he wondered what had happened to her. His conscience was not that of a criminal. In fact, he was extremely remorseful about the whole affair and if there had been any possibility of reconciliation, he would have thrown himself on the Grand Master's mercy and begged for a position at one of the outposts. Anywhere,

94

anything would have been better than his current situation. What good was immortality, if one had no life to speak of?

It was just a matter of time now. The Order had connections. They would be after him and if he was not careful he would also become the victim of a bizarre crime or accident himself.

He had spent the last several days in a deep depression, waiting to hear from Abdul Hafiz al Sajek. He had given the strange man something to think about. He had promised him something even greater than the Key for a much better price, but the man's piercing green eyes haunted his dreams. There was something odd about him. Never-the-less, he needed enough to keep him supplied with funds for a long time if he could but make the transaction without losing his head... literally. Al Sajek frightened him. The man was obviously insane. He did not relish the thought of dealing with him again, but he had no choice. He knew no one else would be interested enough in what he had to offer to pay the kind of money he needed. Al Sajek had known exactly what he was talking about when he mentioned an obscure little chapel in Scotland. Why would an eccentric Muslim know of Glessyn in the first place, but the man had nodded knowingly when he had mentioned the possibility of more Templar treasures being kept there. Over past few decades, a great deal of interest had sprung up concerning another, more famous chapel where Templar treasures were thought to be hidden, but no one ever mentioned Glessyn. What was even more frightening about al Sajek was that he seemed to have no problem with the idea of taking any treasures that might exist. The man virtually smelled of money and yet, like all men of wealth, he was greedy. When Philipe had mentioned the Holy Grail, the True Cross and the Cathars, his eyes had lit up like brilliant torches. Yes, al Sajek would pay a tidy sum for such treasures, but Philipe was loath to deal with him all the same. Of course, there was the risk he would be taking to return to Scotland in order to raid the Knight of Death's precious chapel. It would be very dangerous, but it would be unexpected, wouldn't it?

The church had been deserted for years. No one but Ramsay went there. When d'Brouchart had bestowed the life eternal on him inside the little stone structure, it had been easy to see that it was not in use and was virtually hidden from sight of the main roads. He'd looked for some mention of it in a number of Scottish tour guides, websites and journals, but had found nothing about it. The building was on private property nestled under a stand of ancient oaks, off the beaten path, so to speak. All he had to do was wait for the proper time and he would be able to tear it apart quite leisurely. Surely he could find something there of value to the Pakistani billionaire. If the place were not special, why would the Templars be so hell-bent on caring for it all these years? He had heard many rumors of what might be there. Yes, all he had to do was go and find something and he would be back in business. He shuddered again and finished off the lukewarm wine. Al Sajek was crazy all right. Why else would he have offered a cool million for a chance to 'meet' Ramsay, himself? What would the Muslim do with the Scot? And why? He had declined that offer. No way was he going to attempt to kidnap the venerable Scot again. Not while he was in perfect health. What he and Barres had accomplished had been done only because Ramsay had been physically indisposed. The Scot had been completely incoherent and semi-conscious when they had abducted him from his own bedroom. Besides, they had practically had Simon d'Ornan's full cooperation or else the maneuver would have been completely impossible.

Devereaux had to make a move soon and get himself clear of France and Scotland and perhaps even the entire northern hemisphere. Australia was sounding better all the time.

No more trips to Monaco. He would have to think about his future. Maybe get a good accountant to make some investments for him. The Golden Key had brought much less than he had hoped for and he realized after the fact, that he should have kept it or at least demanded more for it. The Pakistani devil had seemed overjoyed at the sight of it. He had even asked about the Ark of the Covenant. The Templars would have paid much more in ransom for it surely, but he did not want them to have it back at any price. Vengeance was sweet, but not very lucrative. What would Louie do without his key?

Devereaux laughed aloud at that thought, but his mirth was fleeting. All he had at the moment was the location of the chapel in Scotland. If need be, he could just give the man the location. Al Sajek had promised to think it over and get back with him. He had given him enough information to pique his curiosity. To hell with the Templars! Let the two crazy factions fight it out. It would serve them right to have their precious sanctuary looted by Muslims after all these years. How ironic! Infidels, they called them. He only needed enough to get away to the South Seas. He had no use for the occult mysteries. At least he would have the satisfaction of knowing that he had caused more heartburn for the Grand Master. He turned up the bottle, draining the last of the wine and stood up, intending to go for another bottle. He swayed slightly and thought perhaps he should go to bed instead. It was his last coherent thought.

When he turned, he had only a glimpse of the man dressed entirely in black standing in front of him. He saw the deadly glitter coming at him and let go a whimpering sob as it passed completely through him, just slightly lower than his ribcage and to the left of his spine. The Knight caught him roughly by the right shoulder when he slumped forward, grasping the deadly sword by the hilt.

Ramsay pushed him back and wrenched the blade free. Philipe looked up into the face of the Assassin as he leaned forward close to his face.

"Thot was for Ian McShan," Mark Andrew told him in a hoarse whisper. "This is for John Paul," he added before stepping back.

Philipe made a desperate attempt to get away from the lethal blade by turning his back on the Knight and stumbling toward the living room. Mark Andrew caught up with him easily just as he reached the doorway. The man grasped either side of the door as the golden blade emerged from his stomach and more blood sprayed across the bare floor in front of him. He looked down in disbelief at the bloodstained blade and gasped once more when the blade disappeared back the way it had come.

Mark grabbed his arm and turned him around.

"You would see who it is that comes for you, my friend," Mark told him and felt Champlain's hand on his shoulder.

"Brother, your mission!" The Frankish Knight admonished him.

Philipe sank to his knees and Champlain knelt beside him.

"The Key, Philipe? Where is the Key?" He asked desperately.

Blood ran from the man's mouth and he only looked at Champlain in complete shock.

"Tell me, before you go, my son, and I will hear your sins," Champlain pleaded with him. "Make yourself right with God, I beg you."

Philipe drew a ragged breath, grimaced at the pain and then spat a mouth full of blood in the big Knight's face.

"Take my curse with you and share it with your Brothers, Master!" Philipe managed as his breath ran out.

Champlain got to his feet and moved back, blinking rapidly as tears ran down his face, washing away some of the bloody speckles.

Philipe fell forward and caught himself on his hands.

Mark Andrew leaned down beside him and put his lips close to the man's ear.

"This one is strictly business, you understand," he told him and stood up.

He raised the Golden Sword above his head and brought it down swiftly. A fine spray of blood covered his hands and Devereaux' head rolled away from his body. Champlain left the hall, headed for the small bath under the stairs. Mark stood over Philipe's corpse, willing himself to come to grips with what he had done. His sin was heavy upon his soul even before he knelt beside the downed man's lifeless head and closed the staring eyes.

The Knight of Death drew a deep breath, bent over and kissed the top of the man's head before placing one hand on his forehead. He performed his duty without the ceremonial words of honor and released the doomed man's soul to Hell. The experience was another first in the growing repertoire of death that he held in his memories. An immortal without a mystery. Another unnecessary death. Another wasted life. The only other examples had been the succession of men bearing the title *Chevalier du*

Trone. No mystery, but at least he had honored them with the prayer, even Argonne. Devereaux would not receive the benefit of his prayer. It did not fit.

Louis Champlain returned from the bathroom a bit cleaner, picked up the former Templar's head from the floor by the hair and dropped it swiftly into a heavy-duty plastic bag. He dropped the plastic bag and its gruesome contents in his backpack before hefting it unceremoniously to his sturdy shoulder. His heavy features showed no sign of emotion. Before they left the house in flames, they cleaned up most of the blood from floor, dumped the headless body into an abandoned well in the overgrown yard and pushed all of the stones surrounding it on top of the body, filling it with a good four or five feet of debris. They then performed a thorough search of the residence, but turned up nothing resembling the Key.

Mark turned back once before getting into the car to look at the towering pillar of dark smoke marring the clear blue sky. In the distance, they could hear the sirens of the local fire brigade. It was unlikely they would look in the well. The surrounding countryside was bone dry in the midst of a drought. They would be more concerned with keeping the fire from spreading than trying to solve a mysterious fire in an apparently abandoned cottage. The mission had gone even better than he had planned or expected. In fact, it had seemed too easy. The hard part would be getting their ghastly package back to Italy. The Knight of the Golden Eagle would have his gift returned.

((((((((((((((<O>))))))))))))))

Lucio slammed his chair back from the computer terminal and rubbed his eyes. He was tired again. He was tired of being tired. It was almost three in the morning and the information he had found on the Internet concerning the formidable Mr. Sajek was most depressing. The man would be very hard to reach. He was an enigma. Hard to pin down. Very, very rich and very, very private. A great collector of antiquities. A Shiite Muslim from the Punjab in Pakistan. Not much more to go on. If they let him get back to Pakistan with Champlain's Key, they would be very hard-pressed to ever recover it. They could do many things and go many places and speak many languages and wear many disguises, but it would be extremely difficult to infiltrate a culture as foreign as the Punjab. None of the Knights spoke the language as far as he knew and the country was in a constant state of war with the Sikhs on one side and the Hindus on the other. What exactly al Sajek was doing there was another perplexing question.

98

Lucio could not imagine someone like Louis Champlain passing himself off as a Pakistani. Impossible! And Mark Andrew's blue eyes and Scottish brogue would not stand him in good stead in such a place, in spite of his ability to understand many of the dialects from that part of the world. Furthermore, he didn't believe that the columnists had it right to start with. Al Sajek was not likely a Shiite at all, but perhaps a Zoroastrian from the looks of his interests and financial portfolio. And clearly his appearance led one to believe that his mother's nationality might have been other than Arab stock. Green eyes, black hair and light skinned. A handsome man, but hardly a typical Mid-Easterner and even if he was a member of the ancient order of Assassins, he was an anomaly at best. Most likely, connecting him with the Shiites was some sort of smoke screen to confuse the issues of his true identity. But as long as he had money, and enough of it to spare, nobody cared. That was the beauty of being rich. Especially in a poor country. He would have to meet the man and 'see' him to know him. He thought it might be possible that he could lead the mission to America with Louis and Philip when Mark Andrew returned with his life. He would request it. Mark would surely jump at the chance to return home to his bride and a mission would help to take his own mind off of Merry.

He wondered if Mark Andrew and Champlain were having any luck in France. He picked up the phone and dialed the number in Scotland. To hell with it. He would talk to her. What did he have to lose? The worst she could do was hang up on him. He needed to tell her goodbye.

(((((((((((((<O>)))))))))))))

"But she is his great-granddaughter. I'm sure of it," Merry said quietly as Simon paced the floor in the library.

"She called him 'Ian', not grandfather. I see little family resemblance other than the hair. But she cannot stay here," he told her. "There must be somewhere else she can go. We can give her money."

"She says there is no one," Merry reiterated. "Her grandmother is ill. The woman couldn't even come home for her husband's funeral, if you will remember..."

"That's beside the point," Simon shook his head. "She can't stay here. The Grand Master will be coming in a few days. We have to seal the chapel. What will Brother Ramsay say? What will the Master say?"

"I don't know. I asked you first."

Merry was beside herself. She had offered the girl a room for the night. At present, she was in a room upstairs, presumably taking a bath.

99

"I don't like it at all," he said and stopped pacing to look at her, biting his lip. "Why would she show up here? Now?"

"The will of God?" Merry asked him. "Her grandfather's death? Maybe she's looking for an inheritance? You know as well as I do that nothing is coincidental, Simon."

"Oh, no. No you don't," Simon shook his head more adamantly. "We can't become like Brother Lucio. We have to think of something. God helps those who help themselves... remember? We could fill this house with strangers and vagabonds if we're not careful. Would that be right?"

"She seems pleasant enough and she is kinfolk," Merry said off-handedly. The girl was lovely. She had seemed grateful enough when she had offered her a place to stay until she could get things sorted out.

"Porcupines are pleasant creatures as long as you stay away from them," Simon told her miserably. "Just because she is possibly kith and kin does not mean we have the right to open his home to her. He'll kill us."

"Surely not," Merry said doubtfully. Simon was right. Mark Andrew would be mad enough about the wedding, when she told him she was having second thoughts. This unexpected development could push him over the top. Why didn't he call? They could just ask him what to do. She could not imagine him tossing the girl out in the street, but...

"Just until tomorrow then," Simon shoved his hands in his pockets. "I will drive her in to town and give her some money. She can go back to Edinburgh. I have a really bad feeling about this. Something is not right about her."

"All right," Merry nodded. "How much?"

"How much what?" He asked.

"Money."

"Does it matter? Enough to get a good foothold. Surely she can do some sort of work to support herself."

"Well, all right," Merry acceded. "But I want her address or an address where we can reach her. Mark will want that, surely. You find her a place to stay and get her address. OK?"

Simon nodded. The last thing he wanted to do was traipse around Edinburgh with a strange young woman, looking for lodgings. What would the Master say?

The phone on the desk rang and they looked at each other in surprise. It was almost midnight.

"Maybe it is Brother Ramsay," the Healer said hopefully before picking up the phone. "*Oui*?"

"Simon?" Lucio's voice was hesitant.

"Brother," Simon was clearly disappointed. "How are you?"

"Well. I'm well. I would speak to Dame Sinclair, *se'el vous plait*," Lucio immediately took on a defiant tone. Demanding and impersonal. It almost sounded as if Lucio was mad at him. Why?

Simon held the phone out to her. His face betrayed his thoughts.

Merry took the phone and frowned at Simon. "Hello?"

"Sister?" Lucio's voice startled her.

"Lucio?" Merry's frown deepened. The last time she had seen him, he had been extremely angry with her. That he would call her was indeed a surprise. "What is wrong? Is John Paul ill?"

"Does something have to be wrong for me to call you?" He countered.

"I'm sorry. How are you, Brother?" She changed her tack.

"I'm better," he said shortly. "And how are you?"

"I'm fine," she answered, equally short.

"I wanted to apologize for our last meeting," he said in a low voice. "I was... upset."

"Yes. You were," she agreed. "You never answered Mark Andrew's letter. I don't know what he thinks about that."

"I know. I'm sorry," he said. His tone was flat. He sounded ill. Stuffy almost like he had a cold or had been crying, perhaps? "I don't think I could do what he asked. It is... too much."

"I see, but you could have at least answered with a polite no, thank you. He said you would refuse." She looked at Simon who was watching her intently. The Healer looked away. "Lucio... could you... come here?" She asked and had no idea why she would do such a thing. Simon jerked his head around to stare at her, mouth agape. "We have a problem."

Simon shook his head desperately. "No!" He whispered. Mark would kill them for sure.

"What sort of problem?" Lucio perked up. Mark Andrew was in France. There was no telling when he would be back, but...

"It's... well... it's..." Merry made a face at Simon. They needed help. But Simon was right. Mark would kill them.

"It's nothing," she said quickly. "Have you seen John Paul?"

"Yes," he said. "This morning. He looks well."

"Good." She looked at the floor and felt as if she would cry. She wanted to be angry with Lucio, but she couldn't. "Have you... has anyone heard from Mark Andrew, do you know?"

"No, I've been busy. He's still in France, I believe," he said bluntly. "What is the problem? Tell me, Meredith. You know I would do anything for you."

"I'd rather not say," she hedged. What had she done? Now he would be suspicious. She made a face at Simon and rolled her eyes. 'Kick me!' she mouthed the words to Simon.

"Do you still have my letters?" He asked and her heart lurched. What would he think if he knew she had let Simon read one of them?

"Yes. Why?" She asked.

"Read them sometime… please. It's not too late," he said and his tone took another turn. "I still love you, Merry."

"I know. I'm sorry," she said miserably. What was wrong with her? She had made up her mind and now she was unsure. With what Simon had told her and John Paul…

"Let me speak to Simon," he interrupted her thoughts as if he could read her mind long distance.

She handed the phone to the Healer.

"*Oui*?" Simon turned his back to her.

"What is wrong?" Lucio demanded. "If you do not tell me, I'm going to the Master right now. Do you hear me, *caro mio*?"

"Nothing," Simon lied in his usual, poor way. He hated it when Lucio used such a tone with him. It made him feel like a child. An errant child. Lucio had given him a few hard knocks when he'd actually been an errant child and the words '*caro mio*' was more a warning than a term of endearment.

"I know you are lying, Brother," Lucio continued when he didn't answer. "Do you need me to come up there? Is it the relic? Has something happened to it?"

"No, nothing like that at all," Simon told him with appropriate conviction and wished it was so simple. Lucio would never understand. "Nothing has happened to it. We just need to finish the preparations... arrangements for the wedding and our Sister has been having nightmares. That is all. She is… we are lonely up here in this big house… all alone… as it were… just the two of us… with Bruce, that is, of course and the dogs. But that's silly. Who could feel lonely with those two running amuck? Give my best to the boy, will you?"

"Of course. Take care of her, Brother," Lucio told him. "If you need me, you know where to find me."

"*Oui*." Simon closed his eyes. He needed someone, but Lucio would not do. He felt totally inept. Now he had two women to contend with. He was out of his league entirely, but what could Lucio do, except make matters worse. If only Champlain were available. Champlain was always good in a pinch, but he was with Ramsay.

"Go with God, Brother."

"And you, Brother."

Simon let out a great sigh of relief and hung up the phone.

"He thinks I am crazy. Tomorrow, we will be rid of her," Simon said with conviction. "It pains me to turn her out, but I can see no other way. I will do as you ask and then we can tell Mark when he comes home and let him decide what is to be done about her. There may be some personal effects left. A will, perhaps... something. We can give her enough money for a month... maybe more."

Merry nodded. His words made sense. They could not allow a stranger to stay in the house. They simply couldn't. Not with the Grand Master coming. Thank God Simon had been present. If not, she would have begged the Italian to come to Scotland in spite of the danger. She suddenly felt very lonely and frightened. The Italian was nothing if not a 'take-charge' kind of guy.

(((((((((((((<O>)))))))))))))

Lucio debated whether to go to bed or to go to Scotland. He felt completely lost. Something was not right there, but he would be in deep trouble if he left without permission. He stood up and stretched his arms over his head. His joints still ached from the fever and he had a number of sore spots scattered all over his body. His wrists were bruised and cut from the restraints on the bed and his skin was still peeling in places. He had unmistakable cuts and bruises on his right hand and knuckles and wondered who had born the brunt of that attack. Mark Ramsay, most likely. Just another rip in the rotted fabric of their relationship. There were needle marks left by the IV's he had kept pulling from his arms. He shut down the computer and went back to his room. It seemed he had only just closed his eyes when he was awakened by a knock at his door.

Sir Champlain stood on the porch in the gray light of dawn. He looked somehow bedraggled though his clothes were as neat and clean as ever.

"The deed is accomplished, Brother," the man said shortly when he opened the door. "The Council will meet at seven."

Lucio glanced at his watch. It was almost five-thirty. This was good news. Devereaux was dead. His immortality would be returned and he would resume his place at the Council Table. Things were looking up.

Champlain said nothing more before heading down the porch toward his own rooms. Lucio went at once to get ready. It was easy enough. The Master had refused to allow him to return to his apartment. Most of what he had in the tiny closet was old and out-dated and now, woefully, a size too big. Suddenly, he was starving. He looked in the small mirror in the bathroom and pinched his cheeks. He was at least fifteen pounds lighter than before the illness. New clothes would be in order. And perhaps he might even refurbish his apartment and take a holiday in Sicily. There was no sense in spending his nights alone. It hadn't taken Mark Andrew much time

103

to do what had to be done. One thing about the Scot, he was dependable. God's Will. That was all it was. God's Will. Let God be in charge. He was certainly no good at it himself.

Six-thirty found him in the Council Room waiting for the others to arrive. He sat at his place staring at the wall. Contemplating some of the strange dreams he remembered even now from when the fever had control of his mind. The dream about the dragon and the fountain had disturbed him enough to hang on in his memory even days later. He could remember having had it at least a half dozen times while he had been suffering and wondered what it meant. There were passages in the Treatise concerning a fountain with seven heads and a Dragon that had to drink from the waters twenty-one times. But who was the Dragon? And what did it mean to drink from the fountain? He couldn't keep Merry out of his thoughts long enough to concentrate on anything. Personally, he considered Mark Andrew to be the Dragon. In the dream, the golden haired woman had told him to make the Dragon drink, but he had tried to kill the Dragon instead. Had he not only recently tried to kill Mark Andrew? As he sat staring into nothing, he could only thank God that he had not succeeded. In retrospect, he knew quite well that he could never have lived with the guilt had he succeeded and Meredith would never have accepted him even had he won. He fervently hoped that once the wedding was over, she would begin to fade from his mind.

His thoughts were interrupted by the arrival of the Ritter von Hetz and his apprentice, John Paul Sinclair-Ramsay. The Ritter greeted him in the Templar fashion before sitting down at his place near the head of the table. John Paul smiled slightly, nodded to him and took a seat in the rear of the room where the apprentices were stationed in two rows of chairs according to seniority with the youngest members on the front row. The Chevalier de Lyons, Knight of the Sword, arrived with his own apprentice, Cesar Hananaih and was followed by Sir de Bleu, who sauntered in alone, yawned lazily, stretched and then went around kissing and hugging everyone as if he'd not seen them in years. After the greetings, they sat immersed in their own thoughts.

Champlain was next to arrive sans apprentice. Baldemar de Jesus, the Knight's absent apprentice, was currently in Spain, inspecting one of the Templar holdings near Barcelona. Looking into the possibility of adding the vineyard and winery there to the list of so-called 'wine tours'. Something that Montague felt would add a considerable sum of money annually to their investment portfolio. He looked worse than de Bleu and yawned repeatedly, but made no comment before taking his seat further down the table from von Hetz.

A pair of stewards arrived with a cart filled with carafes of strong Italian coffee and proceeded to set them up with steaming mugs rather than the usual wine-filled goblets, plying them with sugar and cream. Morning meetings were rare and especially so early as this one. The sounds of the coffee cups and the boys who served them, seemed to echo much too loudly in the marble room. Time was dragging again.

Lucio was surprised to see his own apprentice, Stephano Clementi sidle in from the front hall and take a seat next to John Paul. The boy glanced at him once, dark circles evident under his darker eyes and then nudged John Paul who turned a strange look on him. He was sorry to have dismissed Stephano so quickly. Certainly it had been a traumatic experience. Again, he had caused someone else pain for no apparent reason. Lucio felt as if he were in one of his strange dreams. He looked down at his hands and felt his cheeks burning. He wouldn't have been surprised to hear that the boy hated him now.

Sir Barry came in noisily from the direction of the front parking area, accompanied by his apprentice, a blithe young English fellow named Robert Atkins and de Bleu's apprentice, Adonaijah Sidzenga, from Ethiopia. Adonaijah's dark complexion and infectious smile always perked up their meetings. It seemed he never frowned and was never caught without a number of amusing stories about his relatives who lived in a remote village in the Great Rift Valley. A spate of conversation erupted as they went about the table hugging and kissing and talking about the rain that had begun a steady downpour outside.

"You look awful, Brother!" Sir Barry told him before clasping him a great bear hug. "You should come by and hear my new music. It'll cheer you up."

"New, is it?" Lucio asked halfheartedly, knowing full well that whatever it was, it would not be less than sixty to six hundred years old. He felt as if they were all staring at him. He suddenly felt uneasy and expected to fall dead at any minute before the thing could be done.

Barry let go of him, but not before giving him one of those looks that said everything. Barry was fascinated by what had happened to Lucio. He'd never known that such a thing could happen to one of them. Certainly events of late had taken a number of precarious turns which had caused even the stern-visaged schoolmaster to rethink his own existence.

Mark Andrew finally arrived at precisely seven o'clock as was his custom. Right on time, looking as if he'd just awakened from a refreshing night's sleep, starched collar on his white on white striped shirt and black herringbone tie. Lucio wondered if he stood outside the door looking at his watch and waiting or if he was just so perfect, he couldn't help it. He also wondered why Mark had shown up looking like a banker, wearing a gray Birdseye suit. He watched in silence as the Scot took off his coat and hung it on the back of his chair before sitting down directly across from him. Was he planning on leaving here and going straight to the preacher?

Mark leaned his forehead against his hands and looked down at the table. He had failed to greet anyone and no one had made a move to greet him. How truly they all seemed afraid of him. What had happened to them? Had the former Knight of Swords been right all along? Would Ramsay, indeed, bring on the complete downfall of the Order? But Lucio knew what was wrong with the Scot. The same thing that was wrong with Champlain. It was not an easy thing, killing a man, beheading him and bringing his head home in a bag or a box. Regardless of the notches in one's sword, it was not something a man with a conscience could quickly put behind him. Dambretti glanced down the table at Champlain. The Frankish Knight's sleepiness did not hide his frustration. His precious Key was still missing.

Lucio closed his eyes only to have a scene from sixteen years earlier plague him. Thomas Beaujold had stood in this very room and slammed his fist on the table, calling for Ramsay's head and they had all been flabbergasted. But now, Beaujold was dead and those who had followed after him, taking up his cause against the Knight of Death, were dead as well. Hugh de Champagne. James Argonne. Philipe Devereaux had joined the list of the departed. And there were others. All lost and for what? Who would be next?

At five after seven, the Grand Master arrived, accompanied by Sir Cambrique. They took their places at the head of the table and Sir Philip called the meeting to order. The Seneschal sat down, opened his book and picked up his pen, ready to take the minutes. Only Simon d'Ornan and Sister Sinclair were missing. D'Brouchart glanced at each one of them in turn, taking a moment to look them in the eyes before picking up his heavy stainless steel coffee mug. He held it briefly under his nose, breathing deeply of the aroma before tasting it. The Knights watched him in silence. The Grand Master's eyes flickered briefly as his gaze crossed over the empty chair next to Dambretti. Too bad Simon was not here. Simon's presence always comforted him with a certain measure of light. There was too much darkness in the room. Death still lingered in the air around Ramsay. In the elder days, the Assassin would have been required to spend time outside the group, fasting and praying in order to get his thoughts together and his heart right, but time was shorter and growing shorter all the time.

"Brothers," d'Brouchart stood to address them and everyone sat up to pay attention. "The first part of our mission has been accomplished with little trouble. Sir Ramsay and Sir Champlain are to be commended on their expediency in this matter. Philipe Devereaux has been eliminated, his head returned to me and his body left to rot in France. The Golden Key was not in his possession. We have learned from our network that it is now in the hands of Abdul Hafiz al Sajek, a purported member of the secret order of the Assassins, a heretical offshoot of Islam, which is not and never has been condoned nor recognized by the Infidels. This greatly complicates our quest for its return. While he surely knows what he has purchased is a relic of some antiquity and very precious, we hope that he does not know the full significance of the Key. It is not likely that Devereaux had much contact with the man and it is quite possible that he may have come on him by accident in his search for a buyer. At present, the target is in Florida under constant surveillance, negotiating the purchase of a resort property. He has rented rooms for a fortnight. Since we have traced his movements subsequent to his meeting with Devereaux in Greece, there is a possibility that the Key could still be in his possession because he has not been home since then. Further, it would not be likely that he would have entrusted such an artifact to one of his subordinates. It appears that our Mr. Sajek is a well known collector and possesses a number of interesting artifacts. As we are aware of his secret order, so they are aware of us, but I am hopeful that he does not know that the Key came from us and with any luck, he will not be expecting us to come claiming it from him. It is imperative that we overtake him in America before he returns to Pakistan where the Key would undoubtedly become even less accessible to us. He passes himself off as a businessman of slightly more than average means, but hardly gives the impression of his true net worth which ranges in the tens of billions. That is to say that he does not flaunt his money or his influence. He does not travel with a large entourage, but relies on his anonymity in the west. That will be a great advantage to us."

D'Brouchart sighed and picked up his coffee cup and took another drink before continuing.

"On matters closer to home. You have noticed that we are presently involved in some… excavations here on the grounds. We are looking for the Stone that is the missing part of the Golden Key. The Stone that has, unfortunately, been lost, apparently in the sewers."

The Master cast a baleful eye on Dambretti who looked away from him, repressing the urge to roll his eyes. How could he have known? De Bleu failed to suppress a chuckle and received a scowl from the Master.

"We hope to recover it soon and be rid of these pesky workmen," he continued. "I cannot stress enough the importance of recovering this Key… or this Stone, Brother Armand. We must strike fast and we must not fail. We know very little about this al Sajek in a personal sense, but he is highly educated and very shrewd and Brother Dambretti tells me that his nation of origin may be in question since he has more the appearance of a European or even American. A formidable foe none-the-less. He has studied the occult arts and is not to be toyed with. Sir Ramsay and Sir Champlain will go to America as soon as we take care of our business in Scotland. Sir Philip will accompany them in case our friend should undertake an occult assault."

At this, de Lyons and de Bleu shuffled slightly in their seats. Sir Philip had not been sent out on a mission in countless years. These two, fairly new additions to the Council, did not think that Sir Philip had ever left the Villa for any reason. Occult assault? The two French Knights glanced at one another in confusion, but asked for no explanation. They had both expected to accompany the Knight of Death on his mission and actually had a bet between them which would be chosen. Now Philip would be going? Unheard of.

Von Hetz sat straight up in his chair and narrowed his eyes. He knew well what the secret order of the Assassins studied and practiced. The Babylonian Book of the Dead, which described details of how to traverse the Abyss along with information about the entities inhabiting its depths. A very dangerous book that few people took seriously these days, though it was no less real and no less potent than some of the Arcanum they kept in their private libraries.

"Sir de Lyons, Sir Ramsay, Sir Champlain," the Master addressed three of his Knights, looking at each of the named men in turn. "You will accompany me to Scotland on the morrow. We will seal the crypts beneath the chapel there."

Lucio cleared his throat loudly. Why were they leaving him out of this?

"Sir Dambretti?" d'Brouchart acknowledged him, clearly aggravated.

Lucio stood up.

"I would like to volunteer for the mission to America, your Grace," he said. "There is nothing to keep me here now. Surely Brother Ramsay has more pressing personal business in Scotland. Considering his most recent misfortunes, I should think that he may deserve some time off."

"Well said and true, Sir. Some of us could use a little R and R, but I would have you well first and foremost before you proceed with your normal duties, Golden Eagle. Your request is certainly appreciated by those present, but I must remind you that you are not quite yourself," d'Brouchart and looked at him doubtfully. "We have not yet located the Stone. Someone will need to oversee these... excavations. Furthermore, I should like to see you put on a little weight before we proceed with the ceremony. You look a bit... boney."

Lucio could not help but sigh in disgust. So he would be left to comb through the sewers? And while he was sifting through the muck, he could stuff himself on pizza and beer. How fitting. He had been accused of stirring up shit in the past. Now he would have the rare opportunity to fill that bill literally. Perhaps his experience with sewers and catacombs made him more qualified for such work.

"But certainly, these things do not require my presence. Shouldn't Brother Louie be best able to identify his Stone?" he objected halfheartedly. "Sir Barry will be here and..."

108

"Enough," d'Brouchart dismissed him with the wave of one hand and the Italian sat down heavily. "I would speak to you alone after the meeting. There is a private matter we must attend to."

At once, Lucio allowed his gaze to fall on Ramsay accusingly. His first thought was that Simon had informed the Knight of the phone call to Merry, but Mark Andrew returned his look with a peculiar expression, somewhat mirroring his own as if he blamed Lucio for being sent away again so soon. Mark had returned his immortality and he could not bring himself to say thank you. He hated the man and yet, he owed him everything.

The conflicting emotions in his head and his heart threatened to overwhelm him and he uttered his favorite epithet under his breath without being aware of it. "Santa Maria!"

"Enough! I will not have another failure," d'Brouchart raised his voice a bit as if he sensed the rising tension in the air. "Our missions of late have been most disastrous. I cannot risk sending you along on this mission."

These words added insult to injury and made his blood boil. He was no doubt referring to the loss of the Golden Key in the first place. Something that had been blamed entirely on him. Champlain shifted in his seat and lowered his eyes to the table. Champlain deserved at least some of the blame. The Key was, after all, his responsibility. Lucio could not bear it. He slammed his chair back and stood up. His face was dark with uncontrolled rage. No doubt, they blamed the flood in Scotland on him as well and the latest typhoon in India to boot. He'd had enough.

"I would wish to be dismissed from this Council!" He said and wondered why he was being so foolish. It was as if he was standing outside himself, watching from a distance.

"You will sit down, Sir!" D'Brouchart shouted at him, now clearly angry.

Lucio ignored the order and turned on the Grand Master, sputtering in anger.

"I have tried again and again to make known to my esteemed Grand Master and my honorable Brothers, that I am in possession of certain knowledge that must be addressed!" Lucio continued in spite of the Grand Master's anger. "I can see no use for my expertise in the Hermetic Mysteries if I am to be ignored and suppressed as if I were a disobedient child! I have done everything I can do to prevent a most grievous action taking place that will have profoundly catastrophic results if allowed to succeed. The powers of darkness are set against us and, in particular, against me. This union between Sir Ramsay and Sister Sinclair must not be allowed!"

"Sir Dambretti!" d'Brouchart shouted at him again as Ramsay stood up. "Sit down! That subject is not open for discussion. Sit down, du Morte!"

Lucio ignored the Master and focused on Ramsay's face instead. He leaned forward on the table and opened his mouth to say something he would have most likely regretted, but was not allowed to speak before a most remarkable thing took place.

John Paul rose suddenly from his seat, closed the intervening space between the apprentices' chairs and the Council table and leapt lightly onto the table. The Knights were shocked to their foundations by this unexpected development. They watched in bewildered fascination as the boy walked up and down the table, speaking in a low voice at first and then raising the volume. D'Brouchart remained standing, but Lucio and Mark Andrew both fell sitting in their seats.

"Brothers! Hearken unto my voice," John Paul repeated these words four times, turning clockwise, addressing each of the four cardinal points in the room. Mark Andrew's face grew dark. This was the voice of his dead brother speaking to him. He had engaged in very little conversation with his son, but he knew that this was not John Paul. "Let those who would listen, hear and those who would understand, be warned."

D'Brouchart raised his hand, when von Hetz made a move to rise out of his chair.

"And he shall give him the daughter of women, corrupting her: but she shall not stand on his side, neither be for him. Though ye have lien among the pots, yet shall ye be as the wings of a dove covered with silver, and her feathers with yellow gold. Many shall be purified, and made white, and tried; but the wicked shall do wickedly: and none of the wicked shall understand; but the wise shall understand. God setteth the solitary in families," John Paul stopped in front of the Master and leaned down slightly, looking at him intensely as he spoke. "Oh hear me, I pray! Hear me!" He removed his shirt and flung it over the Master's head. The Master cleared his throat loudly and the boy turned resumed his walk along the surface of the table to Simon's empty chair. He stopped and spoke to the chair as if someone were sitting there, all the while unbuckling his belt. "A father of the fatherless. But thou art he that took me out of the womb. They shall fear thee as long as the sun and moon endure." The young prophet turned his head slowly and met his father's eyes before continuing to undress. He slipped off his shoes and then stepped out of his slacks, leaving them on the table. "I am become a stranger unto my brethren. They that hate me without a cause are more than the hairs of mine head: they that would destroy me, being mine enemies wrongfully, are mighty: then I restored that which I took not away." John turned quickly and faced Lucio Dambretti pointing one finger at the ceiling before continuing. "O God, thou knowest my foolishness; and my sins are not hid from thee. I sink in deep mire, where there is no standing: I am come into deep waters, where the floods overflow me. Let not the water flood overflow me, neither let the deep swallow me up, and let not the pit shut her mouth upon me. Deliver me out of the mire, and let me not sink: let me be delivered from them that hate me, and out of the deep waters." Once more, the boy moved down the table and stopped in front the Ritter. "For thou wilt not leave my soul in hell; He brought me up also out of an horrible pit, out of the miry clay, and set my feet upon a rock. Thou wilt shew me the path of life." He left the Ritter dumbfounded and made his way down the table to where Louis Champlain sat rigid in his chair, pale as a ghost, unable to speak or react as the boy removed his tee shirt and threw it across the room. "The Lord hath chastened me sore: but he hath not given me over unto death. I shall not die, but live, and declare the works of the Lord. The stone which the builders refused is become the head stone of the corner." Once more, he moved along the table, back to where his father waited. He nodded his head slowly to Mark Andrew and continued his speech. "He shall drink of the brook in the way: therefore shall he lift up the head. This is the Lord's doing; it is marvelous in our eyes. Rejoice in the Lord, ye righteous; and give thanks at the remembrance of his holiness."

John Paul stiffened and stood straight up, looking at the ceiling. His eyes rolled up in his head and the Knight leapt from his seat to catch him as he fell from the table. Mark Andrew stood holding the boy in his arms, looking around the table at the men who stared at him in wonder and disbelief. It was almost as if Mark Andrew stood holding a carbon copy of himself.

Champlain was the first to stand up.

"The boy is a prophet!" He declared loudly and slapped the table with his fist. "It is sign from the Creator!"

"But what does it mean?" Armand de Bleu asked quietly from the end of the table.

Sir de Lyons leapt to his feet and pointed one long finger at the boy who hung limply in his father's arms.

"He is no prophet!" He shouted at them wild-eyed. "He is possessed of demons! I have seen it before. He spoke to the four winds and the four elements. It is witchcraft. Sorcery. He spoke to them!"

Ramsay turned away from his Brothers and looked for an outlet, unsure what to do. The Knight of the Apocalypse appeared in front of him and took the boy from him. Champlain turned his attention on de Lyons.

"Hold you tongue, Brother, or lose it!" The Knight of the Golden Key warned as he was advancing on the tall, slender Knight of Swords. "The boy is a gift from God. Have you not the sight? Can you not see the miracle in front of you?"

Sir Barry tried to insert his body between the two French Knights.

"Miracle?" De Lyons asked. "This is what comes of witchcraft and sorcery! How do we know it is not the devil who speaks through the boy?"

"The boy is the bastard son of an unholy union!" de Lyons continued in his furor, frightened visibly by what he had seen and yet spurred on by Montague's support.

"Oh?" Lucio was quick to turn on Montague. "And what do you know of witchcraft and sorcery, Brother? You wouldn't know a witch if she sat in your lap and licked your ear, you stiff-necked Limey!"

"How dare you, Sir!" Montague shouted and shoved the Italian.

The room was in an uproar and d'Brouchart banged his fist on the table, calling for order. Philip was out of his seat, his notebook discarded on the floor as he tried to get hold of Montague. Ramsay spun around and climbed onto the table intending to tackle the Knight of the Sword as he continued to shout, almost hysterical now. "He comes to me in my dreams!" de Lyons sputtered in Barry's face as Champlain tried to reach him around the English Knight. "He speaks of Dragons and golden fountains! Pagan women accompany him! A golden-haired goddess and another with horns on her head. The Devil's minions! The Dragon! Satan! It's blasphemy and damnation!"

Sir Philip shoved Montague aside, rounded the table and caught up with Champlain as he took the man by his throat in spite of Barry's intervention. Armand de Bleu threw himself on the Knight of the Golden Eagle before he could assault the Knight of the Holy City. Dambretti threw off the smaller man only to be tackled by the Seneschal. Montague yanked de Bleu to his feet and tried to help Philip as he struggled with Dambretti on the marble floor. All four of them ended up on the floor in the midst of the scattered apprentices who fell back against the wall holding up their various coffee mugs and juice glasses in a desperate attempt to stay out of the way. Dambretti was up first, leaning on the table, trying to catch his breath when Ramsay reached the end of the table. He reached for the Scot's leg as he prepared to leap on de Lyon's head, bringing him down hard to the floor. When he came up again, he had a short, black-bladed knife in his left hand and turned on Dambretti in his rage. Lucio recognized the wicked little blade as Ramsay's favorite sgian dubh that he'd carried for several hundred years, usually strapped to his leg above his socks. He never expected to see it in the Council chamber. Nor had he ever expected it to be used against him.

The Italian stumbled back away from the Scot. Lucio had no weapon. Weapons were strictly forbidden in Council... for good reason. He fell against the glass in the window as Mark Andrew crashed into him and they went through the window onto the sun porch beyond with Lucio holding Ramsay's left wrist in both hands as he lay on his back in the shattered glass. The Scot struggled to gain a footing above him, trying desperately to get the blade through to his neck.

The Grand Master stepped over the window ledge behind him and took Ramsay by the shoulders, throwing him bodily off of Dambretti, but neither of them let go of the other. They came up together and rolled off across the paving in a tangle of arms and legs. The apprentices, heretofore frozen in place against the walls, broke and ran in all directions.

The Grand Master shouted at Sir Barry who was attempting to herd the apprentices out of the way while de Bleu and Cambrique continued their efforts to separate Champlain and de Lyons inside the Council Room. De Lyons struck de Bleu on the chin, sending him flying. Philip tackled the Knight of the Sword and Champlain threw his sizable body into the pile. Sir Barry left the apprentices with a shouted admonition to stay back in order to lend his aid to the Grand Master as he pursued Ramsay and Dambretti across the tiles. Ramsay had turned the knife and was gaining the upper hand over his weakened opponent, who still held his wrist in a death grip. Lucio was spared only by their combined efforts when they peeled Ramsay off of the Italian, each one grabbing one of his arms and lifting him straight up. Lucio let go of his arm this time and the two Knights carried the Scot backwards, all the way to the wall. His head bounced off the stones and the sgian dubh clattered to pavement. Lucio climbed to his feet and retrieved the knife as Sir Barry lowered Mark Andrew to the ground where he sat dazed and half-conscious.

Inside the Council room the standoff continued.

D'Brouchart wrenched the knife from Lucio's hand and tossed it into the pool before going back inside. Lucio stumbled across the sun porch and out toward the tables. A sudden pain gripped him and he bent double clutching his stomach. He could hear the Grand Master shouting inside the building, but he could not make out the words. He caught himself on one of the tables and leaned across it, breathing hard. Sir Barry came after him and caught him before he fell.

"Brother?!" Sir Barry held him by the arms. "Are you wounded?"

But Lucio could not answer him. He wanted to cough, but his breath was cut off as something seemed lodged in his throat, choking off his oxygen. Sir Barry spun him around, took one look at his purplish complexion and slapped him between the shoulders. Then they both watched in fascination as a glittering red stone popped from his mouth and skittered across the tiles. Sir Barry let go of the Knight and went after the Stone. He held it up in the light and turned to look at the Italian in surprise.

"Damn it, man!" he said. "What have you been eating?"

"The Stone!" Lucio coughed out the words. "It's the goddamned Stone!"

Sir Barry frowned and then smiled before hurrying back toward the melee, holding the Stone above his head, shouting first in English and then French. Lucio pushed himself off the table and stumbled after him. Mark Andrew was only just regaining his wits and stood rubbing the back of his head. He squinted at Sir Barry, trying to understand what he was saying as he rushed past him toward the Council room from whence the sounds of an all out brawl emanated. The Knight had to dodge left quickly as Guy de Lyons came crashing through the door with d'Brouchart close behind him. The Knight of the Sword fell to his knees in front of Sir Barry and looked up at him. The Master drew up short at the sight of the Stone in Barry's hand. Champlain barged out behind d'Brouchart, tousled and bleary, bloodied from a split lip and a swollen nose. He approached Barry almost reverently and held out his hand for the Stone. Barry placed it gingerly in the big man's palm and then they all crowded around to get a look at it, their arguments forgotten.

D'Brouchart broke the spell at last.

"Back inside!" he shouted. "This meeting is not closed!"

The apprentices crowded back inside the door while the Knights climbed through the broken windows, hurriedly resuming their seats at the table.

Chapter Seven of Seventeen
therefore understand the matter, and consider the vision

Father Simon was in trouble. He lay on his back in a dim stone chamber lit only by the sputtering light of smoky torches. He had no idea how long he had been there with his arms stretched above his head and his feet tied on a cold stone platform. It seemed that days had passed. His head hurt and he could barely open one eye apparently due to swelling caused by the blow he had received at the chapel. The room was cold and he shivered uncontrollably. He could tell that he had lost his clothes because he could feel the cold stone all the way from his head down to his heels, but no one had come to see him since he had awakened some time since. But he was not alone in this place. He could hear others, somewhere nearby, but not too close. Not in the same room. He had ceased trying to lift his battered head because the pain was too great when it fell back on the rock. Why had they brought him here? A nightmare of a different sort in the room with him became evident from time to time as he heard the squealing and skittering sounds of rats in the darkness. One of the ugly creatures had ventured onto the table with him at one point, but he had managed to shout it away. If things did not improve soon, the rats would surely come and eat him if he passed out again and from the feel of it, they may have already started on his feet and hands. After what seemed ages, he heard the sound of human feet, the jangle of keys and the rustle of clothing accompanied by squeaking door hinges. The face of a man dressed in the black robes of a priest suddenly hovered over him. At first, he was relieved to see the face of a brother, but the look on the stranger's face made him cringe.

"You are awake, my son?" The man asked and narrowed his eyes at him. His voice was very soothing and soft, but the slight smile on his face made what was left of his blood feel like ice in his veins.

Simon only stared at him. The question was absurd. The priest sounded as if he were addressing his best friend.

"Do you know why you are here?" The priest asked him in French.

"No," Simon managed to croak an answer to this question.

The man placed a cold hand on his stomach and he cringed again. He nodded to someone else and Simon could hear others in the room, though he could not see them.

"You can save yourself a great deal of trouble, my son."

The priest left his field of vision for several seconds before returning.

"What are the charges?" Simon asked him and was surprised to hear that he even had a voice at all. His mouth was dry and it seemed that his tongue was swollen.

"None. You have confessed to no wrongdoing... yet," the man told him. "We want to know about your... friends."

"My friends?" Simon tried to raise his head again to see who 'we' might be, but the priest pressed his left hand against his forehead, smacking the back of his head on the slab. Stars swam in front of his eyes for several seconds and the pain increased in his head, pulsing with every heartbeat.

"The two men who tried to protect you. You must be of some importance to them, no?" the priest continued. "The two Knights of Solomon's Temple. The Templars who attacked and killed several of the King's men."

Simon said nothing. Sir Boniface was dead. He remembered that much. Had they also killed Sir Ramsay?

"We would know where the one called Ramsay has gone. He is a murderer. He killed four soldiers in the chapel. Tell us where we might find him."

"I don't know where he is," Simon told him. "How could I know?"

"I believe you might know where you were about to go with him. Why else would he have been there?" The priest pursed his lips. "I believe you might also be a Templar, no? One of their heretical clergy? I believe that you are in league with them, which would make you a heretic and a devil worshipper... among other things."

"I serve God, as you do, Brother," Simon told him, attempting to find some common ground with the man.

"But perhaps your god and mine are not the same." The man smiled at him condescendingly. "You have been seen with these men often, Simon of Grenoble. You are their confessor, I am told on good authority. You would know much about them that would be helpful to our cause. It would go well for you to cooperate with the King's inquiry."

"And what is your cause?" Simon asked him. This was not good at all. He would not betray his Brothers and he would not repeat what was said in confession.

"To rid the Holy Roman Empire of the heretics and worshippers of Baphomet."

"That is an admirable goal to be sure, brother, but the men you seek... worship the same God as you. I am sure of it," Simon told him again.

"You are not my brother, Simon of Grenoble." The priest's expression hardened. "But you do know them by your own words. We will have them all no matter. Now it is time for your confession."

"I have nothing to confess to you. I gave my confession this morning before God," Simon told him and closed his eyes. This was not going well. Surely he had not been here more than a day.

"And what is this you wear, my son?" The priest slid one finger under the only article of clothing his captors had left to him. A small, braided cord around his waist. The priest pulled on the string, causing it to cut into his skin reminding him only then of its presence. "Is this not a sign of your vow of chastity? A vow you took when you joined the order of Cistercians, promising to save yourself only for the pleasures of your brothers?"

"That is a lie! I am a child of God. A servant of His will. You profane the children of God with such accusations!" Simon shouted at him, his anger getting the best of him. The pain in his head temporarily blinded him.

"Ahhhhhh, a child of God?" the man smiled and looked around at his unseen companions as if this alone were proof of his accusations. "Are you also not a child of the Perfect Ones? A heretic? A professor of Catharism? Was not your mother a Parfait?"

Simon closed his eyes. This was ludicrous. He was an orphan from birth. He never knew his mother or his father.

"I am a child of God. I serve His will," he muttered weakly, finally realizing that it mattered very little what he said now.

"I think it is you who are lying, my son," the priest said as he twisted the cord. He then cut it with a knife before yanking it free, adding a new pain to the long list he already suffered. "Perhaps this would better serve if it were tied a bit tighter, no? Perhaps somewhat closer to the chastity you would preserve for your brothers. Wear it well, my son, and we will speak again when you have had more time to think."

Simon snapped his eyes open and sat up. Cold sweat covered him and the room was extremely chilly. He climbed from the bed and checked the windows. All closed. He needed something to drink.

His nightmares were getting worse. Where they came from, he had no idea. He had never spent any time in the dungeons. He had never faced the Inquisitors and he had never been accused of Catharism. Heresy, perhaps, but... He had to get a grip on himself. The dreams were obscene, disgusting. What made matters worse was that he couldn't even share them with his Brothers and ask what they might mean. There were no interpreters of dreams amongst the members of the Council of Twelve. Such an ability would have been most useful these days, though he doubted he could have related the contents of his dreams to anyone.

"I am losing my mind," he muttered to himself and then threw open the door to find himself unexpectedly facing the young girl they had taken in. She stood in the hallway dressed in a long white gown with one fist poised to knock. Her eyes were round with surprise at his sudden appearance.

"I'm sorry," he said, automatically assuming that he had frightened her. "One moment." He closed the door quickly and leaned against it a moment before retrieving a tee shirt from the bed post. He slipped it on and opened the door again.

"What can I do for you? Is something wrong?" he asked.

"I heard you shouting," she said and tried to look around him into the room. "I thought you were in trouble."

"It was a nightmare," he said, somewhat embarrassed. He wondered what she had heard and furthermore, how she had heard it. "It was nothing, but surely you are up late…"

"I have nightmares, too," she said. "I like to drink warm wine when I am upset. I hope you don't mind."

"Wine? Warm?" He repeated the word, but paid little attention, still trying to fathom how she had heard him. He frowned and stepped into the hall with her. The floor was cold through his socks. Dressed only in pajama pants and tee shirt, he felt exposed and embarrassed. "I need to…" he looked back into his room. What?

"Yes, you need to," she took his arm and turned him toward the front hall.

"I should get my…" he looked back again toward his open door, but felt compelled to accompany her. "Boots…" he finished lamely and she laughed.

"You aren't going outside dressed like that, are you?" She asked and continued to direct him effortlessly down the hall, around the stairwell and toward the kitchen. "You are a priest? I didn't know that. That should make me feel safe with you. Men are such bastards at times. I don't trust them. They leave us to die."

Her comments made him shudder. Who? Who leaves who to die? What was she talking about? He didn't feel safe with her. He had no idea what to do, but he couldn't seem to get away from her gentle hold. He wanted to tell her to go back to bed, but he couldn't make the words come out. He sat down at the table and watched as she poured wine and milk into a heavy saucepan on the stove.

"I don't care for milk, but the wine makes it palatable," she told him as she sat down at the table with him a few moments later with the steaming pot. The mixture smelled good oddly enough. She poured two mugs full and shoved one toward him. He took hold of the cup as if it were a life ring in a stormy sea. The stuff tasted better than it sounded and seemed to cure his queasy stomach on contact.

"What did you dream, Father?" she asked as she watched him over the rim of her cup.

"I don't remember," he lied and turned up the cup.

"You are lying and doing a bad job of it," she laughed and her voice sounded like the tinkling of glass chimes. Her accent was not Scottish, not English. "You are a very bad liar, did you know?" He could almost hear a French accent in her English, but had it not been Scottish only this afternoon?

"Thank you," he said and smiled at her tightly. She had about her some of the same surreal quality as John Paul. A sort of serene innocence, almost a radiant glow from within. Da Vinci would have immortalized her in oil. Michelangelo would have adulated her in stone. Degas would have made her dance. Lucifer would have fed her apples. Simon would hear her confession... He snapped his head up and wondered if he had fallen asleep. She was still talking. Her voice had an illusory quality to it as if there was more than one voice speaking. Choir-like. Angelic. Elohim. Adonai. Hosanna. Hosanna. He awoke again and blinked at her in astonishment. He was not well. The Inquisitors.

"You are a priest, aren't you?" She asked him. "You would hear my confession?"

"How did you know that I am... was a priest?" He asked her. How long had she stood listening outside his door? How much had she heard of the dream?

"You look like a priest and you act like a priest and I heard you say it in your dreams. You serve God's will. You are a child of God, but we are not always what our dreams would make us," she nodded her head and seemed very wise for her youth and apparent innocence.

"I like priests. I don't like rats!" she added suddenly with some vehemence. What the connection between the two might be, he had no idea and this did not sound so innocent as before. She did not need apples. She already knew the truth.

"And do you know many priests, Miss McShan? Are you so devout then? A devotee, perhaps, or a novice?" He asked with some hint of sarcasm. Suddenly he felt as if she was making fun of him and he felt his cheeks burn with anger. "I used to be a priest. A long time ago. I no longer wear the cloth of the clergy and I do not practice publicly."

Simon finished the drink and poured another from the pot.

"I have known a few priests in my day," she said lightly and twirled one of her long strands of wavy red hair in her fingers. "I used to help Father Mark at the chapel. He's a priest, too, you know."

"You helped, Sir... Mr. Ramsay?" Simon almost choked on his wine. "I thought he was... you don't know Mr. Ramsay, young missy," his voice rose a bit. "He is not a priest. He is a Chevalier. A Knight. A military man in the service of the King."

"The king, of course. Yes, he is all that and more. He knows much of worship and adoration," she countered and smiled again. She was unaffected by his discomfiture. "There was a time when he might have been thought a god in his own right. Long ago, of course."

She spoke like an old, old woman. It couldn't have been too long. She wasn't old enough for anything to have been long ago.

"So just how long have you known Mark?" He asked, trying to sound casual, not saying 'by his first name'.

119

"All my life," she told him confidently. "I used to live here... not here," she pointed down at the table with one finger, "but nearby." She said and nodded her head toward the window. Simon glanced at the window that faced west. The McShan place was east of the house, but he couldn't say for sure what she meant exactly. Nearby.

"With your grandparents?" he prompted her to continue.

"No," she shook her head. "My parents."

Simon frowned. He had never heard Mark Andrew speak of Ian's children. Certainly Ian McShan had at least one son if this was his granddaughter. But then, Mark Andrew rarely told anything he didn't have to, especially things of a personal nature that did not require confession. If Ian had married, there could easily be children, grandchildren. Mark would be their patriarch. There was no sin in it if Ian had tried to live a normal life. No sin that Mark had tried to stay out of it as much as possible. Yet, Ian had remained close... very close, living on Mark's land, as it were, in a house that belonged to Mark. If Ian had hated him so much, why had he stayed? Why had he not moved on? Still, there was no reason to believe that Ian could not have had any number of sons and daughters.

"And when was the last time you saw him... Mark, I mean?" Simon was now more fascinated than angry. The milk and wine had a calming effect on his nerves.

"Years," she said and continued to stare at him as if memorizing his face.

"Years. And what about your parents? Surely you could go home?" he asked hopefully.

"They are lost," she said wistfully. "For a long time now."

"Lost? I'm sorry," he apologized for the third time and looked down at the table. He drummed his fingers on the wood. Her presence was very disturbing, like being in the company of something foreboding, possibly evil. What did she expect from him? What did she want? What did she want from Mark Ramsay? Money? Lost? In a storm? In an accident? At sea? At poker?

"I could help you there," she said suddenly, sitting up straighter.

"Where?" He looked up in confusion, and laid his hands flat on the table. He looked at her wide-eyed and felt his face flush hot and then cold. Perspiration popped out on his upper lip and nausea gripped his stomach.

"At the chapel," she told him. "I helped Mark there and another."

"Another?" He frowned. "Another what?"

"There was another who worked there."

Who? Christopher Stewart? No, she would have only been a child of perhaps eight or nine. Major MacLaughlin? But what could she have been doing at the Chapel? It didn't make sense. Major MacLaughlin?

120

"I think we should get back to bed," he suggested and stood up. "We have to figure out what to do with you tomorrow."

The girl rose quickly, almost as if she had never been sitting in the first place and came around the table. She wrapped her arms around his waist and laid her head against his chest as he stood stock still holding the empty cup in one hand.

"Please don't turn me away, Father," she spoke into his shirt. "Won't you decide what to do with me tonight? Why wait until tomorrow? I want to help you, too, Simon."

After carefully placing the cup on the table, he pushed her away, gingerly pressing only his thumbs against her shoulders. She was attempting to seduce him and he was dumbfounded. Exactly what the hell did she mean by 'help'? If Major MacLaughlin had been taking advantage of this girl...

"You cannot stay here, Elizabeth," he told her sternly. "It would not be proper. You must have family somewhere. What about uncles, aunts, cousins? Miss Sinclair and I will help you find them and we'll make sure you get well on your way. Money is no object. I understand that you are distraught. Death is a hard thing to accept."

"You are very kind, sir," Elizabeth smiled up at him. "If you have any more nightmares, I would be glad to keep you company. As a friend."

"I will keep that in mind," he sighed and started down the hall, leaving her alone in the kitchen. He had to get to the bathroom under the stairwell before he lost the milk and wine on the floor. This was not good. He had no intention of having her in the house long enough to have more nightmares. It was almost dawn when he lay down again, but he dared not close his eyes. He did not want to go back to the dungeon.

((((((((((((<O>))))))))))))

Merry was awakened by the sound of the phone ringing, but it stopped before she got out of bed to answer it. Bruce must have answered it or Simon had. She glanced at the clock on the dresser. Seven thirty. Time enough for a good long bath before breakfast. She felt groggy and irritable. Nightmares had plagued her dreams all night, but now she could remember nothing of them. She started the water in the tub and poured in some of the bubblebath that Mark Andrew liked. The aroma of vanilla filled the air and calmed her nerves. She was terribly worried about Mark Andrew and hoped to hear from him today. If she hadn't heard anything by noon, she would ask Simon to call the Villa and see if they had any news. Certainly this part of his occupation was cause for worry.

121

The Assassin. She had never given much thought to the real meaning of the word. It was hard for her to believe that Mark was actually an assassin in the literal sense. She knew that in Texas and most certainly almost anywhere else, he might have been classified a hit man. A professional criminal. A murderer. But as a member of an elite military order, sniper was perhaps the correct terminology. A better word than assassin. The United States trained military snipers. And what was their job? To shoot people at a distance. Same result. Mark Andrew simply carried out his snipering up close and personal. She knew that Mark did not glory in what he did. He did not gloat or brag, nor did he speak of it in any manner other than official reports as far as she knew. Confession maybe. How could he be a murderer? More than that. How could he be a rapist as well and yet, she still loved him. No one would forgive him. No one would understand her feelings for him. Who did they have but each other? Did a man or woman's actions really portray what they were? Who could forgive Adolf Hitler for his crimes? Who could forgive Jeffrey Dahmer? John Wayne Gacy? Meredith shuddered to her toes. Mark couldn't possibly be compared with them... could he? Surely his other life held more meaning than Charles Manson's. Those men were psychotic, crazy, lunatics... Mark was a Knight of Christ. A Christian warrior. Bound to do the will of God. Ahhh, but had not any number of psychopaths claimed to hear the voice of God telling them to kill people?

All these horrible doubts and thoughts swirled in her head like the water swirling in the tub. It was hard to reconcile Mark with this title, this vocation, except for his temper. She was eternally grateful that John Paul had apparently not inherited his father's temper. At the thought of John Paul, another worry washed over her. She felt uneasy about his safety since he had gone back to Italy where she could not keep an eye on him. Her Brothers had already allowed him to be abducted twice. What was to assure her that it would not happen again?

Merry waited a bit before getting in the tub to make sure the phone call had not been for her. She was lying in the tub of hot water, enjoying the soak, breathing slowly in and out, trying to clear her mind of all disturbing negativity when she suddenly remembered one of the dreams that had plagued her restless sleep. She had been in the midst of a beautiful meadow full of golden flowers. In the distance she had seen a fabulous fountain spraying misty water into the air. She remembered that there were people at the fountain and that she had walked across the grass toward them. Two women. One tall, with golden hair, dressed in white and the other, dark-haired, dressed in crimson robes. The dark one turned and waved her forward. It had seemed that she was drifting across the grass rather than walking. When she was close enough to see their faces, she saw that the dark one had horns on her temples. The blonde had beckoned her to come into the fountain, which sprayed from seven stones shaped like flowers. The dark woman placed a golden chain in her hand when she drew near. She stepped into the spray, following the chain that was attached to something inside the water, something obscured by the fine mists. The mists parted and there in the fountain she had seen a terrible red dragon that was drinking from the fount. The chain, which was wrapped around its thick, muscular neck, seemed far too fragile to hold the beast. The dragon raised its dangerously beautiful, multi-horned head when it saw her there and that was when she had screamed. That was when she had woke up, shaking in fear with her arms wrapped over her head. The dream had been so real. It must have held some hidden meaning. She would have to ask Simon.

She picked up the soap and began to lather her sponge. She needed to hurry. They still had to deal with Elizabeth McShan before the others began to arrive.

((((((((((((<O>))))))))))))

Elizabeth McShan placed the phone crosswise in the cradle with the line open and laid a plaid shawl across it, muffling the urgent tone warning that it was not properly disconnected. Wrong number. She looked up at the library's ceiling briefly. The woman upstairs was in the bath and the priest was outside on the patio. She brushed back her hair and tied it with a green velvet ribbon before making her way quickly to the kitchen where the cook was busy setting up the breakfast table.

"Good morning!" She said brightly to the startled cook.

"Whoo're you?" He asked rudely, dropping his fork in the pan.

"I'm Elizabeth McShan, here at Sir Ramsay's behest. Whoo're you?" she asked, mimicking his accent perfectly. She walked slowly toward him.

"I'm Bruce," the startled cook frowned at her. "I'm Sir Ramsay's cook. I was not informed that we wud be havin' comp'ny in th' Master's absence."

"I know," she nodded and continued to close in on him. "And a verra gud cook ye must be, sair. Sir Ramsay wud only employ th' best."

"Whattar ye doin'?" Bruce's voice went up an octave as she reached for his hand, but he was unable to move.

"I'm 'ere t' 'elp you, Bruce," she smiled at him and he was caught up in her deep green eyes. She was just a child.

"I dunna need yer help, choild. Just 'ave a seat at th' table. Breakfast will be ready shortly," he told her as she pressed his hand to her lips.

"Of course you need my help," she told him. "We all need help, Bruce."

123

She came closer and wrapped her arms around his waist, laying her head on his chest. Her hair smelled of freshly baked bread and violets.

The back door slammed and the sound of footsteps echoed in the back hall. The girl let go of him quickly and sat down at the long table. Bruce stood mesmerized near the stove as if paralyzed.

"Something smells good," Simon remarked as he entered the kitchen.

"Thot wud be th' coffee and bacon, sair," Bruce told him automatically and then plucked his fork gingerly from the pan. "Wud ye loike a cup, Master Simon?"

"I'll get it for him, Bruce," Elizabeth McShan interrupted and rose quickly from her seat at the table to fetch a cup for the Healer. "Cream and sugar?" She looked back over her shoulder at him as he took a seat at the table.

"Both, please," he smiled at her and waited for Mark Andrew's grumpy cook to admonish her for getting in his way. The cook said nothing, but went back to his cooking as if the girl had been working with him for years.

Elizabeth fixed his coffee and brought it to him with a light bounce in her step. She was dressed in a simple, flowered dress much like the one she had worn the day before. The little purple flowers and green leaves in the fabric set off her bright green eyes. She was truly lovely, but not nearly so alluring as the night before.

"Your dress reminds me of something," Simon said as he took the coffee from her. "I want to order in some purple flowers, Bruce. I think I have come up with a plan. I want to make some rows of purple flowers and then put in some of those violets we found on the web and at the back, lilies, pink and white lilies. We could make them butt up to the patio and fan out on both sides, lining the walk and in the center of the patio... no at the rear in the grass, a fountain. And around the fountain more lilies and violets and purple flowers..." his voice trailed off as he looked at the girl over the rim of the cup. She sat listening to his ramblings as if entranced by his voice. He had never had anyone look at him like that before. "What is a good purple variety?" he addressed this question to Bruce, but did not take his eyes off the girl.

"I dunno, sair," Bruce shrugged and chuckled. "If I canna cook it, I dunna know much aboot it." It was the first time Simon had heard the cook laugh.

"I like amaranths," the girl offered. "Purple amaranths. The flowers of immortal love."

"Immortal love," Simon nodded. "A charming sentiment."

"Yes. Quite," she smiled. "Do you believe in immortal love, Father?"

"Eternal love," he corrected her and nodded. "I believe in eternal love. God's love is eternal."

"I mean immortal love. Such as the love between men and women," she insisted.

"I don't think it is possible as such love does not extend beyond the grave. We will all love each other in Heaven," Simon gave her the standard Christian view and put his cup down, wondering if she were not baiting him. Immortal love. A strange question. "Unconditionally. Agape, if you care to give it a name."

"Then you don't believe that lovers will meet again and be together in the afterlife?" she raised her delicate eyebrows and her green eyes sparkled with amusement. Was she making fun of him again?

"No. I don't," he said flatly. "I believe you are speaking of earthly love. We will not be concerned with that sort of thing in Paradise."

"What a shame," she almost laughed. "I think that earthly love is about the only thing we have to look forward to in this life. And how can it be termed Paradise without perfect love."

"Ahhhh, now you speak of 'perfect' love. Only God is capable of showing perfect love, but there are other things for us lesser souls," Simon said off-handedly. "There is work and devotion to God. Service to God's people and His will."

"Such as saving souls, Father?" she narrowed her eyes, but the twinkle did not abate. "If you thought my soul was in danger, would you save me?"

"I cannot save you, Elizabeth," he said and made a wry face at her. "I do nothing of my own accord. Only your belief in Christ Jesus and your devotion to God can do that. You do believe in Christ, do you not? You are a Christian, no?"

"Oh, I believe in many things, Father," she said and tilted her chin up a bit, as if daring him to ask her more. "I believe that anything is possible… anything and everything. It is just a matter of setting one's mind to it. As you say… belief is the first step. Devotion can only improve one's results."

"I see," he muttered and reached for his cup. He had no idea what she was talking about or at least, he hoped he didn't, but he was saved from further confusion by Merry's entrance into the kitchen.

"Good morning all," she said brightly and cast a questioningly look at Simon who shrugged slightly. It was obvious that he had made no headway with the girl. "Something smells good. Is that fresh bread I smell?"

Bruce swiveled his head around like an owl to look at her. "No, ma'am. Thot wud be th' coffee. If it's bread ye want, ye'd best droive into town to th' bak'ry. I'm a cook, not a baker. I'm afraid my bread wud do ye no sarvice."

Merry was taken aback by Bruce's sarcasm. She took a mug from the cabinet and set it by the electric coffee maker, one of the few modern appliances in the kitchen.

"I'll get it." Elizabeth bounced up. "Simon and I were just talking about eternal love."

Merry took a seat at the table and gave the Healer a frowning smile.

"He tells me that you have a son almost my age."

Merry's frown deepened.

Simon looked perplexed. Had he mentioned John Paul? He didn't seem to remember that.

"You don't look old enough to have a son my age," Elizabeth continued as she retrieved a cup for Merry. "Cream and sugar?"

"Just cream," Merry told her then added. "Thank you."

Elizabeth brought the coffee to Merry and sat down again.

"I hope that I can weather the storms of aging as well as you have, Miss Sinclair," she said and winked at Simon. "I hope that my baby will be as loved as much as your son."

Merry's mouth fell open. What was she saying?

"Are you expecting, Miss McShan?" Simon asked her in surprise.

"Why, yes!" She said. "I thought you knew."

"No, you forgot to mention it," Simon said softly. How could they turn out Mark's great-granddaughter when she was with child? "Are you married then?"

"No, are you?" She asked him sweetly. There was no sarcasm in her voice. It sounded like an everyday conversation about the weather.

"And when is the baby due?" Merry asked, trying to remain civil and polite. Things were going from bad to worse.

"The Summer Solstice," she said with conviction. "Won't that be nice? Midsummer's Eve. Such a beautiful day of sunshine, life and festivities. It is truly wonderful that people continue to honor the old ways after so long."

Merry calculated quickly in her head. Nine months from now almost exactly. What was she saying? She had become pregnant yesterday?! Merry was beginning to wonder about the girl's sanity.

"I just love the wheel of the seasons, don't you?" the girl continued. "Vernal equinox. Midsummer. The summer solstice. The autumnal equinox. The winter solstice. All very auspicious days for births and deaths. The beginning of one thing and the ending of another. All the circles and cycles renewing each other endlessly. Babies should be born in the Spring or Summer, don't you think? Like your son."

Merry's heart caught in her throat. John Paul had been born on the first day of spring fifteen years earlier. Did this girl also know his birth date? Merry shot a questioning look at the Healer, but Simon was staring at the girl. The words she used rang an alarm bell in his head. They were pagan holidays. All of them. And circles and cycles. Who was the baby's father? Better yet, where was he? Perhaps they could locate him.

"And the baby's father?" Simon asked bluntly. "Perhaps he might wish to know where you are."

"He is not available," Elizabeth's demeanor darkened a bit as she spoke.

"You mean he is married?" Simon pressed the issue.

"Yes, some say so," she said shortly. "We do not always do as we should. I am no exception."

"Have you tried to reach your grandmother?" Merry asked her as Bruce began to set bowls of oatmeal in front of them.

"I have," Elizabeth looked down at her hands and twisted her dress in her fingers. "I spoke with her sister on the phone this morning. My grandmother is in the hospital. I'm afraid her husband's death was too much of a strain. She had another heart attack day before yesterday. She is not expected to recover."

"Oh, I'm so sorry." Merry sat back and looked at Simon for help.

"We will pray for her soul. But surely there is someone else. Somewhere?" Simon asked. "What about your aunt? Or your parents?"

"I used to live with my parents down under. I really don't know where they are now and I don't get along with my aunts. I'm afraid I'm on my own," Elizabeth told them and looked at him tearfully. "I've been alone most of my life. I'll manage somehow. Don't worry about me."

Simon let out a long sigh. Her words were well worn clichés and sounded as if she had read them somewhere or heard them on television and was now trying to use them to garner sympathy like an actress in a bad movie. They would have to wait for Mark Andrew to return. It could not be their decision. Simon knew very little of Scotland's government. Nothing of their social programs, financial aid for the poor and destitute, welfare systems, but there had to be somewhere the girl could go. A church sponsored shelter or at least some form of government assistance for such cases.

Bruce bustled around the table setting out brown sugar, cinnamon and raisins for the cereal.

"If you dunna mind my sayin', sir," Bruce spoke up. "She cud stay on here a bit. We have plenty of room. I cud use the help around the house. She has offered to help me."

"But what would your... what would Mr. Ramsay say?" Simon looked sharply at the old cook; he was not helping their cause. "We can't hire servants for his household without consulting him first."

"Mr. Ramsay 'as ollways been charitable, sair," Bruce told him sternly. "He wud nae turn out a choild in need. 'e wud know wot t' do when 'e retarns. It wud be nae trouble for a few days."

Merry was at a loss. It was not just Mark Andrew's return that bothered her. The Grand Master would be coming soon. What then?

"You are too kind, Bruce." Elizabeth looked up at the cook and smiled wanly. "But you good people shouldn't worry your heads over me. I'll be going after breakfast. I don't want to put anyone out."

"No!" Merry and Simon said simultaneously. "We'll work something out," Simon added and then crossed himself quickly and began the prayers of thanksgiving for breakfast before anyone could comment further.

((((((((((((<O>))))))))))))

Mark Andrew slammed the phone on the desk in anger. First a wrong number and then a busy signal. He wanted to talk to Merry. To tell her that he would be home tomorrow. He sat down in the chair behind the desk in Sir Philip's office and leaned back, rubbing his eyes. He was tired. He had slept very little since his short 'meeting' with Devereaux. It had been impossible to close his eyes on the plane with the metal case sitting on the seat between himself and the Frankish Knight. They had used the privilege of papal immunity to get onto the plane and had almost been detained at the Barcelona airport by a suspicious customs agent in spite of their credentials. Mark had finally relented and allowed them to X-ray the 'reliquary' box. The skull, he explained, was a religious relic being returned to the Vatican archives from abroad. The skull, purported to be that of an obscure Peruvian padre from the eighteenth century was to be properly blessed by His Eminence, the Pope, installed in a proper reliquary fit for display in the Church of St. Francis Solanus in Cusco. The agent didn't like this story either because he couldn't confirm or deny the existence of such a church. Eventually, the airport security supervisor decided that they could not use the skull as a weapon to hijack the plane, but insisted on taking a peek inside the box because, he said, he'd never seen a holy relic up close and personal and being a good Catholic, he wanted to venerate it... personally. Mark decided that the man simply did not like Louis Champlain's looks, but Champlain insisted that it was Mark's attitude that landed them in a holding cell.

In the end, they had been forced to phone d'Brouchart and he had used his influence with the Vatican to get them through without the case being opened on the grounds that it was the property of the Holy See and thus immune to secular laws by agreements between France, Spain and Rome dating back several hundred years, blah, blah, blah, etceteras, etceteras. It had been close. Too close. Airport security had become a nightmare in the past several years. Why did d'Brouchart want to see the head? His job was becoming harder and harder. The next time the Master wanted proof of an execution, he would simply have to come along for the ride.

And then the meeting after the brawl in the Council room had been equally difficult with the man livid about the presence of the knife in the Council Room and threatened disciplinary action. But, at least, the Stone was found. At the moment, the ceremony restoring Lucio's gift was underway in the underground chapel without his presence. He had declined the somewhat impersonal invitation delivered by one of d'Brouchart's lackeys. He had had enough of the Italian for a while and his attendance was unnecessary.

The statement that Lucio had made in Council was preposterous. A desperate attempt to stop the wedding. And what was he talking about anyway? The union must not be allowed to succeed. The powers of darkness. What did his marriage to Merry have to do with the powers of darkness?

Oh, and yes, of course, not to forget the matter of John Paul's behavior in the Council Chamber. Merry would not be happy to hear that her son was a Prophet. He was still in shock over the boy's strange pronouncements himself. But the real problem was deciphering the words of the prophecy. It seemed the boy had been speaking directly to him and even his voice had sounded different. He pondered the idea of demonic possession and then dismissed it.

The message, he felt, was directed at him. Rarely did anything capture his attention with such intensity. When John spoke to him, it was as if the entire world around him dissolved, leaving only himself and the boy suspended in time and space. He tried to remember when or if he had ever experienced such an occurrence. But he had to assume he was not to be counted among the 'wise' because he did not understand the meaning of the words, nor did he remember any similar incidents in his long history. Furthermore, he could not even say whether it was real prophecy or just scriptures quoted during some sort of brain seizure.

After the personal 'meeting' with d'Brouchart, he had gone over to check on John Paul at the Ritter's apartments. The boy had been sleeping peacefully on the couch in the German's sitting room. Von Hetz had confirmed his suspicions that the words were indeed scriptures, but were mixed up, out of order. Most of the passages had come from the Psalms, but some of them had come from the Book of Daniel, also a gifted prophet of the Old Testament. Mark Andrew had asked the Ritter if he understood them, but the Ritter had only shaken his head sadly. The Ritter had a meeting scheduled with Sir Philip and the Grand Master, where they planned to discuss the matter in depth.

At present, the Master was involved in the matter of de Lyons' outburst in Council. The incident had put them all in mind of the former Knight of the Sword, de Lyon's predecessor, Thomas Beaujold. Thomas had done almost the same thing before apparently losing his objectivity and going on a one man crusade designed to rid the Order of its Knight of Death. Hasty words had been spoken. Old wounds reopened. Things that would have be mended or cured or disposed of. The Master would not take kindly to another vendetta springing up amongst the Council Knights. The Ritter admitted that he was glad he was not at that meeting.

On the other subject, perhaps they could figure it all out. It was beyond the dark Knight's abilities to decipher the meaning of John's words, but von Hetz reluctantly agreed with Louis Champlain that they had the ring of prophecy, but only time would tell.

After leaving John Paul in the Ritter's hands, he found himself waiting again. One of his least favorite activities. Waiting for permission to leave the compound. If Merry was willing, they might be able to get the wedding done before he had to leave again. Would nothing ever work out in his favor? If he could get the wedding behind him, he felt that he and Merry's relationship would improve and they would stop fighting so much. The impending marriage was beginning to look less attractive than he wanted to admit. Almost like a mission that he needed to accomplish. And to top it all off, another problem had developed concerning the Italian. With his immortality restored, Lucio had no reason to stay in Italy and there was no doubt in Mark's mind that Lucio would be going to Scotland, with or without the Grand Master's permission. D'Brouchart was much less aggravated with Dambretti now that the Stone had been found.

One of the few perks of the Grand Master's position was that he needed no excuses or explanations for his decisions though he often gave them. He could command Lucio to remain in Italy, but it was not likely that he would. If he were Grand Master, things would be different. For one thing, HQ would be in Scotland. For another thing, Lucio Dambretti would still be a mortal man. He sighed and picked up the phone again. He also knew the Grand Master would want to throw him and Lucio together as soon as possible so that they could work out their differences. That had always been d'Brouchart's standing policy. Sir de Lyons and Champlain would be together when they went to America. They were still quite angry with each other over the harsh words exchanged in Council over John Paul. Another happy thing to look forward to. The phone was still busy... broken more like, but why? What had happened? Perhaps it was off the hook? Yet another fine thing to worry about. He had a very bad feeling about Scotland. He had not liked the idea of von Hetz mucking about in his chapel and he did not feel that Simon should be exposed to the power of the Ark. Simon's constitution was not strong enough to handle the stress of the thing, though he knew the Healer would feel obligated to do his part regardless of the danger. If he knew Simon's cell number, he could have called the Healer, but of course, his own stubborn refusal to update himself was working against him again.

He searched Philip's desk for an address book or file card or something with Simon's number, but found nothing.

He glanced at Philip's computer terminal. That would be where Philip kept his files these days. D'Brouchart might have had an address book on his desk, but not Philip. He poked one of the keys and the screen lit up. After some trial and error he found the e-mail and then hesitantly and painfully began to peck at the keys. After several aborted attempts, he managed to send an e-mail to his home in Scotland telling them that he would be home tomorrow if anyone cared to read it.

(((((((((((((<O>)))))))))))))

The Ritter paced the floor in his tiny sitting room at the Villa. Something was not right. He had been very disturbed by the activities of the day, the fight and John Paul's words. Nothing but argument and speculation had resulted from his meeting with Sir Philip and d'Brouchart. Each of them had their own ideas about what the prophecy meant. They were most in agreement that the prophecy had referred to Mark Andrew since the first half had clearly pointed to him. Father of the Fatherless. The solitary in families. They shall fear thee... certainly all the Brothers feared Mark Andrew Ramsay. And he had become a stranger unto his brethren. That much was easy. But prophecies usually were clear in regard to whom they were addressing. It was the actual interpretation of the prophecy that was hard to pin down. Something was going to happen to Sir Ramsay and he would not be the one telling the Knight of Death such a thing. That Ramsay did not understand the implications of his son's words, was good because sometimes, ignorance truly was bliss. It was better for him not to know... for now. Besides, he could not elaborate on what might be in the offing enough to help him get around it or over it, but whatever it was would not be fatal. The boy also spoke of the Stone and that had been fulfilled almost immediately with the recovery of the Stone in the midst of the brawl. And had not Mark Andrew's attack on Lucio precipitate the recovery of the Stone from his body?

The first part of the prophecy was very clear. ...she shall not stand on his side, neither be for him. Mark Andrew would not be marrying Sister Meredith.

The German turned his attention to the north and west, focusing on Simon d'Ornan's thoughts without actually prying too deeply. He only wished to get a feel for the Healer's mood, not his personal musings, but something was amiss there. Simon was in turmoil, mentally and physically. There was something very wrong with him other than the burden at the

131

chapel. Von Hetz shuddered at the memory of the evil presence there and felt heartily sorry for having left the Healer to deal with it. The evil presence of the girl was never far from his mind, even in sunny, southern Italy. She had treated him sorely and he felt unclean for having touched her. Allowing her to touch him. Unclean! Unclean! He felt he should run through the Villa shouting 'Unclean! Unclean!' like a leper. Simon was also concerned about the selfsame girl. But how did Simon know about Elizabeth? Had she also appeared to him?! This revelation caused the connection to be broken momentarily. He refocused his thoughts quickly and delved deeper into Simon's mind, searching for the source of the Healer's knowledge of the girl, but he was disappointed. Simon was asleep. He was having a nightmare about the Inquisition... the dungeon... rats... the cold stone... the pain... Von Hetz quickly withdrew his thoughts. He did not want to witness this. But... he hesitated. Simon had not been a victim of the Inquisition. Simon's infirmity stemmed from an accident... or did it? Why was he dreaming about a dungeon? Von Hetz frowned. Of course, dreaming about a dungeon did not necessarily mean that one had to have been in a dungeon at some point. He certainly had dreamt his share of bizarre scenarios in his long life. Some of his dreams went quite beyond bizarre, but normally he dreamed of things he knew.

This too was probably coming from the influence of the Ark and its power. Even the boy had said the girl's name aloud. He remembered it quite well. In fact, it had hit his nerves like an electric shock when they had pulled the boy from the floor and he had uttered the name 'Elizabeth'.

Von Hetz went into the bedroom and sat on the edge of the cot. But John was just a boy... well, fifteen... only half grown. And Simon? The girl could not possibly have the same effect on either of them. If she had appeared to John, she had surely sent him into near catatonia. John would have recognized her for what she was. Simon on the other hand might not readily see through her, but he would have no use for her charms.

"John Paul?" He asked quietly and shook the boy's shoulder gently. It was well after midnight.

The boy opened his eyes blearily.

"John Paul? Did you see Elizabeth at your papa's house?" He asked.

The boy nodded.

"Did she say anything to you?" He asked hesitantly. His heart fell at the thought that the girl had been able to manifest herself inside Ramsay's home. He had not considered the possibility that she could travel far from the Chapel.

The boy nodded again.

"Can you tell me what she said?" He asked quietly.

"I am here to help you, John."

"Did she... help you?" Von Hetz grimaced and gritted his teeth as pain struck him between his eyes.

"Go to sleep, Master. Go to sleep," John muttered and was off again.

Chapter Eight of Seventeen
And he hath confirmed his words, which he spake against us

It was after midnight and still Lucio was sitting in the chair in front of d'Brouchart's desk in the Grand Master's chambers. In all his years of coming to the Villa, he had never been invited into this sanctified space. This was Sir Philip's domain, not his. Sir Philip was there, of course, sitting on a small sofa with his legs crossed and his hands clasped around his knees, a deep frown etched on his thin features. Lucio was tired and growing more exhausted by the moment. He was feeling a bit better since regaining his gift, but he was not quite over the residual effects of the fever and now, regretfully, he would be eternally thinner than he had been before. His clothes were all loose on him and he had actually developed a few crow's feet around his eyes in the short space of time he had been mortal. The scars from the bindings on which he had unmercifully cut his wrists on in the hospital bed and the marks from the IV needles were probably also going to be around for a while.

The Grand Master leaned back in the chair and clasped his hands in front of his considerable stomach. The chair squeaked ominously.

"And so this is your interpretation of the Treatise?" He asked again.

"Yes, yes and yes…. Your Grace," Lucio answered irritably.

"If what you say is true, then we cannot risk a marriage between Ramsay and Sister Meredith," d'Brouchart finally relented and shook his head. "And how will we prevent this, Brother?"

The fatigue faded magickly as this turn of events perked him up.

"I don't know," Lucio told him. "I have been trying to keep them apart, but every time I turn around you or some other circumstance keeps throwing them together. And now you tell me that they have been… that there is the possibility… that she could be pregnant. It is beyond comprehension! How could it have happened? But I am not concerned with that, your Grace. If it is so, then I have no aversion to raising Brother Ramsay's child as my own. I fully expect to have children myself and so there should be no problem."

D'Brouchart frowned and then sighed. Here was the old Golden Eagle. He'd half thought him changed forever. Arrogance and magnanimous statements. Well, he certainly would not repeat what Simon had told him on the phone about the 'bath' and John Paul's conception and the embarrassing position in which the Healer had inadvertently found the prolific Knight of Death. Caught, almost literally in the act. They had enough trouble already.

"The good news is that Simon does not think she is pregnant. It is the Ritter who thinks it is so," d'Brouchart told him.

"The Ritter!" Lucio spat the word. "Why?" Why did the Master always take the Ritter's word as immutable while questioning everyone else.

"The Ritter has also had visions," d'Brouchart shrugged slightly. "It is one thing to have visions, but an entirely different matter to interpret them. Simon's visions were similar to the Ritter's, but he had a different explanation. In fact, he tends to agree with you. He does not want to perform the wedding and feels that if she should marry, it should be you."

"Ah," Lucio nodded. At last, an ally. Simon, of course. Simon had always been the first to listen to reason.

"But we cannot dictate to Mark Andrew and Sister Meredith who they should or should not marry. This situation is what you might call unexplored territory. In the past, such situations were easily remedied. The prospective brides were not Knights of the Order for one thing. It is not... possible for me to interfere without much trouble."

"I understand that, Sir," Lucio told him. "I would just wish to have the opportunity to spend some time with her before they carry through with it. I believe I could convince her if you would but permit me."

"That may be true, but Simon also pointed out something else, Brother," d'Brouchart leaned forward before continuing and lowered his voice to whisper conspiratorially. "Something we all seem to forget. And something that I whole-heartedly agree with. We are not here to enforce the prophecies. We are simply here to fulfill them. If it is the will of God, it will be done."

Sir Philip crossed himself and said a solemn "Amen."

"I would suggest that you go very cautiously, Golden Eagle," d'Brouchart eyed him closely. "I am inclined to allow you to accompany us to Scotland, but I will not have you calling Sir Ramsay out again. And I would not have you provoking him. By God, I believe if you give him another chance, he will see to your demise. The marriage is not his decision alone and will not be decided by a contest. If this is to be God's will, then let it be done. You do not have to force things. At this time, I am not sure what to think, but I am disinclined to support the marriage between them, but that does not mean, mind you that I am in full agreement with you concerning your interpretation of the Arcanum. I will tell you this in all honesty: I advised Meredith to choose one or the other of you and be done with it, but let me also tell you that I encouraged her to set her sights on du Morte simply because he is more stable than you. He owns substantial property. He has deep roots in Scotland. You understand that, if she should wed you, you will be responsible for her well-being for a very, very long time! I have yet to see you do anything that would convince me that you are ready to form a lasting bond with any one woman, let alone any family that might be forthcoming. And I will tell you now, Sir, I will not tolerate infidelity. You will not be allowed to keep your Sicilian concubines if you marry Sister Meredith. Is that clear?"

"I understand," Lucio could barely repress a smile. The thought of seeing Merry again did more for his feelings than anything they could have done for him. He felt almost well, except for the itching, peeling skin on his back. And he did not care what the Master had told her or what the Master thought of him. He would win her. He had always been able to beat Mark Ramsay when it came to romancing the ladies. Of course, he would need more than romance and a few good pickup lines to win her, but that would come. She loved him. He was sure of it.

"You will say nothing of this meeting," d'Brouchart said after a moment and looked at him intently. "There is serious work to be done in Scotland. Do not complicate matters. And understand this, Sir Dambretti, I will not hesitate to kill you... if you jeopardize the Ark!"

Lucio's eyes widened slightly. He had not expected to have his life threatened after having just regained it. Yes, serious business was at hand.

"I will not disappoint you, your Grace," he nodded his head solemnly.

"Good," d'Brouchart said and stood up, extending his hand to Lucio. The Italian took his hand and kissed his ring before leaving the room quickly.

"What do you think?" D'Brouchart asked as he resumed his seat and looked at Philip with raised eyebrows.

"I don't think you could have said anything more to impress upon him the importance of your mission, your Grace. But the company of women is a dangerous thing. Ramsay is easier to understand than Dambretti. Brother Lucio seems to be even-tempered and easy of humor, but he is surprisingly complicated and his temper is bad when provoked. Where Ramsay will seek the straightest path, Dambretti will twist and turn. Where Ramsay seeks the simplest explanation and holds steady, Dambretti looks too deep and then flies away."

"Yes," d'Brouchart nodded. "But they must work out their differences as I have said before. The only reason I restored the Golden Eagle's gift is because of Simon's most recent revelation. If it had come from anyone other than Simon of Grenoble, I would have sent Brother Lucio off to the Middle East and been done with it. I grow weary of the tug of war he plays with du Morte. I have many regrets, Philip, but Dambretti seems to be one of my worst. Sometimes I believe we would be well rid of him. If only Carlisle had not been lost..."

Sir Philip was aghast at this peek inside the Master's thoughts. Carlisle. Carlisle Corrigan! Was a name he'd not heard in ages. He knew that the Master silently blamed the Scot for Carlisle's death and Simon's misfortune. What he had never understood was why the Grand Master set such a store of trust in Simon d'Ornan. Ever since Simon had joined them as a priest just before the horrid events of the fourteenth century, the Master had been inclined more toward tolerance as far as the Healer was concerned than safety demanded. Philip wondered if Simon knew he held so much sway with the Grand Master. The Master seemed taken with the fragile child from the very beginning, placing him with the Cistercians for safekeeping at a very early age. As soon as Simon had donned the robes of an ordained priest, d'Brouchart had recruited him to the Order. And then, one night, he had been called from a deep sleep to witness a most peculiar thing.

At the time, Templars were being sought and arrested everywhere by order of the Holy See and the King of France. He and d'Brouchart were in hiding, desperately trying to arrange passage out of France to friendlier shores. He had answered Edgard's call, fearful of some new and terrible threat, to find d'Brouchart beside himself with fear and outrage. Simon of Grenoble lay almost dead in the house where d'Brouchart had been given sanctuary. Oddly, he remembered Sir Ramsay's face that night more clearly than anything else. He'd rarely ever seen anyone since with a more profound look of devastation in his eyes. It had been Ramsay who delivered Simon to the Grand Master shortly before they departed for Scotland. Philip remembered quite vividly having to literally drag the enraged Master off of Sir Ramsay when he saw Simon's condition.

Had the Master killed Ramsay that night, they would have been completely undone and the Master had seemed intent upon killing the Knight of Death. There had been much turmoil during the early fourteenth century. The Ordo Militi Templi was disbanded and destroyed with the exception of those fortunate enough to escape to Scotland and other places of refuge. Some of them joined other military orders. Some of them drifted into oblivion, but the Order within the Order, the Red Cross of Gold remained intact. Preserving the sanctity of the Order within the Order was hard enough in the face of papal persecution, but killing their only hope of regrouping and surviving in Scotland under Robert the Bruce's protection would have been madness. Ramsay had arranged their flight from France. Ramsay had interceded on their behalf with Robert. Ramsay had found lodging and support for them in his native land when others had turned them out.

After Philip had managed to save Ramsay's neck, d'Brouchart dragged them both into the smoky bedchamber and performed the Tree of Life ceremony on the near dead priest. Sir Philip had thought at the time, that d'Brouchart had lost his mind. Simon had not even been an apprentice, never-the-less, d'Brouchart had bestowed the gift of immortality on him and then commanded Sir Ramsay to impart the Mysteries of the Mystic Healer to his keeping and thus had Simon, the Priest become Sir Simon, the Mystic Healer. Philip had been horrified. He had been afraid that the priest would be unable to recover at all and would languish forever between life and death. But he had recovered completely... almost... and when the priest had finally awakened, he had found himself a Knight of Solomon's Temple, Order of the Red Cross of Gold, the Mystic Healer who could not heal himself. The greatest irony Philip had ever witnessed.

Yes, Sir Philip remembered it all quite well. He had never learned the exact cause of Simon's injuries. D'Brouchart always referred to it as 'an unfortunate accident' and Simon had never spoken of it. Philip had to wonder if Ramsay had somehow actually been responsible, or possibly, the cause of whatever had happened to the priest.

Simon was an anomaly.

Sir Philip sat on the small sofa contemplating the countenance of the Grand Master as he sat lost in thought. That he was being sent to America was still shocking. What did the Grand Master expect them to find there? He shuddered to think that his Mystery might be needed to complete the mission. If that was the case, then this Abdul Hafiz al Sajek was truly the Abdul Hafiz. And if it were so, then they would be up against a most powerful entity. How on earth had Devereaux managed to pull this one off? Perhaps the ex-Templar had not sought out the man, after all. Perhaps al Sajek had sought out the apprentice. Again he shuddered in the cool night air that flowed in from the open windows. A deeper chill coursed through his soul.

(((((((((((((<O>)))))))))))))

Lucio was disturbed much more than he wanted to admit by the Grand Master's threats, but he pushed them from his mind and rushed away to Naples to pack his bag. He would be glad to spend what was left of the day in his own bed. He found the apartment just as he had remembered… trashed. But it was good trash, comfortable trash. He packed his bag and lay down on the bed. He would have to be back at the Villa by noon tomorrow and then he would be off to Scotland. He wondered if Merry would notice that he had lost weight. And then almost laughed at the absurdity of the thought. Vanity! With everything he had to worry about, he could not afford to waste time on such trivial matters. He began to think of different ways he might be able to manage a word or two with her in private. He had, after all, promised the Grand Master not to cause overt problems and Simon was right. He didn't have to force the issue. It was God's will and it would be done. Mark Andrew could not oppose God's will. No one, not even the Grand Master or the Pope could oppose God's will. A sense of well-being and peace washed over him and for the first time in weeks, he slept a peaceful, dreamless sleep after a quick prayer of Thanksgiving to God for giving him this second chance.

((((((((((((<O>))))))))))))

Simon paced his room. The Grand Master would be coming tomorrow and they had made no headway in getting rid of the girl. Why had Mark Andrew not called them? Why didn't he carry a cell phone like every-blessed-body else in the world?! And Sister Merry was driving him mad with her endless questions. He couldn't answer them and she didn't believe him. She was extremely distraught over Mark Andrew's silence. Why had he not called her? Simon didn't know! She wanted to tell him about Elizabeth and ask what they should do. Well, so did Simon! When he had finally called Italy at Merry's insistence, he had spoken with Sir Philip. Mark Andrew had already left the Villa. Philip had no idea where Mark had gone or why or when he might return. Simon could think of nothing that Mark could possibly be up to in or around the vicinity of Naples, Italy, but it was evident that Mark Andrew was not going to call them. He began to imagine that the Knight was angry with them. That he already knew about Elizabeth somehow. Deep down Simon was afraid of the Scot. He had always been afraid of Sir Ramsay, ever since he could remember, but it was not fair to Mark at all. Mark had never done anything to him to cause the fear. In fact, Mark had been extremely good to him when he was just a bothersome brat, then a nosy boy, then a troublesome youth. Everyone thought him beyond reproach, but he had been well on his way to Hell and damnation when Edgard had pushed him into the priesthood. Strangely enough, it had been Sir Boniface who had been leading him astray, but that was all ancient history and after the fall of 1307, nothing had ever been the same. Boniface had died and he had lost his former identity almost as completely as if he had been reincarnated without the requisite death. He had no reason to fear Mark Ramsay, but he did.

Lying down was out of the question. Every time he closed his eyes, he found himself in the dungeon. He needed help and he had no idea what to do. Healer, heal thyself. The words kept returning to his mind. How could he heal himself? What was wrong with him? Every time he went to sleep, the dream took up where it had left off and progressed from there. Each part of the dream more horrible than the last. The things in his dreams had never crossed his mind asleep or awake until about six days earlier or shortly after Mark had taken his leave of them. He had heard many hair-raising tales of the Inquisition, but few had come close to such horrors as these. At least, none of the Brothers of the Red Cross of Gold spoke of any. He wondered at himself. Was he losing his mind? The last dream had been so painful and so unbelievably despicable; he had thought he was going to die even after he woke up. He had spent half an hour on his knees in the bathroom, throwing up. After attempting to sleep three more times since ten o'clock, the third dream was the final straw. He vowed never to sleep again. He feared that a fourth episode would culminate in what he knew could not possibly be.

The dreadful injury that made his stomach churn and his dinner return at the worst possible times had come from an accident, a fall, not from an Inquisitor's dungeon. He did not remember the accident, thankfully, but he had been told of it weeks afterward. His recovery, such as it was, could only be thought of as miraculous. It had been the will of God, the Master often reminded him. And now it seemed God had abandoned him in the night, turning him over to the powers of darkness. Why? He prayed endlessly and asked God to help him. He had to assume that these hideous dreams held some purpose hidden from him. He had mentioned the nightmares, but not the content of them, to Sir Philip on the phone and the Seneschal had mused that his close proximity to the Ark was somehow affecting his mind and suggested that he take one of his own sedatives. It made sense, but he didn't want to put himself to sleep so soundly with the girl in the house. What if something should happen? What if there was a fire? A storm? A meteor? The Ritter had warned him to stay away from the chapel before he'd left. He had no intention of going near it.

At one o'clock, he ventured out to the kitchen to get a bottle of water from the refrigerator. He felt exhausted and physically ill from the imaginary pain he suffered in the dreams and the very real pain he suffered from his bouts of nausea and vomiting afterwards. His last bout had brought pink and red foam which meant he'd sprung a leak somewhere in his stomach. He sat down at the table and stared at the wall, listening to his poor stomach growl and protest at the onslaught of chilly spring water. He felt empty, hollow, and he knew, without looking, that the circles under his eyes were very dark. A cold rush of air startled him and he looked up to see Elizabeth standing near the head of the table, smiling at him.

"I told you to call me if you had more nightmares. I can help you sleep, Simon," she said sweetly.

"I did not think it was proper to call on you, Miss Elizabeth. It would not be proper at all and you should not offer such things to priests... or men in general. You are much too young..." he began to admonish her, but his voice trailed off as he forgot what he was going to say.

"I'm not as young as you think. I can help you," she said again and took a seat across from him. She was dressed in a long white gown tied at the shoulders with many pastel ribbons. The scent of wild flowers drifted to his nose.

"I sincerely doubt that, my child," he muttered. "It is something I must work out for myself."

"No, Father," she said and reached across the table to take his hand in hers. "I can help you and you can help me."

Simon frowned down at her hand. Her touch was like silk. Her voice soothing and melodious. He looked at her face and it seemed she almost glowed in the dim light cast by the small nightlight above the counter.

"You would confess?" He asked her though he did not know why.

"Yes," she answered him. "I would like to confess." She got up, still holding his hand across the table and came around to where he sat frozen on the bench. He turned on the bench to face her and she sat in his lap like a small child. His brain told him that this was all wrong. She should not be doing this. He should not be doing this. "Won't you let me whisper my confession in your ear, Father Simon?"

"I cannot help you," he told her abruptly and held his chin back away from her hair as she leaned her head on his shoulder. He wanted to shove her away, but he felt paralyzed. "I have nothing to offer you. I don't have the means to... help you." He heard his own voice in the room, but in his head, his inner voice screamed at him 'Get away!' 'Get away!' He could not believe that he had said such a thing to her, but what she wanted was quite obvious. She must have been very lonely and confused.

"I told you that anything and everything is possible, Father," she whispered against his neck and then kissed him on his earlobe. "I know that you think it is wrong to desire a woman's company. I know that you have no faith in your ability. I also know that you are not a priest, Simon. You never really were a priest. Not in your heart of hearts. You are a scoundrel and a rapscallion."

"Perhaps you may have been right in the past, but I am what I am, Elizabeth. You cannot change it. No matter how sweet your kisses are," he lowered his head and closed his eyes as she kissed his cheek and then his eyelids. What he was feeling was impossible. Impossible. Illogical. Immoral. Indecent. Infinitely wonderful. And wrong.

"Surely you can believe your own feelings?" She asked him and took his face between her hands kissing his lips. He kissed her back to his own surprise. She was not the first girl he had kissed in such a fashion, but that girl had been centuries ago... lost forever in time.

He could not help himself. He put his arms around her and returned her embraces kiss for kiss.

When she got out of his lap and tugged on his arm, he followed her down the hall to his room. He felt sure that he would wake up any moment or at least, return to the dungeon where things, as bad as they were, made more sense.

She took him into his room and closed the door, turning the key in the antique lock. No locks! No locks! This was against the Rule.

"No," he protested and backed away from her. "We can't do this. You are too young and I am a poor Knight of the Temple of Solomon. It isn't allowed. It isn't possible. I cannot..."

"Yes, you can," she told him and pushed him backwards with one finger against his chest. "You are just a man, Simon, nothing more. You need me. You need to know what it is that your Brothers fight every waking moment. You need to know what your Brothers know. I can help you learn what it is that has been kept from your mind. I can help you know who you are. Simon of Grenoble, youngest son of Solomon the Wise."

"You know nothing of me," Simon shook his head, but he was lost when she put her arms around him and whispered in his ear.

"I can give you what no other can. I can give you love and I can tell you your true name."

"And what is my name?" He asked in a voice barely a whisper now.

"Menylech," she said. "Behold a wondrous restoration and renewal of the Ethiopian!" She quoted words from the Arcanum.

(((((((((((((<O>)))))))))))))

Mark Andrew was beside himself. There was no reason for him to have to wait to return to Scotland with the Grand Master. He had not been given orders to stay and so why not fly on ahead? But it seemed the entire world was against him now. There were no seats going to Scotland. Everything was booked. The best he could do was book a seat on the next available flight out, which ensured that he would not have the distinct pleasure of traveling with the Knight of the Golden Eagle. He had left the Villa immediately after the meeting upon learning that Lucio would be going with them just as he had feared. Waiting at the airport, alone and miserable, hoping for a cancellation and attracting the attention he hated from passersby, he finally gave up and returned to the Villa in defeat, where he remained in his car, waiting for the morning sun to rise above Vesuvius.

Why were they not answering the phone in Scotland? First it was busy signals for hours and then no answer. He fell into an uneasy sleep in the cramped front seat of the rental car and dreamed of Simon. As soon as the first rays of dawn awakened him, he was off to the airport again to wait for his flight.

It was very early in Scotland when he arrived and the drive down from Edinburgh was uneventful. He pulled up in front of his home just as the sun was peeking over the line of oaks to the east. A misty ground fog obscured the normal curves of the meadow and hugged the base of the house, making it appear to be sitting on a cloud. He would have a full four hours before the

142

others were due to arrive. The old house was still sleeping, it seemed. There were no lights to be seen in the dark windows in front. He hoped that Merry would be glad to see him and that nothing was seriously wrong.

He used his key to open the front door and went in quietly, closing it softly behind. The house seemed to loom over him as if it didn't recognize him and the air felt unnaturally chilly. He hoped that the furnace was not on the blink again. The old contraption was on the brink of destruction. Generally, he and his apprentice and servants relied on the fireplaces and stoves to keep the place toasty warm, but with Meredith's recent arrival, he would have to update the heating.

Bruce Roberts was in a very fine mood in the kitchen making breakfast. He was overjoyed to see that his Master had returned. Mark Andrew questioned him about the phone lines, but the man knew nothing of any trouble and told him that they had received calls from Italy the day before. That they were expecting company around noon. It didn't make sense.

Mark Andrew climbed the stairs quietly and went directly to Merry's room. When he knocked on her door softly, she came to answer it, dressed in a long, cotton gown. A worried look on her face as if she expected trouble disappeared when she saw who stood in the hall wearing an equally worried expression.

His fear of rejection was overruled immediately. She hugged him and kissed him so many times, he was unable to say more than one or two words for a full five minutes. She finally calmed down enough to go back into the room and close the door.

She had more questions than he did.

"Why haven't you called me?" She asked at last as he collapsed in the chair by her bed. She rushed about the room gathering her clothes. Her bath was running in the adjoining room and he could smell the scent of vanilla.

"I tried," he said and waved one hand tiredly. "The phone was constantly busy and then there was no answer."

"That's impossible," she glanced at him. "Simon called Philip and then Philip called back again to tell us when they would be here. The Ritter called and I spoke to John Paul a minute." She dashed into the bathroom to turn off the water and then came back.

"I don't know what happened then," he shrugged as she came to hug him again. "I sent an e-mail."

"I checked the computer a hundred times at least." She shook her head. "It never got here."

"I'm not good on computers," he said with some chagrin. "I'm sorry."

"No matter. You're here now. That's all that's important," she smiled at him. "But you are going to let Simon hook you up with a cell phone or a

PDA and then I'm going to teach you how to use a damned computer and that's final!"

Mark had to smile at her as he nodded his head.

"There is a problem we have to resolve before the Grand Master arrives," she continued almost breathlessly. "Simon and I have been beating our heads against the wall..." She stopped at the door of the bathroom and bit her lip. "Won't you come in here? We can talk while I take my bath and save time."

Mark Andrew looked around the room as if looking for the answer to her question. He remembered what had happened the last time he had gone into the bath with her. But John Paul was not here. Surely no one would come to disturb them this time.

He nodded and followed her into the bathroom. The water looked very inviting. The scent made his mind drift back in time.

"Come on, hurry up," she told him as she undressed and stepped into the tub. "We don't have much time."

He was appalled, but not too appalled to follow her instructions.

"Now," she said, after he had sufficiently scalded himself and sat breathless in the water facing her. "I know that you don't like to talk about things from your past, but like I said, we have a problem and you're just going to have to bear with it."

"What kind of problem?" he grimaced as she squeezed hot water from a sponge onto his tired shoulders.

"Your son, Ian McShan," she said and watched his face grow very dark. He seemed to be overcome by rigor mortis at the mention of the name. "He had children?" she asked.

"No," he told her shortly. "None."

"But he must have!" she dropped the sponge in the water and then picked it up again. "There is a granddaughter."

"No, no children," Mark took hold of her wrist and pushed the sponge away. "What are you talking about?"

"Ian's granddaughter is here," she told him simply.

"Here?" He looked around in alarm.

"If he didn't have children, then how could he have a granddaughter?" she asked him and leaned toward him, taking his face in her hands. His eyes were full of something that resembled fear. A chill coursed up her exposed spine.

"He had no children. No granddaughter," Mark said and started to push himself up.

"Wait!" She pulled him back down. "She is here. Downstairs. She came to see him and found out that he had died. She came here looking for you."

144

"For me?" He exclaimed and fell back in the water causing a great surge of bubbles. "Why?"

"She's pregnant," Merry told him.

"That's impossible. I mean, it's impossible. Ian had no children," Mark's voice cracked. "Surely it is a mistake. I would know."

"What about Ian's wife? Could she have had a child before she married him? Perhaps she is a... a... a step-great-grandchild?" Merry asked hopefully. This was not the reaction she had expected. She had expected anger, not this look of desperation in his face.

"No!" He shook his head adamantly. "I will go and see what this is about. It is some trick of the devil or perhaps some enemy of the Order. We certainly seem to be growing new ones every day." He climbed out of the tub oblivious to the water and soap bubbles splashing everything as he dragged one of her fluffy towels from the rack into the bedroom with him. "And Simon let her in?" He called back to her. "What the hell is wrong with him?!"

"Wait!" Merry said as she slipped and slid through the bathroom, trying to follow him. "I'll go with you. You can't just go down and throw her out, Mark Andrew. Whoever... whatever she is. She is very young and she says she's pregnant," Merry pleaded the girl's case as she followed through the bedroom. He dried himself carelessly and put the same clothes back on. "You need to calm down first."

"I knew something was wrong here!" He continued, ignoring her words completely. When he looked at her in panic, she knew it was worse than she had anticipated. "I knew it! Damn Lucio to hell. I should never have left you here alone with Simon. That fucking Italian whore and his woes."

"Shhh. Shhhh. Shhhh," Merry grabbed him and held him tightly. "Don't say things like that. We need to sort this out."

Mark pulled away from her and finished buttoning his shirt.

Merry grabbed her bathrobe and stuffed her feet in her slippers.

"She's very sweet, Mark," she continued halfheartedly. "Mark, please, don't be rude. She's just a child."

"Just a choild?" He looked at her in disbelief as he pulled on his pants and picked up his socks. "A choild o' Satan, no doubt."

"You are overreacting," she told him, feeling her anger rise. She couldn't explain the girl's sudden appearance and her claims to be Ian's granddaughter if he had none, but she refused to attribute it to the powers of darkness so quickly. There had to be some other explanation. A ruse perhaps. A scam, maybe. And she took personal umbrage to his reaction as he made it sound like Simon was the one at fault when it was she who had insisted on allowing the girl to stay.

"I'll show ye overreacting," he muttered under his breath and sat down to put on his boots. "Wair is she?"

"Downstairs," Merry told him. "I gave her a room for the night. Just for the night. Simon was going to take her to Edinburgh today, I promise. It was my fault. Not Simon's. There was nothing I could do. We wanted to talk to you first. We tried to reach you, but…"

"Did she ask fur me by name?" Mark cut her off and took her by the shoulders, staring into her eyes.

He made her feel guilty. He was simply concerned about her welfare and he really was afraid.

"Yes, she did. She said she used to live down under with her parents. Her family is in Australia maybe?"

"With her parents. Down under, you say?" Mark repeated the words. His eyes darted about as if he was trying to remember something. "And what does she want?"

"She doesn't want anything," Merry told him. "She had no place to go. Her grandmother… Ian's wife… Mrs. McShan, that is, is in Wales visiting her sister. The woman had a heart attack! She's not expected to live much longer."

"Wales?!" Mark's agitation returned. "She 'ad nae kith an' kin in Wales! 'er sister lives in Edinborg. Thot's 'er only livin' relation. I may be a callous bastard and piss poor father, Meredith, but I keep an eye on things. I knew oll aboot Missus Ian McShan from birth ere they were married and I know thot she was barren. These things 'ave t' be warked out. Ye dunna think I cud allow a parfect stranger into th' family?"

Mark was out the door with Merry behind him. He virtually leaped down the stairs and stopped by his bags in the entry hall long enough to extract the case containing the golden sword. Merry's heart froze when he strapped the weapon on and then headed down the hall behind the stairs.

In the dim hallway, he stopped to look back at her as he drew the blade from the scabbard. "Which?"

Merry nodded at the door next to Simon's room, wondering if she should go and knock on Simon's door. Perhaps he could mediate this situation better.

"Open th' door!" Mark called through the wood and rapped on it with the hilt of the sword.

Merry held her breath while they waited. Several seconds passed, but nothing happened.

"Open th' door!" Mark tried again and beat harder on the wood.

Why didn't Simon come out to see what the noise was about? Surely he could hear this!

Mark glanced at her again and reached down to turn the brass doorknob. She noticed his hand shaking when he reached for it. The door

146

opened easily, swinging inward, silent on its hinges. A cold blast of air struck their faces. The room was empty. The bed was tousled and the windows were open. The draperies drifted lazily in the early morning breeze. Mark edged into the room slowly and Merry followed him. No one was there. There was no sign of the girl, or the bag she had carried.

Mark turned a quizzical face on her and she shrugged. She had no idea what had happened to her.

"Simon?" He asked suddenly.

He stormed past her into the hall and did not pause or knock before opening the door to Simon's room.

"Simon!" Mark called the Healer's name from the open doorway and then stepped inside the room when he received no answer.

Simon lay on the bed as if sleeping. He did not stir when Mark shook his shoulder roughly and called his name again.

Mark turned to Merry in desperation.

"Wot's 'appened t' 'im?" He asked her in a quiet voice.

She simply shook her head.

"Wot was 'er name? The girl," he asked in the same tone.

"Elizabeth," Merry told him. "The same as Ian's mother, she said."

Mark let go an unintelligible garble of Gaelic and swung his sword about in a fit of irrepressible rage, slashing at the draperies on the windows. Merry stood in shock, watching him as he sank to the floor by the bed and reached one hand up to grasp Simon's forearm.

"Wot is this evil thot 'as come upon us?" He asked no one in particular. "Simon. Simon. Not you, too!"

Merry hurried down the hall to the kitchen to fetch Bruce Roberts. She did not know what else to do.

(((((((((((((<O>)))))))))))))

Konrad von Hetz, Knight of the Apocalypse who Sees, had seen enough. He would have to return to Scotland. He had thought the matter over and that, even though Simon had failed to hear his confession about the strange apparition in the crypt, he had washed his hands of the matter, asking forgiveness of God and leaving the evil behind. Or at least, he had thought so.

Now he saw that it was not so.

He left John Paul with Sir Barry and went ahead of the others to the airport to arrange passage to Edinburgh using his 'official' credentials as a representative of the Holy See to secure a seat on the fully 'booked' plane. As was rapidly becoming a habit, he told no one where he was going other than his old cook in Switzerland... just in case. The others would know soon enough. He needed a bit of lead time in order to 'clear the way' before the Grand Master went to seal the crypt. He kept a constant vigil of prayer in his head as he waited at the airport and during the flight to Edinburgh. It seemed strange that, after so long sitting in leisure at his chalet in the Swiss Alps, he would suddenly find himself cast into such a state of turmoil, personally involved in great and mysterious events. He had been unprepared. He had grown lax. While he had been languishing in his old parchments, evil had come in search of him and he had fallen. Just as Mark Ramsay had fallen fifteen years earlier... though not quite. Ramsay had been a victim and that was something Konrad could not claim. He considered himself an idiot. He wanted to shout and scream and tear out his hair in despair. How could he have been so foolish as to leave Sister Meredith and Brother Simon to face this evil alone, without even a warning? But he had tried to convince himself that it had only been a nightmare brought on by the proximity of the Ark and the spirits surrounding it. He should have known better. Was he not a spiritual guide for the Council? How could he not have recognized the girl for what she was? Evil incarnate in human form!

His thoughts returned to Simon. Simon was sleeping, but it was an unnatural sleep. He could see nothing, but an almost palpable black oblivion filled with tiny specks of light. Had the Healer gone mad? What had she done to him? Of all of them, Simon had the most pure heart. He had a few tarnishes, but nothing serious. His had always been the brightest countenance among the twelve, always been faithful to the Order and to each of his Brothers. Never complaining, never wavering from his duty. If something happened to Simon, he would never forgive himself. Never!

Shifting his thoughts a bit, he saw Mark Andrew, fully awake with nervous energy. The Knight of Death's mind was turbulent. He was at a loss and on the verge of destroying something, anything. He saw Sister Meredith nearby, imploring the Scot, begging him to calm down, to think, to sit, to eat. She had little to no experience with these situations. Her mystical training was far from complete and she was not helping the situation. Ramsay wanted to lock her in the cellar while he collected his wits. She did not understand that just as their mysteries were concrete and divinely inspired, that there were also other mysteries, equally concrete, but far from divinely inspired. True, she had seen the human side and she had seen some of the workings of Light, but she had experienced very little of the workings of Darkness. She could offer Mark Andrew no consolation and he could not understand why she did not see it as he did. Mark Andrew had lived in Darkness for much of his life. It was inconceivable to him that Merry could not recognize it for what it was. And it was also inconceivable to him that she could not accept his word on blind faith.

Merry was still looking for logical, rational explanations like a damned scientist. She would have to experience the evil before she would see it, truly see, for the insidious patches of dark malignancy found even in the midst of bright sunshine. She would see. Von Hetz vowed to make it his primary concern as soon as the business with the Ark and the Key were in hand. He would take on the responsibility of bringing Merry into full realization of exactly what her responsibilities to the Order entailed. He could actually make her see things in a new light. Where Dambretti and Ramsay wished to protect her feelings, he would give her new experiences with the powers of darkness and in so doing, would prepare her for what was to come. If she continued going around, trying to explain things and making excuses for evil, she would not be ready for the Apocalypse.

The presence calling itself Elizabeth that had attached itself to the chapel had expanded its power and scope dramatically. Normally, such a thing would be confined to a small area of manifestation, but to appear in broad daylight in physical form indicated a truly immense power. He would have to meet the thing on its own ground. He would go to the chapel and confront it there. It would require an exorcism of a sort that was more than the mundane rebuking normally used to dispel such infestations and he had done nothing like it in many, many years. In fact, Sister Meredith's Mystery contained more information about such things than his own, but she was far from ready to perform an exorcism of this magnitude. First, he would need to see Simon and try to awaken him. He would have to confess and Simon would have to listen and absolve him or else he feared he would never be able to accomplish what needed to be done. Exorcism required a clean slate and his heart was full of sin.

And John Paul! Another wave of guilt washed over him. John Paul had seen the girl. He should have known. It was unthinkable. But John Paul had not answered him. How could he answer him? What would the boy say? And he could not look into John Paul's mind unless the boy allowed it or wanted him to see something. This was another thing he did not understand. He had to assume that she had gotten to him as well. What had he, in his stupidity, allowed to happen? He closed his eyes and willed the plane to fly faster.

Chapter Nine of Seventeen
therefore the curse is poured upon us

Abdul Hafiz al Sajek looked up just as the sun topped the trees and threw the first golden rays into the pit in front of him. His green eyes sparkled in the first light of dawn. The water fall sent up a fine mist into the air as it plummeted over the edge of the limestone sinkhole, falling almost seventy feet onto the exposed rocks below. Ferns and mosses clung to the sides of the roughly conical depression, giving it an overall greenish hue in the early morning light. Rainbows danced in the mists above the stream. A beautiful place, a perfect place for his designs. Here, where no one would expect it.

These people were too simple-minded to understand what was about to happen. They had removed themselves from the truer nature of the world long ago. He, Abdul Hafiz al Sajek, Supreme Lord of Time, would stop the progress of the impending cataclysm. He would not let the Word fade from the world. The Word that had been all but lost, forgotten by some, never known by others. He would cast their holy relics into the Abyss and give the Ancient Ones something to play with. Something to keep them occupied, something to stop them from coming forth to meet the God of the Jews and the Christians. Al Sajek had no faith in the god he supposedly served. He had seen the power of the Old Ones who lived in the underworld. He would not take a chance on the God of Abraham losing the battle of Armageddon. Against these ancient and evil entities, a solitary presence would not stand a chance. The people fooled themselves into believing in only one god when there were many. And those who venerated the Creator, did not understand His Divine Plan. Did not understand that the Creator had given them the Power of the Word and they had lost it. He, Abdul Hafiz, would do all he could to stop or, at least, delay the impending battle as long as possible.

He turned quickly and walked back into the circle of stones laid out on the soft ground. Turning counterclockwise, he bowed low to each of the cardinal points and then reached up to remove the chain bearing a silver amulet from around his neck. The Amulet of N'ydens. The thing that would protect him from the Old Ones. He shielded it from the light of the sun and wrapped it in its black silk cover, sprinkling it lightly with oil of musk before shoving it into his pocket. Tonight would be the eighth of the nine consecutive nights wherein he must call upon the spirits of the undead sorcerers from times long past and ensnare them in a mirror. He would be ready to act in two more days. He would find the Key of Salvation and the fool would open the door to damnation. He, Abdul Hafiz, would commune with the Keeper of Great Powers and would become one with him... again.

The tall, dark-skinned man glanced back once at the rainbows dancing in the mists above the waterfall and began to pick his way back through the dense growth of ferns and profuse sub-tropical plants surrounding the sinkhole area. It would be nice if the transactions could be made before he came back to complete the cycle, but, if not, he would carry on just the same. In the long run, it would not matter that he did not own the land. No one truly owned the land. The land belonged to none of them, but rather they belonged to it and they all belonged to the Old Ones.

((((((((((((<O>))))))))))))

Merry and Bruce were having a hard time keeping Mark Andrew from going to the chapel in search of the girl, whom he was convinced was connected somehow with the Ark of the Covenant. He paced the library alternately speaking in Gaelic and English or a mixture of both about things of which Merry had no comprehension. Twice he had threatened to lock them both in the cellar if they got in his way. They had gone back to Simon's room several times to try to awaken him, but he was totally unresponsive. His heartbeat was strong and his breathing was regular. Even his color was good, but he would not wake up. The dark circles had faded under his eyes and his skin was not nearly so pale as it had been when the Scot had last seen him.

The only thing Merry could do was sit and watch Mark Andrew wear himself and the rug under his boots out completely. She hoped that he would eventually calm down and then perhaps they could talk. He had rejected every overture she had made, every plea. He needed sleep. Food. A stiff drink, perhaps. She suspected that he had not slept in days, nor eaten properly.

He stopped suddenly and stared at her as if he had suddenly remembered something.

"Your son is a prophet," he said in a surprisingly calm voice as if this one thought was the only coherent thing in his mind.

"What?" She perked up. This was the first comprehensible thing he had said in over an hour and it didn't really make sense.

"John Paul is a prophet," he said again and seemed to have lost most of his former agitation. "And he shall give him the daughter of women, corrupting her: but she shall not stand on his side, neither be for him. Would that it were not so, Meredith. If only I could change that for him." He repeated the first line of the boy's strange mixture of scriptures.

"What are you talking about? Please tell me." Merry got up and took his arm, drawing him to his chair before he started pacing again. He allowed her to push him into the chair this time and then she sat on the arm, pressing his head close to her. Rocking slightly as if she were comforting a small

151

child, doing the one thing that she'd never thought possible. Her actions seemed to calm him somewhat. It was the first time he had allowed her to touch him since he'd scrambled from her tub. But his words, now spoken in calm, even tones, were even more frightening than the previous ranting and raving.

"Talk to me, Mark. Tell me what is going on," she said.

"Your son spoke to us in the Council," he answered after a moment. "He spoke of a woman to be given to someone, but said she would not stand on his side nor be for him. I thought he was speaking of you and me, but he must have foreseen this. Though ye have lien among the pots, yet shall ye be as the wings of a dove covered with silver, and her feathers with yellow gold."

Merry marveled at his ability to remember the words.

"He was talking about Elizabeth," he continued. "Elizabeth is dead, Merry. She has lien among the pots. She was buried long ago. And Simon. God setteth the solitary in families. Simon is an orphan. A father of the fatherless. He is a priest, a father to the Knights of the Order, who are nothing more than a passel of orphans and bastards of little renown. But thou art he that took me from the womb. John Paul was not talking about us. He was talking about Elizabeth and Simon and about someone else in the Council. Someone knows about Simon, Merry. I thought he was talking about you and Lucio and our marriage, but it is far worse. Far more evil than even my poor demented brain could imagine."

Mark wrapped his arms around her and buried his face in her dress.

"He is sinking in the mire, Merry," Mark Andrew told her. "We have failed Simon. She made him do what he could not do. What was impossible."

"What?" Merry pushed him back and raised his chin in her hand to look in his eyes. "Made him do what, Mark? What did she make him do?"

"He can't lay with a woman," Mark looked at her in consternation. "They took that ability from him in the dungeon. They ruined him and it was my fault. I couldn't find him. I couldn't find out where they had taken him, who was in charge."

"Took... his... ability?" Merry's voice was very small as the realization of what he was talking about finally dawned on her.

Mark nodded and then got up again to resume his pacing.

"How do you know?" Merry had to ask.

"I am the one who ransomed him from the Inquisitors. They were above nothing, being nothing more than sadistic criminals themselves. Bribes were paid. But I was too late. I am always too late!" Mark told her with a vengeance. "It has always been me. Why? Why does it always have to be me? But, wait..." he came to take her by the shoulders. "You can say nothing of this. Simon doesn't know he was in prison. He doesn't know what happened to him. He doesn't know what they did to him. He doesn't remember. God was merciful to him, but I have failed him… again."

"I don't understand, Mark Andrew!" Merry threw her hands up in exasperation.

"The Grand Master… all of the Brothers… we were only Knights in the Order of the Knights Templar proper, the original Order. But we had already established the Council of Twelve in secret. He sent me to get Simon from the church. Sir Boniface and myself, but we were too late. I couldn't save him from the king's soldiers. Sir Boniface was killed there. Boniface was the Mystic Healer before Simon. I escaped only narrowly and by the time I was able to find him and take him out of prison, it was almost too late. He was near dead. He would have died of shock and infection most likely since the Master would not allow any physicians near him, but the Master saved him by giving him Sir Boniface's mysteries and making him a Knight of the Council. I was there. I'm always there, late. Meredith, I hate being late! If you're going to be late, just don't fucking come at all! I don't understand it. Simon was only a priest and new to the Order. Not an apprentice. A simple priest. He would have been better off dead. He has suffered for years… centuries," Mark frowned and then continued his pacing. He stopped again. "The Master shielded… used magick to keep the memory of it from him. He was afraid it would make him insane…" his voice trailed off and then he looked up. "There was something… else."

Merry was horrified. There was so much she did not know about her Brothers and how could she ever hope to understand them? Even Simon.

"John Paul said but thou art he who took me from the womb," Mark repeated the words again and went back to pacing. "Someone in that Council room knows where Simon came from. Someone took him from the womb."

"I don't understand at all, Mark. Someone on the Council delivered Simon when he was born?" Merry frowned at him. "What does that mean?"

"It would mean that Simon was delivered by the knife. Someone cut him from his mother's womb. What you would call a cesarean section," Mark told her in aggravation as if she should already know this.

Merry frowned deeply and placed her hand over her mouth. Scenes of bloody horror danced through her head. When was Simon born? In the fourteenth century? A C-section in the Dark Ages? Or was that the Renaissance? She didn't know and didn't care. Anesthesia was a modern medical miracle.

"I'm sorry," Mark said suddenly and stopped once more. His expression softened "I should not be telling you this. I'm an ass."

"Why should you not tell me?" She asked, though she did not want to hear more, she had to know. "I am not that squeamish though I know it must have been painful for his mother."

"It isn't proper and yes, it would have been fatal more often than not. It was used only as a last resort to save the child. The mother did not usually... survive... and was more likely dead before they cut her..." his voice trailed off and his complexion darkened. He remembered the time.

"Don't you think I need to know these things?" She asked. "Why do you insist on keeping all these things to yourself? Does anyone else know about him that you know of? Listen, Mark, I will not say a word to Simon. I swear it! What would I say, for God's sake?"

"Sir Philip was with the Master when Simon was found on the doorstep so to speak. He must know something," Mark told her almost reluctantly. "But you must never tell it, Merry. Simon would not appreciate me telling you what he doesn't even know himself."

"He will never know it from me, Mark Andrew," Merry assured him. She glanced at the clock on the mantel. Surely the others would be arriving soon. Perhaps the Grand Master would know how to wake Simon. He would be certainly be unhappy to hear what had happened and she did not want to be the one to tell him what had transpired concerning Elizabeth.

Bruce came in to announce that lunch was ready. They had missed breakfast and the cook would not hear of them missing lunch. The old man refused to take no for an answer even in the face of his Master's anger.

Mark agreed to eat after a bit of cajoling and they ate in deep silence at the kitchen table. The meal was almost over when someone knocked loudly on the front door. Mark Andrew rushed from the kitchen to the foyer to answer it personally, expecting the Master.

Von Hetz stood on the steps looking like a vision from hell. His long, dark hair hung in his face, his cheeks were sunken, his eyes surrounded by deep shadows.

"Brother Simon," he said without preamble.

"This way," Mark answered without question and led him down the hall. The Apocalyptic Knight's appearance was unexpected, but not unwelcome.

The Ritter bade them wait in the hall while he went in the room and closed the door.

A few minutes later, he emerged from the room and stood silently for several long moments in the dim light. Merry shuddered. He looked even worse than before.

"You knew of this?" The Ritter addressed Mark Andrew.

"What?" Mark Andrew answered with a question and frowned at him.

"Of this... woman?" The Ritter's voice sounded hoarse and raspy.

"I only just learned of it this morning," Mark Andrew answered. "I knew her when she was... alive."

"You knew of Simon of Grenoble?" The Ritter tilted his head up slightly and narrowed his eyes at the Knight.

"Yes," Mark nodded.

"You know who his father is?" Von Hetz continued to eye him steadily.

"No."

Von Hetz seemed to relax almost imperceptibly, then turned his eyes on Merry. "How did the girl get in the house?"

"We invited her in," Merry told him. "She was on foot. We had no idea that anything was wrong."

"How long has she been here?" He asked.

"Two days," Merry whispered. The Knight of the Apocalypse truly scared her. "I swear, Brother, I had no idea. Simon wanted to turn her out. It was my fault."

The Knight seemed about to explode and then his features relaxed completely as he seemed to come to grips with something internally. Mark cleared his throat. He would not see von Hetz treat Merry less than respectfully. Not in his house. If the man had some idea of taking her mind by force, it would be over his dead body.

"And do you have any idea where she is now?" Konrad asked finally.

"No. She was gone this morning," Merry answered a bit louder.

"She accomplished her mission," he told them with some measure of resignation. "Brother Simon does not want to wake up. He wants to die. Before he can come back to us, he must face his nightmare. There is nothing I can do for him."

"But why?" Merry looked at Mark. "It was not his fault! If the girl was... evil, and he didn't know..."

"Ignorance is no excuse, Sister," von Hetz told her. "Believe me, I know. Evil spares none. Not even children. She has caused him to relive something he never knew. Her reasons are her own. I cannot fathom her mind. I dare say she has no mind of her own. Perhaps she wishes simply to hurt or destroy those close to Sir Ramsay or all in proximity of the chapel. I cannot say. I did my best to banish her and thought it done."

"You know her?" Mark Andrew eyed the tall man suspiciously.

"I do," Von Hetz nodded. "I would speak to you alone, Brother."

Mark cast an apologetic glance at Merry and followed the Ritter down the hall. She heard a door open and close. Before following them, she checked on Simon once more and tried in vain to wake him.

While she waited at the foot of the steps like a small child, her initial anger at being left out of their conversation faded. She felt destitute and foolish. How could she and Simon have fallen for the girl's story? It had sounded lame from the beginning, but she had seemed so sweet and innocent. And now it sounded completely ludicrous. She wondered if she would ever learn to be less gullible and more forceful. How could she have been so stupid as to invite a stranger to stay in Mark Andrew's home? It was no wonder that von Hetz did not trust her. And Simon had tried to tell her. He had tried to say no to her and she had pushed him aside. He would have had to treat her like Mark Andrew treated her or like Lucio treated her and he would never be able to do such a thing. He would have had to slap her down and take her by the throat and choke her into submission. She was still a spoiled and foolish girl and, in spite of her long training, she still retained a streak of stubbornness that bordered on insanity in the face of logic. Silly, stupid girl. After all these years.

When would she learn to listen to Mark Andrew? To trust him when he told her things that she had only thought were myths and legends and superstitions. Much of what she had learned in Egypt had struck her as ridiculous and useless, but now the reality of her position came home to roost, digging its claws into her mind like a ravenous vulture.

The two men were still in the library when the Grand Master's party arrived. Merry was unsure whether to knock on the library door or go outside and greet them alone. The library door looked much more formidable than the front door. She straightened her dress, brushed back her hair and opened the front door. The bright noonday sun did nothing to lift her spirits, but the sight of Lucio Dambretti standing by the car, looking up at the house made her heart lurch. Why hadn't they told her he was coming? He flashed her one of his smiles and she closed her eyes momentarily, before returning a very much subdued smile in greeting. She wanted to talk to him, explain things, make him understand. Perhaps he knew something that could help Simon, help her. How could she handle this? On the one hand, she was glad to see him, but the thought of having both of them here again, together, made her want to run away to the cellar and hide forever. She had been foolish to tell the Grand Master that she could handle it. It was just too much. De Lyons took her hand and pressed it to his lips as usual, disdaining the normal kiss on the lips as she mumbled a greeting to him without thought. D'Brouchart stepped into view, blocking the Italian from her sight.

$$(((((((((((((<O>)))))))))))))$$

The Grand Master did not take the news of Simon's mishap well at all. He went directly to the bedroom and closed the door in the same manner as the Apocalyptic Knight, leaving them all in the library, wondering what would happen next. Von Hetz had waited a few minutes before trailing after him. Lucio took Champlain and de Lyons back out to the car to unload the trunk, after receiving rather stilted greetings from Mark and Merry.

"Mark Andrew?" Merry asked and approached him cautiously as he sat in his chair staring at the fireplace.

He looked up at her and shook his head. Whatever the Knight of the Apocalypse had told him was not good. And she could not imagine that things could be worse.

"He looks well enough," he referred to Lucio, no doubt.

"Yes," she agreed. "I didn't expect to see him. They didn't tell me he was coming. You knew, didn't you?"

"We will seal the crypt," he said. "Apparently, the Master thinks we need his presence. I, for one, do not see why, but Brother Hetz wants to perform an exorcism before we go in. It would be a good idea, but he is... afraid," he said and refused to look at her when he gave her this last bit of startling news. "He said that your Mystery contained more information about exorcism than his own. I told him that you were not ready for such a rigorous exercise. I hope that he will not press the matter," he paused to meet her gaze and raised both eyebrows. "I know that you will not volunteer."

She shook her head. Exorcism. Yes. It was there in her mind. All she had to do was think the word and the entire process became immediately accessible. The preparations, the rituals, the proper dates and times. The names of power. The proper clothing. Everything. She could do it. She knew she could, but she had just promised herself that she would listen to Mark from now own. Respect his wishes. Value his opinions. Do as he asked... do as he asked. The thought that she might be asked or expected to play a part in whatever the dark Knight had in mind did not help her feelings of foreboding.

Mark smiled and took her hand, pressing it to his lips.

"And don't let the Master bully you into it," he told her. "Soon we'll be married and I'll have a legal right concerning your... concerning your... future." He ended the statement lamely. Things had changed. He would really have no more rights over her than he had at that moment. Wives were no longer required to love, honor and obey. A husband was lucky to have the first two.

Merry nodded. How could she tell Mark that she had made a mistake in accepting his proposal? She couldn't bear the thought of hurting him again.

"I don't have much time," he told her. "I will have to leave for America soon. I had hoped we might be together at least one night, but with the Master here and Dambretti. I hardly think it would be proper."

"I know," she said miserably and sat down on the arm of the chair, once again holding his head against her. She would never be able to tell him. She would marry him and damn the rest of them if they tried to stop her.

"I don't know how long I will be gone," he was almost rigid. It was as if he was trying to distance himself from her. As if he already knew that the tide had turned against him. "I could be gone... for years."

"Years?" She looked down at him in surprise. Years?! They spoke of years like other people spoke of weeks or days. She was afraid for him to leave and afraid for him to stay. She had never fully appreciated the term 'a rock and a hard place' until now. When she had joined the Order and rejected both Lucio and Mark's proposals of marriage, she had thought herself very clever. She would have her cake and eat it, too, but she had never expected it to turn out this way. She was right back where she had started from. The recent events confirmed something that she had refused to admit even in the privacy of her own mind. She still loved both of them! It was not possible, not moral, not logical, not acceptable and last, but not least, not wise in light of the two very different, but very volatile personalities of both men.

When Lucio had left Scotland and returned to his home in Naples, she had thought it would be long time before she saw him again. Three months was not nearly long enough. Not for the impetuous Italian. He had his life back, thanks to Mark Andrew, and nothing had changed as far as the Knight of the Golden Eagle was concerned. She knew that he would never give up. He might get mad. He might get depressed. He might even become violent, but he would never give up. Merry had to imagine that even if she actually married Mark Andrew, Lucio would come to look at it as only a temporary setback. And there was absolutely nothing that she could do about it, short of killing him herself to be rid of him.

"This is not an ordinary man we are looking for," Mark Andrew's voice interrupted her thoughts. "It could take years to catch up with him. Years to recover the Key. It took... centuries to recover the Ark."

"But you know where the Key is, don't you?"

"But we knew where the Ark was, too," he countered and smiled slightly. "You will take care of yourself while I am away?"

"Yes," she nodded. "I will."

"And you will see after our son? He seems quite capable, but he might need a bit of motherly love," he tried to sound unconcerned, but looked truly devastated and she knew that he felt he might not be back at all.

"Yes, of course," she told him as a sense of alarm grew within her. What was he not telling her? "Mark Andrew..." she began and was cut off by the sound of Lucio's voice behind her.

"Sister?" He called to her from the library door. "Where should we put these things?"

She turned around and found him standing in the door with an armload of white boxes.

"Take them upstairs. I'll be up shortly."

"Go on," Mark shoved her slightly toward the door. "Go with him or else he'll be into everything. Give him the room over the parlor this time."

She started for the door and he pulled slightly on her hand before letting her go. She paused.

"Meredith," his voice was very low. "If I don't come back, you should marry him. I believe he would take good care of you, but make him stay here with you. Don't go to Italy with him."

This was more than she could stand. She pulled free of his hand and hurried from the room before she fell completely apart.

She took Lucio upstairs and showed him to the room at the opposite end of the front hall from Mark's. When she turned away to leave him, he called to her to wait.

He dumped the boxes on the bed and rummaged through them momentarily before picking one out.

"This one is yours," he said and handed it to her. "Your new... uniform. I believe your old one is... ruined, no?"

"Yes," she nodded and took the box.

"Did you read my letters again, like I asked you to do?" He asked.

"Yes. I did, as a matter of fact," she told him and thought he looked somehow different.

"And you understand them?" He asked, raising both eyebrows.

"Yes. I do," she nodded.

"And...?" He lowered his head slightly, looking into her eyes.

"This is not the time," she said already becoming angry with him for pressing her on the matter so soon.

"There is never time," he told her. "We have to make our own time, Merry."

"Mark will be leaving soon," she said offhandedly, trying to change the subject. "He seems to think he may be gone a long time."

"Ahh, si`, that is true. We could discuss it after he is gone." Lucio missed the concern in her voice and smiled at her, totally misinterpreting her comment. "Good thinking."

A mistake. Merry sighed and shook her head.

"And what of Simon?" She asked him.

"He will recover," he told her confidently. It was obvious he had no idea what had actually occurred. He only knew what had been said in the library. That an evil spirit, or presence, as von Hetz had called it, had assaulted the Healer and that he was now in some sort of deep sleep. "He has encountered evil before. It is all around us. Can you not feel it? It is this old house. Brother Ramsay needs to tear it down and build anew... somewhere else... warmer, I think. When we are married, I will buy you a villa in Sardinia overlooking the sea."

"I don't think that Simon has encountered this sort of thing before, Lucio. I am worried about him." Merry ignored his last statement and made a slicing motion with her hand. Something she had learned from him that

159

meant he was tired of the subject. "Basta!" she said the requisite and only Italian word she knew.

He took a step back, surprised by her action. She had learned something from him after all. After a brief silence, he closed the space between them again and pouted.

"And so am I," he agreed and reached to take her hand, looking down at Mark's ring on her finger. "But I am more worried about you. I told you that you must avoid Brother Ramsay at all costs. Have you done that? You are still wearing his ring. He will get the wrong idea."

She closed her eyes. He knew better. Why was he doing this?

"I have to go," she told him shortly. "There isn't much time and I have a number of things I have to do to prepare for this... evening."

"I know," he said simply. He let go of her hand reluctantly as she backed out of the room, but winked at her before she turned away from him.

(((((((((((((<O>)))))))))))))

Abdul Hafiz al Sajek leaned back in the leather chair in his hotel suite in Tallahassee, Florida. He held the golden disc up to the light of the lamp and perused the rather primitive engravings on the back. An odd combination of ancient scripts. The names of the archangels Gabriel and Michael were there in Angelic script, along with the seal of King Solomon the Wise and an admonition to the foolhardy concerning tampering with the things of God engraved in ancient Hebrew. He was surprised it was not a curse. Whoever had written it had truly been a wise man. Curses were indeed foolhardy endeavors. Anyone with any sense of magickal propriety knew that curses worked in both directions with a strange sort of polarity affecting both the curser and the cursee. Al Sajek figured that those who cast curses on others were either overcome with rage and hatred or else ready to suffer the consequences in order to see their enemies suffer. Either way, he had no need for curses.

But here was just a simple warning against using the Word of God foolishly. The Word. That was what concerned him. Was this a warning against a Word, or was it referring to the Word. It would make a difference. A big difference. But he was not concerned with the use of the Key. He did not intend to use it. He intended to lose it. He did not need these mystical artifacts of the Jews and the Christians. He only needed to make sure that they did not have them. Without the Key, the Ark was virtually useless, except for its legendary mythos and the fact that its immediate surroundings held significant danger for anyone nearby. If one were to touch it or try to pry it open without the proper ceremonial preparations... well certainly it

160

could still kill. Without the Key, no amount of preparation or magick could render it useful. And if it could not be opened, it could not be used at Armageddon to wage war against the Princes of Darkness and the Kings of Men. If the armies of Light thought for even one second that they could lose the battle, they would not come. This world was such an insignificant part of the universe; it would not be worth risking everything for ungodly men. As long as he, Abdul Hafiz al Sajek, could postpone this prophesied second coming, he could maintain his hold on life and that was all that mattered. This was his world and he wanted to keep it. He did not mind sharing it with the Prince of the Air. He had protection enough from the Evil One. Eventually, he would have the world just as he wanted it. In another few thousand years, there would be no religion at all. These silly Christians would have given up hope of the Second Coming of their Savior and the Jews and the Muslims would have annihilated each other. Man would rule supreme over the earth. It would be the age of true Enlightenment and he would be their Savior. He would be the Supreme Lord of Time. Science and Intellect would rule. Ignorance would be banished.

He turned the Key over and looked curiously at the indention in the center of the Star of David. He pressed his finger in it and felt a tingling sensation course up his arm. Powerful indeed! And this was the place where the renowned Philosopher's Stone belonged. The powerhead of all alchemy. And those inept, defunct Templars had finally done it! He wished that he had the Stone as a part of his collection, but there was still time to get it from them. The Key had come to him easily enough, once he had perceived its whereabouts. The mind of the fallen Templar had been easy enough to control. Even the Knights of the Temple were simple-minded in many ways and confident in their arrogant adherence to the Rule of Order, which they felt secured them a place in Paradise at the right hand of their god, no matter what they did or did not do on earth. This Key was no good without the Stone, but the Stone, itself, was invaluable. It was a separate treasure in and of itself. It had many uses other than to decorate this artifact. He would have it eventually. He would have everything... eventually.

Abdul Hafiz al Sajek opened a small golden box on his desk and laid the Key inside its blue velvet lining. He closed the box, made a sign in the air above it and pronounced a sacred name of protection over it. He checked the clock. Time for his meditations. The Templar would be coming soon. Perhaps more than one of them. He would be ready for them. And afterwards, he would go for the Ark. Scotland was beautiful this time of year. The brisk winds of autumn would soon be turning the leaves brilliant colors as the world prepared for another deep winter sleep. So different from the temporary home he had made for himself in the Punjab where only the level of the dark waters in the swamp rose and fell with the seasons and tides.

((((((((((((<O>))))))))))))

Von Hetz knocked softly on the door and then let himself in.

D'Brouchart knelt beside the bed with his forehead resting on his hands. Simon lay exactly as he had left him. Appearing only to be asleep.

The Grand Master raised his head and looked at him briefly then returned his attention to Simon's serene face.

"He favors his mother," von Hetz commented lightly, but the anger was evident in his dark face. "I see nothing of his father in him…" he added a peculiar emphasis that made d'Brouchart's head jerk around in his direction.

"You looked into his mind?" he asked incredulously.

"Yes," the Knight of the Apocalypse nodded and then went to sit in the chair next to the bed, slouching down in his usual position, clasping his hands on his stomach. "He did not know I was there. And furthermore, I do not think he knows what has happened to him now. I believe he thinks it is only a dream from which he cannot wake."

"No. He doesn't know," d'Brouchart said softly and reached to touch the Healer's face. "But how did this happen? What is this curse, Konrad?"

"She put him where he is," von Hetz said in disgust. "It was her whole purpose for him. She wanted knowledge about him. About us."

"I have sinned," d'Brouchart did not take his eyes from Simon's face. "I thought it would be better for him, but who is this spirit? This creature? Where does she come from? Do you know? Who sent her?"

"Perhaps she is not a spirit at all, but a spy, your Grace," von Hetz suggested an alternative and wished that it were so. A solid explanation for what he had seen. But he feared that it far from the truth. How could anyone have the power to do what she had done without some sort of demonic connection? "But whatever the case, as far as Brother Simon is concerned, the news would have been far better coming from someone other than from the lips of a stranger and one who would violate him so much so that he does not wish to live."

"Is that what you saw?" D'Brouchart turned his watery eyes on the Knight. "But why would he want to die?"

"Think of it, Brother." Von Hetz eyed him almost contemptuously. "The one thing he could never do. He may be a priest devoted to chastity and the service of God and the Order, but he is still a man. Do you think that he never has dreams? It would be unnatural for him not to wonder how it might have been otherwise and then to have committed the sin in such an unholy manner? Simon of Grenoble? A thousand years in the dungeon

162

would have been preferable to him. He refuses to accept what has happened."

"What can we do?" D'Brouchart asked and the Ritter was astounded to hear the tremor in his voice. The Master was crying. Von Hetz had not thought it possible.

"You are the Master. You must decide." Von Hetz raised his eyebrows. "I will do what I can, but I can promise you nothing. He is the Healer who cannot heal himself. Why have you never told him about his parents?"

The Grand Master narrowed his eyes. He had his reasons. He still had his reasons.

D'Brouchart stood up and looked down at Simon once more before turning on his heel and leaving the room abruptly. Von Hetz remained sitting in the chair by the bed... thinking dark thoughts.

After a few moments, he began to recite the 23rd Psalm for Simon.

"The Lord is my shepherd, I shall not want..."

(((((((((((((<O>)))))))))))))

"Du Morte!" Mark Andrew was startled by the sound of the Master's voice. The big, man stood in the door of the library looking at him. "Come with me."

Mark got up and followed the man down the hall toward the kitchen, but he didn't stop there. He went down the stairs to the cellar and then opened the door to the laboratory. Mark hesitated. What now?

The Grand Master picked up the matches on the cluttered counter and lit the oil lamp. Mark had never come to clean up the glass. It still lay shattered, glittering on top of the worktable, crunching under the soles of their boots. In three months, he had ventured into the lab only three times.

He watched as the man walked about the room lighting the various lamps and candles scattered here and there.

"Here," d'Brouchart said gruffly and removed a small bottle from his pocket. "The Elixir."

He handed the bottle to Mark Andrew.

"Can you make more of it?" He asked stone-faced.

"No," Mark shook his head slowly.

"Why not?" D'Brouchart scowled at him. "You are the alchemist!"

"I have sinned," Mark Andrew told him quietly. "I no longer have the Dragon's blood in my veins."

"Take out enough for Simon." D'Brouchart looked away from him and Mark frowned as he realized that the man was wiping tears from his eyes. "Your Brother told me that there is a way to make more of what we have. I want you to start on that immediately. He said there is a way to expand it." Mark could only assume that the Master meant Simon when he said 'your Brother'. Another good reason why one Brother should not muck around with another Brother's mystery. It was true enough, but he did not want to make more of the stuff. It was dangerous and immoral and could cause men to do great atrocities in order to possess it.

"It can be multiplied, but it would take weeks. And I do not know the procedure by rote. My God, Edgard! Do you realize that we are acting out the Hermetic Library like a troupe of bad Shakespearean actors? These developments have completely annihilated my confidence. I thought I knew what I was doing. It is not in my... it is not my... Lucio Dambretti would know it the process by heart, but he does not have the... he doesn't know the mechanics," Mark frowned and slapped his forehead. "I don't have weeks, your Grace. I have to go to America. And what do you plan to do with it, may I ask?"

"That is none of your concern," d'Brouchart told him roughly. "You will leave instructions with the Golden Eagle. He will finish the work while you are away."

Mark nodded his head ever so slightly. So Lucio would take his place as the Alchemist and the Bridegroom. Why didn't he think of that? What a splendid fucking idea! It was a set up. D'Brouchart had consulted his oracle. He was sure of it. Not that the Master had ever or would ever admit having the ability to look into the future, Mark was sure he could. Michel de Nostradamus could do it using the mysteries. Why not Edgard d'Brouchart? He was about to depart on his last mission and the old man knew it!

"Should I leave him... everything?" Mark looked about the lab forlornly. He had already come to terms with losing Meredith. In his heart he knew. It was with some bit of shock that he realized that he would miss his home and his work in the lab even more than he would miss her company. It was only to be expected, of course. He'd had this lab and these instruments for centuries. They were his closest companions. He would miss his hounds and the meadow and...

"Whatever is necessary," d'Brouchart answered shortly interrupting his grand misery.

Mark set the bottle on the counter and rummaged about for a clean glass straw. He opened the bottle and placed the tiny straw in the liquid and then held his finger over the end of it. The straw held but one small drop of the red Elixir. He laid the tube in d'Brouchart's hand.

"That is more than enough."

"Come with me."

D'Brouchart turned quickly and made his way out of the lab. Mark looked around one last time and followed him out after recapping the bottle and replacing it on the shelf. A few moments later, five Knights of the Council of Twelve and the Grand Master stood at the foot of Simon's bed while Sir Ramsay knelt beside him.

"Hear me, Master and Father, Creator of the Universe, bless this effort of Thy humble servant, Mark Andrew Ramsay, Prince of the Grave, King of Terrors, have mercy upon the heads of Thy people in their time of need. Put forth Thine Holy Hand and quicken this liquor for it rejoices the Soul, it renews virtue, it cleanseth the soul, it strengthens youth and removes old age, for it suffers not the blood to be putrefied, nor choler to be found, nor melancholiness to be abundant, yea rather it multiplies the blood beyond measure and restores and renews all corporeal members efficaciously and preserves them from hurt, and does most perfectly heal all infirmities, as well hot as cold, dry as moist, before all other medicines of Physicians, and to conclude it expels all evil humors and brings in those that are good, love, honor, security, boldness and victory in battle to those that possess it and in this is the greatest secret of nature accomplished which is, a secret not to be valued at any price a most precious and incomparable treasure which God grant to be hidden in their minds that possess it lest it be made known to the foolish and ignorant."

The Knight of Death put the tube to his lips and blew the liquid out onto his index finger. He rubbed it between his thumb and forefinger and then stood up. He leaned over the Healer and wiped his finger on the inside of Simon's lower lip and drew the sign of the cross between his eyebrows with the blood on his thumb.

"Amen let every living man say: Finis."

The small group repeated the word in reverent unison. Mark Andrew turned to them and looked from one to the other of them slowly as if accusing them all of something heinous. How dare they witness this sacred rite? Who were they to demand such performances? Profane! There were all profane! He felt profoundly shaken that his Brothers had heard him say his own blasphemous titles aloud, but these were in his Mystery. These were among his many names and titles. It was bad enough that some of them had occasionally been witness to the Key of Death Ritual, but this...

"Brother Lucio!" D'Brouchart addressed Dambretti and Mark snapped his head around to glare at the Italian. "Go with Ramsay. He has something to show you."

Mark drew a deep breath and let it out slowly before leaving the room with Lucio on his heels. Why? What would it take to get this curse lifted from his head?

Chapter Ten of Seventeen
O my God, incline thine ear, and hear; open thine eyes, and behold our desolations

Lucio was not happy with the instructions the Grand Master had given Mark Andrew. He did not want to delve into alchemy. It was one thing to study the Tractates and the Treatises, but to actually work on the physical end of the art was not his proverbial cup of tea. He did have one consolation and that was, as long as Mark Andrew was gone, he would be staying in Scotland to work on multiplying the Elixir. Not a bad deal, if Merry was going to stay there as well. He only needed a little time with her. Just a little. Certainly it had taken very little time with her before. She loved him. He was sure of it. They were meant to be together and it was God's will combined, perhaps, with a bit of machination on the part of the Master, who had apparently changed with the tide and thrown his weight on the side of right. Who would have thought that he would be here again so soon working with Mark on an alchemical task. Mark had been severely injured and barely conscious the first time, but this time, he was wide awake and angry to boot. Lucio had to fight to keep from slipping into the role of awestruck apprentice as his mind went back several centuries to the time when he had been Mark's apprentice.

He drew a deep breath, willed his heart to slow down and began to recite the requisite verses from the Hermetic writings.

"It behoveth him who would enter into this art and secret wisdom to repel the vice of arrogance from him, and to become virtuous and honest and profound in reason, courteous unto men, merry and pleasant of countenance, patient..." the words came from the Fourth Book of Treatises, but his mind wandered elsewhere, while Mark Andrew scrounged about his cluttered lab, gathering up vessels, burners, jars, bottles, tubes and all sorts of things Lucio did not recognize. His oration was interrupted rudely by a scowl and a growl from the Alchemist.

"Wot ist?" Mark asked angrily, interrupting the Italian's subconscious musings. "Art thou a priest now? Wouldst preach t' me, Brother?"

"It is all a part of the Arcanum." Lucio said indignantly and then continued "...patient and a concealer of secrets. You shall choose a form of glass, round in the bottom, or at least oval, the neck a hand's breath long or more, large enough with a straight mouth made like a pitcher or jug."

Mark looked around and located the required vessel. A large, round-bottomed flask with a long neck.

"The second vessel of Art may be of wood, of the trunk of an Oak, cut into two hollow hemispheres, wherein the Philosopher's Egg may be cherished till it be hatched..."

"Hold, Brother!" Mark spun on him, holding up a round-bottomed bowl made of wood with overly thick walls. "Thinkest thou me now a chicken?!" Mark had become so angry, he had reverted not only to brogue, but all the way back to the archaic language common during the reign of King James I.

"I am only repeating the words, Brother!" Lucio tilted his head back to look at him expectantly. Mark slammed the bowl on the table and then dug under the bench long enough to find another identical bowl made of wood. "The third vessel practitioners have called their furnace, which keeps the other vessels with the matter and the whole work: this also Philosophers have endeavored to hide amongst their secrets."

"Ist thot a cooment, Brother?" Mark asked sullenly and crawled back into the darkness under the bench, cursing and brushing spiderwebs from his face. He located a small rectangular furnace of heavy cast iron, lifted it from the floor and plopped it on the counter. Stepping back, he smiled at it and then blew a cloud of dust from its pitted surface. "I've been looking for you, my friend," he actually spoke to the furnace with more affection than he showed for his Brother.

Lucio ignored his comments and questions and continued, waving one hand in front of his face in the ensuing dust cloud.

"The furnace which is the Keeper of Secrets, is called Athanor, from the immortal fire…"

"Wait!" Mark's smile faded and he turned on the Italian again. "D'thee haf t' name th' 'quipment? We dunna have th' toime!"

"Let the form of the furnace be round, the inward attitude of two feet or thereabouts, in the midst whereof an iron or brazen plate must be set…"

"Hold!" Mark held up his hand and frowned. Wrong furnace. He slid the heavy iron rectangle off the table and plunked it on the floor. He went to a far corner and came back directly lugging a small, round furnace made of ceramic brick. "Go on."

"Below the plate let there be a little door left and another above in the walls of the furnace."

Mark held up one hand. "A lit'l door," he mimicked Lucio's words. "And anoother lit'l door." He spun the furnace around to check for the 'little doors'. He stepped back and held out his hand. Lucio stepped closer to inspect the furnace and then nodded his approval.

"Si`. Due little doors," he held up two fingers and then continued. "Upon the middle of the aforesaid plate, let the Tripod of Secrets be placed with double Vessel. And let there be a little window in which to view the fire with the eye."

Mark sighed and pointed to a dark yellow rhomboid of glass set in the side of the furnace.

"That looks like a jewel or decoration, Brother. Are you sure it is a little window?"

Mark Andrew did not answer him.

"*Si*'. OK, then. And take care that the little doors are always shut lest the heat escape."

"Lit'l doors, lit'l windows. How quaint." Mark crossed his arms over his chest. "Ist more?"

"No, I think that is all," Lucio shrugged and then nodded and poked at the wooden bowls. He picked them up and put them together to see how they worked.

"Then ye wud know th' rest?" Mark Andrew was still angry.

"I would need to know how to kindle the fire," Lucio told him. "And I would need to know what Red Water is and where to find it."

Mark Andrew drew a deep breath, let out a long sigh and then tramped across the lab to a rickety old cabinet nailed to the wall and opened the doors. He took out a large glass jug with a cork stopper sealed with wax and lugged it to the table.

"That should be plenty." Lucio squinted at the red liquid and seemed to be unimpressed with the sizable quantity.

Mark went to another equally decrepit cabinet and took out a metal box covered with a thicker, darker dust layer. He brought it back to the table and opened it up while Lucio looked over his shoulder. Inside were a number of small, white and gray lumps of what looked like course salt crystals. He picked up one of them and placed it inside the lowest door on the furnace. He picked up another smaller box and took out a pinch of deep purple powder between his thumb and forefinger and tossed it through the same 'little' door onto the white crystal. He reached under the table and pulled out three spiders and a tall slender bottle of yellow liquid stopped with a cork-wrapped stopper. He shooed away the spiders and then took the stopper from the bottle. A very foul odor filled the room causing Lucio to cough and gag. Mark used a long glass rod with a tiny, solid glass orb on one end to take out a minute bit of the yellow liquid. He carefully scrutinized the one small drop of yellow clinging to the bulb.

"Now, wotch," he said and held the glass rod over the top of the furnace.

Lucio waited patiently until gravity pulled the drop from the glass rod. It seemed to fall in slow motion into the depths of the cooker's chimney. A miniature explosion followed by a tiny puff of smoke signified the ignition of the fuel at the bottom of the oven. The Italian leaned forward to look through the bottom door. The white crystal was now glowing red and he could feel the heat on his face already. Mark flipped the door shut and engaged a small, rusty latch to hold it in place. "Thot'll last ye aboot two days. An' remember, nevair, evair shake th' yellow. D' ye understand, son?"

Mark inadvertently reverted to the word 'son' that he had used when he was teaching his apprentices some alchemical process. He closed his eyes briefly, disgusted by the faux pas. It was hard to believe that Dambretti had been his apprentice for a short space of fifteen or twenty years. He kicked himself mentally for the slip.

"I think so, Mas... Brother," Lucio nodded, swallowed hard and glanced about the gloomy room full of deep shadows, wondering what other lethal substances might lie in the darkness, waiting for disaster to strike them.

"Gud."

Mark turned on his heel and left him in the grimy laboratory. Lucio stood still for several seconds and then something skittered in the corner and Lucio hurried after him.

"Wait!" He called to the Alchemist. "You didn't tell me how to turn on the lights!"

Mark Andrew stopped at the foot of the stairs leading up to the back hall.

"Th' loights air on, Brother. Make sure ye put 'em out before ye leave. Wudna want a foire down 'ere," Mark called over his shoulder and then added as he stomped up the stairs. "Wot d' ye need loights fur anyway? Air ye afraid o' th' dark now, Brother?"

((((((((((((<O>))))))))))))

Sir Barry was shaken from a deep sleep by Stephano Clementi. The boy was in great panic.

"Sir! Please!" The boy pulled on his arm.

He stumbled from his bed and hurried after the Italian dressed only in pants and sockfeet. They ran quickly through the barracks. All of the boys were gathered at two of the windows facing the inner courtyard. Stephano rushed through the doors, outside and down the steps. Sir Barry followed after him and drew up short at the sight of John Paul standing atop the three-tiered, marble bird bath in the middle of the courtyard. The young man was dressed only in a pair of dark slacks and stood barefooted on the very edge of the top basin, a good twelve feet above the bricked area around the structure. He was looking up at the moon with his arms outstretched, speaking in old Latin.

"And they came into the house of Baal; and the house of Baal was full from one end to another. My daughter is grievously vexed with a devil. There met them four possessed with devils, coming out of the tombs, which

169

remain among the graves, and lodge in the monuments, exceeding fierce, so that no man might pass by that way. For we wrestle not against flesh and blood, but against principalities, against powers, against the rulers of the darkness of this world, against spiritual wickedness in high places. For their rock is not as our Rock, even our enemies themselves being judges. For their vine is of the vine of Sodom, and of the fields of Gomorrah: their grapes are grapes of gall, their clusters are bitter: Their wine is the poison of dragons, and the cruel venom of asps. Is not this laid up in store with me, and sealed up among my treasures? To me belongeth vengeance and recompence; their foot shall slide in due time: for the day of their calamity is at hand, and the things that shall come upon them make haste. So they went, and made the sepulchre sure, sealing the stone."

John Paul dropped his arms to his side and toppled from the monument into the waiting arms of Sir Barry of Sussex. The big Knight fell under the weight of the boy and Stephano helped them up.

"Go and fetch de Bleu. We must record the words," Barry told the Italian as he hefted the unconscious boy to his shoulder. By now lights were appearing in the Knight's quarters and doors were slamming up and down the long portico. Sir Philip rushed toward him.

(((((((((((((<O>)))))))))))))

Mark Andrew was the last to come down the stairs. It was déjà vu to see the group standing at the foot of the stairs in his own home, dressed, once again, in their full Templar regalia. The six Templars turned as one, watching him descend the stairs, making him feel even more exposed, like the unwilling bride approaching an unholy wedding. He was bone tired already. He had not slept in two days. His eyes felt full of grit and his sword slapped his boots and dragged on each riser. His chain mail clinked and jangled and felt as if it weighed two hundred pounds. He brushed his hair back from his face and felt the silver earrings entwined in the white braid scrape his neck. When he reached the bottom of the steps, the six Knights formed a semi-circle and waited as the Grand Master came around, kissing each of them lightly on the lips in the Templar fashion and then hugging each one briefly in turn. Simon had not awakened, but he had turned on his side and his breathing had changed after the administration of the dragon's blood. They hoped that he was only sleeping it off and would soon come around. Bruce Roberts and Sir Guy would stay in the room with him. Sir Champlain would stay on watch in the main hallway in case the girl returned while they were away.

170

They would not have to move the Ark this time. The Grand Master had already replaced the water-stained cover with the new one. They would simply seal the crypt in which it was sitting. They were taking no chances. Each of them wore broadswords, daggers and long knives. Merry had her rapier at her side and an ornate silver dagger made in Spain. Something that Lucio had given her as a Christmas present. She also carried the winged staff of the Wisdom of Solomon under her arm beneath her cloak in a leather and linen pouch supported by a shoulder strap made especially for her by Sir Barry. They filed out into the growing twilight and got into two vehicles. Von Hetz drove his BMW with Merry and Mark Andrew in the back seat while Lucio drove Mark's Mercedes with the Grand Master in the passenger seat.

The chapel was dark when they pulled up in front. Merry got out and stood looking up at the rosette window above the doors. A chill coursed over her body. She did not relish the thought of going inside and would never have been able to do it alone. Mark Andrew went in first and turned up the lights, which cast a warm glow over the interior of the empty building. It seemed uncommonly cold inside the edifice and Merry pulled her cloak more closely about her.

Von Hetz went directly to the bell tower door and pushed it open. Mark stopped at the door momentarily. The Knight of the Apocalypse took down one of the torches from the wall sconce and lit it before going down the darkened staircase. His boots echoed in the stillness as they stood huddled in the apse of the chapel. The Knight of the Apocalypse would go down alone to perform the exorcism before they sealed the crypt.

Von Hetz lit the torches in the lower reaches as he went along. He had been to the chapel earlier in the day just long enough to put fresh torches in the holders in preparation for the ceremony. He was very glad now that he had done so. The deep darkness under the old stones unnerved him. The long passageways glowed with a reddish light as he walked slowly toward the main crypt. Each step was carefully measured as he focused on the task at hand. His footsteps sounded loudly in his ears and he could see a pale, greenish glow emanating from the crypt where the Ark stood. Ducking under the arched overhang, he was immediately confronted by the chaotic whispering of many voices. The spirits surrounding the Ark were in a high state of agitation. He pushed their disturbing voices from his mind. A second, more corporeal presence immediately arrested his attention. A tall Knight dressed in black stood in the aisle between the coffins. Von Hetz drew his sword and held it point up in front of him. The Knight stepped forward. Christopher Stewart. The apparition's skin was stark white against a black uniform. His eyes sparkled and reflected the red light of the torches in the passage. A red cross was clearly visible on the front of his surcoat when he tossed his cloak over his left shoulder and drew his sword. The sound of the blade as it left his scabbard was unnaturally loud in the stone chamber. The Apocalyptic Knight's breath caught in his throat at the sight of the young man, dead now for nine years, dressed in the full Templar regalia. He took one step back and steadied himself with one hand against one wall.

"How comest thou here, Seer?" the Knight's voice echoed within in the room.

"Get thee gone from my sight," Von Hetz commanded him. His own voice sounded unnaturally deep and the fear he felt was clearly audible. "In the name of Christ Jesus, I rebuke thee!"

The Knight's body became thin like vapor and he was gone. A chill blast of air swept over him and he shivered. He silently thanked God that Mark Andrew had not been there to see the specter. A noise to his right caught his attention and he turned to see another form standing beyond the coffins. Another Knight, dressed in red. As with the first, this one also displayed the cross on his surcoat, but it was black as had been the crosses on Dambretti's and Dame Meredith's uniforms after they had been inundated in the red water. He turned to face this new specter.

(((((((((((((<O>)))))))))))))

Louis Champlain, Knight of the Golden Key, sat on the bottom step of the broad stairway in Ramsay's entry hall. He could hear the antique clock ticking in the niche under the stairs and mice scuttling around the floor in the kitchen behind him. Every now and again he heard blips and beeps and chimes from the computer behind the closed library doors. It seemed all his senses were on hyperdrive. He tapped the toe of his boot with the tip of his broadsword and patted the .357 Israeli Desert Eagle pistol in the shoulder holster under his left arm once more. The thing was big, powerful and loud. Just his sort of weapon. If he fired it inside the house, they would hear it all the way to Paris. He yawned and put one hand over his mouth. He did not like waiting, but he used the time by browsing a small catalog that offered golfing gear, planning what he would need to buy in order to take up his next new hobby. He was squinting at the shoe section when his thoughts were interrupted by the wolfhounds in the library. They began to howl mournfully in unison sending chills up his back and over his scalp. He sat up straight and looked around, startled fully awake by the eerie sound of the dogs' mournful howls.

The sight of a tall, well-built Knight dressed totally in black, suddenly standing just inside the front doors, surprised him. The doors had not opened and he'd heard no footsteps. The figure was familiar. He stood quickly and raised his sword to the *en garde* position.

"Hold!" he said loudly and stepped down to meet the intruder. The hounds stopped howling and began barking furiously behind the closed library doors.

The knight in front of him held long Scottish dirks, one in each hand. The blades glittered in the lamplight and he recognized the face of Christopher Stewart, late apprentice of Sir Ramsay and his blood ran cold. The man had been dead nine years gone by. A ghost or a prank? Someone's sick idea of a joke.

"Who are you?!" He demanded.

"Wouldst thou not know a friend, Brother?" The Knight addressed him in French. His voice was hollow and the sound of it almost made Champlain's knees turn to water when the hounds suddenly fell silent and Louis heard them desert the vicinity of the doors that he had been considering opening on the intruder.

"Thou art not my brother, unclean spirit!" Champlain heard a tremor in his own voice. How could he fight a specter? He had seen many things in his long life, but he had never been directly confronted by any such thing as this. This was beyond his realm of experience. Evil incarnate.

"I would be your brother, Louis Champlain," the apparition smiled and advanced on him. "I would make thee my brother and embrace thee in the bonds of death."

His attack was sudden and Champlain had trouble parrying the double assault targeting his neck. The blades clanged in the silence of the big house. The Knight jabbed at the Frankish Knight's midsection with both daggers and brought his left arm up in time to parry Louis' swing, but the Frankish Knight's arm and blade passed through its shoulder. Louis winced at the pain which shot up his arm from the momentary contact with the specter's arm and he jumped back before stepping in with a powerful thrust directed at the ghost's head. The blade of his sword passed cleanly through the Knight's head, making no wound, as if there was nothing there but air. Impossible. His forearm still smarted as if burned from the contact.

Champlain fell back against the balustrade, knocking the breath from his body momentarily. He could hear his own breath in his ears as a fear like none he had ever known engulfed him, threatening to make him turn and run up the stairs in a cowardly retreat. Louis Champlain had never felt such fear. Even when he had been terribly out-numbered by the enemy, he had never felt such hopeless despair as this. Only the blackened blades in the specter's hands had substance as far as his blows went. He would have to disarm the phantom. The thing would not even have to worry about avoiding a killing blow. Meanwhile, all it would take was one good strike in the right place and he would be done for. His broadsword clanged hollowly against the left blade, sending it tumbling through the air. Louis was astonished when the weapon simply vanished midway through its flight and never even touched the floor. He backed away quickly as the onslaught resumed inexorably forcing him up the wide staircase behind him. He crossed blades with the Knight's right knife again and again and delivered many potentially fatal blows to the form in sheer frustration, but there was nothing he could do to stop him. Halfway up the stairs, he sent the second dirk flying over the handrail. Again, it disappeared into thin air. The shade drew a silver broadsword and continued the fight without faltering.

Louis could not kill a dead man! At the top of the stairs, he glanced down into the entry hall to see another Knight in the hallway below, this one dressed in a crimson cloak and surcoat. Giovanni Volpi! Sir Dambretti's former apprentice, also killed by the late Knight of the Throne, James Argonne.

"Holy Mary, mother of God!" Champlain began to recite the Roman Hail Mary in time with each of his thrusts and blows. "Blessed art thou among women! Blessed is the fruit of thy womb, Jesus…"

The red Knight looked up at the fighters on the stairs and then made his way silently down the hall beside the stairs toward Simon's room. Louis drew the pistol between dodging the broadsword and let go a warning shot for the men waiting in Simon's room.

(((((((((((((<O>)))))))))))))

Von Hetz was sweating profusely in the cold air inside the crypt. He had expended little physical energy dispelling the two Knights and knew well that he would be forced to deal with them again before the night was over. It was the mental strain that had almost stripped him of his ability to function at all. A pure heart, pure thoughts, clean mind, mindful of purpose, serving of God, penitent soldier, merciful, charitable, kind, dedicated… He ran through the requirements for successful exorcism. He crossed himself again and turned to the left where he knew something else would be waiting for him. This one made his blood run cold. Sir Hugh de Champagne, late Knight of King Solomon's Wisdom, stood facing him with an almost curious expression on his big face. Yet, another victim of James Argonne. All three of these specters were fallen Templars' whose bodies lay in the crypts beneath the chapel, placed there nine years ago by Mark Ramsay, himself. All three victims of James Argonne's insanity. There had been no services for any of them and for a moment, von Hetz was filled with anger at the omission. Had they received proper burials and last rites, he felt sure that they would not be here under the influence of evil spirits. In the tradition of the early Templars, they had been laid to rest in plain coffins with only the

174

impressions of their broadswords upon the lid. Ramsay had seen to the entire affair all by himself, unwilling to wait for help to arrive.

The Ritter had never asked what might have become of Argonne's remains. He would not have been surprised to learn that Ramsay had reverted to an even earlier and more barbaric Templar custom: feeding the dead to the dogs. Certainly the Scot's wolfhounds would have appreciated the treat. Von Hetz fully believed that Mark Ramsay may have thrown Argonne's body to the dogs in the ancient manner of the Templars. He had counted the number of new coffins the first day he had come here. Three in the crypt and three more in a small graveyard behind the church. Seven had died. Ramsay must have blamed Argonne for Champagne's fall. This grisly specter was not Hugh de Champagne. It was something purely evil.

"What goes here, my Brother?" The phantasm spoke to him and he closed his eyes. Its voice gurgled as if full of blood and a swollen tongue as dribbles of dark liquid oozed from the corners of its mouth. "Why comest thou here to disturb my rest?"

"In the name of Christ Jesus, I rebuke thee, unclean spirit!" Von Hetz shouted the words and held up his sword, deliberately narrowing his eyes to blur his vision of the horrible image.

Champagne was gone, but an even more gruesome apparition waited for him when he turned. He had not expected to see James Argonne inside the crypts, but then he had not expected anything less than this horrendous personal attack on his senses. These things were probably being taken from his own thoughts and fears. The hideously burned face of the deceased Knight of the Throne leered close to him, hissing through its teeth. The flickering light glittered on the apparition's melted features. Von Hetz repressed the urge to cry out in horror and fear.

"Get thee gone, filthy dog! You have defiled the Temple with your wanton lust and vile mutterings. Send down the Knight of Death that I might greet him once again as a Brother." The specter taunted him and held out both burned arms. "Or, better yet, join with us, defiled one! How dare you come here speaking your words of rebuke? Who would rebuke you, Brother, for your sins?"

Von Hetz stumbled backwards and repeated the same line, rebuking him in the name of Jesus. Argonne disappeared only to be replaced by the smell of violets and freshly baked bread. He spun around to face the girl behind him. Elizabeth.

"Why have you come here, Konrad?" she asked him. She wore the same flowered dress and her red hair gleamed in the light of the torches from the passageway. The green glow outlined her girlish figure from behind. "Would you like to see into my mind? I could show you many wondrous things, sir. Let me caress your face as before. Lie with me now, Konrad. Forget this silly quest and follow your heart."

She stepped closer and he backed away. He held up the sword between them. She was as lovely and alluring as ever. A vision of innocence, trust and comfort. She reached toward his face and caressed his cheek with velvet softness. He felt as if his feet had grown roots through the soles of his boots into the stone beneath him and he could not move, could not look away from her. She smiled and placed one hand on her swollen stomach as she moved closer to him. Raising his eyes above her head, he saw the great wooden cross hanging above the Ark of the Covenant. Two of the three most cherished relics in all of Christendom and here, in the presence of God's gifts, was this putrefaction. His fear fled from the onslaught of sheer outrage.

"In the name of Christ Jesus, I rebuke thee, evil one," he spoke the words with perfect constraint and turned his head away from her. "In the name of Christ Jesus, I rebuke thee, evil one. In the name of the one God, the Creator, the Divine Word, the Omniscient, the Omnipresent, the Alpha and the Omega, the..."

"Your spells will not work on me, Konrad," she spoke again. "You have not repented. Your sins are still fresh on your soul and your god has not forgiven you. But I have missed you. You could stay with me."

"Get thee behind me, daughter of darkness, worker of Satan's evil," his voice remained calm and he was able to look at her now as he backed away from her slowly. "I call on thee, Michael. I call on thee, Raphael. I call on thee, Gabriel. I call on thee, Jehovah. Hosanna. Hosanna. El shaddai. I call on thee, Yehushua, Son of God, Redeemer of Men, Son of Light, Redeemer of Men. Aid your servant, Konrad. Aid your son, Konrad, in his hour of need. Get thee out of this hallowed sanctuary, daughter of Satan."

"Satan? You would associate me with Sataniel?" she looked hurt at first and then childlike in her innocent appearance. "After all that I have done for you? All that I have given you? You do me no justice, little one. Am I not more than all these in your sight? Am I not the Queen of Night?"

An overwhelming desire to lay down his sword and embrace her in his arms gripped his mind. Her voice was so soothing and her face angelic. Her skin was milky white and he remembered the cool touch of her fingers on his flesh. He pressed his fist against his forehead and closed his eyes tightly, shouting out a silent prayer inside his head. When he opened his eyes, she was still there, unaffected by his rebuke. His newly found resistance wavered when she began to speak.

"Now those Bodies must be taken, which are of an unspotted and incorrupt virginity; such as have life and spirit in them," she quoted something he had heard in a dream perhaps. Some part of the Arcanum with which he was not familiar. "For who can expect life from dead things; and those are called impure which have suffered combination; those dead and

176

extinct which have poured out their soul with their blood by Maryrdom; flee then a fratricide from which the imminent danger in the whole Work is threatened." She stepped closer to him. Her deep green eyes locked with his. "Thou art Sol and Sol is Masculine forasmuch as he sendeth forth active and energizing seed, Luna is Feminine and she is called the Matrix of Nature, because she receiveth the sperm, and fostereth it by monthly provision."

He shook his head. What was she saying?

"Let none therefore be deceived by adding a third to the two. Now that the progeny may be born more vigorous and active, let both the combatants be cleansed of every ill and spot, before they are united in death." As she spoke she placed one hand on her stomach and he realized that her stomach had grown even more and now resembled that of a woman very near to term and ready to give birth. "Stay with me Konrad and see the fruit of thy labors come to the full power of its majesty. I will give dominion over a kingdom the like of which you have never seen and you will be my King."

Von Hetz could stand no more. His faith left him in that moment and he realized that Christ Jesus was not present with him in this unholy place and he had been a fool to think that he would be allowed to withstand the same temptations as Jesus had undergone at the hands of the Evil One. This place had been made unholy by the acts he had committed here. Turning blindly, he ran toward the stairs. She had spoken true; he had never made his confession and never received his penance. He was unclean!

He heard the melodious tinkling of her laughter as he clambered up the stone steps to the apse.

Mark Andrew caught him as he fell through the belltower door into the chapel, gasping for air, crying.

"Wot ist, Brother?" Mark's eyes were wide at the sight of panic on the Knight's face.

"Unclean!" Von Hetz uttered the one word and looked up at him before wrapping his arms over his head and sinking to the dusty floor. Mark pressed both hands to his temples and stared down at the cowering form of the dark Knight. He had never dreamed such a sight was possible. He looked up at the others who stood staring in horror, unwilling to approach the Knight.

"I'll go," he said quietly and pulled his sword from the scabbard.

"No!" Dambretti stepped forward to take his arm. "I'll go." They stood facing each other, neither of them willing to go, but both of them unwilling to allow the other to make the sacrifice.

"I brought her here. It was through me she came," Mark told him in a low voice. "I'll send her back to Hell."

"That's not true, Mark Andrew," Merry interjected quickly and rushed forward to grab his other arm, inserting herself between them. "It's not your fault. It's no one's fault."

177

"You don't understand, Meredith!" He shouted in her face. "I have to go. She is my devil."

Merry cringed away from him and stepped back against the Italian who, ever ready to make the most of every opportunity, gathered her in his arms and held her close. D'Brouchart took him by the shoulders and turned him around.

"Rebuke her in the name of Christ Jesus," the Grand Master instructed him and then kissed him lightly on both cheeks. "Go with God."

Mark Andrew looked in the Master's eyes and blinked rapidly before taking a deep breath and starting down the stairs in a rush. If he hesitated on the stairs, he would have never been able to continue.

At the bottom of the stairs, he stopped. The silence of the passage was oppressive, but a chill blast of air caught at his face and his hair. He turned toward the crypt and could see the same green glow he had witnessed in his laboratory. He crossed himself and walked slowly toward the entrance. When he stepped inside, he saw nothing at first and then the form of a tall, dark Knight dressed in black, holding a dagger in each hand, stood in front of him.

"How comest thou here, Alchemist?" Christopher Stewart's voice echoed eerily in the tomb.

Mark Andrew thought he would swoon with terror.

(((((((((((<O>)))))))))))

Champlain pushed himself off the upstairs corridor wall, still screaming God's name. He looked about in panic at the empty hallway. The Knight was gone! Just before he had lost his head, the Knight had simply disappeared. He pulled himself together and heaved a great sigh of relief. This was good news and a good sign that something might be going in their favor up at the old chapel after all. Once he had disarmed Stewart, he'd thought himself free, but then Hugh de Champagne had appeared, ready to take up the fight. Exhausted and terrified, he'd thought himself as good as dead, but then Champagne had vanished in mid swing.

The big, Frankish Knight ran headlong back down the hall and virtually fell down the stairs, glancing at the gouges and slashes along the banister where their swords had struck the wood again and again just to assure himself that he had not been dreaming. The wood splinters were real enough. He had to reach Simon's room and see if de Lyons needed help. There were other spirits in the house. He had seen at least one more before he had been pushed back along the hallway. The brief glimpse he'd had of the forth apparition had appeared to be the Knight of the Throne. James

Argonne, also dead. De Lyons was good, but he would never be able to fight off two such formidable foes at once.

When he reached the bottom step he drew up short at the sight of a tall Knight dressed in black standing in the entry hall looking up at him. Christopher Stewart was back at the foot of the stairs where he had started from. The specter stepped forward, daggers held high, ready for close combat. Champlain's heart sank. He was exhausted and bleeding from several small wounds on his arms and legs and his spiritual morale was flagging. What had they done to deserve this new atrocity?

"Wouldst thou not know a friend, Brother?" Christopher Stewart's hollow voice echoed in the high ceiling.

(((((((((((<O>)))))))))))

The words Mark Andrew had spoken in the face of the evil forms confronting him in the crypt had worked on Christopher Stewart and Giovanni Volpi and Hugh de Champagne, but the sight of Argonne's horrid face so close to his own had almost caused his heart to stop. He was back in the passageway now, breathing hard, holding onto the wall for support. The tip of his sword dragged on the stones of the floor. He could hear nothing but his own heartbeat and the sound of his gasping breath in his ears. He pushed himself off the wall and stood up straight, trying to calm his heart and his breath.

Argonne waited for him. The oozing burns on his face gleaming red and white in the torch light.

"Knight of Death. Prince of the Grave. Defiler of women! Join with me, Brother. Share the fate of the Brother you left to die in the flames of your sin!" The spectral form leered at him and held his blackened blade ready in front of him. Mark Andrew suppressed the urge to swing at him and repeated the rebuke once more. Argonne faded from his sight, but his words seemed to echo endlessly in the passage.

Mark Andrew crossed himself again and stepped back under the curving archway. The smell of freshly baked bread and wild flowers filled the air. The odor invoked a long forgotten memory of another time in this same place and though it had been more years than he cared to remember, he recognized the scent at once. Elizabeth!

He could see her petite form outlined against the green glow inside the chamber. She stood in the center aisle, smiling sweetly at him. Exactly the same smile and the same face and even the same flowered gown he remembered from a century earlier. Her red hair caught the light of the torches as it rippled over her shoulders. His heart caught in his throat at the sound of her soft voice and for the first time he realized that he had truly been in love with her. His heart hurt at the sight of her beautiful face now taken in such vile misuse. What evil was this? Had he created it in his own mind?

"Father Mark?" She asked and stepped toward him. "I have waited a long time to see you again."

"In th' name o' Chroist Jesus I rebuke thee!" Mark shouted at her and held up his sword. His hands shook and it took both of them to hold the sword up. "Stay back!"

"That is no way to greet lover, Mark Andrew," she admonished him gently and smiled as she came closer. He could see her eyes now. Deep green, lovely and full of life. "Don't you remember me? You loved me here... in this place. You told me that you loved me then. Were you lying to me? Don't you remember? This is where Ian was conceived," she said. Her voice held no hint of malice or ill-will. She sounded completely innocent and somewhat confused that he would treat her harshly.

"I rebuke thee in th' name o' Chroist!" His voice was shaking as bad as his hands now. "In the name of Saint Michael, Saint George and Saint Andrew, I command thee. Leave this place, child of the Abyss."

She stood barely a meter away now.

"Ahhhh. You do remember me. Child of the Abyss. My lover. My brother. My son. How came you to let our son be killed, Mark Andrew?" she continued and her frown deepened as tears flowed down her cheeks. "Did he suffer long? I have been waiting for you, Father. Tell me, am I not still desirable to you?"

"I didn't... I tried to stop it, Elizabeth, I tried," he told her and shook his head before stepping back. "He was stubborn like his father."

"We can make another son," she told him and tossed her head. "There is plenty of time."

"There is no time for it. There was never time for it. Stay back! You are not Elizabeth!" He shook his head and tried to clear his thoughts. She was lovely. He raised the sword again, this time over his shoulder in preparation to strike. He felt his mind drifting under her gaze. She had been so young. Such a waste and it had been his fault. His fault that she had died, just as it had been his fault that Christopher Stewart had died and Volpi and the others.

"Time is all we have, Father," she said and took another step toward him. "I am here to help you. I like it here with you. Won't you stay for a little while? Let me help you." She reached one hand toward him.

Mark heard himself screaming as he made the characteristic move intended to take her head. He stepped forward, dipped slightly and came up swinging the glittering blade in a full circle even with her neck. The golden blade flashed in the light of the torches as it made the circle. It passed cleanly through her neck and around, taking him with it, as it clanged emptily against the stones of the doorway. He recovered his balance and looked back at her. A sizable chunk of masonry fell from the wall at his feet.

She smiled at him and stepped forward. He fell on his knees in front of her, begging her to forgive him.

"Your pretty blade is no good here, sir," she told him as she reached to take the sword from his hand. His senses left him entirely and he heard the sword clatter on the stone floor. "You have sinned against your God and there is no hope for you. Join the virgin to the second, Mark Andrew. She is not for you. I am for you. You would deny your Brother his rightful place at her side. You are unclean and foul and you have defiled the virgin. I am the virgin. Your god will never forgive you. I will forgive you. Your soul is doomed. I will save you. Join with me, Mark Andrew, and become what you were meant to be. You will reign at my side in the shadows and the Kingdom of Darkness will be yours again. Come and be my King."

(((((((((((((<O>)))))))))))))

Merry's heart froze as she ran forward to the open bell tower door when they heard the echo of Mark Andrew's scream drifting up from below. She stood looking down the stairs at the red glow of the torchlight on the stones.

Lucio was beside her in an instant and pushed her back against the wall.

"I'll go!" He told her when he passed. She heard him utter his favorite epithet under his breath as he started down the stairs before she or the Grand Master could protest. "Santa Maria. Do I have to do everything myself?"

"Let him go, Sister," the Master told her when she looked at him. "Dambretti has no traffic with the spirit. He is not defiled."

Merry's mouth fell open. So he knew that Mark would fail. That von Hetz would fail. What was he doing? Punishing them? She glanced at the dark doorway. What had happened to Mark?

D'Brouchart was kneeling on the floor beside the Apocalyptic Knight, who was confessing incomprehensible sins in his native language. When he looked up, he found himself alone with the downed Knight. Dambretti had disappeared down the stairs and Merry had followed him. The big man got slowly to his feet and pulled the dark Knight from the floor. Von Hetz stood with his head down and his palms pressed to his eyes muttering the word unclean in German over and over. The Master had never seen the man

181

devastated by fear. The sins he confessed were unbelievable. Surely the man had lost his senses.

"Your sins are forgiven, Brother, whether they be real or imaginary," d'Brouchart told him and struck him on the shoulder. He was losing patience with his Knights and he was extremely upset that Meredith had gone down into the crypts. She barely knew how to wield the light rapier that Mark had trained her to use. "Go with God," he muttered as an after thought and dismissed Konrad. They would deal with him later. "Impetuous female," he mumbled and moved closer to the open bell tower door. He could hear various noises echoing up the stone stairwell, but no voices. If they did not come up soon, he would have to go down himself. They could not risk losing the Ark. If the Ark was lost, then it wouldn't matter much if they were all lost.

((((((((((((<O>))))))))))))

Merry held her rapier in her right hand. The slender silver blade caught the torchlight, clearly shaking and wavering back and forth. In her left, she held the silver dagger, surprisingly more steady than the right. Inanely she thought that her left hand didn't have as much sense as her right and attributed it to inexperience. This thought made her smile a tight smile as she realized that she didn't have much sense either or else she would be back home in Texas, sitting in her library, reading a good book and listening to Mozart. A strange sense of calm acceptance overtook her as she thought of home and hearth and all the things that went with them. A breath of cool air struck her face, imparting an exhilarating surge of energy as she focused on Lucio's back. The Italian was walking slowly and quietly toward the greenish glow of the tomb's entrance, subconsciously signaling her to come forward or hold with the blade of his knife in his left hand once he sensed her behind him. The silence in the tomb became so deep, she could hear him breathing. His knees were slightly bent and he leaned his right shoulder into the wall as he edged down the length of the corridor, with both his sword and dagger drawn and ready for anything. She assumed a similar position as they edged their way forward. He ducked unnecessarily to enter the crypt with Merry close behind him. He glanced back at her with a pained look and then almost stumbled back into her when a tall, Knight dressed in black reared up in the center aisle in front of them. Merry caught herself against the wall and fought the urge to scream at the sight of Mark Andrew's long-dead apprentice, walking toward them with Scottish dirks in both hands. Her first thought was that this ghost, or whatever it was, had killed the Knight of

182

Death. The last scream that they had heard from him had been filled with pain.

"How comest thou here, Lucius di Napoli?" Christopher Stewart's voice filled the chamber and echoed over her head.

"In the name of Christ Jesus, I rebuke thee, thou filthy minion of Hell!" Lucio's voice shook and his Italian accent almost obscured the words spoken in English entirely. Merry poked him in the ribs. Surely he shouldn't speak to Christopher in such a manner. It wasn't Christopher's fault that some evil entity was using him to scare them.

Lucio cast a questioning look over his shoulder at her and she gave him a warning glare.

Never-the-less, Christopher's form wavered and disappeared. Lucio straightened up and smiled back at her smugly.

"That was uncalled for," she hissed and then shoved him forward. "Look for Mark!"

There was no immediate sign of Mark Andrew and Merry's eyes darted toward the cross, fearful of seeing him hanging there again somehow. A sigh of relief escaped her lips when she saw the bare wood, dark in the greenish glow emitted by the relic sitting on the altar. She could feel the same pressure in her ears and she could hear the swishing, swooshing presence of the unseen spirits surrounding the relic as they came to greet them.

She jumped backwards and swung her rapier at one of the shimmering shapes as it passed her.

"They are nothing, Sister. Only shells!" Lucio spoke to her. He could see no souls in these grisly entities.

"They are not real, Brother!" He shouted into the tomb. "They are not real! Where are you, *caro mio*?"

Merry spun suddenly to the right and saw Giovanni Volpi approaching them. Her voice stuck in her throat and she stood blinking at this horrid sight as the remainder of her blood drained to her feet. She bumped Lucio's back with her forearm. He turned to face the new apparition and a curse escaped his lips at the sight of his former apprentice. Beyond the specter of Volpi, Mark Andrew lay atop one of the stone coffins. He held his sword clasped to his chest and his feet were crossed. He looked dead, but his head was still attached to his body, so far. She shrieked his name as Giovanni swung his sword at them.

(((((((((((((<O>)))))))))))))

183

Louis Champlain was saved again. This time he had been beaten all the way down on the floor, barely able to hold the dark apparition's blade a few inches from his neck with the hilt of his own sword. Blood ran from new cuts on his throat and cold perspiration had soaked his blonde hair. Pain shot up his leg and through his injured shoulder. He had already sent up his last desperate prayer for forgiveness before dying, when the Knight vanished. The sudden release of pressure, caused him to raise up slightly and then bang the back of his head on the floor as his own sword flew from his hands. He cried out in rage and panic, before climbing quickly to his feet. He searched about the hallway for his sword and then limped toward the stairs, using the sword as a cane. He had to get to Simon's room. He was bleeding profusely now from a bad cut on his shoulder and another one just above his knee. It was quite possible that either or both of these wounds might serve to be temporarily fatal if he lost enough blood. The world spun in front of his eyes and he had to hold onto the banister to keep from falling down the stairs. He shouted for de Lyons, but got no answer. His voice echoed in the vaulted ceiling and he felt utterly alone. When he stumbled into the entry hall, his heart lurched and he knew this would be his last stand.

The tall Knight waited for him yet again at the bottom of the stairs.

"Wouldst thou not know a friend, Brother?" Christopher Stewart asked him for the third time.

Champlain screamed in rage at the sight of the shade, dropped his sword and threw himself at the specter from the third step. He grabbed hold of the only thing solid and rolled onto the floor holding the silver blade between his gloved hands trying to wrench the sword from the evil grip. His own body and limbs passed through and into the specter. He felt bone-chilling cold envelope him as he rolled across the floor, fighting what could not be. Strangely enough, he had inserted himself into the same space as Stewart and now clutched the evil sword with his own hands. Only the resistance of the apparition's opposing power indicated that it was still there. He struggled to his feet and felt ice crystals forming on his eyebrows and eyelashes as he moved jerkily around the foyer, trying to keep himself within the confines of the phantasm's own form. If the thing managed to cut off his head now, perhaps it might kill itself in the process.

(((((((((((((<O>)))))))))))))

Lucio shouted something unintelligible at Merry and thrust his sword between her body and Champagne in time to parry the deadly blow aimed at her neck. Merry ducked under their crossed weapons and rushed forward down the center aisle toward where Mark Andrew lay, screaming his name all the way, but before she could reach him, her way was suddenly blocked by the figure of a diminutive young girl dressed in a flowered gown. Elizabeth! She stopped short of the apparition, skidding on the stone floor and raised the rapier between them.

"Elizabeth!" Merry gasped at the sight of the girl that she now knew was much more than just a young girl in distress.

"Meredith Sinclair. What a pleasure to see you again," the girl smiled at her. She could hear Lucio's voice behind her as he shouted the words of rebuke again. "You are too late to save your lover. He belongs to me now."

"Get away from him." Merry was surprised at the steadiness of her own voice. "You're just a ghost!"

"Am I?" Elizabeth asked and stepped closer. "Would you like to touch me?"

She held out one arm and Merry backed away. The blade of the rapier shook and wavered in front of her face.

"Get out, Merry!" Lucio shouted at her before turning to face the fourth and most horrid specter so far.

He glimpsed the figure of the girl beyond Meredith. She was not a specter, she was something entirely different. He had never seen such a thing. It seemed she had a soul of some sort, but it was nothing he could recognize or classify and he had seen hundreds of thousands over the years, perhaps even millions. It was dark, very dark, laced with flickering colors that changed rapidly from one hue to another. The air around her shimmered like heat waves in front of a desert mirage. "That is not a ghost!"

"Touch me, Meredith," Elizabeth taunted her now and drew closer, reaching for Merry's face. "Touch me and remember what it is to be loved by a woman."

Merry's eyes widened. Her breath came in gasps. She drew a deep, deliberate breath and held it as she allowed the dagger to slip from her fingers. As Mark had taught her, she raised the sword and wrapped her left hand over her right, holding the hilt close to her body and just to the right of her heart with the tip of the blade pointed up. She stepped back with her right foot, dipped slightly and lowered the blade over her right shoulder preparing to swing. The rapier would not do near the damage a broadsword such as Mark's golden sword would, but it would serve the same intent and purpose.

"Be gone, unclean spirit. I rebuke you in the name of our Lord Jesus Christ!" Merry spoke the words and Elizabeth smiled at her. The smile was not sweet any more. It was evil and dripped with contempt; she was not banished by the words, but they did affect her at some level.

"You dare call me unclean?" The girl's eyes flashed with anger. "I have done less than that which you have done. You brought about the ruin of the Chevalier du Morte with your selfish desires and your shameful

185

seductions! He would come back to me now where he belongs and I would have your son's soul as well, as you have caused the death of mine."

Merry swung the blade with all her strength and then shuddered as the sword connected with solid flesh. Elizabeth screamed and reached up both hands, grabbing at the blade that had lodged against the bone at the back of her neck. Blood poured from the ragged wound in her throat and Merry fell back against the nearest coffin, frozen in place momentarily, shocked that her blade had caused actual physical damage. She wrenched her mind from the paralysis and shoved herself forward, reaching for the hilt of her sword. The last vestige of Elizabeth's pretense at being human disappeared in an indescribable and humanly impossible screeching roar that erupted when she pulled the blade free. When the noise died, she heard Lucio again shouting the rebuke behind her. Nothing seemed to happen for an eternity and then the girl reached for her again with blood-stained hands. The creature took one more step and Merry brought the rapier up again in an undercut that sent the blade straight through her stomach just below her sternum and into where her heart might have been, if she had one. The girl fell to the floor and stared up at her in the dim light, a look of disbelief in her eyes. Merry pulled her sword free again and back-pedaled down the aisle until Lucio caught her in his arms.

He took her by the shoulders and pushed her against one of the stone coffins before turning to face the horribly burned visage of Argonne behind him. Merry leaned on the lid of the coffin fighting to remain conscious. The horrid noise reverberated inside her head and when she closed her eyes, Elizabeth's face was still clearly visible. Blackness threatened to overwhelm her. The Argonne specter's hissing voice spouted insults at Lucio, calling the Italian the bastard son of a witch and a practitioner of the Black Arts. His words made no sense to her, but Lucio did not take them very well and began to exchange insult for insult and blow by blow with the specter. She shook herself out of her fear again and then rushed back through the rows of coffins to Mark Andrew's side. He looked pale in the green glow, but seemed only asleep.

"Mark Andrew!" She shouted in his face and grabbed hold of his shoulder, shaking him roughly. "Wake up!"

He opened his eyes, looked up at the ceiling and then came off the stone in a terrible rush, taking her down to the floor with him. Lucio was with them instantly, pulling Mark Andrew up roughly by one arm, shouting something about the golden sword in Italian. Mark's blade passed dangerously close to Dambretti's face in the confusion. The Scot stumbled away from them and Lucio helped Merry from the floor. They stood gasping and panting, leaning against the caskets. Mark turned round and round, looking for anything else that might be lurking in the shadows. The Italian looked around, wide-eyed, expecting more ghosts, but something had changed. The silence in the crypt became even more oppressive and then they heard a strange whispering sound that seemed to emanate from everywhere around them at once.

"*Santa Maria*! Out!" Lucio gasped and shoved Merry toward the aisle with one hand. He had to drag the discombobulated Scot behind him with the other while he struggled to hang onto the golden sword. "Get out! Get out! God save us," Dambretti continued in Italian.

They met d'Brouchart and von Hetz in the passageway. The four of them stood shivering and trembling in the red glow of the torches. Merry pressed her hands against her face and then looked up at the Master. She could not believe what she had done. The silence of the tombs pressed in on her ears.

D'Brouchart handed her a handkerchief and she scrubbed viciously at the blood on her face. The Master took hold of her arm suddenly and removed the staff of the Wisdom of Solomon from the shoulder case, thrusting it into her hands.

"We must hurry, Sister. Calm yourself, focus on our mission. We must not fail," he told. His voice sounded hollow and echoed eerily in the silence. Lucio brought her sword and put it back in the sheath on her belt. He kissed her lightly on the cheek and smiled at her.

"You did well, Sister. A true warrior of Christ," he whispered in her ear and she was surprised how much his words meant to her.

Von Hetz had Mark pinned against one wall, speaking rapidly to him in low tones. His eyes were glued on Merry as if he expected her to disappear. She met his gaze and his face crumpled into a heartbroken frown and she knew that he was blaming himself for everything... again. She tried to smile at him and wanted to go to him and comfort him and tell him everything was all right, but there was no time and Lucio had her arm again, tugging on her. She turned reluctantly and faced the cavernous darkness where even the green glow had faded. Lucio stood behind her, with his back to hers, sword ready in case something came from the opposite direction. She held up the staff in front of her and began the incantation which would bring an angel to seal the tomb.

D'Brouchart and von Hetz helped Mark Andrew from the wall where he leaned, gasping for air, shivering cold in the relative warmth of the passage. They lined up with Dambretti, d'Brouchart facing forward, von Hetz watching with Dambretti. Mark Andrew knelt on one knee beside the Master, still holding the golden sword, ready now to launch himself on anything that might come out of the dark. The four Knights crossed themselves wordlessly and said 'Amen' when she finished the first part of the incantation. A rosy glow was growing inside the crypt now as the spirits regrouped. Meredith took a few steps closer to the open doorway. Shadows of things unseen flickered inside the tomb, making her feel empty inside.

187

She crossed herself and fell to her knees in front of the crypt. Raising the staff of the Wisdom of Solomon with shaking hands, she began to speak "O God, Almighty! Strong in battle, King of Eternal Glory and Pleasantness of whose brightness doth fill heaven and earth, whom angels and archangels do fear, worship and praise saying 'Holy! Holy! Holy!' Lord God of the Sabboth, Heaven and earth are full of thy glory. Thou which didst vouchsafe thy body to be sacrificed to be blasphemed and be vexed with buffets and spittings, to be crowned with thornes, to be nailed to the cross with sharp nails both hand and foot, to drink vinegar and gall, and thy side to be opened..." Merry wavered slightly as the movement of the evil presence on the floor of the crypt caught her eye. She crossed herself again, diverted her attention to the lintel above the door and continued "...with a spear and to be laid in the grave and to be kept by soldiers..." The girl was crawling toward her; felt more than seen. "...and to be kept by soldiers and all for us miserable sinners!" Merry raised her voice and closed her eyes. "Which by thy mighty power and with the sign of the cross..." She opened her eyes to make the sign of the cross in the air with the staff and the specter screamed as if a great pain had taken her. A warm breeze kicked up the dust from behind them, immediately building in strength, blowing bits of sand and silt into the crypt from the passageway. "...with which I do now sign me with mine own hands." She crossed herself again. "In the name of the father..." Elizabeth screamed again. "The Son..." Again the ear-splitting scream surrounded them and engulfed them as the wind grew warmer and more sand and silt began to pelt the backs of their cloaks, whipping the cloth about their bodies and blowing their hair forward. "...and the Holy Ghost and breakest the brazen gates and deliverest thy friends out of the dark places of hell."

The blast of sandy grit buffeted the backs of the Knights behind her as they continued to cross themselves and repeat portions of the Rosary. The Ritter and the Italian turned their backs to the mini sandstorm and knelt beside Mark Andrew. The unnatural wind was becoming so strong that Merry was having trouble staying on her knees as the four Knights moved closer together behind her, trying to shelter her from the onslaught. She fell forward in the gusts and caught herself on the stones. When she struggled to her feet, she was looking directly into the face of the specter. Elizabeth stood at the entrance of the crypt. Her hair was blown out behind her and her body was battered by the hot wind which was growing hotter by the moment. She placed both hands on her bloated stomach and shouted at them above the roar of the wind. Merry felt herself being lifted as two of the Knights crawled to her side and held her up on her knees against the wind. "Also O Lord, by the faith which I confess and know and have in this holy mystery, even so deliver my soul..." The girl began to stumble backwards at last, pushed by the force of the gale and pummeled by the larger pebbles and small rocks which were now being blown into the tomb. The sharp rocks cut her face and blood flowed from the various small wounds. She pointed at them and screamed something unintelligible before disappearing from sight among the stone coffins. "From the darkness of my body that within this corruptible body I may visibly see what the orders of angels may do whilst I live." Merry closed her eyes and Lucio knelt next to her, leaning close to her ear.

"You must finish!" He shouted. "Hurry!"

"Seal this place, most Holy of Holies and keep this place unseen from the eyes of men until that day should come that we may see thy glory again!"

Lucio pulled her to her feet with the help of Mark Andrew. It took both of them on either side of her and von Hetz behind to keep her from being blow into the crypt which was rapidly filling with sand in front of their eyes. The Grand Master stood rooted firmly behind Konrad, holding him around the waist as an anchor. Where all the sand came from was unknown. It appeared to come from the very air around them.

"Amen! Amen! And Amen!" Merry shouted and crossed herself one last time as the two Knights dragged her back toward the stairs. They heard one last muffled scream from below as they stumbled up the steps in a tangled group with the Grand Master bringing up the rear.

((((((((((((<O>))))))))))))

Champlain slammed into the wall and came up with the specter's silver blade free in his hands. He kicked away from a small overturned table and spun around on the floor expecting the dark Knight to fall on him again, but the evil manifestation was gone. He climbed wearily to his feet and stared down at the silver sword in his hands before flinging it away from him with a great shout of rage and started for the hallway behind the stairs.

"De Lyons!" He shouted hoarsely and heard the sound of feet running through the hall. "Guy! Simon!"

The Knight of the Sword skidded into the entry hall in front of him rolling up the rug in front of his boots. His arms and face were bloodied and he stood wild-eyed, looking around the hallway in total confusion.

"Louis! Louis! Where have you been? Where did they go?!" The blonde Knight shouted at him and turned around and around in the hall, holding up his broadsword and dagger.

"I believe it is over, unless something else comes from without," Champlain gasped and went to lower himself onto the bottom step of the stairwell.

"Saints in heaven, preserve us," de Lyons said quietly and sat wearily beside him.

"Brother Simon?" Champlain asked and looked up at him.

189

"He sleeps still," de Lyons answered and let out a long breath.

"And the cook?" Champlain eyed him hopefully.

"A bit tattered, but he will live," de Lyons nodded and then clasped the big Knight in a bear hug. "It must have been far worse at the chapel, Brother. We must prepare ourselves for the worst."

Chapter Eleven of Seventeen
the curse is poured upon us, because we have sinned against him

Louis and Guy met the bedraggled Knights wearily, but loudly on the steps when they returned from the chapel. They all greeted each other as if they had been separated for years instead of hours. Louis' and Guy's enthusiasm would not be denied as they hugged and kissed them all repeatedly while engaging in a rapid-fire exchange of information in French, English and Italian mixed with a tad of Gaelic that made Merry's head spin. The numerous hugs and kisses she received from her Brother's left her breathless as the wind was repeatedly crushed from her body.

"Hold, Brothers!" Lucio finally managed to shout in English as he pushed Champlain away when the Frankish Knight took hold of him for the third time. "Let us calm down and say something we can all understand!"

Everyone stopped talking at once and the silence was almost as bad as the cacophony, leaving Merry's ears ringing in the ensuing silence.

"The devil has been to see us!" Champlain told them simply in English, eyes wide. A crooked grin replaced his worried look and he started to laugh. Within a few moments, they were all laughing hysterically. When the laughter finally died, Louis limped toward the library with Lucio and de Lyons following after him.

"We have fought the powers of darkness and survived," de Lyons added as they disappeared through the door.

D'Brouchart wiped one hand across his sweaty brow and drew a deep breath of relief. No one had died. The crypt was sealed. The evil presence defeated. All in all, a good day's work.

Mark Andrew did not follow the others to the library, but went directly up the stairs without stopping. Merry stood at the bottom of the steps looking up after him as the sounds of a more subdued round of conversation emanated from the library where her Brothers were rehashing the night's events again from the beginning, something she did not want to hear. D'Brouchart sat heavily on the risers and glanced around at the virtually destroyed hall. The tables were moved out their places and overturned, the rugs were marked with dark stains here and there where Louis had fought off his ghastly adversaries. The dark wood finish of the banisters was hacked and splintered in several places that would require expert repair. The Grand Master reached down to touch the blood on the step beside him and looked at his fingers curiously wondering which of his Knights had bled there.

191

Von Hetz, who had sidestepped the initial melee on the stoop, had gone directly to Simon's bedside. He rejoined them with a scowl on his dark face.

"It was a hard-won battle," he said, shaking his head sadly. "We have found favor that none have perished. Bruce Roberts will recover as well."

"What of the Healer?" D'Brouchart asked and looked up at him, his brow creased with worry again.

"He must come up as he went down," the dark Knight sighed and looked away from the Master.

"What does that mean, Brother?" Merry asked the tall Knight.

She was surprised to find that her overwhelming fear of him was gone. She had seen him exposed for what he was and he was no longer a stranger to her. Just a man like any other, encumbered with a great burden and full of fear. No different from Mark or Lucio or herself, for that matter. She no longer saw him as a supernatural creature able to read her mind. She looked into his eyes without fear.

"He must re-live the dungeon, Sister," he told her and she thought he would cry again. "He is still fighting it. He will not face it. He will not wake up. The creature has left her curse on him and we are all at fault. He should have been told long ago."

"Is there nothing we can do?" Merry asked and turned to look at d'Brouchart. He shrugged slightly and looked down at the floor.

"I am at a loss," he answered. "I thought the Dragon's Blood would cure him."

"And so it has," Konrad agreed. "But, this malady from which he suffers now is not related to the demonic attack per se. It is a result of his contact with the demon to be sure, but it is of his own doing."

Merry returned her gaze to the Apocalyptic Knight's face. "Surely there is something we can do? I feel responsible for him. If I had not insisted... if I had listened to him..."

Von Hetz frowned. It was time for her to see. She had made a great stride forward in the crypt and her face was changed now as was her future. She no longer held the same look of childish innocence in her eyes.

"What would you do for him, Sister?" He asked.

"I would take his place," she said. "If I could. If it would help."

"Would you?" He asked and raised both eyebrows.

Merry frowned. "Yes. I would."

"Then so be it," he took her arm suddenly and pulled her down the hall toward Simon's room.

She stumbled along after him, wondering what he was going to do. He opened the door to Simon's room and shoved her roughly across the floor to the bedside. Simon lay upon the rumpled sheets, unmoving, sleeping.

192

"Leave us," Konrad spoke to Bruce Roberts who stood looking at them in surprise. Bruce was as bloodied as the rest of them and had several cuts on his face and arms. He still held a dagger in his hand. "You may stand down, my son. You are to be commended for your bravery. See to your wounds and take some rest."

Bruce nodded and limped from the room, closing the door behind him.

"Sit down," von Hetz ordered and stood over her as she sat in the chair by the bed. "Look at him!"

Merry cast a doubtful look at Simon. He was dreaming now and his face was growing red. His eyes were so tightly closed, it seemed he was about to scream in his sleep, but he made only small whimpering sounds. Von Hetz pulled one of Simon's hands free from his side and forcefully uncurled the cramped fingers before placing it in Merry's hands. The skin was cold, freezing and trembling. She held his hand between both of hers and rubbed it, trying to warm the skin. Simon suddenly gripped her left hand with a force that crushed her bones together painfully and she cried out in pain, trying to pull her hand away from him instinctively. He let go of her hand and turned on his side in the bed, staring wildly at her, but not seeing her. She got up and bent over him, looking into face. He was seeing something else, some other place. He began to speak in French. Merry looked at von Hetz.

"What is he saying?" She asked in consternation. What did the dark Knight want her to see? Simon was suffering terribly now. "What is it?"

"He is answering the questions of the priest. The Inquisitor," von Hetz said quietly. "The priest is asking him about Mark Ramsay and Edgard d'Brouchart among others. Simon is lying to the priest. He will tell him nothing. They are asking him many things. He denies everything. He begins his confession to God and asks to die."

Simon suddenly relaxed on the mattress, seeming to go into a deeper sleep once more.

"Do you understand what you see, Sister?" Von Hetz asked her and narrowed his eyes at her.

"No... yes, I think so," she nodded.

"He will not face what happened there. He will not allow it to become part of his conscious memory as it must, as it should be. He will not allow it to come through to... completion," Von Hetz told her and placed one hand on the Healer's forehead. "He must allow the dream to run its course or else he will never awaken. He must remember who saved him. The why and the wherefore. The demon started this, but he must finish it. He is afraid."

Merry looked about the room nervously. What could she do?

"Are you still determined to help him?" Von Hetz turned to her again. "No matter what the outcome?"

She nodded slightly and raised her eyes cautiously to the Knight's face, locking eyes with him.

Von Hetz pressed one hand against the side of her face and began to speak scriptures. "I am now come forth to give thee skill and understanding. O Lord, according to all thy righteousness, I beseech thee, let thine anger and thy fury be turned away from thy servant, Simon of Grenoble. Let thy servant, Meredith Sinclair understand the matter, and consider the vision. May God have mercy on both your souls. Amen. Amen. Amen."

Von Hetz caught her when she slumped toward him and laid her back gently in the chair. He stood for a moment looking down at her and then glanced at Simon before leaving the room quietly. He retreated into the hallway and sat on the floor beside the closed door with his back against the wall.

Presently, Lucio came down the hall and stopped in front of the door. He looked down at the Knight and then at the door. Von Hetz pushed himself up wearily.

"Hold, Brother," von Hetz spoke in Italian when the Italian reached for the door knob.

"What have you done?" Lucio frowned at him. "Where is Sister Meredith?"

"She is with Simon in his dreams," Von Hetz told him quietly. "Do not disturb them. She must see to understand. And she must understand if she is to be of service to God."

"That is not what we are here for, Brother," Lucio shook his head and reached for the doorknob again. "She has no business in Simon's dreams!"

Von Hetz was on the Italian in the blink of an eye, holding him by the throat. He slammed him across the hall into the wall with his forearm against his neck.

"She does not belong to you, Brother," von Hetz said in his face. "Mind yourself carefully. She went of her own accord as is her right as any Brother of this Order. Primitive Rule number sixty-one: Let sick brothers be given consideration and care and be served according to the saying of the evangelist and Jesus Christ: *Infirmus fui et visitastis me*. That is to say: 'I was sick and you visited me', and let this not be forgotten."

He released the Knight of the Golden Eagle and they stood staring at each other in the dim light.

Lucio blinked angrily at the taller man, started to say something, changed his mind and then turned to walk away down the hall. The last thing he wanted to do was hear another rule quoted to him. Von Hetz resumed his position on the floor by the door. He closed his eyes and seemed to sleep. His lips moved in silent prayer. Lucio paused at the end of the hall, looking back briefly before snorting loudly and turning on his heel. So be it. Let the

194

will of God be done. A little pain was always good for the soul. To that he could attest because he had become an expert.

(((((((((((((<O>)))))))))))))

Mark Andrew sat on the floor in his bedroom, facing the window. The full moon shown down on the meadow and he felt he might be looking at it for the last time. Von Hetz' words had not been encouraging. The man he would be seeking was a great and powerful sorcerer. Older, perhaps, than even the Grand Master. Abdul Hafiz, the mad Assassin. The mythical author and legendary sorcerer, professed to have mastered the occult knowledge concerning the magickal processes handed down from the ancient Sumerian and Akkadian civilizations. He had always thought the man was just a fable. One of the Arabian Nights' tales meant to entertain and frighten young children.

The Knight of the Apocalypse had related a different understanding of the prophecy spoken by John Paul in the Council Chamber, totally unlike his own interpretation of it. Von Hetz thought that the words, for the most part, had been directed at him, especially the part concerning the pit. The land that Abdul Hafiz al Sajek was trying to buy in America was full of pits. Sinkholes. Seemingly bottomless holes in the limestone bedrock caused by years of running water. The place did not fit with al Sajek's previous investments. The land was useless and unstable due flooding and erosion. Only tourists and nature lovers could enjoy its curious attractions. There was nothing there of great economic value unlike the man's other holdings. It was highly unlikely that al Sajek had become a naturalist or conservationist. The proceeds from the campers and tourists were hardly a good business investment and barely paid the yearly property taxes. There was some other, more insidious, reason behind his interest in this property.

Von Hetz had been researching the ancient documents that the defunct order of Assassins held in high regard. Among them were some extremely old and exceedingly disturbing practices including the conjuration of the Old Ones from the bottomless pit and the Ancient Evils from the Abyss and beyond. He thought that the man was looking for a gate to the Underworld. Von Hetz had painstakingly connected Abdul Hafiz' studies and arts with Shaitan, the Abandoner, who, according to the beliefs of the Assassins would lead the world away from Islam. And Shaitan was also connected with the mythical Dragon and the Lord of the Abyss according to the Quran, the holy book of the Muslims.

Von Hetz had proceeded to tell him that Sir Philip was skilled in the arts of the Ancient Babylonians and Sumerians and that the Assassins had

195

gotten most of their secrets from Babylonian and Sumerian texts which were now lost or hidden. The Grand Master knew of these things and that was why he was risking his second's safety by sending him into the field. Once again, he, Mark Ramsay, would be expected to bring back not only the Key, but the Seneschal as well. Louis had been through enough campaigns to know that he had made one of the most deadly mistakes a seasoned warrior could make. Complacency. He had lost his Key due to complacency and carelessness. Ramsay was not worried about Louis. Champlain would take care of himself, but he was not sure of Sir Philip. He had never been on a campaign or even a mission with the man, but he had to assume that he was as tried and true as the rest of them. Certainly, Sir Philip had seen his share of war and combat in his long life, but God had never seen fit to throw them together. Mark Andrew did not like thinking about these things. He only wanted to go and do, not sit and think.

He pushed himself up on his knees and crawled to his bed, where he pressed his forehead against his hands and began to pray. He wasn't quite sure what had happened in the crypt. He remembered seeing Elizabeth, hearing her voice, smelling her hair... like fresh flowers and new mown hay... his prayers faltered. No! Elizabeth was dead! Long gone and the thing he had encountered in the crypt was not her. Not her...

There was nothing left to do but face what had to be done head on. Surely it could be no worse than seeing Christopher Stewart and the horrid features of James Argonne. Was she truly in hell where she might become fair game for the Dragon to use against them? If Elizabeth was in hell, then surely that would be his destination as well. He had sent her there. She had died giving birth to the son he had made with her.

And there was something different about Merry. The very brief moments he had spent with her on the ride home in the back seat of his own car had been tense, silent. Actually, he had sensed a change in her from the moment she had opened her bedroom door to him earlier in the morning. Was she so fickle that only a short separation would bring on such doubts? She had been glad to see him, true enough and she had invited him into her bath again, but it hadn't been quite right. Perhaps it had only been the circumstances. It was the second time he had been in the bath with her and the second time that God had intervened before anything happened, prevented them from committing yet another sin together. In the two-plus months of relative peace that they had shared prior to his trip to the Languedoc, he had managed to avoid encounters with her that would leave him cause to confess. He had thought it a bad thing in light of John Paul's presence and the fact that they were not actually married. Perhaps Lucio was right. Perhaps it was not meant to be.

He could not oppose the will of God and now he would be sent off on a dangerous mission to face someone who could actually kill him, who knew exactly how to do it and would not be afraid to face him. Al Sajek would not waste time fighting him. He would go straight for the kill if given the chance and he was not sure that he could beat the fellow in a fair fight. One thing he was grateful for was that Lucio would remain behind, but where would he be staying?   ... in his place, of course. He'd never imagined something so insidious. The Grand Master had outdone himself again. Lucio in his laboratory, doing his work! Why not marry his woman as well? Sit in his favorite chair. Sleep in his bed. Wear his socks?! His goddamned socks! He had created Lucio Apolonio Dambretti and lived to regret it. Suddenly it did not seem to matter if he ever returned. He might have been better off to have allowed Sir Beaujold to kill him sixteen years earlier in the mud and rain of a Texas flashflood. Now he was committing another sin... self-pity.

"Father, forgive me for I have sinned," he said aloud and began to repent his sins to the empty room. He did not even have Simon to shrive him.

(((((((((((((<O>)))))))))))))

Simon found himself floating near the low stone ceiling. The weight of the massive edifice above him felt as if it rested on his back. He had been on the stone table only moments before with the priest bending over his face, asking him questions and telling him to repent and confess his crimes. But now he thought it was mercifully over. He had died at the hands of these hideous men and not a moment too soon. His only desire was to be shed of this place of horror. Why was he still here? At least he had not given them what they wanted and they would get nothing more from him. The place was dark except for the light produced by the guttering flames of torches set in blackened iron stands near the door. The room was cold, but the air was thick with the smell of mold and sweat and other unspeakably foul odors. He was not the first to have died here in this rat hole. There were no windows and only one door not quite tall enough for a grown man to walk through without stooping. He closed his eyes and waited to be taken away to somewhere else... anywhere, even hell or purgatory might be better.

The priest asked the same questions again and again and nothing changed. Didn't they know he was dead? No angels had come for him and when he opened his eyes, he was still in the cell, still lingering above their heads. The whereabouts of Mark Andrew Ramsay. The whereabouts of other Knights of the Order and names he did not recognize. He didn't know the answers. Why would he know? He didn't hang out with the Knights. Hang out? Hang out? Those words were not from here. Not from this time. He was hanging out at the ceiling... Something was wrong... dreadfully wrong.

197

Scenes of green meadows, sheep and cows flickered through his mind. Stone fences. Horses. Buggies. Ships. Trains. Automobiles. He reached for his cell phone. He had to make a call. But his fingers closed on nothing. He didn't exist. He was a spirit. A ghost. Stone houses. Scotland. Scotland. He was in Scotland, not France. Not this place. This place was a dream... no, it was not a dream. It was a memory.

The priest asked if he was a Templar and if he had participated in the heretical initiation rites. No! The answer was given. No! Not his voice. Not him. Not him. The priest described the alleged heresies in detail and Simon pressed his hands to his ears. No, no and no. He wanted to shout at the man. The priest asked again about Baphomet and the defilement of the crucifix. No, no and no. The priest asked about his chastity and his lust and his... Stop! Wait! It was only a memory. But whose memory?

The priest backed away from the table slightly and Simon saw that it was not his body, but the body of a woman there where he had been. What was this? The priest moved aside and spoke directly into one of the assistants' ear. One of them picked up a knife. "Cut the cord!" the priest told the man. "Get him out of my sight! Bring the payment to my chambers." "Wait, Father. It cannot be cut. Too late." The man bent over the woman and then looked up at the priest. "It is... too late." "Then take the whole thing and try not to kill him! Let them have what is left. If they would ransom half a man, then so be it. But he must live long enough for the exchange. Be careful. If they come for me..." The priest took the man roughly by the front of his robe. "I will come for you. Do you understand? This Scotsman is a dangerous fellow. Have a care! If it were not for his fat purse, we might arrest him as well. I suspect that he may well be one of them and our little fellow here seems to have a greater value to them than we first imagined." He slapped one fist on the stone and then turned on his heel to leave the room. Simon closed his eyes; he could not witness this! It was too horrible. He heard the woman scream and he screamed with her. A chill breeze brushed his face and he opened his eyes.

He lay still for a moment trying to recover his wits. The screams still reverberated in his mind. Not a dream. A memory, but a distorted one. He was lying in a rumpled pile of damp bed linens with his arms pressed to his stomach and his knees practically in his face. He straightened out slowly and tried to remember where he was.

Mark Andrew's house. This was his bedroom at Mark's home. It seemed he did not have enough strength left to get out of the bed. This thought proved true when he crashed to the floor with a resounding thud and then got up slowly on his hands and knees. His stomach heaved and he knew what was coming. It seemed days had passed since he had eaten. There was nothing to throw up. Dry heaves. Newer memories flooded his brain and almost made him almost faint. Elizabeth! What an evil child she was. And he had fallen into her snare. He had sinned greatly with her, but there was something else. His name. His father. Had it been only a dream? A very sick dream? The child was a sorceress, not quite human, with inhuman abilities. Magick.

When the nausea passed, he clung to the bed for support and pulled himself up on his knees. He was shocked beyond measure to find Merry curled into a ball in the armchair on the other side of the bed. How long had she been there?

He got up and stumbled around the bed. His feet were bare and his clothes stuck to him, damp with cold sweat. Yes, sick. He had been wounded.

"Sister?" He reached to shake her shoulder.

She opened her eyes slowly and then looked at him wide-eyed, before coming out of the chair, wrapping her arms around him, knocking him back several steps. He was weak, shaking uncontrollably and could not avoid her desperate embraces.

"Oh, God. Simon! Simon!" She held him tight enough to cut off his breath. "I'm so sorry!"

"It is not your fault, Sister," he protested and pushed her back to look at her face. "I put myself in danger. It is not your fault."

"No. They did it!" She told him and laid her head on his chest. "It's not fair!"

"I should never have stepped between them," Simon shrugged. "It was a stupid move on my part."

Merry started to say something else and stopped. They were not on the same page. He had no idea what she was talking about.

She hugged him less passionately than before and sniffled against his undershirt. Never had she known such relief. There was no reason to tell him. No reason. She understood why no one had ever told him. What possible purpose could it serve?

Simon stroked her hair and let her cry. She must have been having a terrible nightmare. He could certainly sympathize with that. His own dreams had left his mind foggy. When he ran one hand under his damp shirt, he found that the wound from the sword was completely healed. He closed his eyes. That had seemed months ago. How long had he lain here? What had happened?

"Thank you for sitting with me, Sister," he told her softly. "I hope I have not been too much of a burden. But you must release me... it's a... it's...not proper."

When they finally parted, he was shocked to see for the first time that her face and surcoat was stained with blood.

"What is this?" he asked in alarm. "Are you hurt?"

"No, I'm fine," she hugged herself and shivered.

She understood now why he had an air of perpetual sadness about him even when he smiled and why he always seemed to look pale and sickly. The Grand Master had saved him when he had been on the brink of death and had forever captured him in that state. She thought that he must have been very nice looking before the Inquisitors had taken him. Brother Simon, the priest, the gentle Healer, with his large blue eyes and soft blonde hair. A bit on the small side, but sturdy enough to wield a broadsword. She'd seen that much. It was not fair! New tears welled to her eyes and she hugged him to her once more against his protests.

"No. No. It was just a dream," he told her urgently, but held her tight, relenting once more in his weakened state. "We all have nightmares, Sister."

(((((((((((((<O>)))))))))))))

Ninth Degree Assassin, Abdul Hafiz, stood near the tangled overgrowth around the circular hole in the ground, looking up at the nearly full face of the moon rising above the trees. The eighth Name of Power had been invoked successfully. The man pushed up the loose sleeves on his long, baggy over-garment made of black silk and bent to lay out the circle of stones in the soft ground. He removed the silver amulet of N'ydens from its silk wrapping and held up it up to the light of the waxing yellow moon in order to catch the power of the ancient and potent lunar deity on its gleaming surface. He bowed low to each of the four cardinal directions, showing his respect for the elemental forces and then turned to face the pit. He made a sign in the air with his right hand and began to recite the invocation to the Ninth Name of Power in the ancient language of the Sumerians, a language unheard in the wilds for thousands of years, while holding the amulet in front of him for protection against the Old Ones, the Ancient Powers of the Abyss.

When he had finished this incantation, he turned again to the four cardinal points and began the dangerous conjuration which would start the two-night process of binding this last sorcerer to his will. One misplaced syllable and he could find himself bound forever in the Abyss, at the mercy of the unnamed and unspeakable powers he wished to control. Many stalwart sorcerers had preceded him to this point and few had succeeded. Even those who had managed to entrap these names had eventually succumbed under the immense pressure required to maintain control and were now lost forever. The trapped and tortured spirits he would conjure, command and subdue to his will were already howling in protest. Eight names and now the ninth would come under his control. One misstep and he would become one of them and they would be glad to have him join them in the halls of dust and ashes.

200

"Time is short and mankind does not know or understand the evil that awaits it from every side, from every open Gate, from every broken battlement, from every mindless initiate at the altars of madness. Let all who hear these words be warned that the habitation of man is seen and surveyed by that Ancient Race of gods and demons from a time long before time, and that they seek revenge for that forgotten battle that took place somewhere in the Universe and that battle, which rent the Worlds in the days before the creation of man, when the Elder Gods walked the spaces between the worlds, the race of Marduk, as he is known to the Chaldeans, and of Enki our master, the Lord of Magicians. Know, then, that I have trod all the zones of the gods, and also the worlds of the Azonei, and have descended into the foul places of Death and Eternal Thirst, which may be reached only through the Gate of Ganzir, which was built in Ur in the days before Babylon was and was thence removed hitherto and placed in the wilderness where no man had business and no man knew until this time. Know, too, that I have spoken with all manner of spirit and demon, whose names are no longer known in the societies of men, or were never known in the hearts and minds of men. And the seals of these are written herein. Yet others I must take with me when I leave you. O Anu! Have mercy on my soul!" These were words from *the Necronomicon*, also called *the Azif* and supposedly recorded by Abdul Alhazred, the mad Arab according to the works of H.P. Lovecraft. Abdul Hafiz knew the madness. He knew.

Abdul Hafiz' invocation to the gods of darkness continued in his melodious sing-song voice, accompanied by many signs, which he made in the air with his fingers and on the ground with his dagger. These the same words written long ago in eternal madness, recorded and preserved by only a few, known true only to the elect, recognizable only to those with the ears to hear and the eyes to see them for what they indeed were. Not the fanatical ravings of a madman, but the meticulous work of a doomed man, one who had braved to go where none had ventured and survived long enough to return and write down his knowledge. Abdul Alhazred had not returned unchanged, though few living men realized or could begin to fathom what had happened to him. But Abdul Hafiz knew.

By the time the lengthy incantation was finished, streams of sweat poured from under Abdul's turban, even in the cool breeze issuing from the waterfall in the pit. He looked about the darkened undergrowth at the treeline, concentrating hard to hear anything that might be perceived as a warning that the spell had gone awry. In his altered state of mind, preserved by his contact with the powers of the Abyss, he strained the limits of the human body in which he lived. Only the sounds of crickets, cicadas, frogs and nocturnal birds broke the silence of the night, but he not only heard their chirping calls, he heard them breathing, heard every movement of their spiky legs and filmy wings. An ephemeral Luna moth fluttered past his head, the loud beating of its wings making him swing around suspiciously to identify the source of the noise. Soft electrical crackling noises came from hundreds of sources as fireflies blinked in the underbrush all around him. Behind these mundane vibrations from the physical world, he heard the distant cacophony of something akin to howling wolves and barking hyenas. These sounds were said to be the echoes of demons wailing in the pits of Hell. Hounds of the Barrier. The invocation had been successful. Nothing had come to devour him.

He pulled his long knife from his ornate silver belt and drew its blade across his left palm. He pressed the amulet into the blood and then pressed the disk to his forehead, leaving the symbol of protection stamped on his skin. He raised both arms over his head to embrace the moon and then lay down in the middle of the circle, looking up at the face of the silver orb overhead. He opened his mind to the universe and heard the whisperings of the eight sorcerers he had bound to his bidding. They were not pleased at having been subdued by such a lowly creature as his form indicated. Al Sajek smiled at their protests and closed his eyes as one of the sorcerers recognized him as a half-caste and began tossing insults at him and his mother. They would just have to get used to it. Tomorrow night he would call upon the last and most powerful of them all. Subdar, the mightiest of all the great sorcerers who had once roamed free upon the face of the earth among men. The following night, the moon would be ready, the stars would be in perfect alignment and they would open the Seventh Gate to the Beyond for him and he would give them a pretty new toy in return for their services. The Seventh Gate. Adar's Gate. Adar. Would Adar be home, he wondered.

((((((((((((<O>))))))))))))

Merry let herself out of Simon's bedroom and closed the door softly, exhausted, feeling hollow inside. When she saw the dim form of the Ritter in the hallway by the door, she almost screamed in fright.

"Ritter von Hetz!" She said and clasped her hand over her heart. She had had enough frights for one day.

He looked up at her, questioningly.

"It's over," she told him tiredly. "He's awake. He's going to take a shower, I think."

"Good." The Ritter made no further comments and she left him sitting in the hallway. She found Champlain and de Lyons in the kitchen with Bruce Roberts and Lucio. Bruce was trying to round up enough first aid supplies to cover everyone's wounds, including his own various cuts and scrapes. Lucio was sitting at the table inspecting a cut on Champlain's leg when she came in. He got up at once and stood looking at her expectantly as if she might also have wounds that he could inspect personally. It was inconceivable that only a few minutes had passed since von Hetz had taken her to Simon's room. It seemed the dream had gone on for hours.

"Is everything... all right?" he asked and frowned at her accusingly. She felt that she had aged a thousand years. The dark circles under her eyes had grown even darker.

She wiped at the dried blood on her face and ran her fingers through her hair before answering him.

"Simon is awake and well," she said quietly.

"See?" His frown faded and he smiled broadly, taking her by the hands. "I told you he would recover. Simon is tough, though he might not look like it, eh, Brother?" The Italian turned his smile on Champlain who grimaced in pain when Bruce pressed a cloth soaked in alcohol on a nasty cut on his arm, but returned his smile good-naturedly.

"*Oui*! For sure he is that," Champlain agreed wholeheartedly. "For a little man, he can hold his own. I have seen him lose his temper once or twice. I once saw him cut down an entire date palm with his broadsword when we went on a pilgrimage together to worship at the Holy Sepulcher. Someone had tied his camel to the tree in such a way that the knots were... " Champlain redirected his story to Bruce and Guy as the cook continued to ply first aid to his numerous cuts and bruises. Sir de Lyons listened to his tale with rapt attention. Louis was an expert storyteller and he had plenty of experience to draw upon. The Frankish Knight had been on missions and pilgrimages and campaigns with everyone who had ever been anyone within the Order and he never had anything but good to tell of his Brothers, both living and dead.

"Where is the Master?" Merry asked Lucio when she turned unnoticed away from Louis.

The Italian watched her with a mixture of concern and puzzlement as she looked about the kitchen almost absently and then got a bottle of dark beer from the refrigerator. She took the cap off and drank half of it down, spilling it carelessly on her surcoat.

"He is in the library... praying, I believe," Lucio answered after a long pause. "Why?" He wanted to ask her what had happened in Simon's room. Something was not right with her. There was none of the fire he had experienced earlier in the day. When he placed one hand on her cheek, she didn't even look at him, but wiped at her mouth with the back of her hand.

"I need to talk to him," Merry whispered and turned like a ghost, leaving the kitchen and the Italian, making her way to the library. She could hear the low voice of the Grand Master before she even opened the doors. At prayer, no matter. She didn't really care if she bothered him.

"I beg your pardon, your Grace," she apologized automatically without the least bit of sincerity when he looked up. He was down on one knee near the footstool.

He pushed himself up with the aid of the stool. His chain mail jingled and his boots squeaked. The Master was the only one relatively unbloodied by their scrape in the chapel.

"Simon?" He asked shortly.

"He is awake," she told him. "He thinks it was all a dream, Sir. Just as you like it."

"Good," the Grand Master nodded, but cast a warning frown at her. "That is how it should be."

She nodded and turned up the rest of the beer, finishing it off though its bitter taste made her shiver to her toes. When she turned toward the door, she threw the bottle against the stones of the hearth in anger.

D'Brouchart looked at the broken bottle and nodded again before smiling at her.

"That is a good, clean anger, Sister," he told her and then looked past her at the door. "Suffering has a tonic effect, does it not? Where is Brother Ramsay?"

"I don't know. Upstairs, I guess," the anger fading from her voice. A sense of euphoria engulfed her suddenly and she felt light-headed. It was going to be all right. Everything was going to be all right.

She had planned to demand answers from the Grand Master. To make him tell her why the world was the way it was, but she couldn't put it into words. She wanted to know why he felt the need to protect Simon from the truth. She wanted to know why he would be so cruel to the Healer. But she already knew the answers. Simon had told her once that Satan traveled to and fro upon the earth and that the earth belonged to the Prince of Darkness. She had just never taken his words literally until now. Satan had certainly been present in the dungeon.

"Get him for me," he told her simply and then sat down in Ramsay's chair. He knew she was looking for sympathy, but he had none to give. She had offered freely and Simon had needed her services. Only now was she beginning to earn her keep as a member of the Order and he was pleased with her progress.

She went slowly up the stairs and down the hall to Mark Andrew's room. There was no answer to her knock. She opened the door cautiously, one of the fringe benefits of being a Poor Knight of the Temple. No locks. No secrets. Mark Andrew was lying on the floor beside the bed, curled around the golden sword, much like she had seen him in the laboratory in the basement of her home in Texas when Valentino had used hypnosis on him. But this time he was asleep. She sat on the floor next to him and stroked his hair. He moved a bit and she lifted his head to her lap and leaned back against the bed, closing her eyes. The Grand Master could wait. They deserved a break. They all deserved a break.

(((((((((((((<O>)))))))))))))

Mark Andrew was going to fall into the pit and at the bottom, a great red Dragon waited. On its head was a gold medallion and around his neck was a braided cord with an ornate silver buckle. His hands slipped on the wet grasses and mosses at the edge of the pit and he could not hold on much longer. He could see the beast below him as it watched him from eyes that burned like red hot coals, set deep beneath a horned brow. A double row of horns lined its head and twisted spines ranged down its back. Steam welled up around its body, making the ledge to which he was clinging extremely slippery. There was no way to obtain a handhold or a foothold on the slick ground. He looked up and saw the face of the full moon above him. The Dragon spoke to him with the voice of Ian McShan. "Curse ye, Mark Ramsay! Curse ye to the blackest pit of hell!"

John Paul stood at the edge of the pit looking down at him. Mark called him by name, but he looked up at the moon and began to speak in scriptures. "And let not the pit shut her mouth upon me. Deliver me out of the mire, and let me not sink. For thou wilt not leave my soul in hell; He brought me up also out of an horrible pit, out of the miry clay, and set my feet upon a rock. The Lord hath chastened me sore: but he hath not given me over unto death. I shall not die, but live!"

He reached out one hand to his son, but the boy backed away from him. When he looked up again, he saw the face of his brother.

"I canna help thee, brother," Luke Matthew spoke to him. "I canna go into the pit. Tis the will o' God."

Mark could hold on no longer. He heard the Dragon roar as his hands slipped from the stone and he was falling... again.

Mark opened his eyes. He was looking into a cloud of blonde curls directly in front of his face. He blinked away the nightmare and squinted at the hair. Merry?! She lay on the floor in front of him with her head resting on his arm. His other arm was draped over her waist. He tried to relax and enjoy the moment's respite, but it was suddenly very uncomfortable as he realized they were both still dressed in the chain mail under their dirty white surcoats. He tried to ease her head off his arm, but it hit the floor with dull thud.

"Sorry," he said as they both sat up rubbing various sore spots produced by the armor and weapons they wore.

She turned to frown at him, rubbing the side of her head. He shrugged sheepishly and her eyes widened.

"Oh, my God!" She cried and looked about in panic. "What time is it?"

"I don't know," he muttered as he pulled himself up stiffly and sat on the side of the bed. Gray light filtered into the room through the open draperies.

"The Grand Master sent me to get you," she said and took his hand and he pulled her up beside him. "I didn't mean to fall asleep. I only wanted to let you rest a while."

"I'm sorely obliged, lassie," he said and rubbed at a spot on his side where the hilt of the sword had made a deep dent.

"Is that a joke?!" She looked at him incredulously. He never made jokes!

"Yes," he nodded and smiled at her. "Life is just a joke, Meredith Nichole. One long, sad joke. Are you surprised to learn that?"

Merry sighed and stood up. She picked up his sword from the floor for him and he turned it over in his hands, inspecting the perfect edge.

"You'd best get back to your room before we have to go to confession," he commented dryly and looked away from her when she bent to examine his neck. His tone did not suggest that they would have something to confess. He sounded angry, but wasn't that when he was most in danger of sinning?

"I'll see you downstairs then," she relented without a fight and left him alone. He did not respond, nor did he look up at her. She was too tired and too depressed to help him with whatever was bothering him... now. She had helped enough Brothers for one day.

Merry went directly to her room and closed the door softly. She wondered what the Grand Master would say about her disobeying his order. Surely he could understand extreme exhaustion? No matter, at least they had gotten some sleep, such as it was.

She took her bath quickly and dressed in tan slacks and a white blouse. She pulled her curls back and pinned them down in a severe knot on the back of her head. She did not feel like trying to make herself presentable. In fact, she wanted to look as bad as she felt. The dark smudges under her eyes were pronounced and felt sunken beneath her slightly swollen eyelids. She put on no makeup and bundled up her stained uniform intending to take it down to the laundry room. Never in a million years would she have dreamed she would be washing a blood-stained Templar uniform in Woolite. The silly thought made her smile. Maybe she hadn't lost her sense of humor entirely. Mark Andrew's small joke had been unexpected and funny as well, but his successive statement had left no doubt as to the black mood he was in. She knew that he blamed himself for everything that had occurred concerning the appearance of the specters in the tomb. She also knew that he blamed himself for the deaths of Stewart, Volpi, Champagne and Argonne and in this blame, she, too, was partially responsible as was Lucio. But the Italian was much more resilient than the Scot. She doubted that he had ever considered that he might have helped to bring about the terrible slaughter that had occurred in and around this very house nine years earlier. He most likely contributed the entire chain of events solely to God. She paused at the top of the stairs before descending the risers slowly with her uniform tucked under her arm.

Lucio was sitting at the foot of the stairs, leaning against the handrail with his eyes closed. She stepped lightly down beside him and leaned to look closely at his face. He had lost weight. That was the difference, but he was still handsome in spite of everything that had happened. She wished selfishly that he was less attractive. He needed a shave and a lap to lay his tired head in, but it could not be hers. It could not be her hand that stroked his curly hair and soothed his tired eyes with kisses... she jerked her attention away from him. Lucio would have to find his own love somewhere else. Perhaps, if he would grow a beard, he would be less attractive. Maybe she would suggest it. Maybe she would get away from him right now before he woke up. She shook her head and wondered if he was truly asleep and if he had slept on the stairs all night and if he had, why? When he did not stir, she tiptoed down the hall, leaving him on the stairs and made her way through the kitchen.

As soon as she turned her back on him, Lucio opened his eyes and watched her with a slight smile on his lips. He rubbed one hand over his chin and frowned. He needed a shave and he was tired of shaving. Perhaps he might just grow a beard and forget the razor for a while.

Bruce Roberts was at his stove with a number of small bandages on his arms, face and neck. It must have been quite a fight he and the others had put up while the rest of them had been at the crypt. Louis and Guy's stories had been a mishmash of English and French, but she'd heard enough to know that they had paid dearly with their own blood to protect the Healer. Now, she wondered how she was going to react when she saw the Healer again. In her heart, she felt even closer to him than she might have felt for a real brother. The love she felt for him was something akin to the love she felt for John Paul. A protective sort of affection that she knew would be very inappropriate in the Healer's eyes. Sadly enough, she knew that the feeling would not be mutual and he would simply think she had lost her mind if she said or did the wrong thing. She would have to be careful. Furthermore, she hoped that Mark Andrew did not learn of what she had done. He would most likely disapprove loudly.

As for von Hetz, she certainly had a better understanding of the burden of his mystery and how he must feel when he had to perform his duties.

The cook greeted her briefly as if nothing had happened and then went back to his work. She passed the door to the cellar and went into the small room near the back door where the Stone Age washing machine and prehistoric dryer were located. They didn't make them like these any more. Heavy, white porcelain affairs with pewter and chrome knobs and handles... like brand new, clean as new pennies and surprising effective. It was almost as if Mark's appliances had developed some affinity for the Scot or else knew better than to break down.

Even though she tried to focus all her attention on the mundane task before her, the thought of the dungeon made her shudder again as she measured out the soap. She had never realized that the Inquisitors had been priests who had turned on fellow priests as well as laymen and never had she ever given much thought to just how horrible it must have been even though she had read about it during her seven year search for Mark when he had left her in Texas after Valentino's death. It had never been real to her and now she had the urgent desire to lash out at someone, anyone. To demand an apology or to seek retribution or justice or revenge on the behalf of all the innocent people who had suffered and died needlessly. If she ever saw that insidious priest again in this world or the next, she would... Lucio's voice startled her from her dark thoughts. She jumped and let go a small shriek, before looking up at him in consternation.

"Sleep well?" He asked her blandly.

She shook her head and squinted more closely at the label on the soap box to hide her feelings. "If you can call sleeping on the floor wearing chain mail and boots, sleeping well, then, yes."

"Brother Ramsay has always been a bit rough around the edges. Perhaps he prefers the floor to his bed, no?" He continued in a dark vein and she snapped her head up again to glare at him.

He had spied on her. Just when she had been thinking such guilt-ridden thoughts about him, trying to forgive him for his trespasses...

"Don't start with me, Lucio," she told him and slammed the surcoat in the washer angrily. "Nothing happened!"

"I have done everything I can to keep you from making a terrible mistake, Merry," his voice softened a bit. "You are doing nothing to help this situation. If you continue to throw yourself at his feet, he is going to give in."

"Give in?" Her voice rose and her eyes snapped at the unintended insult. "Just what are you trying to say, Lucio? That I am at fault here? That I have to beg you sorry bastards to sleep with me? You are beyond comprehension! How dare you..." she dropped the soap and swung a fist at his jaw.

He side-stepped and caught her fist against his palm and laughed.

"See? You still love me," he said and she jerked her fist away from him.

Merry turned her attention back to the wash. It was a set up. He was trying to make her mad. She suddenly hated herself.

"I guess you think you're trying to help things, I suppose?" she said more calmly than she felt. Three seconds and he had her. How could he do that? She was not in the mood.

"I am," he nodded confidently. "I have told you everything I know. I have told you of my undying love for you. I have told you..."

"Stop it!" she snapped at him and stepped past him as the washing machine began to make strange little squeaking noises. "Won't you just go somewhere and grow a beard and leave me the hell alone!"

Lucio reached to feel his face again with a puzzled frown before following her down the hall and out the back door. He wondered how she had known that he was contemplating growing a beard to add some bulk to his face. Had she become a mindreader?

Merry did not want Bruce Roberts to hear them arguing. If he was going to force her to have it out here and now, then so be it, but they would do it without an audience. She flung open the door, intending to lead him outside, but he grabbed her arm, spinning her around. She backed out the door, dragging him with her and stopped on the top step.

"Let... go of me!" She almost shouted at him.

The Knight held onto her hand and fell to his knees in front of her.

"Merry, Merry, give me just one moment. My life is empty without you. Without your touch. Without your face, your eyes, your voice to soothe my aching heart, I am nothing. You are my life, my love and the only reason that my heart still beats. Marry me, Meredith Sinclair and I will give you the world. I will buy you a palazzo in Palermo. We can live like royalty there and no one would bother us. I swear it!" He crossed his heart and then crossed himself in the Catholic manner. "I love you," he added.

The look in his eyes was hard to bear. When she did not answer, he pressed her hand to his lips and rolled off several lines in Italian. The tone of his voice was unmistakably full of grief and desperation and she thought he would actually cry any moment. Though the words he spoke sounded like something out of one of her hokey romance novels, she knew they came from his heart, unrehearsed and her own heart skipped several beats before catching on again. How could she hurt him so and live to love another man without thinking of him every time she kissed Mark Andrew? It wasn't fair! It wasn't fair to her or them and she hated herself even more.

She stood staring down at him, not knowing what to say. He was begging her and the sight of it made her sick in her soul. What would she do? What could she do? She would much rather have fought with him.

Merry jerked her hand away from him and turned to flee down the steps. At the bottom step, she froze. Simon, Champlain, de Lyons and d'Brouchart sat around the glass-topped patio table looking at them with various expressions on their faces, ranging from barely suppressed laughter to consternation to surprise. She turned very slowly to look back up the steps at Lucio, who was still on his knees with a very peculiar look on his own face.

"What was that, Brother?" Champlain called to the Italian from where he sat. "I didn't quite catch that last part."

Merry's face flushed with embarrassment. How much had they heard?

"I said..." Lucio stood up quickly and spoke more loudly. "Would you please wash my uniform for me, Meredith? I don't know how to use Mark Andrew's antique monstrosities. Do not make me beg any more."

Merry blinked rapidly at him and then sighed in relief.

"Of course," she said stiffly. "Just bring it down to the washroom."

"*Grace, Signorina,*" he smiled and raised both eyebrows before turning on his heel to retreat into the house.

Merry drew a deep breath, calmed herself forcefully and turned to walk casually toward the table as if this had been her intention all along.

"Good morning, Brothers," she smiled sweetly at them and went to sit next to Simon who now seemed her only refuge in the storm. They nodded solemnly to her as she looked at each of them in turn.

"And what did you say to Brother Lucio's question?" Simon looked sidelong at her.

"I said of course I would," she told him. "I would do the same for you if you asked me."

At that, Champlain slapped the Healer on the back nearly sending him onto the pavement and burst out laughing. De Lyons sat shaking his head and chuckling softly. Simon sat staring at her with his mouth hanging open.

"What!" she frowned at them as a terrible suspicion washed over her.

"Simon? What did you hear?" She asked, her voice full of barely controlled anger.

Simon swallowed hard and leaned to whisper in her ear.

"He said that you break his heart, that he lay down his life for you and you step on him. He called you his love and his life and asked you to marry him... twice. Once in English, once in Italian." As Simon whispered to her, the color drained completely from her face. "He also said that one kiss from you would send him to heaven. That one I could use, but the rest..." Simon sat back and tilted one hand to and fro. "I don't know."

210

Meredith Nichole Sinclair, Chevaliere *d'Sagesse du Solomon*, sat stone-faced for several long moments with her hands folded in her lap, staring into space. Then, without warning, she slammed the chair back, turning it over on the bricks and ran toward the back door of the house.

"You certainly have a way with women, Brother," Champlain slapped Simon again and laughed loudly. Simon nodded and smiled sickly at him before turning a frown on the Grand Master. The Frankish Knight's words brought back a terrible memory. Surely it had all been a dream. And what the girl had said about his father... it just could not be true.

Merry burst through the back door and stormed down the hall to the kitchen, intending to find Lucio and make him pay for causing her such embarrassment. Now she would be the butt of their jokes until something else came along and she had already learned that their memories were as long as their lives. She drew up short at the sight of Mark Andrew and Lucio sitting at the table facing each other silently over breakfast. They both looked up at her expectantly. She opened her mouth, closed her mouth and then stomped off toward the front of the house.

Lucio looked at Mark and shrugged.

Mark raised both eyebrows and then frowned. Perhaps she was still mad at him for what he had said earlier. Who could tell?

Chapter Twelve of Seventeen
The beast that thou sawest was, and is not; and shall ascend out of the bottomless pit

The departure of the Knights and the Grand Master at noon left Merry with a number of unanswered questions and an unsettling outlook on the near future and what could and would happen to them next.

They would go back to Italy where they would gather the latest intelligence on Abdul Hafiz al Sajek and then the team consisting of Ramsay, Champlain and Cambrique would travel on to America to recover the missing Key. She had asked Simon in private about the success rate of such missions and he'd assured her that it was quite high in spite of the disasters they had faced in the past fifteen years. The objective didn't sound so terrible now, standing in the bright noonday sun on the steps of the big house, but Merry still had misgivings about Mark's attitude, which seemed to be a mixture of disgust, anger and resignation. He had spent most of the morning in the cellar with Lucio. She had found several excuses to go down the stairs during the morning and stopped to listen, but had heard nothing from behind the partially open lab door. At least they were being civil to each other.

Von Hetz had not come down from his room until just before everyone had departed. He had pulled her aside and told her to keep a close watch on Simon d'Ornan and to let him know immediately if anything seemed amiss with the Healer, promising to come back at once if need be. Lucio had avoided contact with her as if she were a leper. He obviously did not want to hear what she would say to him when she had the chance. Her cheeks still burned from the embarrassment he had caused her in front of the Master. She'd not had the chance to thank him properly for making a fool of her and she was worried that Mark would hear about it from Champlain who was always in the market for entertaining stories. Now the Italian stood on the porch less than three feet from her, watching as their Brothers and her ramparts wound their way down the long drive and disappeared beyond the hedgerow, heading for Edinburgh and beyond. She glanced at him once or twice and made up her mind that she would not be made miserable by his presence. She had enough to worry about with Mark's mission and John Paul's strange behavior in Italy.

Surprisingly, when they were out of sight, he did nothing more than let out a long sigh of relief and she saw his shoulders droop slightly. It was almost as if a visible weight descended on him even as she watched from the corner of her eye. Was her presence that unnerving? She wanted to ask him, but there was no time. Instead of looking at her as she expected him to do, he turned away from her and started for the front door, but the sound of a truck motor stopped him.

A United Parcel Service truck passed the cars in the drive and bounced to a stop in front of the steps.

Lucio glanced at her as a young man slid out of the van and dragged a brown package out of the floor of the truck. The delivery man looked up at them and waved before heading their way.

"My flowers!" Simon's voice startled both of them. The Healer squeezed between them and went to meet the young fellow on the walkway. His face lit up when he examined the paper work and it was the first time she had seen him truly smile in quite awhile.

"Flowers?" Lucio asked and glanced briefly at Merry again before following Simon down the steps to greet the delivery man, leaving her on the steps.

Merry went back in the house, shaking her head. They had all the time in the world. She would have her chance to speak to Lucio eventually and already, her anger was dissipating as she realized that it was virtually baseless. But the thought of spending all the time in the world with Lucio, made her cringe. It simply wouldn't work. At least the Grand Master had the good sense to leave Simon with them. Certainly d'Brouchart would not want to leave the chapel without a keeper while Mark Andrew was away. Even with the Ark sealed in the crypt, there were other things there to be considered. Mark had no apprentice to take care of his work now... or did he? Things had a way of coming full circle it seemed. Dambretti had started out his career in the Order as Ramsay's squire and moved on to be his apprentice. Strangely enough, he was now taking his place... temporarily. Lucio would be working in the laboratory on something for the Grand Master. She had learned this also from von Hetz who had given her a second cryptic warning to keep an eye on the 'activities' in the lab and to let him know if Sir Dambretti needed his help. All these things were coursing through her mind as she made her way to the computer and sat down to find where she had left off her studies in what now seemed ages ago. It was incredible to think that things would return abruptly to 'normal' at the estate while they waited to hear from the mission to America. It was as if they lived entirely outside the rest of the world and nothing else existed apart from the Order. She checked her e-mail and found nothing, but on the news page a story caught her eye on the international front.

A surprise attack by an unidentified terrorist faction in Axum, Ethiopia had resulted in twenty-seven deaths and the complete destruction of the two Churches inside the walls of the compound of Saint Mary of Zion! The place where the Ark of the Covenant had lain concealed, yet

213

unconcealed, for hundreds of years. The article, replete with photos and a short video, showed the devastation. The older cathedral was nothing more than a burned out shell and the newer church built by Ethiopia's president in the 1960's was completely leveled. The Treasury building was a smoking hole in the ground. The article gave several possible motives for the attack, blaming first one and then another of three opposing guerrilla groups. Ethiopia's crumbling governmental jurisdiction was operating in a semi-vacuum inside the country's disputed borders. The same religious war was raging out of control in Ethiopia just as it had been in the middle east for the past 2000 years. Jews, Christians and Muslims. But now she probably understood it much better than most of the rest of the world. The article showed the local populace in an uproar over the destruction of their churches and mentioned briefly that the fabled mystery concerning the Ark of the Covenant had been put to rest, since it was not found in the ruins. Merry marveled at the ignorance of the general population of the world. Of course it wouldn't have been in the ruins. Whoever had destroyed the churches were probably looking for it. Treasure hunters most likely and if it had still been there, it would have been taken or there would have been a much more spectacular tale to tell.

The Grand Master had known this would happen. This was why he had moved the Ark. How had he known? What else did he know?

Simon and Lucio passed the library doors, heading toward the kitchen, carrying two large brown boxes wrapped in plastic. She pushed back her chair and followed after them. They would want to hear this news. If the Ark had remained in Axum, it would now be either destroyed or in the wrong hands at the very least. As she walked down the hall, another, more interesting, thought occurred to her.

(((((((((((((<O>)))))))))))))

The Council meeting was brief and to the point.

The Church of Saint Mary of Zion had been destroyed and most of the clergy there had been killed. The attackers were as yet unidentified and had left no word or indication concerning the motive behind the pre-dawn invasion of the church grounds. Ethiopia was in an uproar. Internationally, everyone was blaming everyone else, but none of the usual suspects had claimed responsibility for the attack. Whoever had done it, was well organized, well armed and completely anonymous. State of the art weaponry instantly discredited the idea that the attack had come from one of the wandering bands of disenfranchised Muslim factions. What was even more interesting was that none of the holy relics and valuable church artifacts and

214

accouterments had been taken after the explosions which had, oddly enough, destroyed the outer walls of the buildings, killed the people in and around them, but left the interiors fairly intact. The videos released by the press, had shown a number of gold and silver items sitting upright in their proper places throughout the smoking rubble. Plunder had not been the motivational factor. That much was certain. And the actual nature of the explosion was left unexplained. There had been no eye witnesses to the explosions.

Of the twenty-seven killed in the destruction, seven had been shot in the head, close-range, execution style murders. Something that the press did not and would not know, was that all seven were members of the Order of the Poor Knights of Solomon's Temple. Lay brethren. And though this bit of information escaped the news reporters and government officials, it did not escape the Grand Master. This was bad news indeed, but not unexpected. He had moved the Ark as a precaution, but his field agents had assured him that the plot to steal the Ark had been thwarted. Whoever these latest attackers had been, they had been after something specific and they had not found it. They would try again.

"The Assassins, or Holy Killers of Islam, were responsible for the attack," d'Brouchart announced with finality. "The object of their search was the Ark. I am not sure why they have decided to go after it now, but we must assume that they have reasons for wanting it. It is quite possible that Abdul Hafiz al Sajek knows what he has in his possession and now wants the toy box. He most likely thinks to open the Ark with the misguided idea that he can use it to add to his mystical powers. He is a formidable foe, but not beyond folly. Make no mistake about his abilities, Brothers." The Grand Master turned his gaze on Mark Andrew and spoke directly to his own Assassin. "He is extremely dangerous and very old. I have heard rumors and rumors of rumors about him all my life. This will be our first direct encounter with him. His only weakness is his supreme arrogance and self-confidence. As with many of the more powerful entities inhabiting the earth's twilight zone, he considers himself invincible as long as he works towards the fulfillment of his own prophetic vision. He carries few, if any, attendants with him and I have it on good authority that he has only two assistants with him in America at the present time. He relies on his anonymity, sorcery and his magickal skills to protect himself. He moves unseen through the world. So far, this has worked very well for him. Most people do not even know he exists. That gives us an advantage. We may be able to take him unawares, but it is unlikely that he would assume that such a thing as the Golden Key would come to him with no strings attached. That he singled out the Templars in Ethiopia and had them executed would indicate that he knows of our involvement there. He will be expecting retaliation. Let us hope and pray that he does not know exactly what or who will be coming for him or when.

"Our sources tell us that he goes out every evening just before dusk and every morning just before dawn, alone. He goes into the wilderness, stays a few hours and then returns to his hotel, where he has been negotiating the purchase of the land he seems to have such an interest in. What significance this particular parcel of property holds for him is unknown. I have some people working on that end, but so far this parcel of land seems no different than any other piece of real estate in the same general area." The Master paused to glance at von Hetz before continuing. "It is a wild area just south of a city called Tallahassee. The state capitol, I believe. It is forested and presently used only for hiking and camping... tourists. Most bothersome industry. Tourists! But I digress. I would suggest, Brothers, that you find this place," the Master paused to tap one meaty index finger on a rather outdated map of Florida. "... and take him in the forest!" The Master gritted his teeth and emphasized his words by clenching one fist in the air. "Take his head, du Morte! I want it here," he pointed at the table in front of him "and I want that Key. You cannot fail in this mission, Sir. Philip will have all the necessary documents for transport after the fact and I have already made a call to His Excellency, the Pope," d'Brouchart paused and frowned at Ramsay. The Knight blinked at him as if only just waking up from a dream. "But mark this, Brother. Do not kill him before you have the Key in your possession. Bury his body deep and come home posthaste. Is that understood?" Mark nodded slightly. "Sir Barry, if you will, Gentlemen." The Master took a seat and the Knight of the Baldric took charge of the meeting.

Sir Barry passed out sheets of paper with detailed maps of the particular area in question for them to peruse. The wilderness area was not vast, but it was big enough to make finding one man lost inside it a considerable task. It was criss-crossed with unpaved roads and hiking trails and not far from civilization on any side. They would have to be very careful not to involve any local bystanders. Barry used an impressive computer generated holographic display produced by Armand de Bleu, showing three dimensional images of the area, maps and local statistical data projected onto a smoky film in the center of the table. Only one blurry snapshot of their target was available and gave little real information to go on. Mark watched only long enough to smile slightly at the pride exhibited by the schoolmaster as he showed off a new skill. Holograms on the Council Table. What would they think of next? Indoor plumbing? The Knight raised his cup and the Master's valet came at once to refill it as had been the tradition for many centuries.

Mark Andrew listened only sporadically to Barry as he concentrated on the map turning in front of him. He had already heard all of this and more from von Hetz. He had already seen the map on paper in von Hetz' quarters. Several points of interest were marked with Xs. Streams, campgrounds, sinkholes and waterfalls. It was fascinating to see them with all the bumps and vales depicted and he had to resist the urge to reach out and touch the image. All the information he needed was already inside his head. The roads were categorized by the type of traffic for which it was designed. Foot, bike, motorized vehicles. The man traveled on foot, they said. He would be making for one of the more remote areas which was also marked on the map in florescent blue lines. This was the property that he was attempting to buy. In the center was a rather sizable sinkhole with a natural waterfall pouring into it. Barry zoomed in on the waterfall and the map transformed into an actual video of the waterfall and the sinkhole that panned a full three-sixty. Beautiful! That would be the place, no doubt.

Mark didn't know why he thought so; it just seemed natural. He would want seclusion to perform his magickal rites most likely. It sounded simple enough, but he knew better. Finding and taking the man might be easy, but making him give up the Key would be something entirely different. It would be very surprising to find him carrying such a relic on his person, alone in the woods, no less. Much too convenient for their purposes. They would probably have to kidnap him and force him to take them back to his hotel in order to get the thing. Coercion was not his cup of tea. He wished that Barry would be coming with them or better yet, the Apocalyptic Knight. Von Hetz could learn the whereabouts of the Key, but then von Hetz had told him that the Master feared al Sajek's powers. The Ritter had actually volunteered for the mission, but d'Brouchart was against having him look into al Sajek's mind, fearing destruction for the German Knight.

They would be leaving in two hours. He had enough time to call home, but he wondered why he wanted to do it. Surely it would be just another of those odd and awkward moments that had passed for communication. The Grand Master was still talking, going on about the Assassins, relating some of the stranger stories he had heard about them and their connection to the ancient knowledge of the Sumerians, the Babylonians and the Akkadians. All subjects Mark Andrew had no interest in. He already had his plan. He and Champlain would protect Sir Philip and Sir Philip would deal with Abdul Hafiz. Simple. They would get the Key and come home. If they had to kill the man, he had no problem with that either, but bringing his head home... why? He only wanted to get home to Scotland and rest. Do nothing. Just rest and take his home back from Lucio Dambretti. If Merry wanted to stay, fine. If not, fine. He was tired of the whole situation. Simple.

"Is that what it looks like to you, Sir Ramsay?"

He looked up quickly when he heard his name pronounced with a distinctively French accent and almost knocked over his goblet in the process. Sir Philip was addressing him and he had no idea what he was talking about. He frowned at Barry who had resumed his seat and wondered when they had changed speakers.

"Your pardon, Brother? I'm sorry. What was the question?"

"Sir Philip feels that perhaps you might have some insight as to al Sajek's motives. The Necronomicon is supposedly similar to some of the darker alchemical wisdom which is your specialty," d'Brouchart repeated Philip's question and scowled at the Knight.

"The Necronomicon?" Ramsay asked in surprise and looked around at them in confusion. "I don't believe it has anything to do with my... field of expertise, your Grace. I have heard it said that only fools would delve into such a dangerous document... if it truly exists and I have heard it said on good authority that it was a fabrication conjured on paper by H.P. Lovecraft, but I hold with the old Dominican claim to fame. Furthermore, it would be in line with Brother Philip's own mystery or perhaps Sister Meredith's Wisdom. I do not believe that any Necronomicon is of practical value to anyone other than the ancients who penned it. I'm not too fond of..."

"Abdul Hafiz is not a fool, Brother," d'Brouchart growled at him, cutting him off. Mark's face darkened with embarrassment. "He wrote the cursed thing. Your H.P. Lovecraft may have been a fool, but this gentleman is not! Your arrogant indifference will get you killed. If you are not practicing your Art, Sir, I suggest you get to it."

The book of the dead concerning the Sumerians dealt with convocations and invocations of ancient pagan gods and evil spirits and something called the Ancient Ones or Old Ones, who supposedly ruled the earth before the time of man. Creatures of the Abyss. He had thought that Abdul Hafiz had only translated the Testimony of the Mad Assassin. But this could not be true. He had obviously missed something in Barry's lecture. The Grand Master's admonition irked him greatly. Practicing his Art? What the hell was he talking about?

"I deal with concoctions and decoctions, your Grace, not rites, rituals and witchcraft. With the help of Sir Champlain and the blessings of God, I will protect Sir Cambrique while he does whatever it is he does. We will get the Key and come home. Necronomicon be damned!" The *Chevalier du Morte* uttered these words with more vehemence than he intended. A round of 'ayes' followed as his Brothers agreed with him and spoke quietly amongst themselves for a moment.

The Grand Master leaned back in his chair and smiled. Mark Andrew was momentarily put out by the Master's reaction to his outburst. Presently, the Master leaned forward and began to speak again.

"Abdul Hafiz is a ninth degree Assassin. He believes that there is no such thing as 'belief'. He believes all that matters is action and these actions are to be carried out only by the leader of the group, namely himself. According to Sir Philip, his workings are closely tied with astrology and the phases of the moon. His rituals are long and involved and he has apparently been carrying on these unholy rites for the past nine days. The present signs in the heavens and the phase of the moon would indicate that he had been invoking the Nine Names of Power to help him with whatever it is he is planning to do. Sir Philip, of course, has not been doing this and therefore will not be prepared to meet him on an equal footing. Sir Philip will be hard-pressed to defend himself against these powers, but will invoke the name of God and of Christ Jesus to help him. He will then ask God to protect all of you and you will have to rely on God's power to overcome the evil ones."

Mark Andrew felt a dark depression coming on. He had had enough of the occult to last him for a very long time. Now he was going to face something much more powerful than a few specters in a dusty tomb. He crossed himself sub-consciously and the rest of the men at the table followed suit. He knew in his heart that, had he asked them, all these good fellows would have accompanied him on the mission.

"I will be in the chapel for the next two hours." D'Brouchart stood up and prepared to leave the chamber. He glanced at Sir Philip before leaving the table. "I expect to hear your confessions before you leave... Brothers."

((((((((((((<O>))))))))))))

Abdul Hafiz al Sajek closed the screen on his laptop computer and sat back in the dim light of his motel room staring into space. The raid on the two buildings in Axum had turned up nothing, just as he expected. He had learned long ago not to ignore his intuitions. Although he had not thought seriously about taking the Ark until a few days earlier, his sleep had been marked with references to the relic too much to be coincidence. The ex-Templar had not been lying about the chapel on Mark Ramsay's property. There were great things hidden in Scotland. Devereaux was dead now, but it had not been by his hand and he no longer needed the man anyway. What worried him was how much he had given up before his death. Philipe Devereaux had simply been a weak link in the Templar chain and they had let him go too far before eliminating him. Perhaps they were growing soft or senile in their old age. He smiled to himself. In the elder days, they would never have let the man go in the first place. One man's loss is another man's gain. Always true. If the Templars sent someone against him, he would use them to hone his rusty personal talents of self defense.

Tonight at midnight, he would summon the keepers of the gate. Tomorrow night, he would cast the first oblation into the pit. It was written in the stars and he had seen it in the waters. The bottomless black waters.

219

((((((((((((<O>))))))))))))

Mark Andrew threw his bag in the trunk of the rented Mercedes and then walked back through the main building and out onto the sun porch. He stood for a moment looking toward the Academy where he knew John Paul would be in class. He stuffed his hands in his pockets and walked slowly across the grounds to the white building accented by tall, darkly tinted windows and a bright, red-tiled roof. He had never been inside the Academy. How long had the building been there? He couldn't remember a time when it had not stood thus, full of sweaty palms and squirrely-smelling boys with wide eyes and devious minds. John Paul was in the third room he checked, along with six other young men. When he opened the door and stepped inside, the old priest scratching on the blackboard with a piece of yellow chalk, stopped in mid-sentence and looked at him expectantly. A diagram of an ancient temple was drawn in blue chalk on the board and the teacher had been labeling it in yellow, in French. Mark had to frown at the thought of his practically mute son understanding French. Archaeology? Six pairs of eyes scrutinized him intently. The Knight of Death, *oui*!

"*Excusez-moi, père.* John Paul, un moment, *se'el vous plait,*" he said simply and turned to walk back down the hall and back outside onto the broad steps.

The boy joined him momentarily, blinking in the late afternoon sunshine that slanted through the oak trees in front of the academy. Mark was surprised to see a hint of greenery peeking from beneath his hair behind his right ear. He frowned slightly and leaned a bit closer. Some sort of fuzzy green leaf protruded from the dark strands of hair. John Paul cleared his throat, but did not look at his father. Instead, he scanned the grounds under the olive trees as if looking for something there.

What had he come to say to the boy? He didn't know.

"John Paul," he said and cleared his own throat nervously. The boy's face lit up and the hint of a smile played about his lips. "I am leaving for America in a few minutes."

The boy nodded.

"I wanted to say goodbye." It sounded so lame. "I wanted to tell you... I wanted you to know that I may be gone a long time."

John Paul nodded again. A small frown creased his smooth forehead.

"I wanted to ask you to look after your mother, I mean, check on her from time to time. Keep in touch with her. She misses you." Mark was screwing it all up. He was not accustomed to saying such things or asking such things of anyone. "She needs you... she loves you."

John Paul nodded.

220

"John…" Mark sighed and looked up at the sky through the tree branches. "If I were falling in a pit, would you… help me out?"

The boy's expression changed. He raised both eyebrows and then turned quickly to face Mark Andrew. He hugged his father, catching him by surprise and then pushed him back and lowered his head to look at him from under his brows. It was almost like looking in the mirror. So solemn. So intense.

"Papa," John Paul spoke to his father for the first time in weeks. "The beast that thou sawest was, and is not; and shall ascend out of the bottomless pit. I will see you when you get back."

Mark stood blinking at him for several seconds, speechless and then the boy turned and went back inside the building without saying anything further. It was more than his son had ever said to him at one time in the eight years he had known him. That John Paul knew of his dream, there was no doubt. At least his words were hopeful. He had seen something from the past. Something that no longer existed. Mark nodded to himself and then smiled slightly before heading back to the parking lot where Champlain would no doubt be wondering where he was. John Paul would be a survivor. The boy had tricks up his sleeve. He'd planned on telling him that he loved him, but it just hadn't worked out.

By the time he reached the car, his depression had returned twofold. And his nerves were on edge. It would be a very long flight and they would have to change planes twice. He hoped the flight and the excruciating process at the airport would go well. He didn't want to have to kill any flight attendants on the way to America just to calm his nerves.

(((((((((((((<O>)))))))))))))

Simon refused to be distracted from his flowers. He was busily laying them out around the bricks of the patio while Lucio and Merry sat at the table, drinking lemonade, watching him curiously. The sun poked its head through the low clouds intermittently trying its best to keep them warm just a bit longer before it retired for the fall's long dream into winter. Merry had tried, quite unsuccessfully, to tell him that gardening was something one did in the spring, not the fall. He had wasted his money and now he was wasting his time. The frost would come and the flowers would die. It seemed a terrible shame to her and she was beginning to become worried about him. Simon had only smiled at her when she had told him that his efforts were in vain. Smiled at her as if she were a silly child and knew nothing of gardening and flowers. He had listened to the news of the attack on the churches in Axum the day before with a frown etched on his face, but had

221

made no comment on it. Lucio, on the other hand, had been very upset. He actually knew one of the priests there. It seemed that the Italian had made more than one pilgrimage to the Church of Saint Mary of Zion.

The previous night had proven uneventful as her anger with Lucio had culminated in a quiet apology accepted and a promised truce in the foyer just before bed. The following morning, Bruce had called them down for a grand breakfast after which Lucio had phoned Italy to check on the affairs of the Villa and to learn what, if anything would be forthcoming concerning the attack in Axum. Sir Philip had taken his call and told him that, essentially, none of their immediate plans were to be affected and to continue on with his work as assigned until further notice. Merry had spent the remainder of the morning studying in the library. After lunch, she and Lucio had followed Simon outside to see exactly what he was up to. So far, Lucio had been a gentleman in every respect and she greatly appreciated it even to the point of making a fresh pitcher of lemonade to take with them and they had sat down together in silence to watch Simon's endeavors.

Lucio had his own reasons for feeling uneasy. If the people responsible for the brutal attack had been after the Ark, their position in Scotland might have just become extremely dangerous. Lucio had expressed his concerns to Philip and Philip had assured him that he would pass them along to the Master. The last thing that Dambretti wanted was the responsibility of taking care of himself, Meredith, Simon and Ramsay's cook against treasure-hunting pirates with superior firepower, looking for ancient relics. He doubted that they were nothing more than common criminals out to make money and had possibly been hired by this al Sajek person. The television had shown him enough to know that whoever they were, they possessed a formidable arsenal and expert demolition talent. He didn't think that a few broadswords and game rifles would profit them much should the same people show up looking for the Ark in Scotland, the second most popular resting place of legend for the relic. Of course, Mark's chapel was not in the same category as the more famous Roslyn Chapel, but Roslyn was not that far away as the crow flies and there were more enlightened individuals in the world than the popular modern day Grail hunters. It was entirely possible that interested parties might know of Glessyn and Mark Ramsay's estate in Lothian. His only consolation was that both Simon and Merry seemed unaware of how much danger they might be in. He would have to talk to Simon and Bruce about it before the day was out, but he wasn't sure how to handle Meredith. Certainly, she had come a long way, but...

"Do you think anyone knows?" She asked suddenly, interrupting his thoughts.

Lucio turned his head slowly to look at her and sipped his lemonade through a twisted straw he'd found in one of the kitchen drawers.

"About what?" He asked almost languidly.

"About… you know," she frowned at him, unwilling to say it aloud. She suddenly felt that even the crows sitting on the peak of the roof might be spies.

"The chapel?" He raised both eyebrows and then leaned back to stretch his arms over his head.

"Si`, the chapel," she nodded in irritation and mocked his accent.

"Of course," he told her and returned his attention to the Healer, who was laying out the lily bulbs in uniform rows in the grass, moving them and rearranging them again and again within the stakes and strings he had strung into triangular shapes around the patio. "There are many people who know of the chapel."

"I mean, do they really know about the chapel?" She asked without looking at him. Simon was opening the second box, murmuring to himself like a madman.

"Does anyone really know anything?" He asked and waved one hand at the Healer. He was surprised at her question and totally unprepared to deal with her. "Look at Simon, for instance. Does anyone really know what he is thinking? Does anyone really know how he feels?" He did not want to talk about the Ark. He would rather hear about what had gone on in the Healer's room.

"You are evading my question," she leaned back in the chair. As to his question, she thought she might have some bit of insight into the Healer's mind, but she would not be telling Lucio about it.

"You are the expert at evading questions," he told her and smiled. "You have been evading my questions for nine years."

"Do you think we should call the Villa again?" she ignored his remarks. "Perhaps they should send someone… soldiers, perhaps. To protect the... our... our interests."

"Soldiers?" He looked at her in surprise. This was exactly what he had requested, but the Master had not answered him either on the subject. "The object you are worried about is sealed in the crypt. You saw it. Even if someone goes down there, they will not know where to look. It's as if the room never existed. Besides, it is protected by Divine Providence." He tried to assuage her fears, but Lucio was not so sure. Who said anyone would simply 'go down there'? He didn't relish the thought of being shot in the head and left for dead. They had blown up the churches in Axum and executed the Templars stationed there. Their deaths could not have been coincidences. Why would the modus operandi change here? He had suffered a stab wound to the brain once before in the seventeenth century and it had taken him years to recover completely from it. Immortality had its perks, but they were not completely immune to destruction. The memory of the excruciating headaches he had suffered before Thomas Willis, a renowned neuroanatomist at Oxford University had finally removed a shard of the blade from his left temporal lobe was still fresh in his mind, pardon the pun. This memory was also attached to Mark Ramsay who had finally convinced the surgeon to perform brain surgery in a time when such procedures usually caused more damage or proved fatal. Why was it that almost all of his significant memories concerned Ramsay? He wondered inanely if Mark still had connections with Oxford... if they might be willing to remove the scar from his face. He had considered it many times, but Simon had chastised him for his vanity and Mark had told him that the scar would come back because it had been there at the time of his induction into the Council of Twelve. Mark was probably right or else the Grand Master could lose weight and grow his hair back, Barry could correct the crookedly healed bone in his left arm that gave him such fits on rainy days and Simon could seek treatment for his affliction. Of course, Simon's problem couldn't ever be healed, perhaps least some of his symptoms could be treated. Lucio patted his chest where the numerous Egyptian tattoos he had earned almost seven hundred years earlier never faded, but remained as crisp and black as the first days after he received them. But then, if the tattoos had not been eradicated by his modified immune system then perhaps...

"I understand that it was taken before. Where was Divine Providence then?" She asked him, interrupting his meandering thoughts again.

"It was Divine Providence that caused it to be taken," he said defensively. "The Israelites had fallen from grace. God intended them to lose it. Now he intends us to keep it for them. We will keep it until He wills otherwise."

"It's so simple for you, isn't it?" She turned a frown on him and then looked away in disgust.

"Yes," he nodded. "Yes, it is very simple. And it should be simple for you, as well. I am here and you are here. And that is the way it should be today, tomorrow, next week."

"And Simon is here and Bruce is here. Are we talking about the chapel now?" She asked.

"Yes and no." He raised his eyes to glance at the crows. There were now a half a dozen on the roof. Crows were never good omens and these looked especially large and unfriendly. "The chapel surrounds its treasures and keeps them hidden. You surround your feelings and keep them hidden. Your heart is sealed. The crypt is sealed. You are inside the walls of your defenses. I am the Crusader outside those walls. But God is on my side. I will break them down. Simon is available to make it all legal and Bruce can be our witness. Simple. When Brother Ramsay returns from his mission, the subject will be closed and we can leave him with his lab and his chapel and his dogs. Meredith, for God's sake. Mark Ramsay does not need a woman weighing him down. He has everything he needs right here... without you. It has always been so. He doesn't know how to treat a lady. He doesn't know how to be a husband and a father. I, on the other, am quite capable of making you happy and I happen to love children."

"Did anyone ever tell you that you are an arrogant bastard?" She asked him in consternation.

"Yes," he said lightly. "The Grand Master told me that less than a week ago, Sister." He sipped on his lemonade and looked away from her. "This is very good, Meredith. It reminds of a little patio party I once attended in Waco, Texas. Have you ever been there? The sky is blue, the land spreads out forever and the women are beyond understanding. We might even want to buy a vacation home there. I hear it's nice in the hill country and that they even have their own wine labels."

He was impossible.

Merry fell silent as Simon began to lay out the purple amaranths in front of the lilies. It made no sense. The Healer seemed to have forgotten they were there. Why was he doing this? Planting spring and summer flowers at the onset of cold weather?

"Brother?" Merry decided to ignore Lucio altogether and focused her attention to the Healer.

Simon twisted his head to look at her from an awkward angle as if startled by her presence.

"Do you have extensive experience with gardening?" She asked him doubtfully.

"Not flowers," he shook his head. "I used to grow herbs and vegetables for eating. We live in a land of abundance, Sister. Things were not always so. It has been a long time since a kitchen garden meant the difference between living well or going hungry."

"Well," she said as she left her seat by the table and went to where the Healer was crawling in the grass. "You have ordered a strange mixture. Are those lilies?"

"Yes. They are called the Sceau du Solomon and these are amaranths, the purple ones, and these blue ones, violets." He pointed at the bulbs and seedlings strewn about the thick grass. His French accent always made her smile.

Merry knelt in the grass and examined the dried out bulbs and tender young plants.

"You want these to bloom all at the same time, I guess?" She raised both eyebrows doubtfully.

"Of course. That is the plan," he nodded and stood up to look at the patterns he had arranged with satisfaction.

"I'm afraid it won't happen, Brother," she shook her head sadly and tried again. "Lilies are early spring bloomers and violets are late spring flowers. Amaranths bloom all summer. You couldn't have gotten a more

225

widely spaced variety as far as blooming times. The violets that bloomed in the meadows here were a wild variety and I'm not sure they were... natural. Too late in the year."

"That's all right, Sister," he smiled. "They will bloom when they are supposed to bloom. You are a woman of science and I am a man of faith."

Merry smiled a frown at him and shrugged. He had a point.

"They will be glorious," Simon announced with confidence.

There was something about his expression that made her wonder. Why was he so seemingly unconcerned about the news from Ethiopia? Just when she thought she was beginning to understand him, she found she didn't. And Lucio's nonchalant attitude about the Ark bothered her immensely. Was he just being over confident to try to make her feel safe, or was he truly unconcerned? She didn't understand him either. And she certainly didn't understand Mark. He had seemed almost cold to her before he had left, barely giving her a peck on the cheek and as far as he should have been concerned, they were still engaged. She was his *fiancee*, his beloved. She had waited all morning in vain for him to arrange some few moments alone with her before he left, but it never happened. Glancing over her shoulder at the Italian who had put on his sunshades and laid his head back on the lounger, she knew that he would have made something happen had he been in Mark's shoes. She wished she had someone subjective to discuss it all with, but who would ever believe it?

Chapter Thirteen of Seventeen
the Lord our God is righteous in all his works

Sir Philip had gotten the odd man out room to himself at the motel and was there praying and preparing himself. Mark Andrew did not know what the Seneschal was doing, nor did he care. The man had been in his room for hours, even skipping lunch with his companions, much to Louis' disappointment. Champlain preferred company and conversation whenever he was nervous and the Frankish Knight was nervous. Mark, on the other hand, had the habit of becoming more and more quiet as the hours passed and the time for action approached. It had taken a great deal of wine to persuade Champlain that the afternoon would be better spent sleeping than talking. The Frankish Knight had drifted off in the middle of a story just after two PM local time, leaving Mark Andrew the peace and quiet he desired. Peaceful except for Louis' snoring, which was formidable. Once he had adjusted to the noise, he felt almost like his old self, with the exception of the depression that still nagged him concerning Meredith and Lucio and the vague idea that he had seen his home for the last time. Now the afternoon was passing at a snail's pace and he knew that he had to brush aside his personal troubles in order to bring his full faculties to bear on the mission at hand. Get to al Sajek and recover the Key. Mark had no interest in America. The place held only bad memories for the Knight of Death and it was a vast, unexplored territory as far as he was concerned, governed by strange gods and even stranger politics. There was nothing to do but meditate while he waited for Sir Philip to knock on their door.

When Champlain finally woke up, feeling a bit less gregarious than before, he sat quietly in one of the chairs by the door, watching the news channel. The story about the destruction in Ethiopia ran over and over, but each time the story came on, Louis would sit up and listen to it intently, before leaning back in the chair, cracking his knuckles, with a frown on his face when nothing new was forthcoming. Mark Andrew thought perhaps the Knight of the Golden Key was trying to memorize the report word for word. They were still unsure who had led the assault on the two churches, but Mark Andrew was glad they didn't know. With a little bit of luck and God's grace, the world would never know the man or the mind behind the attack. He paced the small area in front of the two beds in the room until Champlain threw him out and then he paced the long concrete hallway between the parking lot and the swimming pool until some of the guests complained to the management and then he had paced the parking lot for a while as his mood grew darker and darker. At six thirty, Philip arrived and sent him to get supper for the three of them. He returned at seven thirty with a strange combination of items from a nearby Italian restaurant.

"What is this, Brother?" Philip asked as he looked over the various assortments of bread sticks, cheese-stuffed mushrooms and black olives, fried cheese sticks, three different varieties of cheesecake and two bottles of wine.

"Bread and cheese," Mark told him irritably. "It is a meatless day. I thought that an Italian restaurant would have simple bread and cheese, but this is America. I should have gone to a grocer, but I don't know where one might be. You should have sent Louis or gone yourself, Philip, if you don't like the fare. I seem to have lost my shopping abilities sometime during the 1950's. If you wanted gourmet food, you should have brought Dambretti."

Philip said nothing more, but continued to frown. He'd never had many dealings with Ramsay and the man's obvious chagrin over supper almost made him smile, but he didn't dare. It was his considered opinion that they should have brought de Bleu with them. He was younger and more savvy with fast computers, fast cars and fast food.

Champlain led them in a lengthy prayer while Mark fidgeted with the hilt of his sword. He had been cleaning it unnecessarily and it now lay across his lap under the small table. He could not concentrate. His mind was in a thousand places at once. When the food was gone, Sir Philip prayed some more.

"Is he always like this?" Philip cast a doubtful eye on Champlain as Mark disappeared into the shower directly after supper.

"I wouldn't know, Brother," Champlain shrugged and looked forlornly at the empty wrappers and boxes on the table. His stomach growled, but he knew that going into battle hungry was the best way to go. "He was not like this when we went to France after Devereaux. He knew exactly what he was going to do and just went and did it. Perhaps it is the uncertainty of this situation and it could be the locale. I don't think that America agrees with him. We were far more at home in the Languedoc than here."

"Well, I hope that his thoughts settle before long. I will need to make some more prayers before we go and you and he will need to be protected," Philip spoke softly in French as he stood up and popped a kink from his backbone. "Most likely our subject will have summoned quite an arsenal to surround him by now. I don't know how well we will be covered, but I will do my best. We will have to wait until he is out of the circle and in the open if he is practicing magick. A circle would be fundamental in his work and we would, of necessity, be on the outside. There is no telling what we may encounter in the vicinity of his invocations. And we will have to keep him from getting back to the circle at all costs once we have drawn him out. If he has been successful, he may have an unfair advantage. There will be things better left unknown which may aid us in undoing him. But we won't have the luxury or benefit of creating our own circle and we could be in danger of possession."

Champlain nodded solemnly. He did not understand much of what his Brother was telling him. His own mystery was very cut and dried. He knew how to put the stone in the Key and he knew the proper techniques for using it to open the Ark, but that was the extent of his knowledge. All of this witchcraft was beyond him and he could not think about it without cold fear entering his heart and fear was not something he was accustomed to. He had had enough fear to last for several hundred years when he had faced the specter of Christopher Stewart three times in one night.

"Will we be able to subdue him physically?" Champlain asked after a moment.

"We should, once we break his concentration," Philip nodded. "He is no more or less formidable than any other man when unprotected by supernatural forces. Then we will have to abandon the area quickly. The Nine Names of Power is a very dangerous incantation. He has summoned up the spirits of nine of the most maleficent sorcerers of the ancient world. It would not be in our best interests to stay around when he loses control of them."

"What will happen if we leave them?" Champlain looked worried.

"They will return to the Abyss when the sun rises," Philip told him. "The moon is the source of their power. Once it has set and the sun is on the rise, they will flee or burn up in its glory. It would have been most beneficial to have Sister Sinclair here with us. She could have invoked some of the lesser angels to help us, but the Grand Master felt that we might start something we could not stop."

Champlain shuddered. He did not want to hear more about it.

(((((((((((((<O>)))))))))))))

"And as they came out, they found a man of Cyrene, Simon by name," the voice without a face whispered in his ear. "Him they compelled to bear his cross. And as they led him away, they laid hold upon one Simon, a Cyrenian, coming out of the country, and they laid him on the cross, that he might bear it for Jesus."

Simon shook his head. This not what the scriptures said. This was blasphemy! He opened his eyes and stared up at the stars. The full moon was rising in the eastern sky and he was lying in the chaise lounge on the patio. He didn't remember falling asleep. And this was the third time he had heard the same voice speaking in his head, twisting the Holy Scriptures and making them say what they did not say. Heresy. Simon sat up, rubbing his eyes and looking around the yard. His flowers still lay scattered upon the grass, bathed in the silver light of the moon. He had forgotten them.

Simon walked quickly back into the house and went down to the cellar to find a shovel and a hoe. He went back out into the yard and began to hack and dig at the deep, thick-rooted grass. If he worked all night, he could have the grass out of the way and could plant the flowers before the sun came up. He did not want the sun to burn them. Their fragile spirits could not withstand the onslaught of the sun. He did not want the glory of the Son to burn his plants with too much power. He did not want the Son to burn him. The Son did not want the Father to spurn him. Why did his father deny him? Why had God forsaken him? Why had... Simon's mind was working without regard to his physical endeavors. He lost all track of time as the moon climbed higher in the sky and a chilly wind blew in a troop of ragged black clouds. Would his father also sacrifice him as Isaac's father had done? He would bring a stone here for that purpose. It must be done right! Sacrifices must be done right... If they were to be accepted by God, they must be done right. If it was to be true and right in the eyes of God, he would make the seal upon it. The Seal of Solomon. The Key of David. The insane musings of a mad priest in service to the Knights of Christ. Simon hummed a tune to himself as he worked.

(((((((((((((<O>)))))))))))))

Two hours before sunset, the three Knights of Solomon's Temple parked their rented Jeep Cherokee in a densely wooded section of the hiking and camping area as close as possible to the limestone sinkhole that had been attracting Abdul Hafiz al Sajek every evening and every morning for the past eight nights. They were dressed all in black from head to toe and carried their full repertoire of bladed weapons. Sir Philip had given each of them a silver amulet to wear around their necks and had placed another around his own. He had said prayers over their heads in a strange sing-song language and had then blessed both of them in French and Latin. They made their way quickly through the woods to the site of the sinkhole. They scouted the area and found the remains of the circle inscribed on a bare patch of ground that al Sajek used in his nightly incantations just as Philip predicted. The sight smelled of burned sulfur and the earth outside the circle was scorched bare. Neither Louis, nor Mark knew how Philip had known exactly where to look, but it had saved them a great deal of time and effort.

The Seneschal had led them directly to the spot without a single wrong turn, though he had never set foot in this place in his life. In fact, this was Philip's first trip to America. It was Mark's third in the past century and Louis' second in a long, long time. Louis had commented lightly on the progress that the American 'colonists' had made since his last visit. Of course, he had visited New Orleans before Louisiana had become a 'purchase'. Exactly why Louis had visited the Big Easy was unknown to Mark Andrew and he would not ask. Mark was only now amazed to realize that he knew so little about these two men he had shared acquaintance with for so long. They were virtually strangers to him. Nobodies from a long dead past like himself, without family, without friends other than each other. They were simply poor Knights of Solomon's Temple as far as he was concerned. No matter that his father had been a minor Scottish Laird in service to King William, the Lion, during the Dark Ages.

All of his father's meager holdings and all his family ties were lost long before Mark had returned to Scotland in the fourteenth century. Of course not too many Scots left Scotland for the Crusades and returned there three hundred years later alive and well. There were plenty of Ramsays still left in Scotland, but their relationship to the Knight of Death had been stretched to breaking during the obscurities of those centuries between the fall of Acre and Friday the thirteenth of October in the year 1307. He had had some brief encounters with some of his father's distant relations' descendants from time to time, but he had never pursued any of them. It had seemed pointless. What would he say to them? What would they say to him? He snapped his attention to the task at hand when Louis stepped into a small steel trap concealed in the dead leaves surrounding the circle. The trap snapped on his boot, causing little damage, but making an unacceptably loud noise.

Louis bit his lip and pulled the trap off his foot. Mark helped him reset the trap and replace it in the leaves. Booby traps. It could have been worse. They walked much more cautiously around the area, locating a number of traps before following Philip deeper into the woods. The traps were all small, evidently intended as a sort of early warning system, not intended to inflict real damage. The man was certainly confident that his activities were unknown to any substantial foes. A good sign that they would be more of surprise than he had expected. Philip brought them to a slightly elevated mound of rocky soil surrounded by thick undergrowth and trees which provided them with an excellent view of the open space near the pit where they expected al Sajek to arrive just after dark.

They stayed low and made themselves as comfortable as possible in the ferns and mosses that grew in close proximity to the crystal stream pouring over the side of the sinkhole to the bottom of the roughly conical pit nearly seventy feet straight down to what appeared to be a profusely overgrown bottom. Mark judged the pit to be at least seventy or eighty years old due to the number and size of plants and trees clinging to its steeply sloping sides. One wrong step and there would be little hope of stopping a slide to the bottom and it would be rough going, bouncing over the roots, slamming against the trunks of the trees and rolling through the brush out of control. On the south side, a mass of overgrown roots and tangled vegetation flanked the waterfall on either side, fighting for space in the perpetual mists. A careless move in that area might result in a free fall to the bottom of the falls. They could see no pool at the base, which was another indication that the pit was deeper than it looked, swallowing up the little stream entirely in its depths. Either way, the pit was dangerous and should have been roped off in Mark's opinion. There was evidence of a fair amount of foot traffic in the general area and some of the footprints they saw were small. He shuddered at the thought of what might be found at the bottom of the otherwise beautiful deathtrap. The mouth of the depression was no more than twenty feet across, but plenty large enough for numerous evil specters to come and go, though the scenic natural beauty of the area did not lend itself to the malevolent purposes of the Mad Assassin. It was also Mark's opinion that the man might have done better in keeping to the desert wastelands of North Africa and the Middle East where such activities had been known to exist for millennia.   Such greenery and profuse life gave rise to an abundance of spirits, both material and ephemeral and were usually deterrents to the more profane forms of existence. Mark had never yet seen even a single candle's light put out by darkness. But America was not immune to the spread of evil and already, he had an uneasy feeling in his stomach as he surveyed the deeper shadows under the thick forest trees.

They spoke very little even though the noise of the waterfall masked most of the sounds around the sinkhole. Sir Philip was praying almost constantly and his thin face was a mask of grim determination. Champlain's expression displayed no discernible emotion and he chewed a wad of bubblegum, something he had picked up at the airport. Louis was always trying new things. Sir Ramsay shifted alternately from frowning intensely to staring into space blankly. The sun went down and swarms of mosquitoes descended upon them, but one of Ramsay's numerous pockets had provided them with unscented insect repellent and so they waited with a patience developed over long years of experience. Each lost in his own thoughts.

Just before midnight the objective of their mission arrived. He was dressed in black and white, which contrasted sharply in the bright light of the full moon near perfectly centered overhead, thus shining directly into the sinkhole. The long loose sleeves of his outer jacket were covered with strange symbols embroidered in black thread. He carried no means of artificial light but approached the hole close enough to look over the side into the fine mist that drifted up from below. The three Knights lay on their stomachs watching him with great interest. He raised his hands above his head toward the moon and made several strange signs in the air. In one hand he held a silver amulet about the same size as the ones Sir Philip had provided for them. The moonlight glinted on the silver and a bluish glow seemed to emanate from the object. They heard Philip draw in a sharp breath at the sight of the powerful tool in action. Presently, the magician wrapped the disk in a piece of black cloth and put it away inside his long, loose coat. He walked back to where they had found the remnants of his previous circles and began to carefully lay out the stones, adjusting them and re-adjusting them just so.

"Now would be a good time, Brothers," Sir Philip told them, his voice barely more than air. "Before he completes the circle and calls on the Ninth Name of Power."

Ramsay and Champlain silently drew their swords from their scabbards in preparation of attacking the Assassin. Just as Ramsay got to one knee, Sir Philip held up one hand to stop him. The man had sensed something. He turned suddenly and looked in their direction. They froze. It seemed they could almost see his eyes glowing in the dark shadow cast by his turban. Al Sajek stood staring intently at the spot where they lay hidden for several long minutes before returning to his work. They moved again and he turned again. He was very sensitive to his surroundings. There would be no element of surprise. He already knew something was amiss though he didn't seem overly concerned. Perhaps he thought it only an animal or birds. "Louis, go around the pit," Mark Andrew whispered almost soundlessly to the Frankish Knight. "I will draw him off this way. Sir Philip will come last."

Philip nodded. Champlain moved off soundlessly, a remarkable feat considering his large stature and the heavy weapon he carried.

The Knight of Death took a deep breath, stood upright and stepped out of the brush into the clearing. The sorcerer turned immediately and watched him with an almost animal attitude, swaying slightly from side to side, reminding the Knight of a cobra. Mark Andrew held the golden sword in front of him in the *en garde* position. He walked slowly toward the man, unblinking and unwavering.

Al Sajek moved to the center of the almost complete circle and drew up to his full height, slightly taller than the Knight. He did not seem overly surprised to see the ominous figure dressed in black, wielding the golden blade in front of him.

"Adar! Have you come for your key? I recognize you, Lord of Hunters. You smell of death and antiquity. Lament thy fate, O Adar! The earth shall be void and cast for eternity into the Abyss of perdition and whosoever would forsake the ways of old, will go down amongst the unnamed ones to dwell in the hall of dust and ashes until the cosmos shall pass away." The man smiled at him from beneath his dark turban.

Mark did not let the man's strange address distract him. Al Sajek spoke to him as if he knew him, but this was not possible. The words made no sense and he wanted nothing to do with the man other than what his mission required. A thousand memories came back to him from days long past as he faced this man dressed in the garb of the Infidels.

"Have you not tasted enough of defeat, Adar?" The man continued as he drew a long, glittering knife from under his coat. "Do you not enjoy meeting with your past? And what of that youngest son of Solomon the Wise, of whom you saved from the dungeons of the Romans. Even he has fallen to the dark powers and the spirit of the evil one I have sent to him. Even now he doubts his faith in your God. Where are your brothers? Where are your bastard sons now, Adar? Do you not long for the glory of the elder days?"

Mark Andrew felt the anger rising within him, but he knew that they did not come here with the sole intention to kill, but with only the primary goal to take back what this strange fellow had taken from them. The boasting bastard had him confused with someone else. He was right about only one thing. He was here for the Key, not conversation.

Louis made his way swiftly around the pit, approaching the man from the opposite direction. The Frankish Knight stepped into the clearing and raised his sword in front of him, kissing the blade before making the sign of the cross. He began to repeat the beatitudes of Christ in French and the sound made chill bumps erupt on Mark's spine. It was one of those peculiar habits Louis had developed over the years. Something he usually did just before killing his enemies in battle. As he quoted the Holy Scriptures, he approached the man even more boldly than the Knight of Death. They had to keep the sorcerer away from Philip.

The man turned quickly as he became aware of the second threat.

"Ah, the former owner of the Key!" Al Sajek nodded to Champlain and smiled at him. "What is this little poem? More of your Christian magick? Think you to frighten me with your words? It is no wonder your ancestors so easily gave up what Jehovah had granted them. It is no wonder that the Romans thought you nothing more than wild barbarians. Your slow mind needs time to work its magick and we are out of time, my friend."

The Frankish Knight drew up within a dozen feet of the circle and stood ready to block the man's escape in that direction. The man spoke gibberish. Louis considered himself none of the above. A Knight of Christ, neither Christian nor Jew, but certainly not Moslem. Louis thought ironically that his own faith probably crept nearer to al Sajek's than he felt comfortable admitting.

Sir Philip stepped out of the shadows between the sorcerer and the pit.

"Abdul Hafiz al Sajek, I command you in the name of Yahweh and in the name of his son, Jesus Christ to return that which you have stolen from Him," Sir Philip spoke in a surprisingly calm voice as he held up his medallion to catch the reflection of the moon in its silvery surface.

"You dare to think you can command me, weak one?" al Sajek asked and his smile faded. "Step closer Philip Cambrique so that I might see your face before you die. Do you still tremble in the night when nightmares plague you? You are nothing. A descendent of dogs."

"We are not here to kill you, Abdul. We only want the Key and we will go in peace," Sir Philip sounded almost conversational as he stepped a bit closer.

"Do not make me laugh, Brother," al Sajek spoke, but resumed his swaying back and forth like a snake looking for the right moment to strike. "You are wasting my time."

He put away his knife and went back to completing his circle, ignoring them in his interminable arrogance and confidence.

Mark Andrew looked at Sir Philip questioningly and Philip nodded him forward. Did the man not know how close death was standing?

He took several more steps in the direction of the circle and al Sajek held up one hand toward him without even looking back. It felt as if the hand of a giant struck him in the chest. He suddenly found himself on the ground on his back, with a great, but invisible weight sitting on his chest. He swung his blade up and in front of him, but it passed through nothing. It seemed as if his ears were being crushed by a heavy sensation of buzzing voices he could not understand, as if his head were stuffed inside a beehive. There was nothing there, yet something was holding him down.

Sir Champlain raised his sword and advanced on the man. Within seconds he found himself in the same condition as Mark Andrew. Completely helpless on the ground, unable to move, speak or help himself in any fashion.

The sorcerer began to talk again, almost to himself, it seemed. "I have raised demons, and the dead. I have summoned the ghosts of my ancestors to real and visible appearance on the tops of temples built to reach the stars. I have traveled among the stars, and trembled before the gods. I have seen the Unknown Lands that no map has ever charted. I have lived in the deserts and the wastelands, and spoken with demons and the souls of slaughtered men, and of women who have died in childbirth, victims of the sword and dagger that you bear, Adar. You are no threat to me. I know your heart and your mind. And who is this magician trickster that dares to insult me with his silly trinket?"

"Do not listen to him, Brothers. He speaks words from the Black Book of the Dead! Close your ears and I will provide the way!" Sir Philip called to them. Philip turned to the east and held his amulet up to the moon. He made a sign in the air and began to call upon the Lord of N'ydens. "Great N'ydens of the Silver Hand, I call you forth! Behold the Symbol of your mighty Power! Open the fiery Gate of your Abode and give life to this Emblem fashioned by my Art. See the Name that may not be spoken, issue from the jaws of your servant, Philip Cambrique. See the form of your secret place amongst the stars! I hail you N'ydens! Stretch out your Hand and lend Power to my work that the Elder Lords may assist me in my time of need. In these Names I call upon your Power: Rudabab, Ajuhs, Robbig, Mizrum, Nseb, Airalk, Arabbag, Rabbaj!"

Philip turned back to the north and made another sign in the air.

Al Sajek stopped what he was doing and turned to face the Knight of the Orient. His expression changed from one of supreme arrogance to one of anger and surprise.

"Be gone, defiled one! Unclean flesh! Do you not know who I am?!" he shouted at Philip and then returned to his circle. Philip came to kneel beside Mark Andrew and held out the amulet above his body.

"O great and powerful Lord N'ydens, send away this evil spirit from my Brother. See that he wears the sign of the Silver Hand upon his chest? See that he is a Child of God? The god of your fathers? See that he has the power?"

Mark did not like this. He did not like the idea of calling upon anyone other than God to help him, but the pressure eased immediately and the noise in his ears stopped. Philip left him and went to where Champlain still strained against his unseen attacker. He repeated the same process, releasing the Knight of the Golden Key from the grip of the evil sorcerers, but not soon enough. Abdul Hafiz had completed his circle. Philip tried to approach him, but it was impossible. They could not enter the circle. It was as if it he had built an unbreachable stone wall about him.

Philip called them together and they stood watching as the Assassin began his ritual, bowing to the cardinal points, ignoring them as if they were annoying mosquitoes. Nuisances only. He would not be distracted.

"What do we do now, Brother?" Mark asked and looked at Philip expectantly, and then realized that he was shouting to be heard above the waterfall. It had not been so loud before. They turned in unison to learn the source of this expected noise.

A great geyser of water sprayed upwards from the pit, accompanied by the roar of a wild beast of enormous proportions. A bluish-purple light lit the droplets of water from below, high into the air above them. They stood mesmerized by the sight until the water began to rush back down in flooding torrents. The ninth sorcerer had arrived with a mighty display of power. The whisperings and buzzings in the air increased to a feverish pitch as the water crashed to the ground and rushed toward the three Knights.

"Run for it!" Champlain shouted at them and turned to run off to the left.

Mark Andrew grabbed Philip's arm, but the Knight stood his ground. He held the silver amulet in front of him and closed his eyes. The water parted around the Seneschal, but it did not part for Mark Andrew. He had no faith in the incantations. His amulet was worthless. The water hit him and knocked him backwards. He lost his grip on Philip's arm and was washed away over the rough ground, bumping and knocking against the exposed limestone rocks. At length, the water slowed and dropped him fifty yards from where he had been. He had lost his sword. He could see it lying in a pile of debris between himself and the Knight of the Orient who still stood holding the silver disk in front of him.

Al Sajek reached toward the moon with both arms and stepped out of the circle behind Philip. Mark Andrew was up in an instant, running for his sword. He shouted a warning at Philip and the Knight turned in time to ward off the sorcerer before he could put the dagger between his shoulders. Champlain came in from the left and swung at the Assassin with his broadsword. The man side-stepped Louis neatly and caught the blade with his bare hand, without the least injury from the double-edged sword, twisted it up brutally, and wrenched it from the Knight's hand. Champlain fell back gripping his twisted wrist, grimacing in pain. The Mad Assassin advanced on him and drove his dagger into Champlain's neck without the slightest hesitation, then jumped back nimbly as the big Knight swung at him with his fist. Mark Andrew picked up his sword and ran at the man's back. The sorcerer turned on him and reached for the golden blade. Mark Andrew stopped just short of his reach, dipped slightly and made his deadly roundhouse swing. The golden blade came around in a precisely aimed blow directed at al Sajek's neck. Philip's voice barely reached his brain through the blind fog shimmering in front of his eyes, shouting for him to stop. He had forgotten his primary mission. He was not supposed to kill the man. But the blow was never delivered. Mark Andrew was caught up as if a weightless bit of chaff and thrown backwards by an unseen force.

Sir Philip made his move on the Assassin, reciting an incantation in a language the Knight of Death did not understand. Abdul Hafiz stepped backwards away from him and re-entered the circle. He sat down cross-legged in the center and held out both arms, turning his face up toward the moon. The roar of the beast within the pit split the air. Mark Andrew dragged his sword to him and climbed to his feet, spitting dirt and dead leaves from his mouth. He stumbled back to where Champlain lay on the ground clutching his neck with both hands. Blood flowed darkly over his hands and down onto his shirt. He could not speak. Mark grimaced and took hold of the knife handle protruding from one side of the man's neck. Louis closed his eyes tightly and Mark wrenched the knife free, causing even more blood to pour from a double wound. Philip continued his incantation as Mark Andrew helped the injured Knight to a sitting position. He found Champlain's sword and brought it back to him. Louis would no doubt bleed to death within a few minutes. He shouted at the Knight to stay put, but Champlain staggered to his feet in spite of the debilitating wound in his neck.

The noise level had reach a deafening pitch like a the force of a hurricane. The roar of the inverted waterfall now spraying straight up twenty-plus feet in the air and the bellowing beast in the pit made communication impossible. The Knight of Death had to return to his aid as he stumbled toward the pit.

Abdul Hafiz lowered his arms and glared at Philip menacingly. Philip was standing between him and the pit and he was beginning to be a very irritating distraction. The nine powers he had summoned to his will from the Abyss were extremely hard to manage and the last and greatest was more powerful than all those preceding him combined. He suddenly regretted adding him to his repertoire of slaves. Eight would have been sufficient for his purposes, but once he had discerned the identity of the ninth sorcerer imprisoned in the Abyss, he had succumbed to curiosity.

"Out of my way, foolish man!" Abdul Hafiz shouted at the Knight of the Orient and stood up. His voice was lost on the wind.

Philip ignored him and continued repeating the words of his own incantation to the powers of the Abyss and the Nine Names of Power. By creating conflicting energy flows, he hoped to weaken al Sajek's control enough to gain some advantage over him. If he could distract him long enough for Ramsay to get close enough, al Sajek's conjuring days would be over, but he had been wrong about the powers returning to the underworld at dawn. He also realized that he would have to bind the powers to himself for two reasons. First of all, they could not afford to allow al Sajek to possess such great power and secondly, if they did manage to kill him, the Nine Names of Power would have to be subdued. They could not be loosed upon the world and it would be better done now than later. If they escaped into the open, they would disperse throughout the world. Life would become much more complicated in very short order. It was a contest of wills and Philip could not afford to lose.

Al Sajek advanced on him again with a second dagger, slimmer than the first, but possessing a wicked serrated edge along one side. Philip did not fall back, but stood his ground.

"The Key!" Philip shouted at him when he got close enough. "Give us the Key! Or lose yourself, evil one!"

"Out of my way or die!" Abdul Hafiz countered as he tossed the knife back and forth between his hands, looking for the right moment to strike.

Mark Andrew eased Champlain to the ground as he grew weaker from loss of blood. Within seconds, he inserted himself between the sorcerer and the Seneschal, once more brandishing the golden sword. Al Sajek continued his advance, unimpressed at the sight of the weapon. Mark Andrew swung at him and again, he was tossed aside like a leaf in a gale, but when he tried to stab Cambrique, he was unable to reach him. Al Sajek's face darkened as he struggled against the force of Philip's will. For several seconds, they strained against each without physically touching in a ruthless battle of occult energy, giving Mark Andrew a chance to regain his footing on the slippery ground. Al Sajek reached out incrementally and closed his hand around the silver disk in Philip's hand. Philip tried to pull his hand back, but was no match for the ancient sorcerer enhanced by the Nine Powers he had summoned to help him. The disk began to crumble into a powder in Philip's hand, streaming to the ground in a cone of shimmering dust.

Al Sajek held Philip's hand in his grip and stiff-armed him backwards toward the pit. Mark Andrew regained his footing and ran at the Assassin with his sword raised over his head. Al Sajek turned and at the same time bent Philip's arm in an unnatural position that caused the Knight to cry out in pain as his elbow gave way, bending in the wrong direction. The sorcerer only had time to catch the golden blade in his free hand much as he had caught Louis' sword, but the razor sharp blade that never needed honing was not so easily stopped as a steel blade. He caught the blade long enough to keep it from making a fatal connection with his neck, but blood poured from a terrible wound across the palm of his hand, leaving the bones of his fingers visible. Sajek cried out in surprise and pain and let go of the Seneschal. Philip fell to his knees, cradling his broken arm against his stomach.

Abdul Hafiz turned toward the Knight of Death and screamed at him in rage as Mark regrouped and gathered himself to make another strike. He drew the sword back and gritted his teeth against the horrendous sounds emanating from the pit, but was thrown aside once again by unseen forces surrounding the sorcerer. The breath was knocked from his lungs when he slammed against the ground flat on his back. He rolled to the side and coughed for air, while trying to kick himself as far from the Assassin as possible.

Al Sajek turned away from him and stepped past Philip to the edge of the pit. A reddish mist was now rising from the depths of the hole, the water spout subsided suddenly and the beast's howls intensified, calling for the treasure promised by the magician. Al Sajek pulled a black cloth from his inner pocket and wrapped it around his injured hand. He then removed something from around his neck and held up a long, sparkling gold chain from which dangled the Golden Key to the Ark of the Covenant. He held the chain out in his right hand over the pit.

"Obeel, Dibac, Socab, Sumen! I call you forth by your ancient names. Attend me in my work and behold the Golden Key of the Hebrews, your ancient enemies! I wear the Ring upon my finger!" He held up his left hand where a silver ring glinted in the light of the moon.

Mark Andrew got to his feet more slowly than before. The overwhelming power of the magician was defeating him physically and mentally. He glanced back once at Champlain who sat slumped on the ground with his head drooping on his chest. Philip climbed to his feet behind the sorcerer. Mark Andrew pushed the golden sword into his scabbard and placed his dagger between his teeth before launching himself toward the Assassin's back. He reached the sorcerer before Philip and wrapped his left arm around his neck. He reached for his dagger, intending to cut the man's throat, but al Sajek let go of the Key.

Philip shouted and fell forward at the edge of the pit grasping at empty air in total despair. Mark Andrew let go of the man and reached for the Key as the chain slipped from the man's fingers. He caught the chain on the tips of his fingers, but lost his balance in the process. He held desperately onto the cloth of the magicians overcoat and heard it ripping as he fell over the edge of the pit with the slender chain clutched in his hand. The cloth continued to rip down al Sajek's back when he turned and leaned backwards, struggling to keep from going over the side with Ramsay. Mark turned and caught hold of the rock at the edge of the pit with his left hand. The dagger fell from his mouth as he cried out to Sir Philip for help. Philip rolled along the edge of the pit and grabbed Mark's arm with his uninjured hand. His broken arm prevented him from helping further.

Al Sajek twisted backward, allowing the black garment to come free from his shoulders. It fell over the Knight's head and he ripped it away, throwing it down into the pit behind him.

Philip clung desperately to the Knight of Death, but it was a losing battle. Al Sajek bent over him suddenly and stabbed him under his ribs. Philip jerked away from him, still holding on to Mark, twisting his broken arm unmercifully. The Seneschal turned on his back and tried to shield himself with his broken arm. It was useless. Abdul Hafiz pulled the dagger free and stabbed him again in his exposed stomach. Mark felt Philip's grip tighten and then go limp and then he was falling. The beast below him bellowed in triumph and welcomed him to hell. Mark closed his eyes, and grabbed hold of the key with both hands, bracing for the inevitable impact. When nothing happened immediately, he opened his eyes and looked up at the small circle of silver light above his head.

The Knight of Death would deliver the prize to the beast personally. The last thing he saw before he plummeted into darkness was the sight of the sorcerer's body flying out over the pit, screaming and falling in after him.

$$((((((((((((<O>))))))))))))$$

The Grand Master's sleep was shattered by the sounds of shouting voices in the courtyard. He clambered from his bed and pulled on his boots. Now what?! The Grand Master was one of the few who still adhered to the ancient Rule of Order concerning sleeping fully dressed, except for his boots. He simply could not sleep with his boots on. He paused momentarily to concentrate on the noises that had roused him from his first sound sleep in weeks. He recognized one of the voices as that of Sir Barry of Sussex. The other voice sounded familiar, perhaps one of the boys at the Academy and what sounded like a mishmash of several others, speaking a variety of languages. He stumbled through the anteroom in the dim light and threw open the door to the porch. Stepping out onto the porch, he was taken aback to see one of the boys dressed in nothing but his skin, running barefoot up and down the grassy inner yard in the pale light of dawn with Sir Barry and Stephano Clementi close on his heels. Sir de Lyons and Armand de Bleu joined in the chase as he stepped off the porch, each of them dressed in various states of disarray due to the early hour. Barry still had a towel draped over one shoulder and his face was partially covered with shaving cream.

The naked boy was John Paul Sinclair-Ramsay, of course. He was running as fast as he could from one end of the courtyard to the other, shouting in Latin as he went, easily dodging his pursuers at every turn. The men grabbed for him as he darted past them, but came up empty-handed time and again. De Lyons sprawled on his face and de Bleu tripped over him. They helped each other up and continued the chase.

D'Brouchart drew up short and concentrated his attention on what the boy was saying. It had been years since he had heard the old language spoken aloud and it brought back bitter memories.

"Then I saw an angel come down from heaven with the key of the Abyss in his hand and an enormous chain. He overpowered the dragon, that primeval serpent which is the devil and Satan, and chained him up. And in the first and twentieth day of the sixth month, I beheld a man dressed in black and a dragon the color of blood and in the man's hand was a golden chain and on the chain was a golden key and on the head of the dragon I beheld a golden plate and upon the plate was written the names of the archangels, Michael, Gabriel and was set in the seal of Solomon the Wise!"

D'Brouchart stood frozen as the words came clearly to him in the still morning air. John Paul was speaking of Champlain's Golden Key! His words were interspersed with Holy Scriptures from the book of Revelations.

"And, behold, a hand touched me, which set me upon my knees and upon the palms of my hands.

And he said unto me, O John, a son greatly beloved, understand the words that I speak unto thee, and stand upright: for unto thee am I now sent. And when he had spoken this word unto me, I stood trembling. And he said, O son greatly beloved, fear not: peace be unto thee, be strong, yea, be strong. And when he had spoken unto me, I was strengthened, and said, Let my father speak; for thou hast strengthened me. Then said he, Knowest thou wherefore I come unto thee? and now will I return to fight with the prince of the Air: and when I am gone forth, lo, the Golden Eagle shall come and the daughter of the west will be given up unto him. And when I am come again, the Golden Key shall be forever joined unto its Keeper."

The Grand Master felt a deep shudder pass through him. The words were a slightly modified version of the Holy Scriptures from the Old Testament book of Daniel and the New Testament Revelation of St. John.

John Paul stopped suddenly and was tackled by three Knights at once. They went down in a tangled heap. Sir Barry would deal with the boy. D'Brouchart returned to his desk and sat down heavily to contemplate the boy's words. John Paul had seen his father in a vision and his father had spoken to him. Sir Ramsay would fight the Prince of the Air. This was another name for Satan and while he was doing that, the Chevaliere Sinclair would marry the Golden Eagle. And when Sir Ramsay returned, he would have the Golden Key. That was all well and fine except that there was no way to know if Ramsay knew this. That he or a likeness of him had spoken to John Paul in his visions did not necessarily mean that the Knight of Death knew the contents of the vision. And there were no time frames. D'Brouchart sighed and wished that von Hetz or Sir Philip were there to discuss it with him.

Could this prophecy be so simple? He scribbled the words on a legal pad and scrutinized them carefully, tapping the pen against the desk in aggravation. What if it meant something else entirely? There was little consolation in the decision he had made that left only Simon to mediate or intervene as the case may be, between Lucio and Merry. Simon's heart was too big and he didn't know how to say 'no'. The Grand Master got up again wearily and called for his steward. He would summon von Hetz and discuss this with him after he heard from Sir Barry, who would undoubtedly wish to give him a report on what he had just transpired in the courtyard. Barry had grown much too attached to the boy like everyone else and he would be highly upset by this latest episode. They had discussed the possibility that John Paul might have to be confined for his own protection if these occurrences continued or worsened. There was some concern as to John's sanity. If the boy became dangerous or put the security of the Order in jeopardy... well, it wouldn't be a good day for anyone involved. That much was certain.

242

Chapter Fourteen of Seventeen
cause thy face to shine upon thy sanctuary

Merry woke suddenly and looked about the bedroom, blinking in confusion. For a moment she didn't recognize where she was. It was as if she had heard a shout or a scream that had roused her from her sleep. She climbed from the bed and went to the window overlooking the backyard and parted the draperies cautiously, afraid of what she might see in the moonlight. The golden orb of the setting moon was just beginning to dip behind the trees northwest of the house, bathing the yard in an eerie yellow light as a low ground fog crept furtively in from the meadow. She tilted her head as she surveyed the area just below her windows in the yard. Something was dreadfully wrong. She could feel it in her bones. She raised the window and the smell of fresh earth assaulted her nose. A familiar enough smell but totally out of place. Leaning out the window, slightly, she could see part of the patio behind the house, but the height made her dizzy and afraid of falling.

The moon seemed closer than she had ever seen it before. She closed the window and watched, partially hypnotized by the sight of several ragged, black clouds trekking across its face.

She gathered her robe from the bed and slipped it on before letting herself into the hall. Downstairs, only the ticking of the clock in the foyer, broke the silence. She looked out one of the tall windows by the front door at the drive and saw nothing unusual. The automobiles gleamed dully in the moonlight. Mark's Mercedes made her heart ache to see him again. They had heard nothing from the mission for two days. She wiped away an errant tear and turned toward the kitchen. A bottle of water might help remove the lump in her throat. The floorboards squeaked here and there as she made her way to the kitchen. The water helped, but the uneasy feeling would not be dismissed so easily. She glanced toward the back door and suddenly felt very alone in the big house. Repressing the urge to run back down the hall and up the stairs to her bedroom, she walked past the cellar door, again fighting back tears as she thought of Mark's beloved lab and how it must have irked him to leave Lucio working in it alone. Turning on the light in the washroom helped her feelings somewhat, but didn't shed much light in the darkened hall. Even the moonlight shining through the window in the backdoor looked brighter. She pulled her robe more tightly about her and tiptoed to the door. The sight of the unlocked bolt made her heart skip a beat. She pulled aside the half curtain and squinted into the yard.

A surprise met her eyes when she focused on the brick patio she had built some fifteen yards from the back steps. She could see that the ground around the hexagonal concrete and brick slab had been disturbed. The grass was gone and the dark soil was exposed. There were hundreds of small plants in neat rows in six triangular beds surrounding the patio. She almost shrieked when she realized that she was looking past someone sitting on the porch steps, looking out over the yard. The moonlight shined on the wispy blond hair and she heaved a sigh of relief. Simon, but what was he doing outside in the middle of the night?

She let herself out quietly and went to sit down beside him. He was covered with sprigs of grass and black smudges were visible on his face, hands and arms. His clothes were practically ruined and he held the bloody handle of a shovel in his hands, the spade itself, broken off from the splintered wood, lay on the ground at his feet. The blood was his and came from broken blisters in his palms.

"Simon? Are you all right?" She asked quietly, but he didn't answer.

"There are gardener's gloves in the washroom, Simon. Why didn't you ask me? What happened?"

He turned his large blue eyes on her and a smile crinkled his angelic expression. Again, she felt that he had an unearthly glow about his face.

"What have you done to yourself?" She asked and removed one of his hands from the shovel, turning it over to look at the damage. He had blisters on top of blisters and open abrasions all over his palm and fingers. His fingernails, normally neat and clean, were broken and dirty. Instead of answering her question, he began to quote scriptures to her, causing chills to course up her spine. She had to wonder if it had been Simon's screams that had awakened her. If that was the case, where was Lucio and Bruce? Surely they had heard it, too. And why had the wolfhounds remained silent?

"For every one that curseth his father or his mother shall be surely put to death: he hath cursed his father or his mother; his blood shall be upon him. Shall he then live? He shall not live: he hath done all these abominations; he shall surely die; his blood shall be upon him. Therefore, as I live, saith the Lord God, I will prepare thee unto blood, and blood shall pursue thee. And almost all things are by the law purged with blood; and without shedding of blood is no remission," Simon spoke softly without looking at her as if he did not know she was there. "I have cursed my father."

His words frightened her. What was he saying?

"Simon, please come inside," she whispered soothingly as if to an injured child and gently took his arm. Her heart raced. Was he insane? Had the dream sequence and illness brought on a total breakdown? She wanted to fetch Lucio, but she was afraid to leave him outside alone. He allowed her to push the shovel from his hand and it slid to the ground, rattling on the steps. "What are you talking about? You haven't cursed your father or your mother and you're not going to die."

"I'm tired, Sister," he sighed and frowned at her.

Merry stood up and helped him up from the steps.

"You need to rest, Brother," she told him with more authority than she felt. "We need to get some ointment on those blisters, Simon."

"I am lost. I am as lost as your Mark Andrew," he told her and her blood ran cold. He moved like a ghost through the back hall of the big house. "He will be gone a long time, Sister. What will we do? What will we do when the dragon comes for us?"

She had no answers for him. How long was long? This was very depressing news. And the dragon? What dragon?

Merry grabbed her bottle of water from the table and ushered him to the bathroom under the stairs in the foyer where she took down a first aid kit from the cupboard. The Healer washed his face and hands while staring blankly at his reflection in the mirror above the sink. She fussed over his injuries with ointment and gauze while he watched in silent abstraction. There was no risk of infection, but the ointment contained a pain reliever and a moisturizer which should help at least somewhat. He allowed her to brush the grass and dirt from his hair and wash the back of his neck. When she was satisfied with her work, she helped him down the hall to his bedroom where he climbed into bed, dirty clothes and all. He was asleep before she closed the door. She stood leaning against the door in the hall. The sight of the door leading into the room where Elizabeth had stayed made her shiver. She debated whether to wake Lucio, but she could not tell Lucio about Simon's dreams. She debated whether or not to call von Hetz, but she didn't really know where to find him without calling the Villa and that would raise suspicion when the Grand Master learned that she was looking for the Ritter. He was the only one she could turn to and he had charged her with the promise to call him if anything happened to Simon. Tomorrow, she would try to find him without ringing any alarm bells.

((((((((((((<O>))))))))))))

Mark Andrew struck the water and sank like mercury in the swirling bath. He could not find the surface. He was pulled under, straight down, as if something had hold of his legs. The water was red and green all around him, imbued with a hellish glow when it should have been pitch black at the bottom of the sinkhole. He still clasped the Golden Key tightly in his right hand, refusing to let it go at all costs. With his left, he yanked the silver chain and the pagan silver medallion Sir Philip had given him from his neck and allowed it to slip away in the water. With tremendous effort he managed to get the golden chain attached to the key over his head. If and when he drowned or crashed or died, the Key, at least would stay with his body and

245

there might be some chance that Philip could recover it eventually. He could no longer hear the roar of the beast as the cold water rushed past his ears. When he could hold it no longer, he let out the breath he was holding and breathed in the water. A great pain engulfed him and darkness surrounded him.

When he opened his eyes, he lay curled on his side on a grassy, green meadow with the sun shining on his face. He was surrounded by millions of blue flowers. Straightening himself slowly, he checked for broken bones as he pushed himself up on his hands and knees and raised his head. The silver earrings that had once been in his hair hung from his neck on a braided cord of white hair. The Key and the chain from which it had hung were gone.

When he looked around, he saw a woman dressed in a long, red gown walking toward him across the grass. Her hair hung to her waist and dark and she had small black horns at each temple. In her hand was a thin golden chain. She smiled as she approached him and he waited, unable to stand up or move while she looped the chain over his head and around his neck. The woman held the Golden Key in her right hand. He tried to speak to her, but no words would come out of his mouth and again, he was unable to move when she pressed the Key's cool surface against his forehead.

"Come with me, my Lord," she ordered and took his arm, helping him to his feet.

When he stood up, he found himself looking down on her from a great height. Was she so tiny? A faery perhaps? But what kind? He did not remember a faery of her description in the old stories.

"This way," she said and led him through the meadow by the golden chain around his neck. She did not tug or use force, but he was unable to resist her and further had no desire to do so.

As he walked along behind her, he had to be careful not to step on her. In the distance, where the blue haze of the flowers met the sky line he could see a huge fountain with shimmering water spouting from seven fountainheads spraying into the air, layer upon layer, rising high above the meadow. A fine mist surrounded the fountain. Rainbows danced in the changing vapors. When they drew closer, another woman dressed in a glistening white gown stepped from the mist. Her hair was like spun golden thread and in her hand was a burnished cup inlaid with precious gems. She approached him with the cup held out in front of her.

"Drink from the golden waters, my Lord and take your rest with us," she told him. "Thrice times seven you must drink from the fountain and then you shall part from us for a time and a time again."

If it was a dream, at least it was a pleasant one. He drank the water and great sense of peace washed over him and he felt himself growing sleepy. The horned one allowed him to sit in the grass and within moments he was curled on his side again on the sweet smelling meadow. Blue flowers surrounded him. The woman disappeared and returned with the Golden Sword of the Cherubim. This she placed in the grass in front of his face. The sight of the sword comforted him and he pulled it close as his mind drifted.

"Sleep now," the dark one told him. "When you awake, you will drink again. I will watch over you."

His first sleep was peaceful, dreamless oblivion wherein he drifted weightless, enfolded in a warm darkness that stretched into infinity. Vast was this place beyond the stars, occupied by uncounted multitudes of life forces, also dreaming, sleeping, also at peace with God. But this pleasant existence seemed only to last a few moments before he heard a woman calling his name. He opened his eyes and saw that the second woman was standing over him, leaning down, close to his eyes.

"What you have seen is the time before time when all things are one with God," the blonde woman explained.

"It is time to drink again," a second voice came from his left and he rolled his head lazily in the flowers to find the woman in red speaking to him. She pulled slightly on the golden chain and he sat up in the grass, stretching his arms over his head. An unnatural wind rustled the flowers around him and cooled his ears, the noise of the air rushing past his head startled him and he looked around quickly for the source of the noise, nothing was in sight other than sunshine, green grass and blue flowers. He yawned and a drew a deep breath and it seemed he could hear his own lungs expanding and filling like never before. He couldn't remember a time in his life when he had felt so wonderful. When he raised his eyes to the clear blue sky, he imagined what it might feel like to soar into the heavens like an eagle. When he looked again at the fountain, the golden-haired woman walked toward him, carrying another jewel-encrusted goblet. "Drink and sleep again, my Lord," she smiled at him and held the goblet to his lips. The water was sweet, cold and slightly pungent as if it contained a mysterious spice. The woman in red sat down in front of him with a silver lyre and began to sing a soothing lullaby that drifted across the meadows, carried on the fresh breeze though he could not understand the words. Mark stretched his arms above his head once more and yawned like never before. The same feeling of airy euphoria engulfed him and he truly felt he could fly if only he weren't so sleepy. The bones in his neck and back popped luxuriously when he twisted his head around from right to left. It was not painful, it felt marvelous and again a cool breeze rushed around him when he moved. The woman in white indicated that he should lie down and produced a satin pillow with gold tassels for his head. Unable to resist the invitation, he let all thoughts of where he might be, who these two were and what he was doing there flee from his mind. If he had finally found a place in Heaven, surely someone had made a mistake and would be coming for him soon. In the meantime, he wanted to enjoy it.

The second sleep was filled with dreams of wondrous places. Beautiful landscapes filled with unspoiled forests and rugged, snow-capped mountains and pristine lakes. An untouched land free from the curse of mankind, long lost in the far reaches of the earth's ancient past. He saw long stretches of sparkling white beach as if he were flying over them only inches above the sand. He saw turquoise waters and plunged deep into their magickal depths before climbing out onto fragile coral islands jutting from the froth of gentle breakers. Swarms of oceanic behemoths patrolled the reefs around him, breaking the water's surface in fearless displays of unbridled joy. He saw tropical forests stretching to eternity, filled with waterfalls and rushing rapids, lazy brown rivers and flowers of every imaginable size, shape and color. Life in profuse abundance filled the tops of the enormous trees and their voices filled the air with glorious sound. Even mystical Eden could not have been more beautiful than this place.

The blonde woman spoke to him again when he awoke.

"This is the time between times before Adam and the first cataclysm, when all is well and the world is new and at peace with God and the Cosmos," she told him. "This world that God built for His pleasure and the pleasure of His most beloved creation."

He did not stay awake long, before she brought another cup of water and the dark one sang to him of far away places and dreams of worlds forever lost.

The third sleep took him to a darkened land occupied by nameless, unrecognizable forms and shapes that howled and moaned and groaned within caves and crevices in the burned and blasted rock. Miserable and tormented they sounded. Haunted. Pain-filled voices crying out for mercy. Although he could not understand the words contained within their cries, he could understand the emotion. Something horrible had happened to God's creation. The land smoked and the water steamed and the air was filled with noxious chemicals. The sky was green and gray and the earth was covered with glabrous growths of mold, fungus and slime. There was nothing to drink, nothing to eat and nowhere to rest. This sleep was not peaceful as before, wretched and destitute, he drifted, blasted by hot winds and the foul odor of rot and decay. Thankfully it was as short as the first two. He awoke again to find the golden haired woman bending over him with the dark-haired one standing nearby. The sun was warm on his face, the blue flowers had not changed. He had never taken so many naps in one day, nor did he ever remember having such vivid dreams before. This last dream left him upset and uneasy.

"This is the time of the Ancient Ones. When the powers of darkness descend upon the earth, burning it and scorching it and the angels of darkness and of Satan fight with the angels of light and of God and the land is laid waste and darkness is upon the earth."

Mark Andrew wanted to ask many questions. He wanted to know why they were showing him these things. He wanted to know why the golden fountain was in the middle of a meadow, far from civilization and he wanted to know where its water came from. Where were it's builders? Whose land was this? What were these women's names? Why did he feel that he knew them? He wanted to know how he could get home to Meredith and his home in Scotland and if it was far away. But he asked none of these questions. He wanted to ask, but simply didn't.

Again and again he drank and slept and drank and slept. Never moving from the meadow, never staying awake more than a few moments at a time. Each time his dreams were different. Some were pleasant, some were horrible nightmares. He saw things he recognized and things he did not know. He saw places he had been before and places he had only heard of in legends. In one of the series of ever-changing scenes, he recognized his own life. He saw the birth of his brother and the death of his mother and then his own birth under the knife of the midwife and the reason for his father's disdain for his youngest son. His youth passed like a blurred, disjointed nightmare, ending with his ejection from his father's home. He saw his father force him into the service of King William I, the Lion of Scotland at the ripe age of fifteen. When his service was fulfilled, he saw his brother run away after him. Eventually, they found themselves wearing the white mantles of the Templar Brotherhood on their way to the Holy Lands. Subsequently, he saw his father's decline into despair at the loss of his favored son. He relived the day that Jerusalem fell, his brother's murder and his own fall from grace as a result. Further on, he saw himself with Lucio Dambretti when he had been known as Lucius di Napoli and then, without warning, the dream slowed to a more comprehensible pace and he found himself falling into it, participating in it even as he fought to wake up.

He saw a market place below him and he was there with Lucius di Napoli. They were strolling along the dusty paths between the tables, racks and vendor's carts where men and women were hawking their wares.

"How goes it that she looks so closely after you, Brother?" Lucius asked as he casually plucked an apple from an old woman's basket and paid her thrice its price after flashing her his wonderful smile. He tossed the apple in the air and caught it again before biting into it and making a face. "These apples are not fit for vermin!"

"She is nothin' t' me, Brother," Mark objected, but not before glancing at the 'she' in question before answering. He stopped to look down at a copper vessel on the ground in front of him. He was trying to replace everything he had lost in France. "She is th' woife o' Laird Martindale. She came up from th' south o' Northumbria two years ago t' be wed t' 'im. Th' mon is twice 'er age and 'e 'as a bad cough and 'e dribbles on his napkin when 'e speaks! Oll taken together verra unpleasant and a verra bad match if ye're askin' me, but tis none o' yur business... nor mine!"

"That is a shame, il fratello. She is... well endowed... with such a sweet face. Santa Maria! These arranged marriages are such cruel affairs. I would have fared no better, I'll wager. A withered little hag with a bad temper smelling of onions and garlic with constant headaches and tremors," Lucius laughed and made his hands shake. He looked back at the young woman who was holding a bolt of cloth in her hands while her maidservant checked its quality. Her gown was a rich blue fabric decorated with golden threads and white beads. Her dark hair was layered curls decorated with pearl stickpins. Her eyes were not on the cloth. She was watching Mark Andrew intensely, but when she saw the Italian looking at her, she ducked her head and blushed.

Lucius raised both eyebrows. "There! You see?"

Mark said nothing, but knelt beside the copper pot, inspecting its workmanship critically. "Too thin," he commented abstractedly as he tapped the bottom of the pot and then stood up.

"She doesn't look thin to me," Lucius misinterpreted the remark to have been about the girl. "I'd say she could keep you warm on a cold night better than that blade you sleep with, Brother."

"Moind yur tongue, Brother," Mark frowned at him. "She is none o' our business. Th' comp'ny o' women is a dangerous thing." He glanced at the young woman. A mistake. Her face lit up and she waved briefly to him. "Especially, married women." Mark nodded slightly to her and knew that he was undone.

She dropped the bolt of cloth and hurried toward him.

He turned away quickly, but Lucius caught his arm. "No, wait, Brother," the Italian said in a low voice full of amusement. "She would speak to you, methinks. Do not be rude."

"Ye thinks too damned much!" Mark growled at him from under his brows, but it was too late. She was already upon them. "I dunna hold with thinkin' o'er much, Brother. Twill get ye in tribble sure."

They doffed their caps and bowed lowed before the lady when she stopped in front of them.

"Father John!" The young woman smiled up at him, addressing him by the name he was currently using with a title that he did not deserve. She took his hands in hers and kissed his Templar ring, thinking it a token of the Church. She ignored the Italian purposefully, turning her back to him slightly. "I would have a word with you... in private."

"She thinks you are a priest?" Lucius asked in Italian. The girl shot him a sidelong look of disapproval. "How did you manage this, Brother?"

"M' lady," Mark Andrew inclined his head slightly and then frowned at Lucius in a meaningful way. "You will pardon my companion. He is an

250

uncivilized brute from the barbarian hills of Sicily." Mark resorted to the more formal English, carefully pronouncing his words to hide his brogue.

"Ahhh."

The girl's eyes widened as she looked at Lucius again with a different expression. He bowed to her graciously and doffed his hat again. An extravagant, broad-brimmed affair decorated with a pair of pheasant tail feathers. His shamefully long, curly black hair fell onto the tufted shoulder pads of his short, quilted jacket made of wine colored velvet. They were supposed to be dressed in the local manner to avoid suspicion, but Lucius' taste for finery made him look like one of the Queen's courtiers rather than the local peasantry. Mark's own clothes were a bit more subdued, black and white with silver chains holding his black cloak in place on his shoulders. He wore a much smaller hat with a small fluff of white goose feathers on one side. Not priestly garb, but not nearly as ostentatious as his companion's. She smiled at Lucius and then lowered her voice to speak to Mark, hiding her face partially behind her scarf. "It is... urgent, Father."

She returned her attention to Lucius once more, eyeing him appraisingly while Mark tried to make excuses. She would hear none of it.

"Give me a moment and I will meet you at the Church," he told her and then took Lucius' arm roughly, dragging him away.

The girl watched after them a moment and then went back to her shopping.

"I told her thot I was a priest," Mark Andrew explained as he dragged him along. "Tis a good lie. A man of the cloth is more respected than not."

"It is still a lie!" Lucius laughed at him. "Why would you tell her that, Brother? Were you afraid that she would dishonor you otherwise?"

"Because." Mark bit his lip. The Italian was impossible. "I saved 'er from a well. She threw 'erself in. She thinks I am her... savior. It is her opinion that I saved her soul from eternal damnation."

Lucius could not control his laughter now. He finally regained his composure and then stood leaning against the trunk of a tree, holding his sides.

"And now you have an attachment," he said. "She is in love with you, Brother. I am not stupid. If there is one thing I know, it is love, when I see it. She has attached to you like a gosling to a goose."

"You would do well to be silent," Mark remarked and pulled him up by the front of his coat. "She is nothing to me. I am nothing to her. Laird Martindale would have my head on a pike pole. Your words are as dangerous as they are foolish."

"My words are foolish. That is true, but it is you who are going to meet her at the church." Lucius' expression changed dramatically. "Won't you come with me to the tavern instead. There are some very good wenches there, Mark Andrew, and they would be far less deadly."

251

"Do ye nevar think thot lust moight be a sin, Brother?" Mark asked and shook his head. "Naught passes' between th' lady and meself. Tis but a whim to her. A diversion. Nothing more."

"What will she say to you?" Lucius badgered him as he walked away. Mark turned only long enough to make a rude gesture in his direction. "Will you hear her confession, Brother? I will make a wager with you. Wait! Wait!"

Lucius ran to catch up with him and took his arm turning him roughly.

"Leave it be!" Mark spat the words at him and his face went dark. "And keep yur grimy hands off me."

"She is nothing more than one of these tavern birds in finer feathers," Lucius told him angrily. "Only she will get you killed for all your high-toned morality... Father."

"She is not one of your whores, Lucius," Mark told him darkly.

"She is no better. She would have you in an instant if she has not already and that makes her an adulteress," the Italian emphasized his words by slamming his fist against his heart. "It matters not in the eyes of God whether it is consummate in the flesh. I know what I see. The penalty for adultery is death according to the will of God. I am only trying to save you, Brother. I would show you the truth of my words."

"What do you mean?" Mark scowled at him, but had to ask, knowing full well that the Italian's had a way of getting under his skin with dangerous words.

"I will have her for myself," Lucius spoke in a low voice raised his head defiantly. "I will take her from you like that." He snapped his fingers in Mark's face, which had turned deep red as he shoved the Italian away from him.

"She is not mine to start with and you, Sir, overstep your bounds! She would not have you. You are nothing without your plumes and frippery. A common street urchin and beggar. I daresay it is only my noble blood that keeps me from killing you where you stand," Mark fell back to High English without the slightest hint of his brogue, which indicated that he was beyond reasoning and walked away toward the church without looking back. Lucius was hurt by the reference to his humble beginnings, but undaunted from the test put before him. He had seen Mark's blood on several occasions and had inspected it closely in secret, finding it absolutely identical to his own. Noble blood! A joke.

Mark had been wrong. Within a week, Lucius presented him with a note from the girl addressed to 'Lucius di Napoli, beloved' written elegantly in the lady's own hand. Mark had been devastated and wrongly so. What he had told Lucio had been nothing more than truth. There had never been anything more than words and a few notes passed between himself and the

252

lovely Lady Martindale so miserably wed to her disgusting Laird. Mark had offered to give her the means to escape to Italy, but she had refused his offer. She wanted to go home and she wanted him to take her there. Not possible, but the fantasy had been gratifying enough. His Brother took what he had been holding so dear. He had been convinced that she actually loved him and he had been convinced that eventually, he would have found some way to be with her without losing his head and her reputation in the process. He had been too slow. She had been his first true love and she belonged to someone else.

It was only after he and Lucio had rolled in the mud, ruining their good clothes and leaving each other bloody that he learned of her plan. Lucio had made him listen in spite of the danger. The girl had the foolish notion that she could to persuade some young nobleman to rid her of her husband by hook and crook and take his place as her new husband. This, of course, neither Mark Ramsay nor Lucius di Napoli could do. All the while he had played out his little fantasy with the girl, he had been forced to use his entire strength of will to keep from touching her, profaning their "love" with lust, but then it was all for naught. He could have had her a dozen times and yet... he had not. This was his one saving grace concerning the lovely Lady Martindale. Lucius had very nearly lost his head on that occasion, but Mark Andrew had been unable to justify his anger and Lucius had made sure that Mark's Golden Sword had been securely out of reach before making his point. In the end, the point was well taken. Mark never spoke to her again, nor did he ever ask just how far the Italian had gotten with her. Lucius had cleverly declined any more discussion on the subject.

Lucio had saved him from himself. That was what it amounted to.

Once this portion of the long dream had left him bereft, he passed along rapidly through many more incidents involving the fickle friendship he shared with the Italian. He wondered how much more such 'saving' he could survive. If Lucio thought of himself as his Brother's keeper, Mark felt perhaps he might be better off lost. The flight continued until he found himself, apparently sitting on his own roof, looking down at his back steps while Lucio begged Meredith to marry him in Italian while four of his Brothers watched from Simon's patio. This vision enraged him and he came awake with a roar of anger, but he found himself in the presence of the two women beside the golden fountain. The dark one stroked his face and whispered soothing words in his ear.

She spoke to him of Lucio, but he was unwilling to listen to her. There was no turning back the ages. What had passed had passed. Lucio had always betrayed him. There was no doubt in his mind that Lucio was betraying him even now. He sincerely felt that one day he would have to take his Brother's head if he lived long enough to get home. The woman insisted that he would understand the meaning of the dream when the time came, but

253

he did not want to believe her; he did not want to understand Lucio Dambretti. He only wanted to be rid of him.

The rest of the dreams were less personal and more involved with worldly affairs. Politics. Religion. Things he had no interest in. Some of them he had witnessed or even participated in, but none that he cared to remember or contemplate. Mark Andrew was not a contemplative man and would not be coerced to become so even in his dreams. When he had finally taken the twenty-first drink from the golden cup. The one in red helped him to his feet and pulled the golden chain from around his neck.

"Now the time for sleep is over, my Lord," she told him.

"My Lord! The dragon approaches the border of our land. Follow the seventh river flowing from the seventh fountainhead and slay the beast, for he is the evil one who would destroy our lands," the golden haired one told him and for just a moment, he thought he knew her voice, knew her face and then it was gone. This was a dream and she was a goddess. "Once you have slain the dragon, you may sojourn with us here, my Lord and we will care for you. If you desire, you may return to your home."

A dragon? They wanted him to destroy a dragon. He knew there would be a catch. He had never even seen a real dragon. Perhaps this dragon was no more real than this dream and he would wake up in his own bed. He drew the golden sword from his scabbard and turned away from her. If he couldn't wake up, then he might at least change the scenery.

Running across the meadow was far more invigorating and enjoyable than the endless catnaps, but the green grass and flowers gave way to rocky, barren ground and he soon came upon the stream flowing from the seventh fountainhead. The stream, sluggish and dark, snaked through a scorched, burned landscape. The horizon was dim and covered with storm clouds where green and red lightning flashed continuously. A single raven flew toward him, cawing persistently as it passed, dipping low over his head, before swerving off and disappearing over the horizon. From across the wasteland he heard the roar of the beast. The same sound he had heard coming from the pit and the sound stopped him abruptly as a forgotten scene flashed through his mind.

The pit! The sudden memory of how he had gotten here came back to him. He had fallen into the sinkhole with Abdul Hafiz al Sajek, but he'd had the Key. The Golden Key. Where was it? Now the beast that had been roaring in the sinkhole would come and destroy him and the Key would be lost forever. The woman in red had the Key. He remembered seeing it in her hand and feeling the cool gold against his forehead. Subconsciously, he reached up to touch his forehead and found the disk of gold still on his forehead. His stomach lurched when he tried to pull it off, but it would not come free. It was if it was attached to his skull, in fact, and when he tried to pry it off, the pain was very real. When his panic settled down, he stepped forward cautiously to the edge of the stream and leaned over the water, trying to see his reflection in the murky depths. Trying to learn what terrible magick had attached the Key to his flesh and bone.

What he saw made him scramble back in fear. The glowing eyes of a great horned dragon with glistening crimson scales stared back at him from the surface of the water. Between the horns on its head was the Golden Key. He spun quickly, holding up the sword, expecting to find the beast that could be only scant inches from devouring him. Nothing was behind him. Nothing, but barren land without even a blade of grass remaining upon its scorched surface. He looked down at his hands. The hands of a man. He looked down at himself in wonder that he was still alive after the fall, but what of the dragon? Was the dragon invisible? Could it be that only its reflection was visible to the human eye? Did not the legends of old tell of such things? Panic rose in him again and he slashed the air in front of him desperately, stopping only when he heard the roars of the beast rumbling off to his left. He stood still and listened intently. The roars were not nearby, but they were approaching rapidly. He squinted at the horizon. As the bellows grew closer, the more it sounded as if they were coming from the air above him. He went back to the edge of the water and cautiously peered into its dark depths again. The face of the dragon eyed him with a curious frown. When he reached up one hand to touch his forehead where he'd felt the Key, the dragon mirrored his movements, reaching up one clawed foreleg to touch the golden disk on its head. He brushed at his shoulder and the dragon followed suit, hooking one claw around a folded wing as if preening. He opened his mouth and the dragon opened its mouth, displaying a double set of very impressive teeth with gleaming, filigreed gold caps on each fang. This was the most remarkable dream he had ever had. He smiled at the image, but the dragon grimaced, seeming only to snarl at him. Perhaps dragons could not smile… He raised the golden sword in his hand and the dragon held up a tiny sword, flashing gold, no bigger than a toothpick, it seemed, clutched between two clawed toes. Mesmerized by this magickal phenomena, he continued to strike various poses and expressions while the dragon tried to mimic his every move. Perhaps this watery specter had been provided to help him do battle against the beast of which the women had spoken. Ironically, he thought of Lucio and how pleased the Italian would be to see this image. Lucio had called him the dragon.

A sudden blast of hot air snapped him out of his trance and he looked up from the enchanted stream to see his adversary for the first time. But Lucio was not his problem at the moment. A rolling, thunderous grumble announced the arrival of the baneful dragon.

A tremendous, greenish black dragon fell from the clouds across the stream and touched down lightly upon the burned and blasted rocks lining the heavily eroded stream bank. The great beast raised its head, folded its wings and drew itself up to its full height, rearing on its muscular hind legs while its forelegs pawed the air. Mark was surprised to find that he was looking directly into its glowing eyes rather than looking up at it. Perhaps it was a small dragon?

No! He suddenly understood the meaning of the images in the water. He, too, was a dragon. A red dragon. Like all dreams, anything was possible. Anything. Only a dream. Only another of his unending repertoire of nightmares. At least this one was decidedly different and refreshing and did not involve beheaded specters or blood-washed fields of battle wherein everyone was dead and he was left the only survivor.

He replaced his sword in its scabbard. The golden sword would not be effective against such a monster. The black dragon roared again and green flames spewed from its nostrils, searing the burnt ground in front of it, turning the dark water of the stream to hissing steam. It turned its horned head to one side and eyed him from one dark green eye as if challenging him to make some similar display. Mark Andrew drew a deep breath and felt his chest puff up unnaturally. He let go of the breath and was surprised to see a red flame shoot out across the water toward the far bank. Certainly, breathing fire was a dangerous trait when not properly controlled or realized. He shook his head and the flames wavered back and forth before dissipating

The black dragon spread its wings and took to the air with a great flapping and roaring. Strangely enough, but not surprisingly under the circumstances, he had the sudden, irresistible urge to follow. He felt his own red leather wings unfold from his back and then watched the stream grow smaller as he was lifted into the air with little effort at all. He soon found himself flying through the dark clouds close behind his hideous opponent as it flew toward the golden fountain. The black dragon swished its tail at him, slapping him soundly in the face, spinning him over on his back. He flapped his wings desperately in order to right himself and then redoubled his efforts to regain the lost space between them. The slap hurt! Staying clear of the whipping tail, flying swiftly now through the clouds, they alternately swooped close to the ground and then rose high above the clouds. The landscape rolled away from them and everywhere the shadow of the black dragon fell on the green meadow a black trail of charred ground followed him as he repeatedly belched searing plasma onto the grass.

Mark drew alongside the beast and used one clawed hind leg to tentatively grasp the edge of the black dragon's wing on the upbeat. The slight interruption sent the black beast into a spin that ended only a scant few feet from a close encounter with the meadow. It righted itself with a terrible screeching growl and turned back toward its attacker. Mark threw his head back and presented his chest and claws to his opponent. They crashed together, locking hind legs and claws in the air. Both sets of wings flapped and beat fruitlessly as they began to spin out of control toward the ground.

Just before they crashed to the earth, they separated and rose again into the air. They met once more higher than before, crashing together with painful inaccuracy, but did not lock together as before. Mark felt the dragon's claws scraped along his belly and close around his left leg. The beast drew a deep breath, drew back its head and prepared to burn him to a crisp as he dangled head down by one leg. Mark threw himself backwards again and tumbled head over heels, ripping his leg from the deadly grip. He folded his wings and plummeted toward the ground in a harrowing descent that ripped the breath from his lungs. The great blast of greenish fire flashed dangerously close to his head, almost blinding him, but leaving him untouched by the deadly flames.

He caught himself before he smacked into the meadow and flew swiftly away, close to the ground. When he had accelerated to his maximum speed, he flew upwards in a great loop, reaching far above the clouds where he glimpsed strange stars in a cold, black sky. When he emerged from the clouds again, he was behind the dragon, which had resumed its course toward the golden fountain. Mark could see the fountain in the distance as he slipped stealthily into the slip stream created by the black dragon's tremendous wings. He dove under the dragon's belly suddenly and came up in front of him slapping him roundly with his tail before flipping on his back. He raked down the length of the beast with the horns on his head and heard the creature roar in pain and frustration.

The black beast rolled away to Mark's left and turned long enough to spit fire at him again. Mark avoided the gouts of flame and noxious fumes, swerving around in a horizontal loop that brought him back beside his adversary. Turning quickly, he laid hold of one of the dragon's wings with his fore claws and clamped his teeth on the back of the dragon's neck. The dragon shrieked in pain and confusion and spun over and over in his grip, slinging him off. He rolled away, righted himself and came back around in front of the single-minded creature. It was very obvious that it was bent on destroying the beautiful fountain and the two goddesses living within its golden mists.

As they approached the fountain at breakneck speed, Mark was unable to get close enough to attack the beast again as it weaved and bobbed erratically to avoid its pursuer. The black dragon began to slow its pace as they drew closer to the golden mists above the fountain. Mark flew on and around the fountain, turned back and flew directly through the mists. The water cooled his back and coated him with golden droplets. He emerged from the mist directly in front of the other beast. They crashed together violently, sparks flew from their scales and they bounced off each other's belly, touching lightly on the ground before leaping back into the air. The black monster rose straight up into the air directly above the fountain. Mark Andrew followed him and then swooped under it as it began to make another hurdling descent on the waters. The black dragon tried to maneuver around him, but he rolled on to his back and locked with him from below. As they fell, Mark reached for the Golden Sword of the Cherubim, hoping that it was truly at his side where it was supposed to be. He came up with the sword in his claw as he fought for a position against the dragon's flailing claws and beating wings. The black dragon drew back its head, puffing out its chest, preparing to send another blast of fire into his face. Mark raised the sword and jammed it hilt-deep into one of the dragon's huge green eyes. Blood and water gushed from the wound, pouring into the fountain, turning its shimmering spray red momentarily.

The beast screamed a powerful blast of heat into his face as they spun in a close circle and plummeted toward the fountain. The black dragon, mad with pain, managed to cling to him with tooth and nail, taking him down as well. Mark Andrew struggled desperately to free himself from the seeming death grip. It was hopeless. The dragon's talons were tangled in his wings and he could not break free. Sickening, ripping noises told him that his own wings were shredding as the talons ripped through the webbing stretched between the bones, though he felt no pain. He managed to get the upper hand by keeping the fallen monster's body below him, but the ground was coming up much too fast. He would never survive the fall, but at least this nightmare would very soon be over.

The two beasts crashed into the grass beside the fountain, the impact of their bodies shaking the meadow. Darkness surrounded him and the green grass shrank to a tiny spot of light and he knew he was dying. So this was his fitting end? At least he had taken the evil beast with him and left the golden fountain intact for his two lovely goddesses. Semiramis and Diana. Those were their names! And his last coherent thought.

(((((((((((<O>)))))))))))

"Uncle!" John Paul shouted at Lucio who sat on the front steps of his father's house, scraping the mud from his boots. He had just returned from the chapel where the heavy rains had washed out a gully across the road. One of his less pleasant jobs since taking over Ramsay's duties in Scotland in the Knight's absence was caring for Glessyn Chapel. It seemed things around the old place were perpetually in need of repair. If it weren't the road, it was the roof. Taking care of the old stone building and the grounds around it was a never ending battle against the elements. He was bone tired and ready for a good glass of wine and a nap in front of the television.

Lucio turned to frown at John. What now?

The prophet rushed through the door, grabbed his arm and dragged him almost bodily into the entry hall, leaving his boots outside before the Italian could protest. He started to turn back, but found himself being pushed up the stairs quite forcefully. Lucio put one foot against the bottom riser and gripped the rail in consternation.

"What is wrong?!" he asked when John tried to pry his hands from the railing. Why didn't the boy ever just say what was on his mind? Why did he always have to act things out like some sort of mime?

John Paul looked up the stairs when a long wail echoed down from the second floor hallway, making Dambretti's heart lurch and his hair stand on end.

"Oh! Santa Maria! Why didn't you tell me?!" Lucio muttered under his breath as he bounded up the stairs with John Paul on his heels. He met Simon in the hallway and knocked the Healer against the wall as he, too, made his way toward the Chevaliere's bedroom.

"Hold, Brother," Simon grabbed his arm. "This is not the place for you. John Paul, don't let him in. I can't handle both of them at once."

"Let go of me," Lucio told the shorter man and shook him off easily. "She needs me."

He pushed past the Healer and reached the door, but barely had his hand touched the doorknob before he found himself sliding down the hallway on his back with John Paul on top of him. He scrambled up on his hands and knees, glaring up at the determined scowl on the face of Mark's son. John Paul was a very literal young man. It was obvious he had every intention of carrying out Simon's instructions or die trying, if necessary. No matter, Meredith needed him and nothing was going to stop him from getting to her.

Simon opened the bedroom door and stepped inside as another muffled wail reached their ears.

"Dammit, John Paul!" Lucio cursed as he climbed to his feet and dusted off his black slacks. He stomped back down the hall to the bedroom door and tried the knob. Locked! What was Simon doing? "Simon! Brother! Open the door!" No answer except for more cries from Merry. Something was terribly wrong. "Simon! Dammit! I'll break it down! I swear I will! I know I will!"

He beat on the door, shouting for the Healer to open it for several seconds and then backed across the hall, lowered one shoulder, preparing to break down the door. John Paul caught him broadsides in a full body tackle when he was half way across the hall and knocked him to the floor again. They skidded to the edge of the stairs, teetered on the top step and then rolled in a tangle of arms and legs to the stone floor at the bottom of the steps.

Lucio kicked away from John Paul and got up slowly, checking his arms and legs for broken bones. Finding no serious injuries, he started back up the stairs, determined to answer Meredith's cries. He would have bruises everywhere in a few hours. With some satisfaction, he noticed that blood ran from John Paul's nose and it was swelling already. But his gloat was short-lived when he felt the sting of blood in his left eye. He found a cut on his own forehead and pressed his fingers to it gingerly, before continuing up the stairs.

"No!" John Paul shouted and grabbed his leg before he reached the landing.

"Let go of me! Santa Maria! For the love of... " Lucio shouted at him in Italian. The Italian used the handrail to drag himself and John Paul along the landing.

The real cause of the tussle was already lost on both of them. They were fighting now, just to be fighting for domination. Lucio twisted around and put his sock foot against John's shoulder, trying to shove him away. His foot slipped and he landed on his butt on the rug, cursing anew as he lost ground on the landing when John Paul dragged him backward. His sock came off and the Prophet fell back against the wall as Lucio staggered up again.

John Paul lunged forward, grabbed him around one ankle and hooked his own foot around the newel post and hung on. Lucio pulled with all his strength, but could not extract himself from the desperate grip. Lucio didn't want to hurt John, but this was not working. John Paul had lost his ever-loving mind. He bent down and grabbed two hands full of the young man's hair, pulling his head up. He drew back his right fist, preparing to put an end to the thing when another figure appeared on the second floor landing, shouting something in German. This new peril rushed down the steps, scooped the Italian up and literally carried him back down the stairs to the foyer again, dragging him along painfully before dropping him unceremoniously on the flagstones near the open front door.

"You forgot your boots, Brother!"

Lucio got up even more slowly. He felt dizzy now and had more than one pain in more than one place from the tumbles. He looked into the face of the Knight of the Apocalypse and put one hand against a pain in his lower back. Merry screamed again. John Paul stood on the bottom step, rubbing his arm and then his leg and then his shoulder, making faces at his own pains. Lucio scowled and started for the stairs again stubbornly.

"Hold, Brother!" Von Hetz scowled at him. "It is not your place!"

Lucio threw up his hands and stalked away stiffly down the hall to the kitchen muttering under his breath "To hell with all of you !". If she wanted him, she would have to come looking for him!

(((((((((((((<O>)))))))))))))

260

The fall had completely winded the red dragon and left him struggling weakly to get away from the green and black monster on which he lay. The black dragon sprawled, unconscious on the scorched earth with its head thrown back, exposing its long, greenish-white neck to all who might have had the strength to hack its ugly head from its body. But the red dragon could not get his feet under him. His tattered red wings flapped listlessly against the ground, throwing chunks of charred dirt, small rocks and fine dust into the air as he tried to right himself. He could see the neck of the black dragon and wished only to sink his teeth in the unprotected flesh there, but he could also see that the black dragon was not breathing. Two thin wisps of noxious yellow smoke trailed from its nostrils. One of its wickedly clawed front feet twitched and he could hear a burbling, hissing sound as the his adversary's gas bag deflated. It was dead.

The red dragon managed to sit up haphazardly on his haunches and let go a pitiful roaring moan as his own distended gasbag expelled the last gulp of super-heated air he had planned to use against his enemy. The red flames evaporated in the purplish night and the dragon shook his head, causing the braided cord and silver ornaments around his neck to jingle. He clawed briefly at an insistent itch between the horns on his forehead and was surprised to see the golden disc fall to the dusty ground in front of him. He leaned forward cautiously and snuffled the device, blowing up puffs of steam mixed with smoke. The metal medallion glowed briefly from the contact with the hot air. Dragon breath. Quite lethal.

Recovering more quickly now, the red dragon stood on his hind legs and stretched his neck upwards, relieving the kinks in his spine. The aerial battle with the evil beast had left deep wounds on the right side of his belly below the ribcage. Blackish blood glittered beneath the torn scales there and the pain was sharp and burned intensely. He pressed one of his front feet against the offending wound and then let go a stupendous roar that filled the night sky when a dislocated rib snapped into place. When the pain subsided, he crept slowly to the side of his fallen foe and examined him carefully, lifting scales here and there along his belly, checking for any sign that the beast might recover. He moved along the neck, sniffing and snuffling until he reached the ghastly head. One eye was partially closed, but the other was open wide. Gouts of black blood clotted on the dragon's jaw and horned head around the fractured eye socket. A golden pin protruded from the midst of the open eye.

The red beast carefully clasped the pin between the tips of two clawed toes and pulled the tiny weapon from the eye. The Sword of the Cherubim sparkled in the dim light. Its twisted golden blade was stained black. The red dragon thrust the sword into the ground and pulled it out cleaned of the gore before tucking it through the braided white cord around his neck.

He sat back again wearily as fatigue overcame him and his eyelids drooped. He wanted only to sleep. In the distance he saw a luminous white figure approaching, riding a magnificent white horse, but he could not muster enough strength to flee from this new danger. When the horse drew nearer, he recognized the form of the golden-haired goddess who lived in the midst of the seven-tiered fountain. Not an enemy. A friend. Semiramis.

She rode directly to him and dismounted. He watched as she tossed her white fur cloak over her shoulders and drew a jeweled sword from her belt. She approached the black dragon with extreme caution. Nothing stirred as she poked and prodded the beast's neck and stomach. When she was sure it was dead, she came back to where he rested on one elbow. He could hear his own labored breathing as he struggled to keep his eyes open. Whether he was dying or just exhausted, he didn't know.

"You are weary, my Lord," she spoke to him and smiled as she stroked his lower jaw gently with one hand. Her beauty was unsurpassed. "Well done. The beast is dead and the land is safe. Your work here is over, my love. You are welcome to stay with us as always. Would you not care to pass some bit of time with us?"

The red dragon did not care to pass anything. He only wanted to sleep. For a hundred years. A thousand... If only he knew where his den might be. If only he had but the strength to fly there. He could not stay here. He didn't belong here. He wanted to go home. Home. To sleep.

"Sleep, yes, my Lord. Sleep and all will be well," she told him in a soft, soothing voice as darkness took him. "You are free to go, my love." Her words were like music to his ears as his eyelids grew heavier with sleep, he hoped or death. He did not know and did not care.

The goddess knelt beside him and disentangled the hilt of the sword from his hair. She kissed his cheek and wiped the sword on her cloak before laying it in front of him. She retrieved the golden disc and put it where he could easily find it. The sight of him sleeping peacefully made her smile. Before she left him, she pressed one hand against the gashes on his stomach and passed her healing energy directly to the ghastly wounds. After a long pause, a long sigh and a long last look, she whispered goodbye and returned to the mists of the fountain.

Mark Andrew snapped his eyes open and then blinked against the glare of the midday sun shining in his face. He sat up slowly and looked around. He was sitting in the middle of the patio that Merry had built for Simon behind his house. It was now surrounded by flowerbeds. Hundreds of white lilies with delicate pink markings, purple amaranths and blue violets surrounded the bricked area, all blooming in glorious splendor. In the center, directly in front of him was a large unpolished rectangle of dark stone. He pushed himself up slowly and then reached up to feel his forehead where the Key had been stuck during his battle with the black dragon. The Golden Key was gone. A dream. It was only a dream. He checked himself quickly and found his dagger in his belt and his sword at his side. In one of the numerous pockets of his black cargo pants he found a small bundle wrapped in white linen. The Key! He still had the Key. He had escaped the pit somehow, but had no recollection of how he had gotten home or why he was lying on the patio. A bump on the back of his head might explain his memory loss. He sat down wearily on the rock and then frowned down at the strange device adorning the top of it. A bronze and copper six-pointed star with a strange symbol carved in the center of the hexagon. What sorcery was this? He surveyed the immediate area and discovered that the flowerbeds had been laid out in the same fashion as the star on the stone: Six-points with the brick patio forming the central hexagon.

Mark Andrew looked up at his home and shuddered. The house hadn't changed and though he should have been overjoyed to find himself home no matter how he had gotten there, he felt uneasy and unwilling to go inside. He wondered if this was still a part of the nightmare? How much had been real and how much had been a dream? Where was Abdul Hafiz? And what had happened to Sir Champlain and Sir Philip? The sight of the flowers in bloom and his memory lapse did not bode well. Meredith couldn't possibly have gotten the flowers planted and blooming in a few short days. He saw no movement around the house. He glanced at the garden shed, but it was closed up tight, nice and neat as always.

He drew a deep breath and started forward up the brick path to the back steps. At least, Lucio had not blown up his laboratory in his absence and it wasn't raining or blowing snow. He wondered vaguely if Merry was still there or if everyone had left the place abandoned or under the care of old Bruce. Anger flared momentarily at the thought of Bruce living in the old place all alone. And who had been taking care of the chapel if that was so?

Inside the house, he relaxed a bit. The place had a definite lived-in feeling. There was a pile of dirty laundry on the workroom floor and basket of clean bed linen sitting atop the dryer. He smelled all the normal odors associated with daily life: tea, coffee, roasting mutton, as he entered the kitchen, but still he heard nothing but the humming of the freezer in workroom. The sight of Meredith's clothes in the floor lifted his spirits. At least she had not abandoned him, but where was she?

He started past the cellar door and then decided to go down and make sure everything was in order. The Scot was nothing if not methodical. He would start at the back door and go through the house room by room until he found someone or someone found him. Lucio had probably fouled it all up. He went down the steps and into the cellar. The cellar was in perfect order. Everything was in place and... clean... clean! Spotless, in fact. Bruce must have made good on his endless threats about cleaning the wine cellar. Green, brown and clear bottles gleamed in the old wooden racks.

He opened the door to his laboratory and the breath caught in his throat. The lab was as clean as the cellar. All the spider webs and dust had been cleaned out of every nook and cranny! Where his ancient wooden worktable had stood, he found a shiny clean stainless steel table with orderly rows of bottles and equipment in glass and steel cabinets and plastic covered wire racks. The bottles themselves were new, topped with metal or plastic lids which gleamed under a long, fluorescent light fixture overhead! He was stunned. Anger boiled to the surface. Bruce knew better than meddle in his lab. This was the Italian's doings!

His old wooden shelves had been replaced with modular steel shelving. His cabinets were gone and in their place stood red and yellow metal cabinets with the words 'toxic', 'flammable' and 'combustible' painted in block letters across the front along with the appropriate universal symbols stenciled in red and white. The large brick furnace had been scrubbed clean and the broken bricks along the top replaced. The skylight was opened and the glass panes were sparkling clean. New glass panes had been installed in place of some the older broken panels. The floor had been scrubbed, leveled and shiny new tile gleamed in the sunlight pouring through the skylight. All of his chemicals, herbs and minerals were contained in uniformly ordered and carefully aligned bottles, jars and ceramic crocks, replete with neatly printed labels. There was even a new bulletin board on the wall, replete with stainless steel clipboards and safety goggles hanging from pegs. He picked up a bottle of red liquid from the worktable and peered at the label. Red Water. Written neatly in Lucio's perfectly printed letters. He opened the red cabinet to see jars of sulfur, bottles of mercury and the yellow all lined up on the shelves in impeccable order.

There were rows of brand new beakers and flasks with red and blue gradient markings. Graduated cylinders with plastic holders on the bottoms, Bunsen burners, boxes of glass droppers with rubber bulbs, stainless canisters full of glass straws and metal stirrers, cotton balls, various colored plastic tubing in a number of sizes coiled on metal spools, shiny clamps and metal rods and stainless steel tripods. There was an electric cooker, a steel blender, a digital centrifuge, electronic thermometers and a number of electric appliances he did not recognize on the table. Everything was plugged into surge protectors fixed to the back of the table. He shook his head. What was wrong with candles and oil lamps? This was too impersonal for him. None of his old equipment was to be seen anywhere. A new glass bell jar sat in the center of the table over a ceramic trivet. On the trivet was a crockery bowl full of gold-colored powder. Was he making gold as well now? It hadn't taken him long to fall right into his old job, but how on earth had he figured it all out so quickly? The whole place reminded him of Valentino's laboratory in Texas. Apparently, Meredith had lent a hand here.

"Dammit!" Mark cursed and slammed the cabinet door. "Wot 'as 'e done t' me lab? *Basta!*"

He looked around once more, completely flabbergasted. A small wooden rocking chair sat next to a black miniature refrigerator with a matching microwave on top. It hadn't taken the Italian long to take over his lab. He looked in the refrigerator and found Italian beer, string cheese, bottled water and a bag of grapes. Atop the microwave was a box of crackers, two packages of microwave popcorn and an open box of macaroons, Lucio's favorite. He slammed the door and in turning focused on the area under the stairs where Lucio had put in a full shower and an eyewash station... had he taken over the rest of his house as well? With a dark anger rising in him, he wondered what else the Knight of the Golden Eagle had done in his absence. Not only that, but how long had he been gone?!

A series of chills flowed up his spine as he climbed the stairs to the kitchen holding onto a new ornately worked wrought-iron handrail with a bottle of white wine in one hand. At the top, he glanced back at this cellar and saw that it had the look of a goddamned rathskellar or one of the underground bistros in Paris. The wine he carried wore an Italian label, no less. But he needed a drink and there was no Scotch to be found amongst the well-stocked cellar. Not even the hounds had come to meet him. Surely they had heard him come in the back door. He pulled his dagger from his belt and continued down the hall with more caution than before.

In the kitchen, he found more changes as he searched for a corkscrew to open the wine. Everything had been rearranged and modern appliances had been placed on the re-tiled counters. A microwave oven, an electric can opener, a shiny toaster with six wide slots, a small convection oven. Merry's additions no doubt. He had intended to buy these things long ago, but Bruce never complained. He stopped to look at the blender and remembered that Merry like to mix things up and drink them rather than eat them. Something she had called 'fruit smoothies'. Strawberries and kiwis, no doubt. He drew up short at the sight of a new stove with shiny knobs and a built-in grill on top between the burners. He slowly scanned the wall next to the stove where a free-standing cupboard had once stood as he uncorked the wine and saw that several new appliances had been installed in the wall. He examined them carefully, running his hand over the smooth stainless steel surfaces, peering inside the dark glass windows on front. Inside one of them a leg of lamb was sizzling in a glass Dutch oven. Next to these additions stood a glass-doored cold box displaying an assortment of desserts.

They had turned his kitchen into a goddamned cafeteria!

The only thing remaining was his long, wooden table with benches and chairs now made more comfortable with tufted, ruffled seat cushions.

He left the kitchen in growing alarm. His library. His books. The house remained eerily quiet and he found himself walking on tiptoe. He made his way silently to the front entry hall. Most everything looked the same here at least, but the library was another frightening development.

No one was present, but neither was his favorite chair. There were two leather recliners and a matching leather sofa. The furniture had been rearranged around a new focus: a wide-screen television hanging on the wall by the double doors. A blue light glowed around it and though there was no sound, a man dressed in khaki shorts was pointing and gesturing to a group of monkeys feeding in a banyan tree. On either side of the television, he found his oldest leather-bound books, neatly arranged in new bookshelves. He tore his eyes away from the picture and scanned the old bookshelves. All present and accounted for. A relief, but the hearth had a spit and polished look about it and there were shiny new fireplace tools in the rack along with a brass fan-shaped fire screen. The mahogany desk was gone. It had been replaced by a modern thing made of glass and steel tubing. A fancy black computer sat on the desk mocking him as he saw his own reflection in the blank monitor. All of this he took in with one inhaled breath and felt the hair on the back of his neck rising in anger. Even the wall papering above the wainscoting had been changed. He stepped closer and ran one hand over the embossed designs in the vinyl. Not too bad. He could live with that, but the other?

He spun on his heel as a muffled sound drifted down the main stairway to his ears. The sound of a door opening and closing upstairs. The doors to the parlor were closed as usual. Checking them quickly, he found them locked. He would look in there later. He put one hand on the rail and then his heart lurched when Simon suddenly appeared at the top of the stairs. The Healer's face was smeared with blood. His white shirt was stained terribly with the same. There was blood on his hands and he held a bundle of bloodied white towels in his arms.

"Brother, what happened?!" Mark shouted up to him, just as he stepped on the top step. Simon looked up, faltered and missed his step. He came bouncing down the stairs, tumbling head over heels, and landed at Mark Andrew's feet. Mark turned him over, but he only groaned slightly before slipping into unconsciousness. Mark stood quickly and pulled the golden sword from his scabbard. He raised the sword and placed his back against the railing, rushing headlong up the stairs. He stood in the dim hallway and waited for another sign or sound to tell him which way to go.

There were subdued voices coming from somewhere down the hall. He pressed his back against the wall, and edged toward the sound in complete silence. Merry's bedroom. The door not quite closed. The voices came from within. Still he could not make out the words.

Mark Andrew drew a deep breath and kicked the door open, stepping inside quickly, holding the blade straight up in front of him, expecting the worst. What met his eyes was beyond comprehension.

Lucio Dambretti and Konrad von Hetz stood near the bed with their backs to him. They turned abruptly at his noisy entrance. Each of them held a squirming bundle in their arms. Babies? Babies! Two of them. Lucio's mouth fell open and he heard Merry shriek. Mark took a step backwards and lowered his weapon slowly. Nine months? He'd been gone nine months? Impossible!

He lowered his head and tried to regain his composure. He'd made a fool of himself, bursting in on them, carrying his sword and dagger like the madman he had become, but when he looked up again, intending to apologize, his shock was made complete by the sight of his dead brother, Luke Matthew, who suddenly appeared in front of him, near enough to take hold of his shoulders with a huge smile on his face. He stared into the crystal blue eyes momentarily before blackness threatened to close in on him. His brother? Alive? How could it be? He almost fainted, but found himself supported in a bear hug that threatened to smother what life was left in him completely out.

"Papa!" John Paul cried as he picked Mark up from the floor and swung him around as if he were a child.

Chapter Fifteen of Seventeen
Know therefore and understand

Mark Andrew stood in front of the fireplace in the parlor staring up at the portrait of Lucio and Merry that hung above the mantel, clasping a glass of very old Scotch in both hands. In the painting, the unsmiling couple stood next to each other, dressed in the pristine white uniforms of the Order. Lucio held Merry's hand in his, but seemed to stare back at Mark defiantly with just the slightest hint of his famous smile on his face which was turned just enough to hide the scar on his cheek.

"Twins?" Mark asked simply.

"A boy and a girl, just as the prophecy said, born on Midsummer's Eve," Simon answered him softly. "The boy looks like his mother. The girl is the image of her father from what I can tell so far."

"How long, Brother?" Mark asked and turned to look at the Healer who had a big bruise covering a sizable lump over his right eye, the results of his tumble down the stairs.

"Almost twenty-one years. You went missing in 2016. It's 2037," Simon raised both blonde eyebrows. He sat on the green velvet sofa with his elbows propped on his knees. This was the only room that had not suffered changes except for the portrait above the fireplace. He rubbed his elbow and then his knee. He had bruises all over him from the tumble down the stairs.

"And Bruce?" Mark looked pained.

"He's gone, Brother," Simon told him reluctantly. "He retired to Edinburgh and died last year. I'm sorry. He didn't suffer long."

Mark nodded. He reached up to unhook the portrait and then walked it carefully across the hall to the library and leaned it against the wall below the television before returning to the parlor without a word. Simon looked at the floor, unable to watch as the Scot moved the portrait of his mother, which had been relegated to the western wall, back to the nail above the fireplace. Her rightful place.

"What will you do, Mark Andrew?" Simon asked him point blank.

He stood looking out one of the tall windows beside the fireplace. His cook was gone, his dogs were gone. His life was gone. Everything had changed. The babies that he had, for one fleeting moment thought might be his own, belonged to the Italian. The painting was their wedding portrait. They had been married in his chapel at Glessyn by his priest, no less! And they lived in his house. And his son was no longer a boy, but a grown man, thirty-six years old now and the image of his own dead uncle, Luke Matthew. It was almost more than he could do to keep from completely breaking down into a lump of flesh, blood and bones on the rug.

"I will have to go to Italy," he said quietly. "I have to return the Key to Champlain or is he dead as well?"

"No, he lives and Sir Philip also," Simon answered and shifted uncomfortably on the sofa before standing up. "They managed to throw the sorcerer into the pit after you fell. It took both of them to do it. Champlain's injury was more severe than Philip's but they mended rightly."

"Oh," Mark nodded. It was too much to absorb all at once.

"I would suggest that you wait a bit before you do anything. Try to get your wits together. Try to remember what happened after you fell. The Master will want the full story for the records, of course and he will want to know what happened to al Sajek," Simon said quietly, but there was a note of desperation in his voice.

There was no doubt that the Healer expected him to explode in a fit of murderous rage at any second, but Mark did not feel angry. He felt bewildered and heartsick.

"Who lives here, Simon?" He asked and raised his chin slightly. "Are they so afraid of me, they won't even come down to see me?"

"John Paul lives here and the Ritter comes fairly often these days," Simon answered the first question. "I stay here as much as I can. It is a beautiful place. You say you saw my garden?"

"Yes," Mark nodded and turned away from him. "I woke up in it. Is there an empty bed?"

"Yes, of course," Simon answered more brightly. "It's still your home, Brother. We... I mean, you have a new gardener and a housekeeper downstairs and I stay downstairs as well, but John Paul and... well, John Paul has your old room right now. Brother Lucio stays with Sister Meredith... in her room. Von Hetz has a room he keeps upstairs. I'm sure John Paul would be more than..."

"No!" Mark shook his head. "Just have a bed brought here." He waved one hand about the parlor. "I'll stay here. If I decide to stay here."

Simon glanced around at the beautiful room full of antiques. If?

"I'll go with you," Simon told him. "A number of things have changed and much more has occurred in the world. Politics. Religion. Finances. You'll need me to... catch you up to speed."

Mark nodded and then looked up to see Lucio Dambretti standing in the doorway looking at him with a peculiar expression on his face. He could not tell if it was fear or concern.

"Brother," Lucio said and looked at him from under his brows, obviously ready for the worst.

"Brother," Mark returned his greeting with a short smile. "You have outdone yourself this time. I must commend you on your efforts to usurp my entire life. Well done." He retrieved his glass of Scotch from the mantel and raised it in salute.

"I did what was to be done," Lucio told him flatly. "We can leave as soon as you like."

"There is no need to hurry," Mark told him. "I will be going on to Italy. Simon will go with me. There will be time for it."

Lucio walked into the room and took him by the shoulders to greet him in the Templar fashion, kissing him lightly on the lips.

"It is good to see you again, whether you would have it so or not," he told him and then turned abruptly to leave him standing in front of the hearth, closing the door behind him.

Simon let out a sigh of relief and Mark Andrew closed his eyes, dropped his head and covered his mouth with one hand.

"I'm sorry, Brother," Simon apologized. "I know this must be hard for you."

He was startled by the excited voice of an unfamiliar female from the doorway.

"Simon! Merry needs to..." the voice faltered when he looked up.

A woman stood in the doorway. She was about his own age and dressed in pair of faded jeans and a blue tee shirt with a colorful sailboat embroidered on front. Her brown hair was pulled up in ponytail on top of her head. She stared at him, mouth agape.

"Close yur mouth, lassie, lest th' floies get in," Mark said after a moment. Just what he needed. A female servant! "Do ye not know th' value of knocking?"

"I'm sorry. I forgot to tell you," Simon said quickly and went to take her hand. He dragged her into the room to stand in front of him. "This is your daughter-in-law. John Paul's wife. Michele. Michele, this is John Paul's father, Sir Mark Andrew Ramsay."

The woman swallowed hard and stuck out her hand nervously. Mark Andrew crossed the room and took her hand automatically, frowning in confusion. She was not a beautiful woman, but she had a fresh clean look about her like many of the local Scottish girls. A smattering of freckles dotted her nose and she had bright, clear eyes of sparkling blue.

"Mark Andrew," she repeated his name. "My God. I thought you were John Paul. I never realized... I mean, no one told me that... I'm sorry. I... I.... I didn't know... realize that you were back from..." she turned on the Healer, her complexion growing somewhat pale. "Simon? What is this? I thought he was dead. John Paul never..."

Simon took her arm and sat her down in one of the velvet chairs.

"Michele, I'm sorry. I didn't have time to tell you. He just came in. Everything happened so fast. We weren't expecting him and... Be still now, my child," he whispered to her. "There are complications in the family. Surely John has told you about his father. Do not upset yourself and I will be with you in a moment." Simon turned to Mark and shrugged apologetically.

"Michele and John Paul have been married for twelve years," Simon explained quickly. "She lives here, too." Simon still wore the same bloodstained clothes. He looked down at them in frustration.

"I'm verra pleased t' meet you," Mark Andrew told her darkly. "Wot ist ye wanted? Did ye say thot Meredith needed something?"

John Paul's wife swallowed hard and looked at Simon before answering. How could it be that John Paul never told her about his father? That he was alive? That he was so... that he looked... that his father was younger than himself?! She found her voice and cleared her throat nervously. And rude! How could John Paul have such a wonderful mother and stepfather and have a rude father?

"Merry... Meredith wanted to get up, Simon. John Paul has to go over to the chapel. It's time for Mass. He has a meeting with the secretary and... there's the matter of... the matter of the new cistern." Michele got up and backed away from them slowly. It was very clear she was highly disturbed by Mark Andrew's appearance and demeanor.

"If she feels like it, tell her to go ahead," Simon shrugged. "I'll be up directly."

The woman turned quickly and made her escape.

"Such a sweet girl," Simon said quickly when she was gone. "You'll like her, I'm sure. They make a good match."

"We need t' talk, Brother."

Mark headed for the door. Now, he was feeling angry.

He dragged Simon out of the parlor and down the hall, past his new kitchen and outside to the patio. The blue flowers hit him in the face like a fist and he grimaced at the sight of such a happy color when his world was entirely black. He walked to the middle of the paved area and looked down at the stone, before going on to the glass topped table to sit down in one of the chairs. Simon sat down across from him and chewed his lip nervously.

"Now let me get this straight, Brother." Mark Andrew set his jaw. "I've been gone twenty-one years. My son is... thirty-six, probably a bit older than me. I have a daughter-in-law named Michele who seems to be American, judging from the accent. Merry and Lucio are married. How long?"

"Six years," Simon answered his question bluntly and set his own jaw. Mark Andrew was hard to cope with and Simon did not feel like dealing with him, but he saw no one else coming forth to handle him. Simon really hated his job at times like this. "She waited fifteen years for you, Brother."

"And Lucio stayed here all that time?" Mark frowned.

"Most of the time," Simon nodded. "He worked in your lab. As I said, I came as often as I could and stayed for as long I could. You needn't have worried about Sister Meredith's love for you, Brother. I can assure you that there was no... trifling here. After she accepted his proposal, he moved

271

some of his personal belongings here and stayed, but they were married right and proper before sharing a bed. He has kept your house and your duties well in order."

"So I noticed," Mark said darkly, remembering his re-modeled lab. "So he has been making gold for the order?"

"Yes. Don't ask me how. I don't know," Simon shrugged.

"And John Paul is a... priest?" This was the strangest development.

"Yes," Simon nodded. "Not an actual priest, but he has a following. They call him Father John. He isn't ordained if that's what you mean. He majored in Theology at the University in Edinburgh and he spent a few years studying at Oxford... your old alma mater."

"And he uses the chapel to... lead his flock?" Mark made a pained face.

"He cares for the chapel as you did and he conducts masses there on Sundays and Friday nights." Simon also looked pained. "I don't understand it either."

"And these twins..." Mark looked away across the meadow. "Are they immortal?"

"Who can know?" Simon shook his head and looked down at his hands again at the blood there. "They only just arrived, Brother. The delivery was not easy. Sister Meredith lost a great deal of blood."

"What will happen, Simon?" Mark asked him and looked him in the eyes for the first time. When Simon did not answer, he pulled his black shirt over his head. He couldn't possibly have worn the same clothes for twenty-one years. The tee-shirt was as clean as the morning he had put it on in the hotel in Tallahassee. His trousers were equally pristine as were his boots and everything in his numerous pockets. Where had he been? He tried hard to remember details of his last memories, but there seemed to be gaps as if he were trying to remember a dream that was just on the verge of his conscious mind, but not quite. He looked down at his stomach and was surprised to find four long, pink scars starting just right of center under his ribcage. He remembered the green and black dragon raking its talons across his belly when they had been fighting in the air. They looked like old scars, very much like the dagger wound he had suffered in Jerusalem almost nine hundred years earlier. So it was all true, not a series of disjointed nightmares. He'd lived as a dragon and he'd killed the black beast threatening the golden fountain. At the moment, he couldn't explain it, but he was delighted to discover that he wasn't quite as crazy as he'd first thought. He looked up at the Healer in amusement and then smiled, before pulling the Golden Key from the pocket of his cargo pants to lay it on the table in front of Simon. At least there was some bit of good news.

"What happened?" Simon stared at the scars on Mark's stomach in abject horror. "Where have you been, Brother?" It was the first time that

272

Simon had actually had time to ask where Mark had been, realizing that Mark Andrew had not simply appeared out of thin air. There was no car out front. He didn't fall from the sky and he'd hardly crawled up from the well. The meadow behind the Knight spun slowly and the Healer thought he might faint. "How did you get here?" He asked in a hoarse whisper when his throat constricted. "Are you spirit or flesh?"

"Hold, Brother," Mark had to laugh. "I suppose I'm flesh enough to feel pain. I met the beast, Simon," Mark told him. "It was in the pit. The one John Paul warned me about. It wasn't a dream or a metaphor after all."

"Don't speak to me of dreams and beasts, Mark Andrew," Simon let out a long breath and shook his head sadly. "I have had enough of them over the past few decades. I still dream of the crypt."

They both turned when the back door slammed.

Von Hetz appeared on the back stoop, looking very distraught. So far, von Hetz had managed to avoid speaking with Mark alone. A few brief words after the initial encounter in Merry's bedroom and that had been all. The Apocalyptic Knight had announced that he would share the good news with Italy, handed over the baby and left them.

He walked hurriedly down the path to join them. Mark automatically attributed the man's attitude with some piece of bad news from the Villa.

"You'd best come inside, Brothers," he said without preamble. "We have a problem…"

Chapter Sixteen of Seventeen
they would desire mercies of the God of heaven
concerning this secret

Lucio Dambretti, Knight of the Golden Eagle, and very recently new father of twins, sat on the floor of Mark Andrew Ramsay's laboratory with his head in his hands. He was beside himself with fear and bewilderment. Ramsay had barely returned and already the world was falling apart again. He had a million things on his mind and first and foremost was the fact that he and Merry would no longer be able to stay in Scotland. He did not necessarily love Scotland, though it was sometimes a beautiful place when the weather was pleasant, and one wherein he would not mind bringing up his children. Merry loved it as if she were a born Scot and had even developed a slight brogue during the fifteen years she had lived here. She would not want to leave. Already, she had asked him what they were going to do, how they were going to move with two newborns and where and what would Mark Andrew do. He'd had no answers for her, but Mark's seeming calm in the parlor might have been a good sign, but for this latest development.

Now, he had another problem. Much larger and much more in need of immediate attention than their dilemma with Mark Andrew's unexpected return from never-never land. Where his Brother had been was a mystery unexplained as of yet. What had he been doing for twenty-one years and how had he suddenly reappeared in Scotland in his own backyard, seemingly out of the clear blue sky. Was it all a joke? Something the Grand Master and the Scot had cooked up together? Was the Grand Master after the twins and nothing more? Would he now be eliminated with the birth of the prophesied babies and his wife be given over to the Scot? A million questions and insane scenarios raced through his brain.

When Konrad von Hetz entered the laboratory, with Mark Andrew and Simon d'Ornan in tow, the Knight of the Golden Eagle raised his head and looked at them accusingly.

Simon drew up short at the sight of the three willow baskets sitting in front of Lucio on the tiled floor. In each basket was a child, newborn. Each child wrapped in a different colored blanket. Two of them had pieces of parchment paper neatly rolled and tied with black ribbons attached to the basket. Mark Andrew pushed Simon out of the way and knelt beside Lucio, frowning deeply. One blanket was red, one blanket was black and the third blanket was blue.

"I thought you said twins, Brother," Mark looked up at Simon in confusion. "Fur pity's sake, mon, why did ye bring them to th' cellar? Tis no place fur a babe!"

"These are not my children," Lucio answered him in a voice broken with panic and despair. "My son and daughter are upstairs with their mother. I found these babies here, in the lab. Someone left them here. How could someone get into the lab in our house with three babies unseen?" Lucio's head snapped up and his eyes blazed momentarily. "Are these your children, Brother? Did you bring them back with you from Perdition?"

He handed a piece of parchment to Mark Andrew. It was from the basket of the baby wrapped in the blue blanket. The child was asleep. Its small, almost bald head was covered with a thin layer of silver hair.

The Knight of Death looked up at Simon again and then at von Hetz. He had no idea where he had been, nor what he had been doing. They stood watching him as if they expected him to read it aloud and so he did.

"What locks the Gate beneath the serpent's eye? This child is Elizabeta Simone." Mark Andrew read the words written in heavy black script on the unlined paper. "Wot th' divil ist?!"

He dropped the paper to the floor and reached into the basket, carefully picking up the baby wrapped in blue. It immediately began to wail at the touch of his hands. He had no experience with babies, but laid it very carefully on the stainless steel table. If someone were playing a trick on them, it was damned strange that it happened the very day he returned home. Lucio got up from the floor and joined in with Simon and von Hetz as they crowded around him. Mark Andrew gingerly unwrapped the blanket to look at the child. It was still unwashed from birth and wore no clothing. A girl, small, but very healthy in appearance, pink under a bluish white coating on her skin.

Von Hetz turned on his heel and reached down to pick up the basket with the black blanket. He laid it on the counter and pulled the tiny scroll from the basket, untying the ribbon with utmost care as if he were defusing a bomb.

"What dwells within the tomb after the spirit has departed? This child is Konrad Eli," the Apocalyptic Knight read from the paper. He unfolded the black blanket to expose the child, also unwashed, newly born and decidedly healthy in appearance. A boy with dark, olive skin and dark hair. The baby awakened at his touch and began to cry, adding a second voice to the first. Simon stood mesmerized, staring first at the one and then the other.

Lucio removed the third child from its basket and uncovered it. Mark took the third parchment roll from the basket and Lucio snatched it away.

"What hand harvests the soul at death? This child is John du Morte," Lucio read the paper and then threw it to the floor and stomped on it. He yanked the red blanket from the child and its cries joined those of its brother and sister. A boy! Dark hair, light skin. Three babies. Triplets, but all very different and only hours old. The umbilical cords were tied with red strings.

Mark took a step back, shaking his head. These were none of his doing. He had come to the lab even before going upstairs and they had not been here. Their sanctuary had been invaded under their very noses. He reached for his sword, but he'd left it in the parlor.

"*Che cosa e` esso?*" Lucio asked looked around in dismay. "What cruel joke is this? Whose children are these? Who brought them here?" He spun on Mark Andrew. "Is this your doing? Did you bring these babies here? Where are the mothers? What have you done? Why? Are you in league with the Grand Master? I won't stand for it!"

Simon backed away from the table, unable to drag his eyes away from the red-faced baby girl who was now crying as loud as its tiny lungs would allow. The room was filled with their cries. Mark Andrew scooped up the baby and put it back in the basket on the floor and covered his ears with his hands. Von Hetz retrieved the parchment papers and stacked them together, smoothing them out. Simon turned and ran out of the room with one hand over his mouth.

Mark once more ignored the Italian's questions and accusations and started after the Healer and von Hetz grabbed his arm.

"Brother, something very evil has happened here today. Take this!" he shoved the papers into his hand. "Tell no one. Fetch your daughter-in-law."

The Apocalyptic Knight turned to Lucio.

"Brother!" Von Hetz took Lucio by both arms. "Look at me!"

Mark stuffed the papers in his pocket before hurrying after the Healer. He did not want to hear any more. He followed after Simon and stopped in the kitchen. He could hear the Knight of the Serpent throwing up somewhere near the rear of the house. After a quick drink of water that did little to loosen the knot in his throat, he went in search of his daughter-in-law. He could think of nothing better to do than to follow the Apocalyptic Knight's instructions. His mind was still reeling from everything he had learned in such a short time. He was ready for someone else to take charge. Surely von Hetz knew what was going on if anyone did and he had experience with orphans. Plus he had the ability to delve into their minds and learn the truth. They needed to know the truth, if the truth was amongst them. Perhaps these were foundlings or... or... He pushed the tangled thoughts from his mind as he tried to think where he might find the girl. What was her name? Melinda? Melanie? Michele, yes that was it. Damn it! John Paul married. How could it be so? He dragged his shirt over his head as he climbed the stairs.

The impression he had made on his daughter-in-law had not been very favorable. What happened next added nothing positive. He ran up the stairs and down the second floor hallway, shouting for Michele at the top of his lungs. The frightened girl stuck her head out of John Paul's bedroom, staring at him in shock.

When she stepped into the hall and shushed him, he grabbed her arm and dragged her, shrieking toward the stairs. He did not look back when he heard another door open and heard Merry calling his name. No doubt she was thinking he had killed everyone in the house and was now about to slay her son's wife as well. He couldn't deal with her now... not yet.

(((((((((((((<O>)))))))))))))

A few hours later, when things had calmed down a bit, Merry had the triplets brought to her room and laid out on the bed. She examined each one carefully before saying anything. Michele brought warm, soapy water, clean cloths and soft blankets to clean them and they soon had them dressed in newborn clothes and swaddled tightly in new blankets which seemed to have a calming effect on them.

The four Knights of Solomon's Temple waited almost breathlessly for Merry to speak after making her examination as if she would somehow miraculously know what was going on. Michele sat on the edge of her chair with her eyes riveted on the three squirming bundles on the bed. John Paul had not returned from the chapel. He knew nothing of this development... yet. Michele, who normally accompanied her husband in his mission work, had stayed behind to care for Merry, but the young woman was in shock. First John's father's arrival and now five babies and none hers. It didn't seem fair. Not fair at all.

"The Master spoke to me of certain prophecies," Merry said looking at each of the men in turn. Mark Andrew found it hard to meet her gaze. It was the first time he had heard her speak since his return and he could think of nothing beyond the fact that he had lost her again. "He told me there were two prophecies concerning the birth of twins. He felt that my marriage to Lucio was the fulfillment of one of those prophecies wherein twins would be born of the Virgin and the Eagle or 'the second' as he called Lucio," she paused and a flush of pink colored her cheeks. Speaking of her own marriage, pregnancy and the involvement of two lovers, both present in the same room was difficult to say the least, but none of them seemed put out by her words. After swallowing hard, she continued "He said that these twins would be a boy and a girl, immortal at birth. This, he said, was the will of God."

Lucio glanced at Mark Andrew as if to say 'I told you so'. The Knight of Death averted his attention to the view outside the window beyond the bed. It may have been twenty-one years for them, but it had only seemed

277

like hours to Mark. Perhaps a day or two at most. And he had to fight with himself every minute to keep from beheading the Knight of the Golden Eagle for taking her from him... again. It was inconceivable to him that she could sit in front of them so calmly, as if nothing were wrong. He stood with his arms crossed over his chest, his fingers digging into his own flesh in an attempt to keep his mind off his mental pain. He glanced at Merry and found her looking directly at him once more.

She couldn't believe he was there. Somehow, she felt that he was just a ghost, not real. In fact, she wished that he was ghost. It would have been easier to go on believing that he had died loving her, knowing that she loved him as well. Just when she was finally on the road to recovery after losing him, here he was again, standing at the foot of her bed as if nothing had happened. Where had he been? Why had he stayed gone so long? It was the second time he had disappeared from her life without a trace. Surely he could have returned before now? She fought to control her voice and her temper. She fought to keep her attention focused on the babies and the problem at hand. They would have to do something about the babies first and then she would have to deal with Mark Andrew's return. She drew another deep breath and continued.

"The second prophecy concerned the birth of another set of twins, born of an unholy union between the Virgin and the Lion. He thought the Lion was you, Mark Andrew," she did not take her eyes from his face. He did not flinch nor seemingly bat an eye. Beautiful blue eyes. Why did you leave me? She silently screamed the question at him. "Evidently, he was wrong."

She shook her head as she shuffled through the papers Mark Andrew had given her. How could she remain angry with him? She loved him too much for that. Whatever he had been doing and wherever he had been, she would forgive him, but she knew that he would not forgive her for marrying Lucio. Fifteen years she had waited. Fifteen years. John Paul had grown up without his father. John Paul didn't understand why he had three uncles who cared deeply for him and no father.

Mark looked down at the floor and then at the two white cradles sitting near the window. Lucio's children. So, they thought that if she had married him, the twins would have been unholy? This was more news he did not want to hear. Of course his children would be unholy. How could they be otherwise? He closed his eyes and drew a deep breath before focusing on her words. Why had they not told him this to start with? Why had they let him think he would be her husband? How could she have let him go on with it? Suddenly, he detested all of them for having played him for a fool. If he were not already home, he would have walked out the front door and left them with their woes. This obviously had nothing to do with him. He'd been gone for twenty-one years, living somewhere in a nightmare where he dreamed that he was a dragon. Suddenly, he wished he were back at the golden fountain in the meadow with the two beautiful goddesses who had fed him sweet water from a golden goblet. Even if he had to remain a dragon, their company was much preferable to this.

"I don't know where these questions came from, Konrad," Merry was speaking to von Hetz. "Do you recognize them, Lucio?"

The Italian shook his head. They were not part of the Hermeticum.

"Mark?" she turned her attention to the Scot.

"What questions?" he asked and shot a cold glance at her.

"On the parchment," she said and fought the urge to cry. "The questions... the riddles."

"Oh, twud be naught I ken," he deliberately let his worst brogue through.

"Riddles?" Lucio perked up. "You mean like puzzles?"

"Yeah, they're puzzles and I would assume that whoever left them here knew about us... somehow. We need to figure out the answers to the questions."

They shook their heads in unison and she concentrated her will on the papers.

"Look!" She said excitedly. "Konrad Eli. What dwells within the tomb after the spirit has departed? Eli... zabeth. Konrad, you were the first to see her there. This child is yours, isn't it?" Her excitement was cut short and her smile faded when she saw the look on Konrad's face.

Von Hetz was utterly devastated, as if she had punched him unexpectedly in the stomach. He drew a sharp breath and reached for the bedpost. The boy was his as his own suspicions told him. His unholy union with the evil presence in the tomb had produced a child, but how was it possible? He felt his knees grow weak as he clung to the bedpost for support and crossed himself as the truth of it sank into his brain. Hearing it from Meredith somehow made it real. He had all but forgotten the strange encounter that he had experienced whilst cleaning the crypt at the chapel. But that had been twenty plus years ago. Elizabeth? Surely not. It had been a dream... a nightmare and this was some sort of tasteless joke. But who would use real babies to perpetrate a joke on them? The children were real enough... weren't they?

Mark turned a suspicious eye on the Knight. Konrad von Hetz and Elizabeth? Impossible. Preposterous! But the Knight of the Apocalypse' expression told the truth of it. Mark's anger turned to icy fear as he realized once more that whatever this thing was, it had nothing to do with Elizabeth McShan. She had been dead almost a hundred years when the specter had shown up in the Chapel. Dambretti had been tampering with the alchemical processes. Perhaps these children were not real at all. Perhaps they were the work of some dark sorcery that the Italian had blundered on to. There were many source books stuffed in old trunks in the attic. Mark squinted at the child labeled with Konrad's name. The resemblance was remarkable none the less. Olive complexion, dark, straight hair and a rather stringy build even for a newborn, being at least two to three inches longer than the other two children.

Simon sat down heavily on the velvet bench at the foot of Merry's bed. Elizabeth. Not that name. Not again. He was still feeling the residual effects of the ordeal he had helped Meredith through only hours before. She had been suffering so much that he had taken some of her pain from her. Never in all his long life had he ever expected to feel the pangs of childbirth. And then Mark Andrew's appearance had wrenched his remaining strength. When the babes had appeared in the lab, he had suffered another form of torment. What had they done? Who was responsible? Was Mark Andrew's return connected to this mystery? Had the Knight of Death brought these children here and, if so, from whence had they come? And to what purpose?

Merry went to work on the second piece of paper. It took a few moments longer.

Lucio stood stock still, watching his wife as she studied the puzzle attached to the girl child. His day had been utterly spoiled. He turned his head towards Mark, glaring at him. This should have been the happiest day of his life. A father! A fine son and a beautiful baby daughter, but now they had taken a back seat to more of Ramsay's grandstanding. He had no doubt where these children had come from. Spawn of hell. That's what they were and he knew who had brought them there. They had come here by the same means as Mark Ramsay. Magick. Sorcery. Devilry. Mark Andrew should be burned at the stake! How dare he return... now! He gritted his teeth. On this day just to wound him. Just to take away his happiness? These were not real babies. They were creatures!

"Elizabeta Simone," she said quietly and looked at the back of the Healer's head. Merry laid the paper on the girl child's blanket. "What locks the Gate beneath the serpent's eye?" The puzzle held only one clue. The serpent's eye? The Knight of the Serpent? That was Simon's title. "This is your daughter, Simon," she said quietly, but Simon did not turn his head, did not move.

Lucio jerked his head around and stared at the Healer as well. What was Meredith implying? That these children belonged to von Hetz and Simon? Where were the mothers? How could all three of them be born at the same time without some form of magickal application? It was not possible. Unbelievable. It was a trick.

Mark Andrew moved away from the bed and stood staring quietly out the window. Anything was possible. He knew this from experience. If he could be a dragon, the priest could be a father. Simple. Why not? Konrad and Meredith had failed to tell him what sort of attack had been perpetrated on the Healer. Always conspiring against him, it seemed. He had thought it a bit more mundane. He subconsciously toyed with the hilt of his dagger as he stood thinking over what seemed absurd. A knife through the heart, perhaps or a gunshot wound to the head... Something that would have been less surprising. Nothing was ever simple any more.

Merry picked up the last piece of paper. What hand harvests the soul at death? This child is John du Morte. Her hand was shaking as she read the words. Mark Andrew was the answer, but John was not his name. John Paul had suffered an encounter with the spirit, but his name was not du Morte. Taken literally, the name meant John of Death. It made no sense.

John Paul. Was this John's child? She looked up at Michele and her daughter-in-law frowned at her. And where was John Paul at that moment? Michele had told her that he had not returned from saying mass at the chapel. Her brow crinkled in consternation. Was he collecting orphans? Was this one of John's little games? She had come to expect all sorts of surprises from her son. She never knew what he would do next. His most recent habit had not only caused a great deal of grief for her, but for his wife as well. He'd taken up disappearing sometimes for days on end and then he simply showed up again, just in time for supper as if he'd only just been out for a walk. And never an explanation. Nothing, but smiles and shrugs and some extraordinary trinket or gift for his mother and Michele. So far, neither she, nor her daughter-in-law had been able to fathom what lay behind these strange occurrences. And neither had they been able to remain angry with him about them. One look into his bright blue eyes and all was forgiven. But this? What did John Paul have to do with these children? It made no sense. Were they perhaps an extravagant gift for Michele who wanted children but could have none of her own?

The babies began to cry in unison again and Lucio looked to Michele for help. She got up reluctantly with a worried look in her deep brown eyes and helped him cart the three unexpected guests from the room. They were hungry no doubt.

Dambretti offered to help her take them out to the kitchen where they might find some baby formula and bottles to feed them. Lucio really wanted nothing to do with what was going on in Meredith's bedroom and he was glad to get these interlopers away from his own children. There was no way of knowing what evil forces might surround them. All the same, he had never seen such well-developed souls in babes so young. The energies shrouding them were thick with swirling colors and each one of them had a decidedly different aroma, each pleasant in its own right. The Italian, however, determined that he would not be taken in by the deceit whatever it was. Not everything that glittered was gold and had not even Lucifer been endowed with great beauty? Evil had returned to Scotland on Mark Andrew's heels and he was suddenly very glad that he and Merry would be taking their leave of the place very soon. Scotland was cold, dark and damp for most of the year and he saw no real reason to stay around.

The Master would have his Alchemist back and they would no longer live in fear of disaster around every corner. The mists would roll in and eventually all would smooth over and things would take on a more normal feel. If something had befallen one of the immortals during the past twenty-one years, it would have been a horrible situation with no Knight of Death, no Assassin to set their spirits free. The topic of death had come up between the Brothers on more than one cold night spent in front of the fire, but they had discussed the thing in hushed voices fearing to speak too loudly lest something happen immediately. The Brothers of the Red Cross were well aware of the creative properties of thought and word. Lucio had begged company more than once since he'd been exiled to this dreary land, but even the good company of his Brothers could do nothing to cheer him for long. Von Hetz and Simon came regularly, but the others always had excuses even though he'd managed to have them all up for extended holidays from time to time. Edgard d'Brouchart, himself, had come three times bringing along Montague. It seemed that none of them wanted to stay long in Scotland.

Even Stephano Clementi, his latest apprentice now knocking on forty's door, avoided the place, coming only now and then at the behest of John Paul. They had been inseparable in their younger years, but John's college and his subsequent marriage had put too much distance between himself and his childhood friend. Stephano had excused himself, complaining of heavy workloads in Italy left by his absentee Master. Lucio knew that Stephano was actually doing his job for the past ten years, but so much the better for him. At least he'd had some respite from the Master's constant nagging. But he felt guilty about Clementi's situation. His apprentice loved him, enjoyed his company and never complained. Stephano wanted his own family and yet, he never pursued the matter seriously even when Lucio offered to help him find a "nice Sicilian girl". Stephano claimed that his Master was too old fashioned, that there were no longer any such things as "nice girls" any where, let alone Sicily. The world had changed and women had changed. Even though he truly enjoyed his vacation from the Villa, deep down Lucio wanted nothing more than to return to Italy and take some of that 'heavy workload' off of his apprentice's shoulders. Get back to being the 'Golden Eagle, Chief of the Dumbfuck Tribe'. He never thought that he would miss his life at the Master's beck and call.

In the ensuing silence after Michele and Lucio took their leave, Simon remained sitting on the bench with his head in his hands. He knew what this was. No one had to tell him. How it was possible made no difference. He had convinced himself that the night he had spent with Elizabeth had been a sick dream or imagination, perhaps an illusion she had created. Just as he had assumed that von Hetz' confession of the same bizarre contact with the girl's specter had only been a dream. But they had not been dreaming. It had been real. Real enough to have produced tangible results in the form of these devilish children. What would the Master say? He knew that he had never reported the incident to de Bleu for the archives. Dreams were not worthy of record. But who had he been kidding? Twenty-one years late, but... he raised his head and looked at the open door where Lucio and Michele had disappeared with the three babies only moments before. John Paul, Konrad von Hetz and himself. All three attacked and used by the same foul presence. Why?

Von Hetz went to open the window and leaned out, breathing the fresh air into his lungs. He felt as if he would collapse at any moment. This was too great a penalty to pay for his sins. God had surely abandoned him. What unholy offspring had he begotten with a demon in human form? A son! It could not be. It was as if a deeply hidden desire had become manifest in a most horrible fashion. He had always wished for a son. Someone that he could raise properly, with love and understanding. Now this? Of course, the Master would have plenty to say about it, but how could it be so? That had been twenty-one years ago. Devilish sorcery, this. Only the devil could make such a thing work. The girl had been a ghost, a spirit of the long dead Elizabeth McShan in thrall to some evil power, perhaps even Satan himself. Ghosts could not conceive, nor could they bear living children... could they? A horrid legend from ages past blurred through his mind. Some nonsense about a Templar who had ravaged the corpse of a dead maiden and got her with child. A child that was supposedly born in the grave. The German shuddered to his toes and banished the ridiculous tale from his thoughts.

"What was the question?" Mark asked quietly when Merry gave up in frustration and tossed the pen across the room. He went to retrieve the pen and brought it back to her. She touched his hand as she took the pen and he hesitated too long before releasing it. His eyes locked with hers and she blinked first.

How dare he accuse her? He was the one who had left her. Not the other way round. But the question was in his eyes. As plain as day. Why. He wanted to ask her why.

"Why?" she blurted the question in her mind, but it was not what he had asked. He dropped his eyes. He could not answer her question.

"The question on the paper?" he said without looking up. "Perhaps I can help you."

She looked at the paper as if seeing it for the first time. "What hand harvests the soul at death?" she read it aloud, fighting back tears. Why? Why? Why?

"My hand," he said simply and then tilted his head at an unnatural angle that made the bones in his neck pop. He looked at his hands. They were perfectly clean, uncalloused, almost like a surgeons' hands. Not the hands of a warrior or even a metal worker. They should have been scarred and rough, but it seemed that they mocked him with their perfection and he wondered if they had always been so. The two rings he wore sparkled in the bright sunlight streaming through the open window. "My hand harvests the soul at death, but this is not my child Meredith. Contrary to what you may believe, I have not been vacationing in Monte Carlo and I have not been unfaithful to you though it seems to be of little import now."

She jumped when another small voice cried out in the room. She had almost forgotten her own children. Simon got up quickly and went to retrieve his namesake from her crib. Merry watched the Healer in fascination as he handled the baby with utmost care. Simon would make a wonderful father. In a few days, she would be healed completely. No stretch marks, nothing would ever show that she had borne twins if she were to be examined under an electron microscope.

"Shhh! Lucia Simone," he smiled sadly at the little girl who already looked much like her father with dark curls on her head and a deep olive complexion. "Be still, my sweet. Mama` is here."

Mark watched in silence until Simon placed the baby on his shoulder and then he left them. He would not be a part of it. He could not be a part of it.

Simon handed the baby over to Merry and looked up at the ceiling. Nausea washed over him and he fought the urge to run from the room. Lucia Simone! Elizabeta Simone! Not possible and yet... he frowned and forced the nausea away. What if the child was really his? A daughter? A little girl for him to love and call his own? Was this not a gift from God?

"I failed you when you were in need," Simon spoke to Konrad when he turned. "I thought you were dreaming, Brother. I tried to fool myself as well. We have been visited from the beyond. Perhaps there may be some good to be had yet." With this last statement, he bolted from the room, no longer able to overcome the urge to lose his lunch and unable to face them, knowing that they knew what he had done. He wanted them gone so that he could talk to Meredith alone. She would understand. She would know what to do about the baby.

Merry could not quite get her hands around the situation. Triplets? How had John Paul gotten into this equation and what were her Brothers hiding from her? There were far more questions here than answers and she intended to find the answers. Had she become a mother and a grandmother on the same day? Elizabeth had dishonored their house and violated their trust. Had she also violated a fifteen year old boy? But then Elizabeth McShan had been only a few years older than her son at the time. The girl who had visited them couldn't have been a day older than eighteen, but Elizabeth had not been a girl at all, had she? Merry needed answers! She tucked the baby close to her and gave her a bottle that had been warming on the bedside table. Her daughter's first meal and Lucio had wanted to give it to her, but where was he? What was he doing? Had he abandoned his children already? Because of Mark? Of course.

"Konrad... Brother? Is there another John? Does this mean... Is this talking about John Paul or... or... is there some other John? What does it mean?"

"I don't know what it means, Sister," Konrad said as he collapsed into the chair Michele had vacated. "Brother Ramsay went by the name of John a very long time ago. I believe that John was part of his given name about the time he went to Cyprus after the Inquisition."

Merry frowned. She learned something new about Mark Andrew every time she was around him for more than a few moments. John? And he had never mentioned that John was his name and she had unknowingly named his son John? Her temper flared just a little at the thought that he'd kept it from her. But then it was probably not something he would have thought overly important.

An hour later, the five men met in Ramsay's kitchen in an impromptu conference called at Dambretti's insistence. They didn't have much time. Mark Andrew had been commanded to Italy immediately, just as they would have expected. Simon was to go with him while Konrad remained behind. Ever since Merry had become pregnant with twins, the Grand Master had always made sure that there were at least two Knights if not three in Scotland with her and Lucio. Champlain's turn was up to spend a few months with the 'family' as d'Brouchart called them. It was as if he expected trouble to come with the impending birth.

They sat around the table, glancing at each other expectantly as if waiting for the Seneschal to show up and call the meeting to order, each somehow feeling that this meeting was somehow treasonous in and of itself. They needed a plan and they needed it quickly. Something had to be done about the babies and a decision had to be made, right or wrong.

Von Hetz unfolded himself from the bench after a few stilted moments of silence, leaned both hands on the table and studied their faces individually for several seconds. His face was a mask of irrepressible emotions as he discerned each of his Brother's mental conditions.

"Brothers," his deep voice cut through the uneasy silence and caused them all to jump though they had known he would speak. "We have a grave problem other than just the welfare of these three foundlings and we have very few options. If we take this matter up with the Grand Master, we can expect only one outcome. I have come to the conclusion that Master d'Brouchart will have no choice but to sentence these babes to death due to the unnatural circumstances surrounding their... due to their mysterious origins and the date and time of their arrival. Someone... somewhere is playing with us. Someone, apparently quite powerful and knowledgeable is using our own fears and emotions against us.   The second prophecy concerning twins indicates that one of them would be of a good and noble heart, whereas the other would be of quite the opposite demeanor.   The existence of a third presents a vexing problem and seemingly precludes the possibility that these children are not associated with the second prophecy at all, but serve some other unknown purpose.   Triplets were never mentioned in any of the prophecies nor do the Alchemical texts mention triplets according to both Sir Ramsay and Sir Dambretti.   The scriptures do not mention triplets.   Since we have surmised the identities of the fathers of the three, we can be quite sure that anyone of them could be a true and faithful child, but likewise, any one or all three may be the product of evil.   We believe that this... creature, whatever she may have been, returned to the tombs expecting to meet with the Chevalier du Morte.   Instead, I was the one who was there.   It is possible that she came to the house looking for Sir Ramsay, but found his son instead.   And likewise, when she came the third time, she asked for him by name and found Simon of Grenoble instead of Brother Ramsay.   Hence, the three children instead of two.   It would also seem that each time she appeared to us, she was stronger.   It is evidenced by the fact that Brother Simon and Sister Meredith report that she seemed completely corporeal during the time that she masqueraded as Sir Ramsay's granddaughter, eating, drinking and apparently able to perform actual work.   Since we did not openly discuss our experiences with the apparition at the time, we may have caused something that will be difficult, if not impossible, to correct let alone explain."

Mark had to accept von Hetz' logic. For once, Mark had come through unscathed and there was no need to add his experience with her to theirs because he had resisted the creature when she had tried to seduce him in the crypt when they had gone to exorcise the evil presence before sealing the chamber containing the Ark.   Though he had not completely confessed his entire conversation with her at the time, she had told him that they could produce another child together, making a reference to poor Ian McShan. He wrapped his arms around his shoulders and shuddered in the warm kitchen, wondering what might have happened if she had found him at home.   Only Lucio had been spared one on one contact with her... he glanced at the Italian who appeared to be sleeping... or had he?

"The third child is an enigma which lays some doubts as to these children actually being connected with the prophecies and hence, they may simply be the victims of an extraordinary hoax perpetrated against us," the Apocalyptic Knight continued.   "It is very likely that should the Master choose to have all three put to death, we could be murdering three innocent children. I cannot do this with a clear conscience. That the Master is capable of carrying out such an action is certain..." he paused to look at Dambretti. The Knight of the Golden Eagle had been present at the Council Meeting now twenty-eight years gone by when the Master had called for the death of John Paul Sinclair-Ramsay and the Council had drawn straws to determine who would carry out the execution. Now John Paul sat with them at the table, watching the proceedings with a bland expression in his crystal blue eyes. His feelings were unreadable. His own experience with the abomination called Elizabeth known only to himself.

Lucio opened his eyes and nodded his agreement. He remembered the Council meeting quite well. It had been one of the low points of his long existence. He had been unable to do anything to help Merry when she had almost lost her son to the Order. All the Knights at the meeting with the exception of one, had refused to draw the straws from the box and John Paul had lived. He also remembered his own encounter with the specter they were now discussing. A vampire. That was his estimation of her. An unholy creature that takes its life and existence from the life-forces of others. They had created her. The Italian did not, for one moment believe that these three healthy children belonged to a figment of their collective imaginations. Elizabeth McShan had been nothing more than a thought form. The babies were real... flesh and blood. Certainly their appearance in the lab was strange enough. And the evidence showed that they had all been born at approximately the same time which was also strange. The fact that they had appeared almost simultaneously with the Knight of Death made him believe that Mark knew exactly where they had come from and he could not imagine what the Scot had up his sleeve. Dambretti chewed his lip, trying to decide whether to point out the coincident. His suspicions of what might have occurred whilst the inestimable Knight of Death had been gone twenty-one years were growing. What had he been doing all that time? Why come back on this particular day?

"The woman was not... real," Lucio told them bluntly. "You all speak of her as if she was flesh and blood. I looked at her soul. I have never seen such a thing. To think that it could produce innocent progeny is unlikely, Brothers. These babies, on the other hand, are within what I have come to recognize as normal parameters. I have examined them. Their souls are... unique in my experience, but they are not like the creature that we met in the crypt. I believe that they came from separate parents, perhaps three couples, and are not triplets at all. Remember, my Brothers, human females are not like dogs as some might think. They do not conceive multiple children from multiple partners. It is simply not possible that one human female could give birth to three babies on the same day by different sires unless this is some freak medical experiment," he turned a hostile eye on the Ritter. "You should know better. I have no answers, but we must look for them in the realm of the natural world. These children are human. That is my opinion for what it is worth."

"I am only summing up what little evidence we have," the Ritter answered Lucio's unasked questions. "If Brother Ramsay has nothing to say about them, then what have we to go on? Who else might have brought them here? Where are their parents?"

"And have you looked at your own children?" Simon directed his question to Lucio. "Are they... normal, Brother?"

Lucio turned to glare at Simon. He regretted having mentioned to Simon that the twin's souls possessed a quality that he had never seen before... also unique. The Master would no doubt want to know if the twins were immortal, but how could he tell?

"Are they? Are your children... normal?" Mark leaned forward to put the question to Lucio more forcefully.

"No! They are not normal, but neither are they evil, wicked or profane," Lucio almost shouted at him and then looked away, crossing his arms over his chest. "Whatever trick you are trying to play here, Brother, will not work. Wherever these children came from, they must be returned. I suggest that you take them away the same way you brought them. Sorcery or what have you..."

Mark's face lit up with understanding. Lucio was blaming him again for the appearance of the children. "Would that it were so," he said and smiled ruefully. Children, what did he know of children? "Unfortunately, I did not bring them here; therefore, I cannot take them away. For once, I wash my hands of the entire affair in good faith and with a clear conscience. They are no more my concern than your own children, Sir. I care little what you decide to do with them."

"That may be so, Brother, but you realize that, if there is any truth to the cryptic notes attached to them, one of them is either your child or your grandchild. I'm afraid that you may not wash your hands so easily," von Hetz told him harshly.

"Then what in the name of God would you propose that we do, Brother?!" Mark growled at him and then looked away in obvious annoyance. He was tired of all of them and their mystic bullshit and he'd been home less than six hours. How would he ever make it through an entire day with them? A week? A month? He groaned inwardly and closed his eyes.

"I would propose that we swear an oath of silence in this matter to one another," Von Hetz continued. His own words pained him. They were about to commit treason against the Order. No secrets. No secrets. What good is a Council if it is not utilized properly? "I will take these children and scatter them to the four winds. When sufficient time has passed, we may find ourselves faced with destroying one or more of them, but I would rather it come to that in the future than slaughter innocent children in the here and now." The dark Knight resumed his seat.

Mark Andrew wanted nothing to do with this one way or another. It was treason and he'd been accused of enough for one day. Why should he risk what was left of his life for the sake of three foundlings? He was for killing them all at once and being done with it and would almost have suggested that they throw the twins in a well along with them, but this was not a good thought, in fact it was quite evil and smacked of jealousy. He crossed himself and closed his eyes for having thought it at all. When he opened them, he was looking directly into John Paul's crystal blue stare. It was as if his son had read his mind. His face darkened and he looked away quickly. One of them was his grandchild. Lucio was wrong. The evil that had come upon them was as real as the table in front of them. And one of the children was John Paul's son. How could he murder his own grandson?

He stood up. "I am for taking them to Italy. Just as you once took my son to the Master, Konrad. You had no problem then. Why do you shy away from your duties now? It would be our only just recourse to allow the Grand Master to make the decision. We could wash our hands of the matter once and for all," his words cut the German to the bone.

Mark Andrew resumed his seat and lowered his eyes to the table. They would have killed his son.

Lucio stood up. "I will second Sir Ramsay's motion," his statement was even more abbreviated. He glanced briefly at the Scot and then sat down quickly, unable to believe that they were in agreement at last.

Simon pushed himself up more slowly. His eyes were filled with tears and he looked extremely bad. The dark circles under his eyes had grown to alarming proportions and his eyes were bloodshot behind the tears. His nose was red and his voice sounded hoarse when he spoke. There was no doubt he was suffering greatly and, unlike von Hetz and John Paul, his emotions were clearly written on his pale features.

"I would not have the blood of these children on my hands. Taking them to the Master would be tantamount to condemning them to death. I can appreciate the circumstances that surrounded this same issue when John Paul's fate hung in the balance, but we knew who and what our precious John was. Who his father is and who his mother is. This is not the same. I cannot... I would not be able to do my duty to God if I were to allow them to be killed. I hold with Brother Hetz. The Master must not be informed of this... development... at this time," he concluded with a disclaimer of sorts and looked down at Mark Andrew's head before sitting down. They could hear him breathing in the ensuing silence.

It was John Paul's turn to speak. Mark looked up, willing his son to see reason. He stood up, a terrible frown etched his features. As his eyes fell on each of them, they returned his gaze, unable to look away, wondering if he knew what had transpired in Council when he was only seven years old.

Wondering if he knew that the Master had ordered his death and then expected his father to participate actively in his execution.

"Why is this decree so hasty from thee, Fathers? Blessed be the name of God forever and ever: for wisdom and might are his. Destroy not the children of Babylon. But there is a God in heaven that revealeth secrets. But as for me, this secret is not revealed to me for any wisdom that I have more than any living. And wheresoever the children of men dwell, the beasts of the field and the fowls of the heaven hath he given into thine hand, and hath made thee ruler over them All. And in the days of these kings shall the God of heaven set up a kingdom, which shall never be destroyed: and the kingdom shall not be left to other people, but it shall break in pieces and consume all these kingdoms, and it shall stand for ever. Forasmuch as thou sawest that the stone was cut out of the mountain without hands the great God hath made known to the king what shall come to pass hereafter: and the dream is certain, and the interpretation thereof sure. I hold with the Ritter von Hetz."

The Ritter raised his eyes again to John Paul with a look of profound gratitude. The words he had spoken were, in the most part, straight out of the Book of Daniel wherein the prophet Daniel spoke to the King Nebuchadnezzar of Babylon concerning the interpretations of the King's dreams. John Paul had received a gift from God and the gift was bestowed on him by the Holy Ghost. The gift of prophecy. John Paul used the scriptures to speak his prophecies, stringing together quotes in order to say what had to be said. He rarely used his own words to say anything over four or five words in length. Now he was using the prophecies of Daniel to make his decision concerning the disposition of the three children. Von Hetz had no intention of further damaging himself in the eyes of God. The Apocalyptic Knight stood swiftly and leaned on the table, directing his words to Dambretti and Ramsay.

"The matter is settled. We will swear the oath of silence and I will take charge of the babes. May God have mercy on our souls. Amen. Amen. And Amen."

"And what of Sister Meredith?" Lucio looked around at them with the question. They had left her out of the meeting for obvious reasons. Too emotional. Too soon after the birth of her own children. Her logic would be flawed in regard to the welfare of newborn children with her own so close at hand. No mother should ever be put to a question such as that on the table before them. If nothing else in the world was left to the sole discretion of men, this had to be it.

"She will swear to the oath," Von Hetz told him confidently. "I will speak to her of this meeting and its outcome. Tomorrow morning, Brother Simon and Brother Ramsay will go to Italy. We will meet at sunset in your chapel, John, to take the oath. There you will baptize the babies and give them names. I will arrange for their papers through my contacts in Switzerland."

"I have something to say, Brother," Lucio spoke up and stood across the table from the German. "I will take the oath with my Brothers and I will go down with them, but I will make it known here and now that I am against this action. Whatever issues from this insurrection will be the Will of God and I wash my hands of it. I will not betray you or your actions, but neither will I support you in the future concerning this matter. I want no part of." The Italian cast one look at Mark Andrew, before leaving them.

Simon leaned his head in his hands and Mark Andrew stood up. He had nothing more to say. He had no idea what the Will of God was and his mind was blissfully blank. His only thought was to find his clothes and his personal belongings and see what was left of his wardrobe that might be salvaged. The last thing he needed to do was to go on a shopping spree for new clothes. Normally, he would have had his cook or his apprentice take care of that type of business. Now he had no cook, no apprentice and did not have the heart to enlist new ones. Sir Barry would be hounding him to choose one of his students as soon as possible. Major would have been near retirement by now. The thought of Major MacLaughlin, his last apprentice who had received impromptu Knighthood without immortality, made him smile in spite of his troubles. A trip to the frontier might be in order. At least Major would be glad to see him and he would be glad to see some different scenery.

He found his clothes packed away carefully in sealed plastic bags inside wooden chests in the attic. Each chest had been labeled neatly, dated and stacked very carefully near the head of the stairs. Lucio's handwriting again. The Italian obviously never expected him to return. He wondered if Meredith knew about this and if she had agreed to packing him off to the attic like so much used furniture. But Lucio had done a good job. His clothes were clean and practically ready to wear after a few good shakes and a spritz of cologne. No need for a shopping trip. Small consolation. He dragged a leather suitcase over to the chests and began to pack for his trip. He needed to pack for the trip to Italy and he wanted only to find something to eat and then rest before sunset.

A short time later, he found himself alone in the kitchen, opening the cabinets in frustration. There was plenty of food. All of it was Italian with only a smattering of American favorites like macaroni and cheese and canned chili. Linguine, capellini, rigatoni, farfalle, pene and fusilli. There were numerous bottles of olive oil, extra virgin, special reserve and tomatoes, sun dried, crushed, chopped, pureed. The seasonings were equally as strange including pine nuts, peppercorns in three colors, oregano and garlic. Olives, stuffed, Olives, chopped, Olives, sliced, Olives, black, Olives, green, Olives, red. Marinated artichoke hearts in brine. Marinated eggplant. In the refrigerator was Italian mineral water and cheese, mozzarella, Romano, parmesan and leftover stuffed pasta shells in what appeared to be clam sauce. Some kind of Italian bread lay on the counter. He had no idea what most of these things were. They were definitely not Scottish fare and it appeared that Lucio had been doing most of the cooking in the kitchen as well as the lab. He checked the pantry for canned goods. A big box of frosted shredded wheat biscuits sat on the shelf. Bran flakes with raisins. Instant flavored oatmeal. Americans and their dried cereal. Detestable. He plucked a red can with a blue label from the shelf and looked closely at the wrapper. Wolf Brand Chili without beans, he read the proud announcement. Without beans. Another can proclaimed just as proudly that beans were included. He wondered what the ultimate difference would be. To gas or not to gas?

"Can I help you find something?" a timid voice asked from behind him and he turned quickly to find John Paul's wife standing in the door of the kitchen watching him from wide eyes. She carried a plastic tray full of empty baby bottles, glasses and other assorted things he did not recognize.

He put the can of chili behind his back.

"I thought I might find something to eat..." his voice trailed off. He was starving and so far, no one had said a word about dinner or even tea time. He could tell by Michele's accent that she was American though she was definitely not from Texas.

"You don't cook like Uncle Lucio, do you?" She asked hesitantly.

He shook his head and she sighed in relief and smiled.

"Do you like Italian?" she asked as she dumped the contents of the tray in the sink.

He misinterpreted her question and thought she was referring to Lucio Dambretti.

"It doesn't really matter," he said shortly, wondering why she would ask such a thing. "Does it?"

Michele nodded her head in confusion and turned off the water.

"How about cannaloni and bruschetta?" She asked as she left him standing in front of the pantry and went to open the refrigerator.

"Whoor they?" He asked and looked about, expecting some more Italians to pop out of the woodwork. Cooks, perhaps?

"Uncle Lucio does most of the cooking, I'm afraid," she answered, looking back at him from under her arm as she rummaged through the packages stored in the fridge. "I really don't know what they are exactly. I just know I like them pretty good."

"Oh," Mark sighed and his shoulders drooped. "A roast beef sandwich would be nice. Hold the mustard."

Michele frowned into the refrigerator. Somehow, she did not think that she and Sir Ramsay were on the same page.

292

"We don't have much beef around here. Lamb, chicken and fish mainly. How about bologna? It's beef. John Paul loves it," she said hopefully and turned around, holding up a plastic box in each hand. "And we have Miracle Whip if you don't like mustard, sir."

"Miracle whip? Aye, thot's exactly wot I need, lassie."

Chapter Seventeen of Seventeen
a king of fierce countenance, and understanding dark sentences, shall stand up

Mark Andrew spent four very tiresome days in Italy at the Order's headquarters in the Villa north of Pompeii, answering hundreds of questions once, twice and again, relating every possible detail he could remember about his strange experiences during his 'time away' as Philip Cambrique called it. He had hundreds of questions for his Brothers as well, but they could not or would not answer. It was almost as bad as the time that he had spent with Lucio at the infirmary when the Knight of the Golden Eagle had been suffering from 'appendicitis' during the last stage development of the Philosopher's Stone. But instead of babysitting the Italian, he was spending this time with Sir Philip and the Grand Master in closed meetings. He could not even drink wine or throw an occasional temper tantrum as he had at the infirmary. They plied him with strong Italian coffee in the mornings, tea at mid-morning and afternoon and little glasses of sherry after supper, but nothing he could sink his teeth into. When he was not in the confines of the Seneschal's office or the Grand Master's sitting room, he spent his time in one of the living quarters reserved for visiting Knights, military commanders or the occasional VIP from Rome.

The tiny, two room apartment was barely livable in his way of thinking. Spatial frugality was something he'd never cared for or understood. He needed wide open spaces, grass and trees to enfold his sanity and keep it from disintegrating. His only respite was Louis Champlain's visits after hours. The Frankish Knight was fascinated by his story and constantly had new questions for him concerning the fountain and the two women and the dragon and the Key. Mark had to wonder if Louis was writing a book about it all.

Scotland was becoming more and more precious to him as the days passed. He mourned the loss of his old cook, Bruce Roberts, in silence and he dreaded replacing his former apprentice Major MacLaughlin. Major had been a good friend and a trusted member of the Order. He didn't want to start over again with another stranger. Another chance to grow attached to someone he would eventually lose. He wished that he could be home with his old wolfhounds, wandering the meadows and fields, but even Luke and Matthew had died within two days of each other in his absence. He had already decided that John Paul and his wife could stay on in Scotland with him as long as they like, but he would have to work on his relationship with his daughter-in-law. He'd not made a good first impression. Meredith and Lucio on the other hand, would have to go and the sooner the better. It would be a great pleasure to 'remodel' his lab back to its original condition and he longed to get started on the project. He needed to make something with his hands. To get back into the swing of things as they said. A sword for John Paul perhaps or a ring for Armand de Bleu. The young Knight did not have a Templar signet ring yet and time was wasting. He'd read the most recent report from Montague's London office and it seemed the accountant might welcome a 'deposit'.

D'Brouchart had already struck him down twice when he'd tried to leave the Seneschal's office in fits of rage brought on by their prying personal questions and he sported a knot on his left jaw and sore spot on the back of his head. He didn't understand what his thoughts on love, marriage and sex had to do with the current situation. He could well imagine what might happen if he told them about the triplets, but he had promised von Hetz and Simon that he would not mention them just yet. D'Brouchart had resorted to having security lounge around the halls while they talked and that little development did not lend to lightening his mood. Two Templar sergeants stood nervously outside the office doors to make sure that he did not escape and even accompanied him to the dining hall when he went for lunch or dinner after he threatened to disappear for another two decades. It was all terrible, but Simon kept his promise and stayed with him the entire time, though he was forced to remain outside some of the meetings.

The only thing that kept him from killing the Grand Master outright on several occasions was the fact that they had not allowed him to wear his weapons during the sessions. The golden sword had been removed from his reach entirely and placed in Sir Barry's armory for safekeeping.

The Healer repeatedly mediated, redirected and pleaded with the Master and the Seneschal to cease and desist when things heated up, but the reprieves were always short-lived. If Mark Andrew had had a hard time believing what had happened to him, these two, who had not experienced the thing, were impossible to convince. They did not believe his story about the dragons, but rather brushed it off as some devilishly-inspired dreams. They believed that he had spent twenty-one years in a coma at the bottom of a pit in Florida in spite of his denials and evidence to the contrary. How, he asked them had he suddenly awakened, climbed out of the pit, cleaned himself up and got back to Scotland without remembering how he did it? They didn't believe that he didn't remember. They practically called him a liar and wanted to him to confess what he knew and why he was not willing to tell the entire story. The Grand Master went so far as to accuse him of deliberately deserting the Order and then changing his mind after a long respite from his tedious duties as Assassin and Alchemist. This was the most logical answer to the question. The only thing that they believed was that al Sajek was dead and this was simply because it was what they wanted to hear and the fact that he had suddenly dropped off the face of the earth after falling into the pit in America. But Mark was not so sure. If he had suddenly reappeared at his own home in Scotland, then had not the sorcerer also perhaps returned? He had even pointed out that perhaps al Sajek had survived much as he had and was now somewhere regrouping. They didn't want to hear it.

The Knight of Death could not believe that they did not believe. His resentment toward the Grand Master was rapidly turning into something far more sinister. He had finally, in another fit of desperation, ripped off his shirt and showed them the scars on his stomach where the green and black dragon had raked him with its claws. They had been suitably impressed, but still unconvinced. He could have been injured in the fall. He could have been injured in an automobile accident. Any number of things could have caused the wounds that had left the scars even though he pointed out that the immortals did not suffer scarring. They brought in the now much older obnoxious doctor from the Infirmary, but Mark Andrew refused to allow him to inspect the wounds. It took four soldiers, Armand de Bleu and Barry of Sussex to hold him down long enough for the doctor to announce that he could not say what had caused the hideous wounds, but they did appear to have been caused from a close encounter with a large predator. A lion or a tiger, perhaps. The doctor did say that the injury might have been fatal to a normal human being. The fact that the scars had not faded as the days wore on, meant that wherever he had been, he had not been immune to injury in the usual sense while he was there. Mark Andrew then pointed out that if he had been mortal and the wounds should have been fatal to a human, then he must not have been a human when he had suffered the injury. A dragon. He had been a dragon. One positive thing that did emerge from the meetings and the constant badgering was that he convinced himself of the truth of his adventure.

They did not want to believe him. The newest doctor assigned to the infirmary had been running some tests concerning their immortality at the behest of the Master and suggested that rarely had the Knights experienced such severe wounds and been allowed to live. He even suggested that had Mark Andrew been in Italy or Scotland when the injury occurred, he might have been dispatched to the hereafter rather than saved. Mark Andrew did not like the new doctor any more than he had liked the old one. One thing that Mark Andrew and the Master had in common was their mutual dislike of modern medicine and the persons who dispensed it. The medical exam and resulting consultation had degenerated into a war of words betwixt Mark, the doctors and the Grand Master. Mark clung to his story of being transformed into an actual dragon during his absence, citing obscure alchemical papers and documents. The Grand Master was torn between what he considered plausible and what he considered possible. The doctors as men of science, naturally rejected the story, but their knowledge of the mystical truths surrounding the Council of Twelve caused them to wobble between scientific fact and science fiction, what ought to be and what ought not be.

These shouted debates brought new perspectives to the questioning, but Philip had countered Mark's reasoning concerning the scars, asking if Mark had been mortal, even though he may not have been human, for the past twenty-one years, why had he not aged? Why did he not have gray hair and wrinkles as a fifty-sevenish man might have? Why did he still look exactly as he had when he had last seen him at the pit in Florida except for these scars? Mark had no answers for his questions except to say that perhaps dragons do not age as fast as humans. Philip had actually laughed at the idea and they had another struggle to pull the enraged Knight of Death from the Seneschal's throat. They were out of control. Philip was beside himself. He'd heard the beast in the pit. He knew the Necronomicon, but he was terrified to admit that there might be some truth to the story.

The Grand Master and the Seneschal retired together for several hours to discuss the merits of believing Mark's story as opposed to writing it off as fantasy or fabrication. When they had returned, their attitudes were changed. They finished their questions quickly, made summations and notations and released him, apparently satisfied that he had not committed treason in an attempt to gain his freedom. The investigation was closed with questions unanswered and suspicious unvoiced. They would not totally discount his story, but they would only admit that something very mysterious had happened to the Chevalier du Morte and that the inquiry might be reopened if new information should surface that might give some indication of where he had been. They would record his words in the archives as spoken with commentary from the Master.

At last it was over and Mark Andrew knew no more than he had before he had come to Italy. Somehow, he had expected the Grand Master or Sir Philip to know what had happened to him. He came away with a somewhat lowered opinion of the Master's abilities.

Sir Philip caught up with him at the pool as he hurried away to his room to pack.

"Brother Ramsay!" Philip caught his arm and then looked down as if embarrassed for having touched him. "The Master has instructed me to tell you not to go back home... just yet. He wants you to take some time off."

"Time off?" Mark frowned at him. "Time off from what? I've been gone for twenty-one years. Isn't that enough for the man?"

"Just time off. Nothing to do with the inquiry. Take a holiday? You know what a holiday is? A holiday?" Philip added and smiled at him. "Go to Rome. See the sights. Go to Germany or Austria. Take some time off. Do something recreational. Skiing perhaps or backpacking?" Mark's expression made him change direction. "Hunting! Yes, hunting would be good for you, I think." The Seneschal had no idea what Sir Ramsay would do for recreation. In fact, he'd never thought of it at all. He personally liked backpacking through the Alps in late summer. And he enjoyed sailing. He kept a fourteen footer in Naples and often took weekends there with Champlain or Sir Barry when he could pry them out of their lairs. Barry was a capable sailor, in fact, though Champlain simply enjoyed the rides. Philip could not imagine Mark Ramsay on a sail boat that was not full of Viking marauders bent on pillaging some unsuspecting village. His face reddened at the unworthy thought.

"How long?" Mark asked curtly. He was not happy and he recognized the Master's ploy for exactly what it was. D'Brouchart needed some time to work things out with Dambretti. Meredith and Lucio would have to find another place to live... in Italy, he hoped or Mongolia... even better. Normally, in years past, he would have thought of Lucio first when thinking of something recreational. Fishing in Scotland. Hunting... Scotland. Backpacking? Scotland. Golfing? Scotland! Where else was better this time of year? "Aye. Fishing the River Spey is good this time of year I hear. Plenty of whiskey," Mark nodded. "Would that be far enough away from home?"

"A month... or longer, if you like," Philip shrugged and cringed before adding. "Not Scotland. Somewhere else. Greece, perhaps."

"I can go home in a month?" he asked after a moment. Greece was not his cup of tea. Rome? Too crowded... but better than Greece and not that far away. He could rent a nice suite, order up a case of Scotch and stay drunk for a month and when he wasn't drunk, he could sleep. Perhaps he did need a holiday. "Rome, then."

"Yes," Philip nodded. It was hopeless. "Brother!" he caught his arm again and then let go very quickly. The Seneschal fell on his knees in front of the startled Knight. "Brother, I would ask... no beg your forgiveness for my part in this. I am sorry that you had to suffer this interrogation. I feel that I have wronged you and I would beg your forgiveness for allowing you to fall into that hellish pit. I should have been the one. It was my mission and I failed you. I don't know where you've been or what has happened to you, but I beg you to forgive me. I was weak and unprepared. You have no idea how I have suffered, believing that I had caused your death and the loss of your mysteries. When I learned that you had returned, I prayed to God that I would be able to..."

Mark's first instinct was to run from the man. Philip Cambrique had always grated on his nerves just slightly less than fingernails on a chalkboard. The man was too... French, too secretive, too calm and cool and collected... but here he was, on his knees. Not a good thing. He looked around quickly and pulled the man to his feet.

"Sometimes our duties call for extreme measures, Brother. You have done nothing more than carry out your duties to the Order as far as this inquiry. I am accustomed to the Master's badgering. About the mission, do not worry yourself. We all did our parts. There is nothing to forgive."

Mark walked away from the Seneschal shaking his head. He did not want to go to Rome, but it was close by and he knew the city fairly well. It couldn't have changed much in the past 100 years or so since his last visit. Rome had been standing over 2500 years in the same place. The city was too old for his tastes and too much blood had accumulated in its soil. It was rank with evil and the Vatican City was nothing more than a European version of an Aztec sacrificial temple. The only difference between the two was that the Roman Church had evolved and put on a face of civilization. At least the Aztecs were out of business and no longer persecuted their people while the Vatican tried to hide its bloody past behind Michelangelo's cherubs. France was out of the question. Morocco might have been interesting, but it was too far away. And Major MacLaughlin was on a mission in South America, working undercover in Venezuela. A visit with Major was impossible at the moment. At least he knew a little about Rome. He'd been there on numerous occasions. He would go to Rome, stay a month and then go home. Perhaps they would have sorted everything out in Scotland by then and he could have his old room back. If not, he'd take the parlor until they were gone. He didn't care. He just wanted to go home to Scotland. There were plenty of places he could go within easy reach of his home. Perth and Aberdeen. St. Andrew's and Loch Ness. He could always cross the sea and visit Ireland or the Isle of Man. Great hunting and deer stalking there. Hell, he could take up golfing if need be to keep busy and Louis would be a good companion in that respect. The Frankish Knight had already volunteered to do what he could to help him if need be. Surely they could find an apprentice in Sir Barry's academy that knew the sport well enough to teach him. He had been remiss in his patriotism since he'd never bothered to take up the national sport of his beloved homeland. If he really felt game, he'd take up wearing a kilt and playing bagpipes! Sure, sure, there were plenty of things to occupy his feeble brain other than Meredith Sinclair... Dambretti!

In his mind, he had only been gone from home a few days, however, twenty-one years had passed in reality. One month couldn't be that long, could it? He had expected the search for the Golden Key to take longer... but then it had taken longer, hadn't it? Too long. Mark frowned. It was hard to comprehend. He simply could not grasp the concept of being gone for twenty-one years that seemed only a few days.

Surely he could find something to do in Rome. Something that normal people do, but he had no idea what normal people did. Christopher Stewart had been the last 'normal' person he had known very well. Certainly Meredith did not fit the normal category very well. He might go to the Vatican after all, see the Sistine Chapel, perhaps. Michelangelo had been a very good painter; perhaps they had not painted over his work... yet. He'd put nothing by the Holy Fathers. Maybe he'd visit the Coliseum, take a walk on the Appian Way, drown himself in the Tiber River.

((((((((((((<O>))))))))))))

Simon saw him off with a big hug and assured him that he would get
everything ready for him in Scotland. What things Simon would get ready
were uncertain. He did not really care to know. In fact, he didn't really care
about much of anything at the moment, but he was glad that Simon would be
there waiting for him when he did go back. At least the Healer believed him.
He got into the rented Mercedes and drove away from the Villa headed north,
wondering what on earth he was doing. Sir Philip had sent a cell phone
along with him and he didn't even know how to use it properly. Too many
buttons without instructions on them. Furthermore, he was barely able to
recognize the basic controls in the car; everything had changed, but he
managed to get the hang of it after a few miles and soon found himself on the
outskirts of Rome where very little had changed and, yet, everything had
changed. The traffic was still as horrible as ever, but the streets had been
made a bit larger and he was appalled that the 'improvements' had improved
nothing in that respect. Who were all these people and where were they
going? He found the hotel where Simon had reserved a room for him using
the GPS device embedded in the Mercedes' dash. Even that had been a
harrowing experience and had required pulling over several times while he
punched the buttons and listened to the instructions several times. After
parking and registering at the desk with only his credit card, he escaped from
the crowded public places to the luxury suite Simon had selected for him and
sat for a long time, staring at the reflection of himself in the mirror over the
dresser. Yes, he had lost his mind somewhere. He wondered if he would
ever get it back.

The Hotel Domus Aventina on the Via di Santa Prisca, was a very nice
place just next door to the temple of the god Mithras, above the house of
Aquila and Priscilla where Saint Peter had lived during his sojourn in Rome
after the Crucifixion. It was located between the Colosseum and the Roman
Forum, the Circus Maximus and the Baths of Caracalla. His balcony looked
out onto the Church of Saint Prisca's for whom the street was named. Simon
could not have picked a more beautiful place for him to stay, but he hardly
noticed the scenery when he moved to the tiled table on the balcony. He sat
sipping Scotch from a thick tumbler as he glanced over a multitude of
colorful brochures listing all the local attractions that the Healer had also
supplied him with. When he was sufficiently numb from the alcohol, he
stuffed the papers in the waste basket with a twinge of remorse at having
wasted Simon's efforts.

Simon was such a thoughtful person, always thinking of others. What would make a man such that he would put absolutely everyone's needs before his own? The Healer was an anomaly, an enigma and a mystery and it was a privilege to know him as a Brother and a friend. He lay down on the bed, fully intending to make good on his promise to stay drunk and/or asleep, but Simon's sad eyes haunted his dreams. The Healer wanted him to forget his troubles. Wanted his wounds to heal. Simon wanted him to enjoy himself. He could not stay in the bed, nor could he stomach another round of Scotch without something to eat. Getting drunk was one thing. Getting sick was another.

After dark, he ventured out to the street and began to walk in no particular direction with nothing on his mind except finding something to eat. He ended up sitting at a table in an open-air café, drinking red wine, and feeling totally miserable after indulging in a fruit, bread and cheese platter big enough to feet six people. In spite of his misery, his presence at the café did not go unnoticed. Three young ladies sitting at a table very near his own, soon took an interest in him and with a sort of careless indifference, he took notice of them. They were all about the same age, very well proportioned modern ladies wearing outlandish costumes in his opinion. A blonde and two redheads. They began whispering behind their hands, giggling and flirting openly with him. At first, he did not realize what they were about and watched them in idle fascination. He'd had quite a bit of experience in harmless flirtations in his life, but they were amazingly adept at conveying intriguing information without saying a word. Before he had finished his second glass of wine, he already knew what sort of underwear the blonde was wearing under her short skirt and he also knew that one of the redheads liked dragons, displaying several dragon tattoos in some interesting places. They had literally managed to show him these things and more. The second redhead seemed a bit more serious than the others and wore a large silver cross on a chain around her neck that vaguely resembled a St. Constantine's cross. She also wore a Celtic cross on her little finger and little silver oak trees dangled from her ears and an Eye of Horus was tattooed on her neck. She had the look of a wise woman about her that made him feel uneasy when she looked his way. He wondered if she knew what the symbols she wore stood for? He suddenly wanted to ask her, something totally out of character for him. He glanced around at the other tables, but he and they were the only patrons remaining at the outdoor tables. Everyone else was inside the café. His ears burned when one of them blew him a kiss and his discomfiture made them giggle all the more. One of them made a more suggestive gesture that made the hair on the back of his neck stand up and he suddenly wanted to get away. Before he could pay his tab and make good his escape, they were dragging their chairs to his table. One of them took his credit card from the waiter when he returned with it and slipped it into the front of her blouse.

He could cancel the card. Retrieving it would be far more dangerous than an unexplained shopping spree on company money.

Though he made no comments or asked none of the questions he wished to, he learned a great deal by simply sipping his wine and nodding his head occasionally while wondering what was so funny. AS they chatted together around him, he learned that all three worked for the same 'spa' and that the sleeveless blue smocks over very short skirts, had the name of their establishment embroidered across the front. When he finally smiled and said something about the weather, they were genuinely impressed by his Scottish brogue. Supposedly, they had thought him one of their countrymen and had pegged him for some minor aristocrat or another. His foreign origin piqued their interest even more. The mystically inclined redhead, a self-professed hair stylist, got up immediately and moved around behind him. He turned to look up at her and she took a handful of his hair in her hand and bent to smell of it, exposing a great deal more than her tattoos for his perusal in the process. He closed his eyes automatically and crossed himself subconsciously, bringing on another round of giggles from her companions. Words would not come. He had nothing of substance to say to them and he was sure they were about to take him for a ride and he was quite sure he didn't want to go.

"I have seen you before, no?" She asked in Italian, leaning unnecessarily close to his ear. He could feel her breath on his neck and her nearness caused goose bumps to rise on his arms and his neck. "Are you a priest? You keep crossing yourself, signor?"

"Do I?" he asked in English. He had been unaware of the action. He dropped both hands in his lap. The waiter appeared and brought two more bottles of the expensive wine he had been drinking, along with three more glasses and another receipt from his own credit card. The wine was not as strong as Scotch, but it had a kick. His head swam and he felt warm all over. A good drunk was coming on.

"Oh, but you are not from Rome. Only a priest would cross himself like that here. But I am certain I have seen this hair before... somewhere," she insisted in fairly good English and resumed her seat at the table. She took his hand in hers. His earlier desire to leave had faded, replaced by the daring irresponsibility brought on by the alcohol. "What a peculiar ring. What does it mean, I wonder? IAAT?"

He gave no answer, but smiled instead. It took only one smile from him and she offered herself up with a detailed description of what she would like to do for him. The other two added their own comments, trying to top her offer with their own.

He raised one hand and begged them to cease and start over so that he might record it all in writing.

They giggled, but agreed that they had not been properly introduced and were much too forward for complete strangers. They needed his name in order to address him properly. A joke.

He cleared his throat and stood up a bit shakily, but with just the right amount of Scottish arrogance to impress them. To hell with Meredith and Lucio and the fucking Grand Master. If they wanted him to stay out of trouble, they should have let him go fly fishing on the River Spey and sent Simon of Grenoble to chaperone him.

"Sir Mark Andrew Ramsay, of Lothian, Scotland. Eldest son to Sir Timothy Ramsay in the service of King William the Lion, comrade in arms to Robert the Bruce, King Richard the Lion-hearted, crusader and Chevalier. Doctor of Medicine and Alchemical Arts, philosopher, etceteras, etceteras, et--cet--e---ras at your service, ladies," he told them magnanimously and wondered what the hell he was doing. He'd not been introduced by such titles in ages and never in such a ludicrous combination.

The ladies, on the other hand, were suitably impressed, but oblivious to the absurdity of his grand introduction. Naturally, they didn't believe a word of it and in return, each of them stood, introduced themselves and gave their occupations, allowing him to kiss their hands. One was a hair dresser, one was a massage therapist and the third specialized in something she called 'body art and piercing'.

He drank a few more rounds with them while they talked at him and then tried to leave, expressing his regrets that he could not stay. The girls did not allow him to get away with it and soon they had him up, walking down the sidewalk, each one vying for a spot next to him. He needed three arms. One on each side and the third dancing around in front of them.

He spent the next three days and several thousand Euros on the charge card, following them around the city on an all-encompassing shopping spree. Mark Andrew had never been in so many different shops in his life. In fact, he had not even been aware that most of the establishments even existed. He allowed the sheer volume of sights and sounds and smells to envelope him in a sort of bizarre cocoon that left no room for outside thoughts to enter. Before he could digest one thing, another would intervene to take its place and soon he was totally overwhelmed and existing in a state of semi-shock. After the third day, he spent the next three weeks at their apartment in the strange haze of an alcohol and drug-induced stupor while they continued to use his credit card without his presence or permission. But he didn't care. They made good on all their promises on a daily basis.

Lost in a constant miasma of blissful poison, he found the peace that he had been seeking when he'd left the Villa, though it had not come in the form he had imagined. Not once did Meredith Dambretti or Scotland cross his mind. Not once did he think of Lucio, the babies, the Grand Master or Abdul Hafiz and the odd things that had so recently happened to him. It was as if he had dropped out of the sky onto another planet where he was literally worshipped by three beautiful acolytes who seemed to hang on his every word... at first. They were so far removed from the life he knew, they were like alien creatures to him. They dressed him. Undressed him. Bathed him. Took him out. Brought him back. Fed him the best liquor and the best food. Talked endlessly to him about things he'd never heard of and couldn't remember for five minutes. The mystical redhead was into occultism and considered herself a student of the ancient Kabbala. He listened more carefully to her musings much more than the others and it seemed that she was desperately trying to teach him something or perhaps learn something from him. The other redhead and the blonde were attending school of some sort, though he could not say what they were learning. It seemed that they already knew enough to get by quite well on someone else's money. They knew everything that a girl should know and much that they shouldn't. In fact, they were teaching him things in certain subjects concerning sex and drugs that made him wonder if he were not dreaming again.

When the talk turned to vampires and blood and the dark forces of the Universe, he was somewhat shocked and horrified by their fascination with such a dangerous topic, but they knew very little about what they spoke. It mattered very little that he rarely said a word to them about anything, he was never alone and never had time to think about going home or anything else to do with the Order or his wrecked life in Scotland.

As far as he was concerned, he could stay on holiday forever.

FINISHED.

Quotations taken from the Old Testament Book of Daniel and the Revelation of St. John from the King James Version of the Holy Bible and the Rosarium Philosophorium, the Pretiosissimum Donum Dei, and the Treatise of Hermes from the Ars Notoria and the Testimony of the Mad Assassin from the Necronomicon by H.P Lovecraft.

Made in the USA
Lexington, KY
19 February 2010